Geertje Suhr

Love Me, Your Daughter

A Novel

Culicidae Press®
PO Box 5069
Madison, WI 53705-5069
USA
culicidaepress.com
editor@culicidaepress.com

LOVE ME, YOUR DAUGHTER: A NOVEL

This book was previously published in German as *Baby im Dritten Reich: Dichtung, Lügen und Wahrheit* by Grupello in 2016.

Translated by Roland Grefer

Images on pages 72 and 177 are reproductions of artwork created by Geertje Suhr. All other artwork is either in the public domain or was generated by Midjourney.

ISBN: 978-1-68315-101-2

Library of Congress Control Number: 2024945583

Our books may be purchased in bulk for promotional, educational or business use. Please contact your local bookseller or the Culicidae Press Sales Department at +1-515-462-0278 or by email at sales@culicidaepress.com

x.com/culicidaepress – facebook.com/culicidaepress
threads.net/culicidaepress – instagram.com/culicidaepress

Cover design and interior layout © 2024 by polytekton
Cover image from *Young Boys Playing Dice* (c. 1675), a work by Spanish painter Bartolomé Esteban Murillo (1670-1682), modified by polytekton

Table of Contents

Gifted For Love or Love Me

Love as a means of rescue

Benn and Brecht couldn't
Hold a candle to me
(they were too dead for that)
But the living Rühmkorf
Told me the pure truth
When we were dining together on fish,

Using the comforting words
Cheer up, girl
Hardly anyone understands poetry
But yours has a tone all its own
And only your skin is as smooth
As that of a child's bottom

Against the great merits of another
There are no means of rescue other than love
Was said by the great Goethe
Who wrote humbly
"Love me"
At the end of his letters

And thus I loved them all:
Goethe and Grass
Heine, Lyngi and Hölderlin
And also Hahn and Kirsch
(No pantheon without the ladies)

"Love me"
Is written invisibly at the end
Of all great poetry

Jakob Kollhofer, Director of the DAAD, Heidelberg.
Behind him on the wall the portrait of Geertje Suhr's
mother (painted by Rudolf Führmann) in Chicago

Preface by Gorda Selig, Author

Although I knew back then that my biological father had been a war criminal, I was not able to write about him. Instead, I wrote about the difficult relationship between a mother and her daughter …

Ines and Her Mother

(attempt at a novel by Gorda Selig, author)

"Get up", said mother. But Ines didn't feel like getting up.

"Bring the bedding to the bedroom," said mother. But Ines didn't want to bring the bedding to the bedroom.

"We have to hurry", said mother. But Ines didn't feel at all like hurrying. There was no need to hurry at all, they still had plenty of time to do some shopping, but her mother needed to get some exercise in the morning.

"I need exercise in the morning," said the mother. "And I need rest in the morning," thought the daughter. Nevertheless, she got up like a scolded child, took the bedding from the couch in the living room and carried it into the bedroom, where she had previously slept with her mother in a double bed until she could no longer bear it. She had told Karin: "To be a child at night is too much, at least at night I want to be allowed to be forty." Also, her mother often yelled out like a stabbed animal when she slept, but she didn't tell Karin that.

"Open the balcony door," said mother, "it smells like sleep in here."

"It doesn't smell like sleep in here anymore than it does in your bedroom," said the daughter, "and open the door yourself if you want to have it open." With these insubordinate words she laid down in the corner in front of the television to do the back exercises the doctor had prescribed.

"Don't turn on the TV so loud," said mother, "it's still early and the balcony door is open." While saying that, the mother already stomped past her legs to the television to turn the volume down. Nothing annoyed Ines as much as when her mother stomped past her swinging legs so that she had to stop the instructed swinging movements. And every day, mother stomped past the swinging legs, although Ines had jammed herself in a corner of the living room that was far away from the breakfast preparations, in order to let her limbs swing a little bit undisturbed, as prescribed.

"Do you want breakfast before or after the shower?" asked mother. Every morning, the mother asked the daughter who was rolling on the floor, waving and panting, whether she wanted breakfast before or after the shower.

"I'll have breakfast whenever you are finished," said the daughter. "Are you finished?"

"No, but I'm surely allowed to ask," exclaimed the mother, who felt hurt in her thoughtfulness.

"Stop asking," muttered the rebellious daughter, "just make the breakfast and set it down over there."

Mother shouted, "Stupid brat!" and hurried into the kitchen, with her heels clattering loudly, while the daughter locked herself in the bathroom. In fact, she took the ridiculous trouble to lock the door, although it was quite difficult to turn the key in the old lock. But she needed the comforting feeling of being locked in.

"Open the door, quickly," yelled the mother and shook the handle angrily. "My God, why do you always have to lock it? We're among ourselves!"

"I did tell you," said the daughter, "that I don't want to be disturbed when I'm in the bathroom."

"Well, don't make such a fuss," cried the mother, "we've never been embarrassed in front of each other!" But the daughter had always been embarrassed before her mother, before her friends, before all the men in the world, even before the cat, when it stared at her knowingly.

"What do you want now, again?" Ines asked with as little desperation as possible.

"You know that I always have to go to the bathroom when I know that the door is locked," the mother said angrily, "so leave it at least open!"

"But I need my peace and quiet," said the daughter.

"Peace and quiet from what?" yelled the mother. "You haven't done anything yet this morning at all."

At the breakfast table it seemed as if mother had mysteriously lost her voice while cooking eggs and buttering the bread. Exhausted, she chewed on the jam roll as if she had already taken a hundred bites and didn't want any more. On the other hand, the daughter loved long discussions over breakfast. The bad mood resulting from the carrying of the bedding, from the waving of the limbs as prescribed, from the tiresome duty of having to brush the teeth and the showering with way too much water that splashed everywhere was now forgotten. In addition, the light in the bathroom came from the left, and when the light came from the left, the daughter didn't like to see her face in the mirror. She found herself to be ugly when illuminated from the left. When the light came from the front, she found herself to be beautiful, or at least pleasant to look at. Seeing her face in her mother's mirror annoyed her every morning. That made her grumpy for a little while. In the lonely apartment in America, on the other hand, she had dreamed of a scintillating breakfast conversation over a German egg with crisp German rolls and the tasty German coffee. The sweet heathland honey loosened her tongue, the gentle rays of the sun smoothed her wrinkled soul, and the coffee revived her mind.

Ines started to speak. She said: "Jane Austen actually only ever loved her sister."

"My God, don't you start on Jane Austen again," exclaimed the mother indignantly, "and so early in the morning!" Well, if not Jane Austen then, thought Ines, then just the weather.

"Lovely day today," she said, as if she had said "hello!"

"No," said her mother, "it's supposed to rain today."

"But the sky is totally blue," said the daughter.

"It's not blue, it's gray," mother stated.

"This is probably a mirage then here, and not a sun," wondered the daughter aloud, without making the slightest daughterly effort to hide her irritation.

"That is still sunshine and will soon be rain," replied the mother.

"Look, I'm getting a rash here, and right now," said the daughter, to be done with the tiresome subject of the weather.

"My God, you have to get city spectacles to be able to see that," sneered mother.

"What is a pair of city spectacles?" asked the daughter, puzzled, and worried because she feared she had lost part of her precious German during her long stay in America.

"Well, it is a kind of pair of huge magnifying glasses," said the mother. "And anyway, you know that I don't like to talk in the morning. I have a long wind-up time." The daughter knew very well that she only had to ask the mother about old friends or the time in Lübeck or the trip with the Paul family to Vienna to get her to start talking, but now it was too late or too early for that. Now her mother insisted on her chronic breakfast problem, the long wind-up time.

Chicago, dated: ....

(Letter by Gorda Selig, author, written at a time when people still wrote letters to each other.)

Dear Friederike,

Please read this beginning of my new novel (*Ines and Her Mother* or something like that), which might not remain the beginning, which could become a middle part or be deleted, you never know whether you have already started. At some point you know that you are in the middle of it and that you are, so to speak, unstoppable. But in the beginning, everything is unstoppable and is clamped down in the machine for tearing up (yes, imagine, I'm still using the old rickety typewriter!). That's why I need you, especially at the beginning, because otherwise it would never be the beginning, but would rather always remain just word clutter, fantasy play, written thoughts. I'm telling you this so that you can say, just go on, because I would rather be modest and discreet like you, too. Only know-it-alls, cheeky, indiscreet people talk a lot about themselves, meaning they don't write: talking much about oneself? I ask you, who wants to write under these circumstances? And despite that, everyone wants to write, at least that's how it appears sometimes. Every author knows that: I know I have a novel in me, says the strikingly young secretary with the funny owl glasses after the reading, who is at an age when you should still have big ideas and think of young men, but don't have novels in their head. But of course, I know that Thomas Mann at this big-ideas-and-young-men-in-the-head age was already working on the *Buddenbrooks*. I, on the other hand, didn't even have that gin in my head at the time: I, too, shall write a novel one day. I wanted to study literature and become a teacher, nothing else. Ten years later I thought for the first time: I want to write a novel. That was when I was about thirty. Three seconds later, I heard an inner voice mocking me out loud: My dear child, you must have gone completely crazy! Was it the voice of my reason or that of my mother?

Friederike, Thomas Mann says that an artist is a combination of tenacity and fragility. And even though I may not be a real artist, I have always been fragile. Imagine, when I go down to the mailbox here in Chicago, I always get a mild asthma attack, just as I used to get a kind of anticipatory cough some time ago. Wonder what is in that mailbox? I think worriedly, instead of: I hope that there are some friendly air-mail letters from Germany in there. Then, when I read the letters, I chugged a drink down beforehand, so that the knives that the letters might contain would be plunged into an alcoholic mist and not into my unprotected poet's heart.

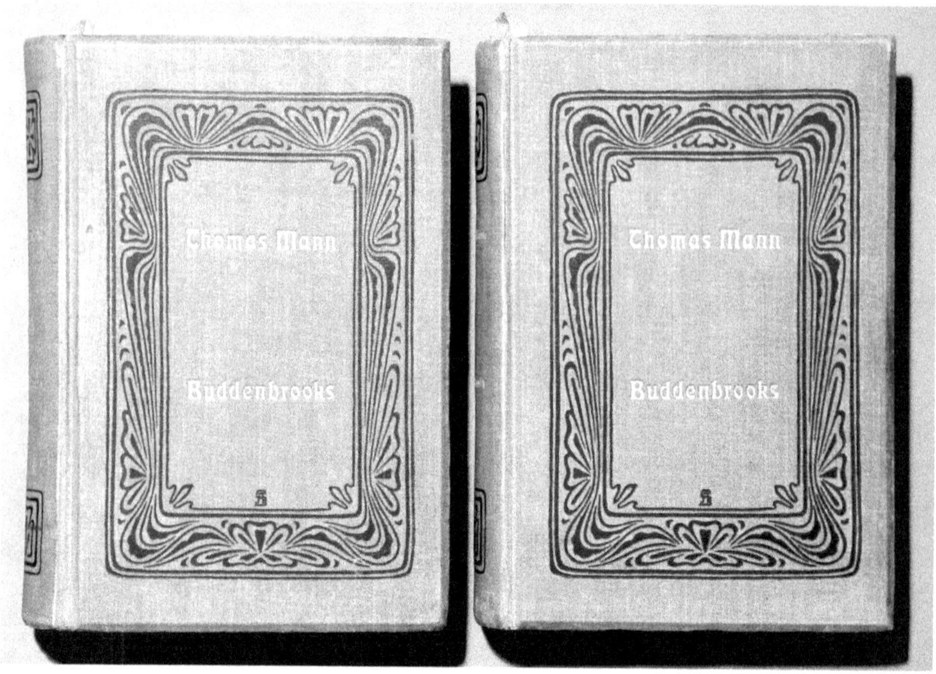

THOMAS MANN

Buddenbrooks

Verfall
einer
Familie

DEUTSCHE BUCH-GEMEINSCHAFT
G.M.B.H.
Berlin

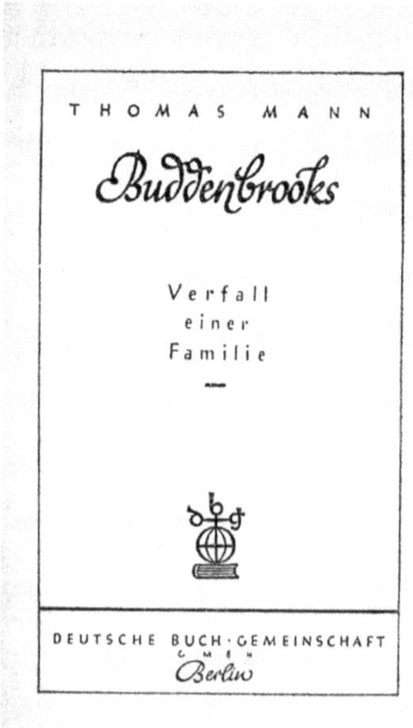

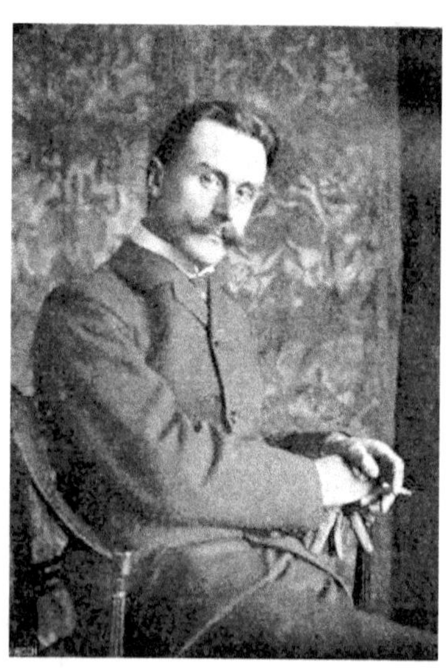

Thomas Mann, *Buddenbrooks*

Do you remember, Friederike, how I named my hero after your dog? We were sitting in your garden in Lilienthal, drinking East Friesian tea sweetened with rock candy, and I said that I still needed a name for the woman. And you said: "Why don't you call her 'Vita'?" And I thought the idea to be funny: now, whenever I see a black Scottish terrier somewhere, I think about how my novel is just disappearing there. And then I get one of those strange German vitriolic attacks — because how can attempting a novel cause hatred? Boredom, desperation, laughter, pity maybe, but not hatred — then I know that my Vita has bitten my attempt somewhere. And I get my stomach cramps. The dead poets must have been constantly ill, Friederike. The biographies are teeming with stomach ailments, headaches, brain blocks, love sickness. They were unstable fellows, all of them. But stable enough to leave us a few unforgettable lines:

> Illness was probably the last reason
> for the whole creative urge;
> While creating, I could recover,
> while creating, I became healthy.

Heinrich Heine never became healthy, but without such lines of poetry, I would not be able to go on. Dearest friend, I couldn't have continued without you., either. When I wrote down the first fifty pages of my 'Vita', which at that time was not called yet 'Vita' but rather 'notepad', I only wanted to distract myself from the fear that the doctoral thesis might cause trouble. Back then, calling Jane Austen a feminist was a sensitive topic. And there were almost only men in my dissertation committee. I wrote down my half invented, half rediscovered childhood of a nameless heroine and drove to you, sat in your beloved garden with the childishly lined notepad, and you listened to me as if I had something to say to you. And I thought: I would always like to be allowed to tell it to her that way. Not a single line of the earlier attempt to write survived, ever new layers of words were added to the old ones until the new ones completely obscured the previous ones, but behind my last 'Vita' there was a glimmer of the first nameless one, of which you said: That's good, you have to continue that.

If you had said at that time: That doesn't work, that stuff is not worth anything — and in retrospect I am convinced that it was worth nothing, just something for your loving ear in friendship — then I would have never continued. Praise gives more support than criticism, the great poet Peter Rühmkorf said to me and encouraged me with his praise. And yet, I later asked him full of self-doubt: So tell me, did you really mean that when you wrote to me that I am capable? He just looked at me in amazement. But by then I was already thirty poems ahead.

Yours, Gorda

Portrait of Heinrich Heine, 1829

Ines and Her Mother

(attempt at a novel)

Although Ines had told her mother, "we don't need an umbrella under this blue sky," her mother had put the heavy cane umbrella into the large brown bag. Now you carry it alone, Ines thought stubbornly, but then, after a few steps, she took the bag. But actually, she took the bag from Klara. Whenever Ines walked next to her mother or a friend, she also walked a little bit next to Klara. That made her soft. Until her thirteenth birthday, Ines had never gone to town without Klara, or to school or to her friends. She never stood alone in front of strangers who so often pulled at Klara's red braids and said: Look, she has hair like in the movies. However, there was no hair like Ines' in any movie. But Ines didn't care: Klara's hair is my hair too, she thought, after all we are twin sisters. And twins are a single hair and a single soul. And that was also the case with their soul, even though the hair couldn't have grown on the same head, because Ines hair was thin and brown, and Klara's hair was thick and red and slightly curled and reached to her shoulders. On the whole, heaven had spilled its cornucopia unevenly over the two sisters: Klara got the golden-brown eyes, the sun-loving light complexion that turned soft brown with the first days of spring and dark brown from July on, the thick rosy lips that seduced all people to smile at her, while Ines stood beside her as if she were waiting for a present and not receiving it. And yet, heaven had shown its understanding in its impenetrable way: This here will become a sister tragedy, an angel must have thought, and took Klara away with him before Ines could notice the damage done to her by Klara's beauty.

That was a short time before puberty, which surely would have blown up the twins' lovely unity. What had so peacefully gone through life hand in hand until then, would undoubtedly have been separated into the beautiful and the unendowed, to the chagrin of the unendowed. But this way only one piece of the entity of Ines-and-Klara remained, the piece of Ines with a heart full of love for Klara. For all the Klaras, who were later called Barbara, Gisela, Karin, Helga or had other names. And love and grief are easier to bear than envy and jealousy.

But the most beloved of all later Klaras was called Henriette. When she met Henriette, Ines knew immediately: here is my Klara! And she put aside her lifelong mourning for her beloved twin sister to wear red to celebrate her reunion: for red is the color of joy. And that of blood. And Henriette was of her blood. That is what Henriette thought at the time, too. For Henriette's sister had been less a relative than a stranger, because she was ten years older than Henriette. And she had been more of a brother than a sister, because she would have preferred to become a boy and fight with the boys of the neighborhood and not run away girlishly, like Henriette and Ines. And yet, Ines felt proud and brave to be in Henriette's presence. This was because Henriette seemed fragile and sickly, although she actually didn't have anything, just a little anorexia and a pale complexion to go with her reddish-blond hair, while Ines showed early signs of chronic body ailments, mostly stomach trouble and vomiting, diarrhea, and inexplicable heart cramps. But in Henriette's presence, Ines felt that she would become healthy and brave, because Henriette seemed tender and sickly.

"You know, Mom," said Ines on her way into the city while walking along the park, "it's been two weeks since I came over from America and still no call from Henriette. And I am sure that I wrote her: I am arriving in Hamburg on July 12. "In the old days I would have gotten a phone call right away."

"In the old days, in the old days," said the mother, "in the old days isn't today."

"But she must know that I feel insecure. In May I said to her on the phone: Do you actually want to forget me? I mean, when someone says, "Do you actually want to forget me," they are expressing their insecurity, aren't they? I would have written to her immediately. But not a word from Klara."

"Klara, Klara, why are you talking about Klara?" said her mother.

"I mean Henriette, you know that, mom."

"Do finally stop it with Henriette," said the mother.

"But I have a problem and I need to talk to you about it."

"I have really heard enough about Henriette," said the mother.

"When you told me about your problems, I did listen to you," said Ines.

"I really don't bother you with my problems," the mother replied mockingly. That was true, mother hardly had the desire to talk about her problems because she hardly had the desire to talk about anything. But that had been different once upon a time. For example, when Dad died. But they never talked about Dad anymore.

"If I don't get a call from Henriette tonight, I'll call her myself. I just have to know what's going on," said Ines. "You never give up, don't you?" said her mother, "I wouldn't let myself be humiliated like that." That was true, mother would not let herself be humiliated. When her then best friends, the Petersen family, hadn't been in touch for several weeks, mother slammed the receiver on the cradle when they dared to finally call again. Not like that, she said, and the Petersen case was closed for her. There was no talking and pondering about it, as Ines did, who had been wondering about the break with Henriette for three years.

Well, it had not been a real break, after all. Only a little bit of this and that had been broken, above all the need to tell and the ability to write to her; Ines always felt a pain in her hand when she wrote to Henriette. She could no longer write long letters. Have writer's cramp, she wrote to Henriette with a cramped hand and a cramped soul, but she preferred not to talk about the soul. So, in turn Henriette hardly wrote any more, no surprise. Or she wrote about the chickens and that felt to her as if she didn't write at all.

"I mean, who cares about chickens?" said Ines to her second-best friend Karin.

"But chickens are really cute things," you said.

"Well, if chickens could be cute, then these chickens would be cute, so silky-brown with a few colorful feathers on their heads, so very cute, to whoever likes chickens, but I don't like chickens. I eat chickens. And I can't like what I eat, you know. Otherwise, I can't eat it anymore."

"But you do like chicken," Karin said, astonished. "After all, you eat it almost every day."

"That's just it", Ines said, irritated. "I eat chicken and I like chicken meat — but I don't *like* chicken, meaning liking within the meaning of loving. Could you maybe eat cat or dog?"

"Of course not", said Karin, who owned three dogs and two cats.

"Henriette writes to me about the chickens as if they were pets. They all have names: Frauke and Katja, Gerda and Elke; those are their names. And then she tells me how sweet they are, and how they jerk with their heads and scratch with their feet and pluck their feathers... Well, that's too many chickens in the house for me. During the last visit, I couldn't stand the fried chicken. I don't eat a chicken that has a name."

"What was its name?"

"Irmgard or something like that. It doesn't matter."

Mother and daughter turned to the left, toward where the winding city center opened up.

"How long are you going to stay here?" the mother asked. "I have to know when you're leaving again."

"Roger will call me tonight, then we will arrange where we want to meet", said Ines. "My travel plans depend on that."

"Roger, Roger," said the mother, "I wish this thing would finally come to an end." A good end or a bad end, thought Ines, and didn't know herself what to call good and what bad. She only knew what she wanted. And she wanted Roger to finally separate from his wife, although there was a child, the daughter, who would have to be about seven years old by now. Ines never asked about the child or the wife. Had never seen a photo of them, either. Karin had once met the Seifert couple in Hamburg — at that time, she lived not far from them — and had told Ines: "You know, such a tall, dull blond, nothing special." And Ines had repeated the words to Roger — admittedly, she enjoyed repeating them — when he jumped up and screamed: "You leave my wife out of this!" So, Ines knew that Roger somehow still loved this woman, even though he always said: "I don't love her; I only feel responsible for her." But hadn't he also said the following to Ines when they were sitting together in Murten am See for the first time? "When I read your novel, I knew what made us different; you are able to love, and I can't." So, hadn't he loved Ines either then?

But that couldn't be possible! Oh, how easily all wounds opened in her; it was a miracle to see such old wounds bleeding freshly. She had once read that Rahel Varnhagen had been a 'spiritual bleeder'. She had never been able to forget that, because she herself was such a bleeder of the soul, the smallest pinch and the blood flowed, oh heaven help, who will save me from old pains (Klara, Klara, where are you?). And she had said to Roger: "But didn't we once love each other so much?" And he comforted her and again didn't comfort her with the words: "You know how much I loved you. But you are the one who left. You wanted it like that, all by yourself!" And Ines had done everything this way and wanted nothing this way.

"I didn't leave, I was made to leave," she said for the hundredth time.

"Stop it now," said her mother, as they stood in front of the butcher's store. "I'm going to get some sausage and some chops; your brother wants to come for dinner. "

"Alone or with his wife?" asked Ines.

"With his wife of course," said the mother. Oh dear, exclaimed Ines, but only towards the inside, showing nothing on the outside.

"And then I'll buy chicken," said the mother, "you love chicken so much."

"Well," said Ines, "just don't give me a chicken that has a name, or I'll get sick.

"Names, names," said the mother, "who is talking about names here?"

Chicago, dated ....
(Letter by the author)

Dear Friederike,

please read the new parts of the not yet started novel (*Ines and Her Mother* or something like that). On Monday morning, I liked the beginning, and on Tuesday afternoon I knew it wasn't worth anything. And so it swings back and forth until my stomach turns over. I once read that of all professions, artists get the most heart attacks because they suffer so terribly from stress. And I tell you, this going back and forth will yet drive me crazy, there is no security and comfort anywhere, only with you. At the same time, I'm telling you that I want to hear the truth from you, but who wants the truth when it kills you with a dagger? This means that I want tact, but tact is no truth. And where do I find a truth that doesn't hurt? And in a moment, I will eat baked chicken that has no name. Thank God, dear Friederike, that you don't breed chickens, only rabbits, and rabbits are thick balls of gray wool that everyone must love, including me. And I don't need to eat rabbit meat.

Since I am so afraid of writing, I always tell myself: You don't need to write more than two typed pages a day; that's about four handwritten pages. And sometimes I even allow myself only one page when I feel bad, like last summer when I suffered from a pinched nerve in the neck, and my left hand was paralyzed (thank God not the right one like my 'heroine' Ines!). Then we bought the wrong mattress — one without springs, very hard, which was supposed to be ideal for back pain and was instead brutal. My whole body hurt, and I took Valium and painkillers like Tylenol every night, so I could hardly read in the mornings, let alone write. And often I just watched TV.

And now I understand a life in front of the television! Only two years ago I didn't know what was going on in the TV box during the day, and maybe it was not yet going on, yet, what is going on today, is hell. Well, sometimes I cannot believe that I see and hear what I get to see and hear. And no writer could step into more blunders — or perhaps taboos — than such a program does portray on the TV. On Channel 5 a daughter tells how her father forced her to sleep with him for years, how she aborted his child and later took him to court, on Channel 7 a murderer sits there and tells how his father beat him with a rubber truncheon, how his uncle raped him, and how his mother humiliated him, and on Channel 2 — but I think I'll tell you that some other time, otherwise you will never want to read my banal stories of failed love and failed life again, but will want to turn on the TV right away. But thank God, you still have some neat, middle-class talk shows in Germany about class reunions and reunions with your first great love and the funny quiz show of 'What's my line?" An almost intact world. And who hasn't longed for that world, the more broken it really is? As a result, I write about the unbroken world, in which one can still speak of misguided loves and misguided writings.

Yours, Gorda

Ines and Her Mother

(attempt at a novel)

All the stores that were important for mother and daughter, such as the butcher, the baker, and the Spar grocery store were all located on the main street of Hallwede, and mother and daughter completed all the shopping in just under an hour. They bought mainly rolls, cold cuts, and canned soups, because they mostly ate that, because they both didn't care much about cooking, but a lot about reading and watching TV. "Cooking is work and fattening," Henriette had always said, when she still treasured reading and walking and lollygagging about. But now she no longer thought much about all that. It all changed after Herbert came into her life.

"What do you mean by 'came into'?" Karin had asked.

"Well, since he arrived on her doorstep."

"And when was that?"

"That was about three years ago. Or has it been four already?"

"The cans are so heavy", Ines said to her mother, "mom, we have to go home now, I can't carry that heavy stuff anymore." The mother, who had wanted to still go quickly to the pharmacy to flirt with the young, handsome pharmacist while buying her pills, made her way to the bus stop.

"I'm telling you, we have to get a wheeled shopping tote," said the daughter. "My back can't take it anymore."

"Oh, that stupid wheeled shopping carrier," said the mother.

"They're not stupid at all," said the daughter, "they're highly practical."

"And where do I put that thing in my little apartment?" asked the mother. Since the mother was older than seventy, she refused to buy any more things, be it an urgently needed new TV, a video player, a better mattress for the double bed or a matching shower curtain.

"I'm too old for that now," she said, "I could drop dead tomorrow." Since it was true that her mother could drop dead tomorrow, Ines dropped the subject of wheeled shopping totes. Anything but that, she thought, her dropping dead is

Ines and her mother shopping in Hallwede

the last thing I need. Who will I then have left in the world? No Klara, no Henriette, no dad, no Ronald, no Roger. Only Jane Austen, my beloved Jane and, of course, Karin, how can I forget them? In the stairwell, the mother barely made it up the five short flights of stairs, and Ines remembered that ten years ago, when she had just moved into the apartment, the mother had already said that I hope I can still make it up the stairs. Dad had just died back then.

"I have to leave Münster," said her mother. "Everything here reminds me of your father." But she had already given away his suits, his shoes, his ties, his pipes. She had taken his photographs off the walls and broken up with his side of the family. Now she had to break up with the city, too, because Dad had gone to work in its streets, bought things in its stores, walked in its parks. My mother didn't want Dad in her life anymore. So she moved to Hallwede, where her sister Käthe lived.

"Blood is thicker than water," she called it. And Dad was the water. Back then, Ines and her mother had been close allies. After Klara it was also still Dad, thought Ines, about whom one was no longer allowed to talk.

Chicago, dated ………
(Letter by the author)

Dear Friederike,

You know, it is my ideal writing style to sound as intimate and soulful as possible. Because, actually, I prefer to read memoirs, books of letters, and diaries. That's why I often write prose that seems to be taken from memoirs, letters, and diaries.

I am always happy when, after one of my readings, the audience asks: You have experienced all this yourself, haven't you? And their eyes shine like those of children in front of a piece of sheet metal twinkling golden in the sun. Then I can't disappoint them, after all, and say: But no, half of it is invented, a quarter comes from reading, and the last quarter has been experienced, by me or my characters.

But there is one mistake that I would never make again: To give something that I wrote to my mother to read. She can be found on every page, she says, in every person, in every scene. And when I read the beginning of the 'Vita' to her, she screamed: "I do know how you talk about me, but you leave our family out of it, I can tell you that!" But the author leaves nothing out. Otherwise, the author is not an author, but a polite individual who doesn't wash their dirty laundry in public. Yet, every author is also a polite individual who prefers to wash their dirty laundry in their own basement alone. And that is why they invent the stories they tell. So that they can't do the telling while they are silent.

Yours truly and untruly,

Gorda.

Ines and Her Mother

(attempt at a novel)

After they had eaten the rolls spread with liverwurst and a cup of spring vegetable soup, mother and daughter went to bed: the mother laid down on the living room sofa, the daughter went into the bedroom to sleep in the double bed. It was a misfortune that, after the death of the father, the mother had moved to an apartment where there was no guest room. But the mother had been in such a hurry to move away from the town of Münster that she had taken the first apartment she found in Hallwede. And the first is never the best, at least not for Ines, who now always had to squeeze by, as she moves from the bedroom to the living room and from the living room to the bedroom, just as her mother happened to like it at that moment. The worst thing was trying to use the phone. If someone called Ines and she answered the phone in the living room, then the mother talked from the sofa and Ines had to give her a finger signal: Now do shut up, why don't you! And then the mother was offended. So Ines took the phone into the bedroom whenever she could. But the mother also had to be able to go into her bedroom: This is my bedroom after all, said the mother. And the daughter went into the living room. But after all, the mother had to be able to go into her living room at times: After all, this is my apartment, said the mother. And the daughter went out onto the balcony. When the weather was nice, the daughter lived on the balcony. Of course, a balcony in Tuscany would have been cheaper than the one here in Hallwede. In Northern Germany it simply rained too much. And in summer, it was mostly cold. Heinrich Heine wrote that the summer in Northern Germany is like a winter painted green. And then he fled to Paris, away from a cold, rainy, anti-Semitic Germany that had more or less forced him to convert. That was in 1831 and not in 1933. She had written her master's thesis about Heine.

Ines went to bed with four books. As far back as she could remember, she had read more than one book, but for some years now she read four or five at a time, sometimes up to seven. Some books were for work and therefore not much fun, although they used to be great fun, when they were not books for work but fun books, such as those of Jane Austen and Virginia Woolf. There were only fun books in bed, so today I need my rest, thought Ines, and looked into her book about the structure of the cosmos. Actually a religious book, she thought, because who could write about such things without worrying about the genius in the universe? But too difficult before falling asleep, so she picked up the book by Hitler's architect Albert Speer, the memoirs of the German Faust at the side of the Austrian Mephisto, who laid the world of monumental construction at his feet — to the feet of the unemployed nobody and architect. Who could resist that? Would I have resisted if I had been faced with this choice? A pointless life without work or a hideous monumental building for the devil? The devil came in quite a conventional human form, without a goat's leg or a horse's foot, and he didn't eat flies, either. To the contrary, he hated meat in any form and lived a vegetarian life like a Buddhist monk. Who would have been able to recognize him as the devil? Certainly not Speer. And he had probably not read Hitler's *Mein Kampf*, either. For example, who still reads the Bible today? The Bible and *Mein Kampf* are certain to be among the most unread books in twentieth-century Germany. God's book and that of the devil, that's actually funny, don't you think?

Like my own ones, Ines thought, and was suddenly depressed. And she remembered what the female editor of a huge bestselling publisher had once said about her manuscript: "Our readers of today can no longer identify with that. So much fear of life is not 'in'!" And she recommended to her that she read Angelika Maria Dämmer, whose female characters came across as proud amazons, completely without fear and blame in the daily battle in the office and the marital bed, while her own now and then — quite often, to be honest — descended from the high horse of life to take refuge under a comfortable cover where they had time to read and brood. But then Sabine Wenger, the young editor of the Gutenberg publishing house, told her that Angelika Maria Dämmer refused to present one of her great texts in Klagenfurt at the Ingeborg Bachmann Literature Competition. "If I were to be torn apart there, I would take my own life," she is said to have said.

"What!" Ines exclaimed indignantly. "She always writes about such daredevil women in leather gear and then has a soul like a scared rabbit! That is the purest fraud! At least I don't cheat my non-existent readers when I ..." And at that point Sabine Wenger had said: "Mrs. Smith, be patient. Next time I will know more about the fate of your novel in our publishing house." In the next few days Ines was supposed to meet Sabine Wenger in Düsseldorf.

"If only the day would never come", Ines thought like the convinced pessimist the publishers had made her into. Actually, the last two weeks had been very pleasant, because the light skirmishes with her mother didn't count. I mean, at least you still have some hope left at that point. And without hope, you can pack up and bury both yourself and your writing materials. Back to the universe, Ines thought. Because then you had to think in billions of years as a distraction, and not in months and weeks and hours and seconds that could hurt so terribly when, for example, Roger said, "I can't meet you next week, it's my daughter's birthday." The year she separated from Ronald, she preferred to read about the terrible conditions in Moscow before the fall of the Wall, where people had to stand in line for many hours to get bread and meat and a dried-up piece of fruit. They didn't even have paper, she thought pityingly, as she wiped her eyes with a Kleenex, and no soap to wash their hands, and no toilets, while she cleaned her own on her knees. And two families in one tiny apartment, my God I'm lucky with my cozy two-room apartment. Of course, she couldn't keep the big, beautiful apartment after the separation, but the Russians often couldn't get one at all, and you have to look down on the dirt on the work shoes of the many, and not always up to the palaces of the few. Her aunt Käthe did the exact same thing. She always walked across the cemetery, the old, beautiful one in Hallwede, and said to herself when she was annoyed about something: At least I am still alive, like her sister Frauke, the mother of Ines, when Frauke hit her with these words:

"Don't keep telling me about your diseases! Somebody who travels as much as you do cannot be ill!"

"That stupid birdbrain," the mother had said to Ines. "She tells me constantly, and for hours on end, about her travels or about her illnesses. If she is as ill as she claims, she should stay at home!" Nothing annoyed Ines' mother more than her sister's travels. And even though she had moved to Hallwede because blood is thicker than water, Aunt Käthe's blood was in increasing danger of turning into water.

"She's talking about Venice, as if I hadn't been to Venice before."

"But you have never been to Venice," said the daughter.

"Well now, don't you be on my sister's side, too. That's more than enough of that, my own daughter!" Ines, too, always traveled around when she visited Europe from Chicago.

"Just what am I going to tell the neighbors, where you always hang out," raged the mother.

"That's none of their business," said the daughter dryly.

"My God, they ask me, where has your daughter traveled to again?"

"Well, then tell them the truth," said Ines.

"The truth, the truth, what truth?"

Chicago, dated …
(Letter by the author)

Dear Friederike,

You won't believe what I've been through during the last few weeks! You know that my story 'Aviva' is about my girlfriend Gwen, who was not my girlfriend back when I wrote the story — I think it was fifteen years ago now — or not a real girlfriend at all, otherwise I couldn't have written 'Aviva', a story full of biting irony about myself and Gwen. In it, I portray myself as a poet consumed by envy, who doesn't have her head full of poems, but rather of stories of 'Aviva', because otherwise there is probably not much for her to think about, while I have better things to do than think about Gwen day and night. About three months ago, I gave Gwen the volume with the new story, with the story 'Aviva' in it as a present without thinking too much about it. Gwen doesn't know any German, so what could happen? So she calls me not too long ago and says, I have to talk to you. In the Pancake-House restaurant, she told me that her friend Alexandra, who understands German, had read the story, and told her that I wasn't a real friend, after all. Which was true, at least back then. But today, that is no longer true. What was I supposed to do now? Deny the truth, which no longer existed anyway, call Alexandra a liar, denounce myself or speak of poetic license? In the end, I denied the truth, called Alexandra a little liar, denounced myself and otherwise blathered on about poetic license. I did it so long and so intensely until thin Gwen, who herself would terribly love to write, as you know, threw the fork down on her enviably untouched omelet, and said:

"Stop it, Ines, I do believe that you didn't want to hurt me!" But that was not yet the end of it. Every day I talked either with Gwen or with Alexandra or with Gwen's daughter Sandra or with Alexandra's friend Helen, until I never wanted to talk and never write or publish again. And here I sit and write to you... And tomorrow I'm writing a story in which a woman writes a story about a friend who... Even though I swore I would never write about Gwen again. But I am not writing about Gwen. I'm writing about an 'Aviva' that doesn't even exist in this form...

Your girlfriend and — then again — also not your girlfriend

Gorda

Ines and Her Mother
(attempt at a novel)

The mother only rested for a short time, because at two o'clock her favorite show began, a crime series called "Murders in the Afternoon." Ines heard the voices of the actors through the wall in the bedroom, as if they were all using a megaphone. For a few years now, the mother had been hearing poorly while watching television. But otherwise, she heard very well; for example, when Ines whispered on the phone, she could call from the hallway: "Just don't think I didn't hear that!" But when she watched television, her hearing was oriented to two places, and she had to turn up the volume to such an extent that every stay in the living room became a torment to Ines' ears. To muffle the noise, she stuffed ear plugs into her ears. She did this even now, while she took the women's magazine *Brigitte*, which contained this year's winning stories of the Droste-von-Hülshoff-Competition: Three short stories that Ines studied through-and-through with the despair of the ungifted. Just like thousands of others as well, Ines thought, why these and why not mine, and saw herself sitting in the hall of the ceremonial 'Festhaus' in Düsseldorf last year, Karin beside her, who had not wanted to come at all because she was exhausted by her work as a translator.

"Translators are the slaves of the literary business," she used to say.

Feeling indignant, Ines had spoken to the editor Sabine Wenger: "But my generation is not dead yet, there should still be readers who don't only want to read about intrepid Amazons ..." The strange thing was that the editor from the Gutenberg publishing house had hair that is supposedly only found in films. Thick blond curls with a touch of red in them. Klara's curls. And that made Ines weak. To have such an editor as a friend, she had thought, that would be a great luck. A Klara-type luck, a Henriette-type luck. With this friend by my side, I would never have to get drunk again, she had thought, when the bad letters came from the publishers.

Since her break-up with Henriette — but no, it wasn't a real break-up, just one in the heart of Ines — she even read Henriette's letters only while submerged in a haze of alcohol, although they were quite harmlessly about Frauke and Katja,

From left: Frauke, Katja, Gerda, and Elke

about Gerda and Elke, or whatever the chickens were called. But that was just it, they were about chickens and not about Henriette, and that was as if Henriette hadn't wanted to write at all. In the past, they had told each other everything, really everything, the difficulties with the mothers, the quarrels with the men. But then Henriette's mother bequeathed her an apartment with the so-called 'warm hand' and Henriette had thanked her for it by never talking about her mother again; that's how decent and loyal she was. Ines had to admire that, although she continued to talk about her own mother, only now in a solo voice, where earlier a duet used to sound. At the same time, down deep inside her, Ines loved her mother — and also further up — very much, I mean, mother is mother. Henriette didn't seem to really love her mother at all, at least not on Mother's Day two years ago, when Ines sat with her in the living room and Henriette screamed into the phone with her tender little voice; really, she screamed:

"No, Mummy, you can't do that!" Then she slammed the receiver down. "She actually wants to visit me on Thursday with her friend and she knows that I always go to the hairdresser then!" Ines remained silent, because Henriette had yelled at her the year before, when she had wanted to visit a second time in the summer, but now there was Herbert in her life, and no more guest room.

"No, you can't!" Henriette had shouted: "You know that the guest room is Herbert's study now! Anyway, we're happy if we're left alone here!" And Ines had not dared ask:

"Does that only apply to Herbert's abandoned family or also to me, too?" for fear that Henriette might say yes. In the first months after Herbert came into her life, Henriette and she had still talked about him, Ines with a feeling of panic in her stomach:

"He doesn't like women, Henriette. He told me he couldn't stand being friendly with women. Only that coming from you." Later, at lunch, Henriette spoke in the most delicate voice, her 'Herbert' voice:

"Listen, Herbert, Ines read one of her beautiful stories to me while I was cooking the beans..."

"Unfortunately, you cooked them a few minutes too long," Herbert blurted out, having a hard time tolerating Henriette's pleasantries if they were not directed at him alone.

"Say, isn't he a bit tactless?" Ines had said when Herbert was sitting in his study again. And Henriette told her how, while among the teaching staff — Herbert was a mathematics teacher in the morning and a pig farmer in the afternoon — he snarled at his colleagues who didn't want to teach mathematics the way he did.

"Herbert," I said, "you must take part in a seminar in human management", and then I ordered him a course at the adult education center with the title: "How to manage my subordinates". Ines had thought that his colleagues are not his subordinates as such, but said nothing more, because Henriette was already talking about her mother.

I said, "Mommy, you can't criticize Herbert, really, Mommy, I have to protest you doing that!" So it was no longer permissible to talk about the mother because of her warm hand and about Herbert because of his warm love for Henriette. Then only the beloved books remained as a topic of conversation. But, with time, Henriette didn't want to talk about them either, only about Frauke and Katja, Gerda and Elke or whatever the chickens all were called. Probably to get Ines thinking about something other than the Bloomsbury group around Virginia Woolf, whose books had been their favorite reading together for years. Now Henriette said things, without blushing, that one would never have said in Bloomsbury, such as:

"Herbert's wife is not a topic of conversation here. Just imagine, she always wanted to play tennis only!"

Or: "My divorced husband had better not dare to call here." But Volker and she had separated in the spirit of Bloomsbury, in the English country house style of the fine people, so to speak.

"We will remain friends," Henriette had said to him.

"Will you give me one of Herbert's pork roasts?" Volker begged her.

"Out of the question," Herbert had refused, "do I perhaps have to invite my wife's divorced husband to my wedding as well?" He didn't have to. He didn't even have to invite Ines to the wedding, demonstrating that he determined the rules of the game in this relationship. And Bloomsbury and Virginia Woolf were no longer topics of conversation for Henriette. After all, they had almost all been bi- and homosexual (bi and ho, they called it!). Herbert could have gotten the wrong idea!

Chicago, dated …
(Letter by the author)

Dear Friederike,

What love makes of people! You would think it would make us better, but it also makes us blind and stupid and greedy and jealous and pushy and stubborn. Some time ago, I visited my friend Brunhild who remarried a year ago after being single for four years. You remember, Bruni with the short brown curls on her head; well she is so happy to be married again that she left the beloved SPD (Social Democratic Party) and maintains no more contact with the women's association, which she had always found so stimulating, because her new husband is in the CDU (Christian Democratic Union) and a passionate hiker. And Bruni, who only walked from the sofa to the fridge and took the car to run all other errands, now wanders around in the Eifel mountains, every free minute she has, with a CDU badge in her buttonhole. Last evening, when I sat in front of the TV with her — we didn't even watch it, her new husband rushed in and roared:

"Can I at least see here how the elections turned out?" as if there was a bush fire in the Eifel mountains. And Bruni cheered:

"But of course, darling, this is incredibly important, especially for us!" Later I asked her: "Tell me, why are the results of the elections so terribly important for you? Will you lose your jobs if the SPD wins?"

Then she explained in a voice that was very normal and sober again: "Nonsense, Gorda, it doesn't have anything to do with the elections!"

That's what I call love, Friederike. Stupid love.

Yours, Gorda

Ines and Her Mother

(attempt at a novel)

Plato says that in heaven all men used to be one entity. Then they are torn into two pieces and sent to earth. This idea of Plato had made sense to Ines at an early stage of her life. To her, all humans seemed like poor broken things, searching for their healing half. She, too, was on such a quest — only much more than everyone else, since she had not only been a whole being and intact in some gray prehistoric time or in heaven, but also on Earth until she was thirteen years old. This unit was called Ines&Klara. Until Klara's death, Ines didn't have to search for friendship and love. Klara was everything that Ines could long for: she had been her beautiful, perfect, beloved half. But after Klara's death, Ines turned into an open wound for which she desperately sought balm and comfort. With rum-raisin chocolate and sparkling wine from Aldi, with trips to Egypt and California, with books and cats and men; and again and again with female friends. Even when she thought she had found the man-for-life, she needed friends. And as it turned out, just then she needed girlfriends.

She met Roger for the first time when she was twenty. He was as beautiful as another woman's husband, the French writer Sacha Guitry would have said, if he had been a woman (in fact, he had said: "She is as beautiful as another man's wife"). Or as beautiful as a lucky-dream man in a movie. Like the million-dollar man, Lee Majors, who had once been the husband of Farah Fawcett. Ines knew she was not a Farah, by no means, rather, that would have been Klara, but *she* no longer existed. To Ines, therefore, Roger seemed to be an unexpected gift from heaven, as if Ma Kettle had married a

Robert Taylor in a Jane Austen film adaptation of the witty love and life. Yet, the men around her loved insipidly, as she knew. They were so distracted by beautiful faces that they had no time to listen.

Nietzsche once said: "Marry the woman to whom you can talk to best" and "the face fades, it is the talking that persists." And that's why he wanted Lou Salomé as his wife; she must have spoken wonderfully, because the much younger poet Rilke had also fallen in love with her. And even later Sigmund Freud was fascinated by her. Ines would have passionately loved to meet Lou and to listen to her with open mouth and mind. Now she had no choice but to speak beautifully herself. In fact, Roger's love seemed to go right through his ear. He was so happy when Ines found fresh images and words. And seemed not to notice that her face was not quite symmetrical, and her lips were too short (unlike Klara's full lips). Roger, like her, had studied English and loved books as much as she did. When other couples went to the movies, he had read to her, preferably from *Pride and Prejudice*, *Persuasion* and *Mansfield Park*. Then, together, they saw the events in the books roll past in their own minds.

One day, Ines had said to Roger: "Why didn't they film Jane Austen's books much earlier? I mean, they are written like perfect scripts and just need to be shortened a bit."

"It's much better for people to see the film in their heads," Roger had replied, "everyone is their own director there."

"A fascinating thought," Ines opined, full of admiration. Shortly before the end of his studies, Roger had shifted the focus of his studies to economics. From then on, Ines had to shoot her films alone in her head.

Lou Salomé with Paul Rée and Friedrich Nietzsche,
1882, photograph by Jules Bonnet

"Being such a thought director doesn't help," Roger had suddenly realized. "One exists for the money, for that which really counts in life. And that is still the man." Ines had not objected to the change of study subject, only that Roger seemed to develop an anger towards everything she read and wrote without him, as if he saw an enemy to be shot down in English studies. Soon, Ines no longer knew whether he saw the enemy in her studies or in her person: he fired around wildly and hit not only Virginia Woolf, Jane Austen, and George Eliot, but also her person. To her, it sometimes seemed as if she was buried under a heap of authors' corpses, barely alive or almost dead.

On a particularly bad day, he said to her: "I can't stand your half-literary babble anymore." That was the day everything changed. I might as well take my own life, she thought in the fifth year of her love, as she sat on the beach on the island of Mallorca, looking deeply saddened at the funny blue waves of the sea where she had fled with her mother and father.

And, yet, he had just given her the engagement ring that she had wished for so much. Such a narrow golden ring and not one with a chunky diamond like the ones you get in the States.

"People in Europe were too poor for something like that, I mean, those who are always killing each other need weapons and don't have any money for useless stones," Ines had later explained to her American husband.

"What kind of death are you engaged to?" she hummed to herself and couldn't remember who the author of these strange lines was. Suddenly a young man sitting next to her on a grass-green towel asked in English or rather in American: "What are you singing? It sounds very pretty."

From then on, Ines spoke English in Mallorca to Ronald — her beloved English — and no one took a shot at her with a rifle any longer to shoot her down or her studies or her joy of life. Because Ronald studied history in Chicago and was completely happy in his subject, World War II.

On Mallorca, Dad already had death in his veins, Karin. And an arrow in his heart. The love-and-passion arrow because of the unknown woman in Hanover. Only his body was lying on a deck chair on Mallorca's beach. His thoughts wandered to Hanover. That's probably why he had always said: "Do go there alone, I prefer to sit here and look at the sea." He didn't like to look at the sea that much in the past — he loved to hike in the mountains and point his finger at unknown heights: "We still have to go up there," he always said, to our horror. Only once, while in Mallorca, did he come with us: on a bus trip to Valdemosa, where George Sand and Chopin and their two children spent such a terribly cold and rainy winter. They had come to the island to enjoy the healthy warmth of the sun, even in winter. Away from grumpy, foggy Paris. But then the sun was spending the winter somewhere else, maybe in Rome or Madrid, but definitely not in Mallorca. Chopin brought back from Paris not only his piano, but also his death, or tuberculosis, which was the same at the time. And his ravishing spirit composed the most beautiful preludes ever written on this planet, while the malignant tubercle bacilli were eating away at his body.

Dad's veins were already worn out when we flew to Mallorca, Ines had told her second-best girlfriend. Most likely, he wrote letters to this woman when he was alone and never saw the sea. But he could dream of a new beginning as much as he wanted: death was going to be his new beginning, but not this woman. Dad was tanned deep brown when we came back from Mallorca, Karin. Deep brown and slim and very young-looking, not sick at all, not eaten up by a yearning love for a strange woman and for a new life.

Back in Münster, my mother found a letter in the pocket of his coat, which she had wanted to bring to the cleaners shortly before his next cure stay at a health resort. He had always gone to the health resort alone, ever since the doctor prescribed one for him, right after his first heart attack. She came along only once but fled after a few days.

"You can't imagine how boring such a stay at the health spa is," she had said to me: "Always eating apples and carrots, going swimming and drinking tea." Probably also because she wasn't allowed to talk to anyone, and Dad loved silence. At least where his wife was concerned. But he must have spoken to the strange woman, you can see that in her letter. She knew about his life, his profession, his wife, and us children. She also knew about his hope for a new, wonderful life after sixty. So he talks to a strange woman, but not to his own. The strange woman, on the other hand, talks to Dad, but probably hasn't talked to her own husband in quite a while. And if the two of them had lived together for a few years as married couples, they likely would also have kept silent around each other. That is the course of passion in marriage. Roger had nothing more to say to me after five years of love, when I spent the vacation with my strangely silent parents on Mallorca. No, they were not crazy funny, just normal funny.

"And Ronald had nothing more to say to me after three minutes of marriage," Ines told everyone who wanted to hear it. "When my husband said 'I do' at the wedding ceremony, he opined that with that, everything had been said. That no further word would be necessary. And when he listened to the news on television or radio or read the magazines, he demanded silence from his wife."

"Today's news is tomorrow's historical events," he used to say. He really believed he was seriously studying history when he read the daily newspaper or watched the news on television. And he did so as soon as he came home.

"It is only when my husband sleeps, that he takes a break from his history studies," Ines said angrily to Karin. And to Henriette. And to her mother. And to Roger. During the day, he taught World War II at the University of Illinois. His favorite teaching material were the newsreels from World War II. He could never get enough of them: bombs over Germany, bombs over England, bombs over France. We owned the TV series *The World at War* and he showed it to his students year after year. And to me. And our cat. And our friends. Books about Churchill and Hitler filled our bookshelves. I have a beautiful photo of our beloved tomcat Felix, which I can't show to anybody, because behind his left ear there's the name 'Adolf Hitler' on the back of a book; that's the title of this thick biography about him — and now it looks like our tomcat is named after the horrible Austrian, who was dictator of Germany and half of Europe for a while. I never understood how an Austrian could become Chancellor of Germany. Although Napoleon was an Italian and not a Frenchman, either.

If I had said to Ronald during the news that his father had been killed in an accident, he would have just looked at me with glassy eyes and said: "Shut up! Don't you ever notice that I listen to the news?"

"Now you're exaggerating," Karin said and laughed out loud.

"Every writer exaggerates," replied Ines. "In earlier times they called that 'making a mountain out of a molehill'. Without such molehill-to-mountain work or exaggeration, nothing affects the reader." But to herself she thought: If you just knew how little I exaggerate.

Chicago, dated …
(Letter by the author)

Dear Friederike,

In two weeks, I'll fly to Hamburg and then I'll drive to my mother's in Lüneburg like I do every year. But I also want to go to Switzerland to visit my girlfriend Hanni. Therefore, I'll hardly have time to write and therefore you'll receive nothing in the mail for a while. All in all, in general, I find it terribly difficult to continue writing the text. The portrait of mother and daughter is drawn so without love, even if it can be called tender in comparison to the one in Elfriede Jelinek's novel *The Piano Teacher*. Did you ever read that book? If not, you absolutely have to. It is gruesome and ingenious at the same time. It pokes around in the most disgusting human areas, in the sadomasochistic mud of humanity. You ask yourself: are people really like that? Yes, people are like that, Elfriede Jelinek knows. The author is always also a drill into the soul, someone who drills and drills until he encounters underground streams.

Streams of violence.

Streams of lust and violence.

Streams of blood and pus and lust and violence.

And up here we go about our ordinary business as if we were quite safe from the stuff way down there.

But the pus rises.

Yours, Gorda

Lüneburg, dated …
(Letter by the author)

Dear Friederike,

My mother has gotten old: her hearing has become much worse; she walks with timid steps and only watches TV, although she used to read constantly, Marcel Proust's complete works three times, I think, everything by Theodor Fontane and Thomas Mann, plus the history of the world in twelve volumes many times over until she knew them by heart, and every week the magazines *Die Zeit* and *Der Spiegel*. And, of course, the daily newspaper. I used to be able to ask her about the political events in Germany and she knew how to give a detailed answer to every question. I think she became so interested in politics at an advanced age because she was not interested in it at all during the Third Reich — that is, in her youth. And when the Third Reich came to an end, she was complicit in crimes that she had ignored while dancing or of which she really knew nothing about; who wants to say that with certainty?

I often asked her. "What did our father do in Prague?"

She answered: "I don't know. When I asked him about that he said he was not allowed to talk about that. He said he had sworn an oath not to. But if he could talk about it, I would not want to know." You know, Prague was for her an island of happiness in the raging sea of war.

"The bombs were falling," she always said, when she pointed to the photo in the silver frame showing her as a young woman, with a baby in her left arm and a small boy on her right hand, my brothers Max and Heiner, and me in the bulging stomach. Already the second unwanted child; it was only the first one she had wanted. The bombs were being dropped all around, but not on Prague. The beautiful Czech city of Prague was, thank God, sacred to the Allies, because the Germans had raided it. And it was sacred to the Germans, because they had made themselves at home there. And that is also how Paris, which I loved above all, was spared. If only the precious baroque Dresden had been sacred to all countries! During the war, the entire German film industry had moved from Berlin to Prague — away from the bombs and into a sealed-off paradise of peace. On the radio, Hitler and Goebbels alternately crackled and shouted for victory, and the newspapers brought beautifully dressed-up reports from the front. If you didn't listen on purpose and looked away, you hardly noticed anything of the war there.

The things I've heard and seen for myself at the age of twenty-five, Friederike. Apart from my love for Remo, nothing else counted, only the lust for my love, only the agony in my lust, only the violence in love to the agony of my lust.

Yours, Gorda

Dear Friederike,

Something terrible happened, but it was bound to happen. Just last Friday, I was sitting with Hanni at Lake Thun, looking out over the beloved elongated, almost narrow-looking lake, to the famous mountain, the Niesen, which rises like a huge pyramid on the opposite shore, and to the mighty jagged Bernese Oberland. Where could it be more beautiful? For twenty years, I missed the high mountains behind the lake so much in Chicago that I couldn't find anything beautiful about Lake Michigan. It is only when the clouds on the horizon clumped like mountains that I could love it. And not to love what you have is a great misfortune.

At Lake Thun, I said to Hanni: "Today I am in paradise, but tomorrow all hell may break loose. I have to go to Lüneburg, I know something is going to happen." And then it happened. And nothing helps you, you can prepare yourself mentally for it however you want. On Saturday afternoon my two brothers and their wives came to visit us. My mother had asked me not to invite them all together, she couldn't stand so much work and excitement. But I thought I was smarter than her and I did it anyway. Because I wanted the two couples to get closer. You know that my lawyer brother's wife doesn't like any of us. Why not? Don't ask me. Or, do ask me. Most likely she thought that we didn't like her when she was introduced to us more than twenty years ago. In actuality, it was not her that we didn't like. I mean, we didn't know her at all. But I will tell you about that another time, now I have to tell you what happened to my mother.

The four of them had hardly left, around nine o'clock in the evening, when my mother started to clean up and wash up.

She always had to clean and put everything away at once. That couldn't wait until the next morning.

"I don't feel well," she said as she bent over to organize the silver cutlery into the cabinet drawer.

"Why don't you stop cleaning?" I kept saying. "Lie down, I can do it tomorrow." But no, that was neither her way nor her nature and she went at it until she had cleared up all traces of the visit. She would not stop before having that finished. Whenever I came from Chicago, she made me unpack everything right away and hang it in the closet. Sixteen hours on the road, all sweaty and smudgy and still: everything must be in order here. It was enough to drive you mad.

"I'm going to be sick," she moaned when she was finally done with the removal of all traces of the visit.

"Go lie down!" I yelled because I was afraid. She was so white in the face. At that point she finally laid down. But too late. I'm always thinking that maybe nothing would have happened if she hadn't thought that she had to clean up the whole apartment. But it would have happened in the end, anyway. It always happens, at some point in time. Then the most terrible night of my life began: every quarter of an hour my mother shouted: "Gorda, Gorda!" At first still full of anger. I had to take her to the toilet every time. Something was wrong with her bladder. Full of anger, she screamed for me, and I answered full of anger: "What do you want now? Let me sleep!" But while she kept screaming for hours and hours, I suddenly knew, now it has happened, this is our last night together in this apartment. And I became very calm — calm and patient.

"I'm coming, Mom," I said, "I'll take you to the bathroom."

"Gorda, Gorda," my mother only just whimpered in the morning. I almost had to carry her and push her. She could no longer walk at all. I would have preferred to carry her like that all my life: only not that, only not a stroke, I thought. That would be the end! But, of course, it was a stroke. After all, she was like paralyzed. Remo's mother was also paralyzed like that after her stroke.

"She's having a stroke," I said to him at the time.

And he answered: "Nonsense, my mother will recover."

"She has to go to hospital," I told Remo.

"Oh nonsense," he said for another three weeks, then she was paralyzed to the point where the doctor couldn't do anything more for her.

I tell you, Friederike, that was the moment when ten lights turned on for me. A whole chandelier of lights! I thought, I have to get away from here. I can't marry that man: he'll let me croak when I get sick. For him, illness is a disgrace, a punishment from God. And no doctor can cure that. Suddenly I was disenchanted by the Thun and Lake Geneva, the Niesen mountain and the entire Bernese Oberland, as well as the beautifully painted old capital city of Bern. I didn't want to die in the Middle Ages. I wanted to be saved in an exquisitely sterilized twentieth-century clinic. From whatever it was. Especially from my love for Remo.

Yours, Gorda

Diary of the Author Gorda Selig

Peter Rühmkorf has always advised me to write a diary. Now it is high time to start. I won't be able to continue to work on my novel for a long time. I'm missing the necessary lightness of heart and tone to do that. And I also lack the strength to write letters.

Two weeks ago, I had my mother taken to hospital. My two brothers had been here with their wives and when they left, my mother fell ill. She cried for me all night, and in the morning, I called the doctor. He told her to drink a lot and sleep. The next day as well. And again, on the third day. Drink and sleep. That's when I said: "No, she has to go to the hospital."

"Do you want to go to the hospital?" the doctor asked her. As if my mother would still have been able to decide anything. She just looked at him in despair. In the meantime, I had called Larry in America and he said: "She has to go to the hospital and get an IV immediately. Otherwise, she'll dry out." As an internist, he has to know that, after all.

I said the same thing to Dr. Werner, and he finally said: "Well, if you insist!" and called the ambulance. At the hospital, the senior physician said that Dr. Werner was a fool:

"Your mother should have had an IV drip immediately." And whether he had never noticed that she was suffering from Parkinson's disease. The doctor is deaf and dumb and my mother smokes as if she wanted to get into the *Guinness Book of Records* for it. Her room is so full of smoke that I cannot breathe in it. I became allergic to cigarette smoke because of my mother's smoking.

"You have to stop smoking," I said to her, which I'm sure she was not happy about. She can read lips and also speak properly, but with a frightening gurgle in her throat. The Germans continue to deny the dangers of smoking — while in the States, we hear and read about it day and night. Larry quit smoking twenty years ago, because his father said to him: "Leave it be, both of your grandfathers died of lung cancer." And Larry is an internist and can't fool himself with sentences like: I know somebody who smoked until ninety years of age.

And you can get lung cancer even without being a smoker. When he hears something like that, Larry says: "For the one who turns ninety, I'll show you a thousand graves."

Here, I am sitting in mother's room, writing at the small table at the foot of her bed. This way, I can always keep an eye on her. She sleeps all the time; they give her sleeping pills to keep her calm. Many years ago, I slept with my mother in the marital bed when I visited her in Lüneburg, but at night she screamed so often that I moved to the couch in the living room. I needed distance from her despair, or I would have become desperate myself. Things have been going downhill with her for a long time. I saw it more and more clearly every day. For more than two years her jaw has been hanging down and her eyes have been staring and protruding. Her hands tremble, asking for the mercy of God and man. She could hardly follow the news on TV anymore, so she turned the volume up so loud that it was booming in the room. I put earplugs in my ears or went into the bedroom. I bitterly missed a third room that could have been my guest room. My mother's cousin, who owns the apartment, had transformed it into an entrance foyer during his bachelor days, which was supposed to give the small apartment a certain elegance. And which drove me from the bedroom into the living room and from the living room into the bedroom. The last night with my mother in the apartment, where we had spent so many days together when I came from Chicago, was terrible. I suddenly knew: we will never again be together in this house. Here, we read together, argued, and made up. We watched political programs on television and read, discussed, argued, and reconciled over and over again. There was no holding grudges. Or was there? She was my confessor and my worst critic.

"Who gives you the right to write about others?" she once said to me angrily. Yes, who gave me the right? I often asked myself as well — and who should take it away from me?

She never said to me: "You are the child of a war criminal." That would have shut my mouth and tied my hands early on. Writing means keeping a Judgement Day on one's own self, Ibsen had said. And so I tried to keep Judgment Day about my own self until a friend once said to me: "In the story, you really exposed yourself; I would never have written such a thing. That sounds like an orgy of pure misery." Whoever judges himself so harshly is allowed to judge others as well, I think. Or am I wrong?

When my mother was hospitalized, I was sitting in the registration room in despair because I had lost my mother, my confidante, my enemy, my beloved friend. How could I continue to write without her and her daily opposition? On the wall of the otherwise bare room hung, to the comfort of the relatives, a print of Klee with the Niesen mountain of the Bernese Oberland on it. I considered it a good omen. That mountain that I know so well and love with all my heart. How often have I sat with Hanni in the restaurant Hirschen in Gunten, with the Niesen on the other side like a mighty Egyptian pyramid in front of the mountains of the Bernese Oberland. Many years ago, Remo and I were officially engaged on September 29th in the Hirschen; his mother and my parents were there. And my parents gave Remo golden cufflinks with his initials on them. And mother Glück said: "We thank you." And gave nothing to me. In a strange way I still feel 'engaged', connected, angry, desperate, driven out of the Swiss paradise.

Every year, I drove from my mother's house to Hanni's house, and we drank coffee and had an ice cream at the Hirschen. Then we wrote a funny postcard to Remo. Year

Der Niesen, painting by Paul Klee, 1915.

after year we wrote the same sentence on the card: today we celebrate the broken engagement at the Hirschen at Gunten. Unfortunately, the fiancé couldn't be there. Until Remo angrily explained on the phone: "Don't you do that! It is an impudence, what you write there. The whole office is laughing about me!" And I laughed, because I could only drown out my pain with laughter; my heartache, several feet deep, is called: you have destroyed my life. No, writing had not only been a liberation, but also a curse. When I sent Remo the manuscript, which ends with our engagement, he threw a terrible tantrum in Bern when he returned it, which I will never forget.

We were sitting in a small pub in Bern and the anger was booming out of him. "You should not have shown me the manuscript. With every page I thought: Now what did I do again? I can never love you again!" I hadn't even described, yet, how our separation came about. In the manuscript, he seems like an overly obedient son and loyal brother who cannot or will not protect his beloved (me) from the jealousy of his mother and the rejection of his brother. Who is writing and rewriting his doctoral thesis until spring has come and gone many times over and winter prevails in our relationship, where instead apples and pears should have hung from the trees? How did our engagement catch pneumonia and then die? Not through the jealousy of the mother and not through the pressure of the brother to separate from me, but because of Remo himself.

Finally, the doctoral thesis was finished, a proud eight hundred pages long, where four hundred would have sufficed. And Remo came to Lausanne to buy with me the ring that once seemed so important to me and now was no longer. The narrow golden ring still sits in my jewelry box among the many rings and necklaces and brooches my husband bought me, not because he loves jewelry on women, but because he wanted to make me happy. On the day we got engaged — it was out first engagement, because two more were to follow — Remo bought me five blood-red roses, and then he left again to quickly take the train to Bern. Because his mother was not to know that he was going to Lausanne as usual, where this time he wanted to betray her with a secret engagement.

She, the most powerful woman in his life — his first love and his general — who didn't want to be pushed away by the strange female from the far north — and that in her own house, too. According to the inheritance laws of Switzerland, at least half of the house belonged to her, the widow, and the other half to her two sons. But, of course, that didn't matter to her: the house was her house, the apartment her apartment, the furniture her furniture, even though she had once taken over all of it from *her* hated mother-in-law. Fortunately, she had died in time before a murder occurred between the women.

When I returned to the dormitory as a newly engaged bride, I immediately placed the roses with their alarming color in a vase of water. There was a knock on the door and my roommate Larry, the American, came in. He was a good friend of the fiancé of my girlfriend Katja. All three of them were studying medicine: the dormitory had originally been intended for medical students only, but then other branches of study pushed their way in, among the men the women, who should have lived strictly separated. And the dormitory became a marriage institute.

"Look, I got engaged," I said to Larry and showed the disappointed man my roses. And the ring. Then I saw that a pain ran across his face, like a knife from his forehead to his chin, and I felt pity for him. I remembered that a few weeks ago he, his best friend Arnaud, and I had had a beer in a shack, the cheapest beer in Lausanne, because Larry was one of the poor students and he had said to me in a cheap beer frenzy: "One thing I swear to you — I'll marry you one day!"

Not that, I had sworn to myself, because Larry not only liked to drink cheap beer, but he also studied listlessly and once stayed in bed in a cheap-beer buzz when he was supposed to take an exam. His best friends had had to wake him up, get him dressed and drag him to the exam place, and I definitely didn't want to marry a man like that. Plus, his nose was too long. But he had a beautiful broad-shouldered figure and blond hair and a high forehead like my stepfather did. He looked like Dad, if you overlooked the tip of his nose. Dad was always with me a little bit when I sat with Larry. That's why I stupidly felt so comfortable with him. Love is a trap.

I had gotten into the habit of knocking on Larry's door after the unfortunate telephone conversations with Remo to have a bottle of beer with him, of which he always had many in stock. He bought a case of it at the beginning of the month and by the middle of the month he had hardly any money left for food. He had fifty cents left to him per day. To eat he went to the student restaurant, where he was well known, the tall, handsome man with the long nose, who always swayed back and forth slightly from the cheap-beer buzz and hence spilled his soup on the tray every day. The good-natured spirits in the kitchen gave him mountains of potatoes and vegetables and as much bread as he wanted, soup too, only he didn't get the meat for his ridiculous fifty cents; but who needs meat every day? We eat too much animal meat anyway. This man, whom I never wanted to marry because I loved Remo and he drank and smoked instead of studying, he got one of Remo's blood roses, as if I had guessed what was to come: from day one, my engagement roses turned into separation roses. Where the first one went, the others had to follow, and I myself should follow them. That is how fate wanted it. Man thinks and God determines the way to go where one absolutely doesn't want to go.

I went into town with Larry to buy some rolls. When I came back, there was a piece of paper pushed under the door. "My beloved honeybunny, I didn't take the train after all; it had already left; my desire for you drives me back to you. But my bunny had already hopped away. But where to, where to? I love you, yours, Remo." I still have this piece of paper today, and I tear up when I look at it, and the migraine-rat takes up residence in my head and gnaws away at my brains: how could you have left this beloved man?

So it was Parkinson's disease that made my mother think she couldn't hear. It wasn't her ears that suffered, it was her brain. And her quarrelsomeness in the last years was desperation because of the trembling hands, the slowness in her head and the ears playing deaf. In the evening, she drank gin mixed with water. At first sight, the drink looked harmless like pure water, but when I smelled it, I knew she drank it to feel happier, younger, and mentally brighter. My mother had always loved to read: history books, world literature, and political treatises. She'd had an excellent memory and was proud to have memorized the most important dates in world history that had slipped my mind during endless study. In the end, she was the more educated of the two of us — and I, with my long studies, played the role of the fool. But last year my mother had stopped reading, she started to look only at the pictures in the magazines and on TV. She often faltered when she spoke. And when she had drunk enough, she started to rage.

"You just want to argue," she yelled a few times in the evening, until I didn't say anything anymore because I didn't want to argue with my drunk mother. Her hands trembled so terribly when she raised the glass. And through her eyes, her mind seemed to fall out of her head.

"I know what you think about me!" she cried angrily. I often heard this sentence after I gave her the manuscript of my first novel to read, a big mistake. In it, I describe how she beat me up when I was a child doing my schoolwork. Maybe, in my naivety, I thought she would apologize to me for that. But that Nazi generation never apologized. Not for beating their own child and not for the murdering that went on during the Third Reich.

"We didn't know any better," she just said. "And if you do it right, one look is enough, and the child obeys." She mastered this evil look toward the child well. My brothers had feared this look, too. But especially me, the little intimidated girl. I am convinced that I was afraid even in the womb because of my mother's fears during the Second World War. Almost all of my friends are such frightened, fearful creatures who don't tolerate stress — while our Nazi mothers were strong, always ready to criticize and ready to fight. The terrible fears when I was traveling alone. A few times, I went to Oberstaufen for a mud-pack health cure. On arrival, the humiliating fear of the hotel, because no one was expecting me there. That's why I preferred to go to my friends, who were all my substitute mothers, the caring, loving mother.

My mother could also be like *that*, now and then; for years on end. Until she had read the manuscript and screamed: "I know how you feel about me, but leave the family out of it, I advise you!" I then erased everything that concerned the family members — and was therefore allowed to keep them in my life for many more years. I first had to learn the consequences of publishing what had been locked in my brain up to then for good reason. Thoughts are free, they say so naively. Yes, the thoughts perhaps, but the printed matter murders, first those described, and then they murder you, the author, as punishment. A mass slaughter begins. A psychological final war. And in the end, you are completely alone. You, who wanted to be loved for your writing. No wonder I don't like to write anymore and tell myself: you have missed your profession. You should have become an actress! Then you would have slipped into other people's roles and your brain would never have had to empty itself. Your truth is a lie for the others.

"You lie before you even open your mouth!" my beloved brother once shouted when I told his wife what happened on the first day of our meeting. My brother wanted to sign over his fortune to her, his share of our inheritance from our grandmother, because as a lawyer he was threatened with a lawsuit from a big company. Then I said to him, in a fit of madness: "I don't want to be community of heirs with a woman who hates me."

"She doesn't hate you at all!" he shouted.

"But she does, too!" I yelled back.

And then she came to the phone and screamed: "Do you think, maybe I want to take my husband's inheritance? I'm not at all interested in that! I have enough money!" Which was true.

"You've hated me for thirty years!" I shouted.

"And you want to draw all the love and attention to yourself!" she shouted. After the phone shouting, she wrote me a letter describing the engagement day in our house in detail: "Your father made an angry speech, his hands trembled when he poured the champagne, so that the glasses began to clink. And you fled into the garden and sat down in a deck chair and couldn't get your backside up again." From this, she concluded that I had not liked her from the first day. "You didn't even know me, so how could you behave so terribly?"

So I was forced to describe the first day to her. My truth of the first day? My beloved brother Max wanted to marry a young student of German Studies who, like him, had been in the States on a Fulbright Scholarship. On the return trip, she was impregnated by an American student whose name she hardly even knew. Of course, she didn't want to marry this strange man and she also thanked him for his child. All that remained for her was the shame of becoming an unmarried mother or have an abortion. At that time, abortion was not directly forbidden, but unfortunately, doctors were prohibited from providing them. We are talking about dinosaur times. My good, well-behaved brother wanted to marry the intelligent student to save her from the Gretchen shame of having an illegitimate child in her Catholic village. He had also fallen in love with another student, who must have been very pretty, lively, and charming, but she didn't reciprocate his feelings at first. I never got to see Rosmarie, but my uncle Willi, my mother's brother, thought he had to tell me: "That's the one he should have married, she was so charming, maybe, but you couldn't keep up with her."

When my parents learned that my brother wanted to marry a girl who was not impregnated by him, they angrily made him think that this brat would one day be heir to our houses — and that would be impossible under any circumstances. Without family blood, no family inheritance, they commanded: "You will not marry her under any circumstances! We forbid you to!"

"I'll marry whoever I want!" yelled my brother: "I love that woman!"

"You only think you do!" my mother yelled back. "And besides: You don't love another man's child!"

"A child is a child!" cried my brother, an outrageously modern thought for those times back then. Yet, we three brothers and sisters were the children of an unknown war criminal who had taken his own life, and not those of our name-father, who loved us, too — at least to a certain degree. However, when the first grandchild was born, he claimed not to have become a grandpa, only my mother Grandma, since Max was not his own son. We three stepchildren were baffled beyond all measure! My dear, good-natured brother and the female student of the German language and literature finally found a helpful doctor. But by then our family was already worn down by the quarreling over the illegitimate child. The young woman, who immediately after the abortion of the child, whom we would certainly have loved very much, went back to Erlangen to study, wrote my brother a love letter from there, which he had not expected: "I thank you so much for your help; without you I would not have survived that difficult time. And now I also know that I return your feelings. I love you. Rosmarie."

But at that time, my brother had already met the lady doctor from Bremen, who immediately lent him her car, an Opel, although it was not entirely new. And she owned a beautiful apartment with Persian carpets, at a time when there was a shortage of housing everywhere. She invited him to dine in elegant restaurants that the young lawyer, who had just passed his exams, could never have paid for. All this delighted my brother, who loved the beautiful, harmonious, and prosperous. And without thinking about it twice, he transferred his love from Rosmarie to the young doctor. And he wrote a strange engagement letter to my parents, which read something like this: "My bride is perhaps not as pretty as R. And she speaks German with a harsh accent, because her mother is Norwegian. Her character can be called rather more reserved than charming, but she has a self-sacrificing heart and gives me her Opel whenever I want. She earns a lot of money with her large practice and ten employees in the best area of Bremen, you know. And since falling in love always feels the same, I can also look out for myself."

"She bought him," my Oma called that. But that is not true: the truth is, my brother was looking forward to being bought. And she lived near him and had the necessary financial means to do so. And finally, a woman went to bed with him, because in those days girls wanted to be engaged before they slept with a man. Just as today, old-fashioned women still want to know the last name of their bed companion before they bed down with him. Dinosaur times, times without the pill and without abortion doctors and us women were threatened by Gretchen's fate. How could we have 'opened up', as my friend Cornelia demanded of us at the class reunions? And with that she didn't just mean our hearts and our arms and our purses.

On a Sunday, my brother came to us from Bremen with his newly engaged bride. She stood there, like a sinner, with her blond hair cut short, which Jean Seberg looked so wonderful in, and with her head bowed as if she was to be beheaded by us. And we looked at her with executioner's eyes, or so it seemed to her. First, I had to go to the toilet in shock that we would now be six instead of five in the family. To get back to the living room, I had to traverse a large hallway. At the same time, my brother came from the left, where our bathroom was: he might have had to wash the fear sweat from his hands. And our stepfather came out through the living room door, pointed with his left hand behind him and mumbled something I didn't understand. To my horror, my brother suddenly bent his knees down and held his fist under his father's chin and hissed threateningly: "If you don't accept her either, you'll never see me again!" That's when I saw a side of my good-natured brother that had remained almost unknown to me until then: if you got in his way, he would get into such a rage that he couldn't control himself. Max and I then went into the living room as dignified as possible, and our stepfather went into the kitchen to get the bottle of champagne from the refrigerator. Back in the living room, he filled the glasses, which were already set on a tray, and handed them around. The glasses began to clink conspicuously, and to dance and clatter, that is how much his hands trembled with anger. While doing so, he gave an engagement speech of a completely new kind: "As I see it, I am still the master of the house here and can say and do what I want. I won't let a young hothead threaten me and put his fist under my chin. I have never seen such insolence in my life! As long as you still put your feet under my table…" And so on, and so on. My mother looked at her husband in horror and didn't understand the purpose of his speech. But I understood him well and disappeared as quickly as I could into the garden, sat down in a deck chair and couldn't get my backside up, as my sister-in-law Astrid had so rightly written to me.

"Why did you never come to me?" she asked me in the letter. I wrote that I came often. She just hadn't noticed. For a while there, I had tension in my neck and back and went to Bremen to be treated by her. She wore the white coat of a doctor in her practice with those numerous employees and displayed there the fine, distinguished behavior of a woman who knows what she is worth. There, she listened to me in a kind manner and answered my nervous rant in the most understanding way, while she never spoke to me at home. There I was nothing but air for her, but not good air. She hid behind her Norwegian language and acted as if she suddenly could no longer understand nor speak German. She just meaningfully turned her back on me and drank six portion-sized bottles of Underberg digestif bitter out of outrage at my unwanted presence. And I became more and more talkative and funny out of embarrassment, and my beloved brother and his children, whom I loved very much, laughed heartily at my cursed humor, and the louder they laughed, the thicker the air around Astrid became, until she filled the whole room with it. Finally, you would have had to open a window to breathe. But back then I couldn't find any window. My brother's children, who are the adopted children of my heart because I couldn't have any, had been watching their aunt's exuberant wit and their mother's eerie silence with concern and interest for years. This whole drama of "I hate you" and "Couldn't you love me a little, after all?" Until both Hannes and Rieke said to me: "Stop worrying about our mother. She simply doesn't want to. Why must you forever beg for her affection?" I repeated these sentences to my brother and asked him if I could see him alone. To that he answered angrily: "I must ask my wife whether she wants to come with me or not!"

And from then on, my beloved brother didn't speak to me anymore or he told me only the most necessary things at family meetings. And Astrid suddenly spoke German when I was around, and the air was no longer thick as molasses between us; you could breathe in and out really well, even though now I was running out of oxygen where my brother was concerned. And that was when I found the window to Astrid: the window to my brother had to close first before hers opened. Both windows couldn't be open at the same time. One day, my brother confessed to me that he had said to Astrid when he met her: "I would like to marry a woman like my sister," and, surely, he meant the vanished Rosmarie. It must have been already back then that the window between us must have slammed shut very loudly. And not just on the day of the engagement.

There was another such window in our family, which sometimes opened and sometimes closed, depending on how the family wind blew. That was the window between the wife of Richard, my mother's cousin, and me. This second-degree uncle was only fourteen years older than me, more cousin than uncle. When I was twenty, I had a little love affair with him, which lasted only two weeks, but ended happily, namely without quarrelling or accusations. Hans had separated from me right after graduating with the Abitur from the German high school, where I wrote the Math and English papers for him, so that I was so enraged about his ingratitude that I didn't know whether to poison or stab him.

"Go to Lüneburg to your cousin Annie," my mother said to me, "you're hanging around here like a wet sack!" A tear-soaked sack.

Today is the first day of September, the day on which Nazi Germany invaded Poland in 1939, after it had already taken possession of Prague. There, my war criminal father sat with his young family in a huge gray house, a fortress of a house with a high fence around it to keep the real owners out. The fortress has now been given a friendly yellow paint scheme and, after the division of Czechoslovakia, has been converted into the Slovak embassy. Last year, Larry and I went to Prague, and I saw the creepy home for the first time.

In 1939 I didn't yet exist, and neither did my brother Heiner, only Max. My mother was young and stupid and didn't suspect — or didn't want to suspect — that the house might have been stolen from rich Jews, who hopefully managed to escape in time and didn't end up in the concentration camps of

Theresienstadt or Auschwitz. In the giant box there was a glass elevator, my aunt told me one day, which had been installed by the family for the paralyzed daughter. And I couldn't stop thinking about this daughter, how she floated up and down in a glass cage, like an angel at Christmas time: from heaven Above to Earth I Come, To Bear Good News To Every Home. What a terrific fairy tale that the Nazis proclaimed in Europe, the story of the devil in the shape of a Jew whom they had to kill before he ate the souls of the blond Aryan children.

Just now, something creepy happened. Mom woke up and asked me stutteringly: "What has actually become of Dad? Did he die, or has he left us?"

"Mom, he died a long time ago," I answered.

"But he was with me," she said. "It must have been a dream." And I was afraid she would die. Because Dad had seen his dead mother shortly before his death and also his father, whom we never knew. He was the director of an insane asylum and Dad grew up among harmless lunatics who were allowed to help in the house and in the garden. When he was forty, his father went for a walk and sucked on a blade of grass on which a poisonous mushroom had grown. It took seven days for him to die in misery. Unfortunately, penicillin had not yet been discovered. His widow, Marie, was left with her four small sons and a tiny pension, even though she had once been a rich heiress. But her entire fortune was eaten up by the 1917 Revolution in Russia, because it consisted of Russian railroad stocks. At that time, people didn't know that you should not put all your golden eggs in the same basket.

When my mother fell asleep again, I went home exhausted and laid down in her bed, which had already been the marital bed of her cousin Richard and his wife Rosie — the same bed in which I had lain smooching with him when I was twenty, where he unbuttoned my blue jacket and I closed it again because I wanted to be a student and not a mother. One day, Rosie found a charcoal drawing of Richard in the closet of his office that I had made of him at the time. Rosie asked him a lot of questions, why, what's wrong, how far did it go, and even now, still? And he calmed her down and didn't calm her down, because one day, in her presence, he told me that after I left, he had been standing in the entrance to the living room for a long time in the evening, calling for me.

"And why didn't you come in the summer next year, as you had promised me?" How could I tell him that my parents had made a big scene on the phone: "You are coming home right away! The man has a reputation in Lüneburg like a thunder roll!" I had to pack my bags and leave and wasn't allowed to go to him in the summer. As a young preppy he had insulted the cake of my step-grandmother Marie with the words: "I am not eating any of that. That looks like shit!" My father never forgave him his pubescent arrogance. But with us children, the sentences of Richard, whom we all loved for his comedy, became a winged expression: "I am not eating any of that. That looks like shit!"

Richard's father had a thriving office supply store on Bäckerstraße, but my great-aunt Wanda married him without any enthusiasm anyway, because, in her opinion, he was ugly like Peter Lorre in the film 'M'. Richard himself looked lovingly like Arnim Müller-Stahl and his wife Rosie was a blond Leslie-Caron beauty and was bitterly envied by us cousins because of her expensive clothes from the best boutiques in Hamburg while we wore Lüneburg chic from the C&A department store there. For this reason, Annie always said to me: "I'm not going into that store; the woman causes me to have inferiority complexes."

Charcoal drawing of Richard, by the author

And I caused Rosie to have complexes, because I studied in Switzerland and inherited a third of the houses where she once had had to work as a saleswoman — probably to her shame. In the meantime, she had become the boss of Richard's store. And, as my friend Petra always said: "Beware when the employee becomes the boss, then you'll get slapped!"

The big, beautiful office supply store was often empty, while customers crowded into a much smaller store a few blocks away. Rosie developed such a bossy tone in the store that you would never have suspected that her mother was not called Frau von Essen (Countess of Essen), but only Mrs. Essen, and that she had saved the family from starvation after the war by working as a cleaning lady. Rosie herself was extremely bright and extremely efficient and read very good literature under the guidance of Richard — but I read the books in the original in English and French and one day I wore a doctor's hat on my head, which was unusual for women at that time, and it ruined all her boutique splendor. In her eyes, not mine. Instead, I yearned for her bird-of-paradise glamour and often felt like a grey sparrow amongst colorful parrots. Once, Rosie visited me in Chicago — to my great astonishment. She seemed depressed and kept saying for no reason whatsoever, as it seemed to me: "It's all a bunch of crap!" And she told me she had to spend every weekend in Lauenburg in her vacation home.

"I can't tell you how I hate the word Lauenburg. Sometimes I can't stand it there anymore." And I had always envied her for this vacation home with a view of the Elbe River. And in the summer, the two of them flew to Africa every year to a hot beach at the same magnificent hotel; but what curious person wants to lie on the same beach and have the same view of the sea every year? And the beds are the same and the breakfast and the dinner. And the same people come to visit every year. Rosie felt like she was buried in the sand in Africa: only her head was still stuck above ground — and the stoning could begin. Because Rosie, the bird of paradise, had been seen smooching at night with the city's most beautiful playboy, a successor to the womanizer Richard, who had retired into marriage and was only smooching at home, if at all. It would have been better in the small town, of course, if Rosie had not appeared to be a bird of paradise for a while, but a sinner in a gray sack dress. But, with that, she might have lost Richard, who saw a kind of advertising sign in his wife's bird-of-paradise look, even though his store specialized in office supplies. Before the wedding, he had said to Rosie: "Getting fat is grounds for divorce." No wonder Rosie ate only one meal a day and was always hungry and angry and grumpy in the store. To me, she was the sweetness herself when we went to eat a piece of cake together that had to replace her lunch. The city gossip about Rosie smooching with the Playboy had finally reached my mother. And that's why one day, I knew why Richard had sent Rosie to Chicago, just as my mother had sent me to Lüneburg after the break-up with Hans. Rich people used to go on a trip around the world when they were lovesick; today, a flight across the ocean had to suffice. And here I thought that during this visit I had become Rosie's friend for life. How wrong I was.

One day, Richard also came to Chicago — to my amazement and horror. Because he didn't come as himself, but as an elderly clown who was always on stage, making jokes and telling jokes like during our puberty. And he bought himself a hat on which three disgusting snakes wound themselves around. And I had invited my Israeli friend Aurora, because she was so beautiful, and he loved beautiful women. But Aurora was disgusted by the snakes, and then Richard started telling stories about our family's Nazi past, stories that I didn't even know: that our grandparents had sewed Nazi flags. I thought the ground would open up and swallow me. And how my grandparents always took advantage of his parents: that, on trips, our grandfather would only pay for the coffee and his father would then have to pay for the whole dinner. In all that he forgot to tell that his parents had been wealthy during those difficult times, while our grandparents were not. And each of his sentences began with the words "Now that we've become rich," even though half of my friends were rich themselves, while the other half weren't, but nobody wanted to hear that. He also always mentioned that we now would have to sell our houses in Lüneburg.

"Why is that?" I asked him.

"Well, your brother Heiner is very ill, and the inheritance will go to more and more people after his death, so you have to think about selling." Does he want to buy them? I asked myself and thought of my architect uncle, who also had both houses in his sight. That is how possessions destroy the closest of family ties.

I was glad when Richard left again. Only my husband had found him and his snake hat funny and had taken many photos of him, which he sent to him for eternal remembrance. A short time later, when I traveled to my mother in Lüneburg, I visited them at the Bäckerstraße. Rosie stood in front of the store, colorful and beautiful like a bird of paradise. But when I tried to take her in my arms for a greeting, she pushed me back in an unfriendly way and hissed: "Do go to the back of the store; Richard is showing the whole town his Chicago album." In his office, Richard was actually standing in front of a thick album with my husband's Chicago photographs. And in the tone of a town barker and clown, he showed them to me, even though I knew almost all of them. Nevertheless,

I said tirelessly: "Ohh" and "Ahh." While Rosie was standing next to me, in a bad mood, Richard was beaming with happiness, having gone to Chicago to his old two-week love without his wife and having thus given Rosie the conjugal kick that he thought she deserved. I just didn't understand why. Until I learned that Rosie no longer wanted to ride with him at tournaments but had become a passionate golfer. Not only did they watch TV separately like most married couples, but now he was on a horse, and she was hitting a ball with a club and running after it, which was good for health but not for marriage.

My mother lies sleeping in bed, a ghost of herself. To think that she once walked proudly through life like a queen who left her crown at home but knows for sure that she owns one. Not only did my mother know all the data of world history and literature better than I, but she might outlive me, or so it seemed for a long time. She was the winner in her fight for supremacy, and she had beaten me with respect to health many years ago, she just didn't know it. So she fought on by herself, knew everything better and more thoroughly, had read more and gave the orders in a non-existent war.

She had always mocked my sickliness: "My god, still so young and already so frail! You are really amazing, a walk into town and you have to go to bed to recover!" I was always tired, for years on end, while traveling; I could hardly keep up with her. When she was sixty-nine, she had run through the streets of Rome like a young girl next to me and had never once complained: "Slow down a bit, I can't keep up with you going that fast!" It had been me who was in bed with a migraine at the time, and my mother had to go downstairs to eat by herself in the restaurant. All the while I was vomiting upstairs. Or I had my 'nervous trembling', which raced in my arms and legs, in my heart and at my temples.

"Whatever you have," my mother said contentedly: "Leftovers from the war, I do declare! What all we accomplished way back then, during the bad times. I raised three children and still worked for the dentist Müller. And you, you can't even do your homework!" That was true. How often did I lie in bed in Chicago with stomach aches or migraines or run to the bathroom for hours on end because of inexplicable diarrheas, or sneezed all morning long, because I was allergic to my beloved cat Annina. I couldn't live with Annina, and even less without her. So I went to a specialist for allergies. He said I was allergic to house dust and cats:

"Get rid of the animal and get plenty of fresh air." Instead, I got rid of myself: I went to bed and slept as if numb from the many drugs and injections he gave me. I am writing here in a race against death.

An hour ago, my mother woke up and said to me: "I feel so sick. Take my hand, and don't go away, do you hear me?" I didn't go away, and I held her hand. She stuttered something over and over again; I didn't understand a word, then I rang for the doctor in desperation. A nurse came and said with a look at my mother: "Oh God, she has to get into intensive care right away." And my mother rolled away — forever, I thought. Don't leave me, I prayed, I won't be able to bear it. Abandoned by God and family in this small town, where I was once so happy with Grandma and Grandpa and aunt and cousin Annie, the most beloved sister of my heart.

My mother had a second stroke, a small one, as the doctor assured me. She's sleeping again. I write myself back into the past, so that I don't have to live in the present. My mother's death is pulling the German soil out from under my feet —

and I have been living in Chicago for years. But mentally I had remained in Germany and Switzerland. My mother's home was my European home — and I am losing that with her. Even if my mother survives this time, she can never go back to her apartment; she has to go to a nursing home, whether she wants to or not. And, of course, she doesn't want to. And I have to liquidate her apartment for her, whether I want to or not, and, of course, I don't want to. A psychic in Chicago once prophesied me that I would have to take care of my mother in old age, that it was in my 'karma.' And I thought, what nonsense, I live in Chicago. And now I sit here and have to take care of my mother for as long as it takes, and that can take a long time.

My psychologist in Chicago, Dr. Sacks, has advised me: "Don't move back to your mother after a divorce, you will always be her child and you will have to take care of her in her old age. Most of the time, only one child takes care of their old parents, and the others live as if it were none of their business."

"It is only when it comes to inheriting that they reappear on the scene," my old friend Erich Meyer-Schomann told me: "And then the dispute regarding the possessions starts. Are you siblings still friends or have you already inherited?" he asks his many friends jokingly or seriously and wants to laugh himself half to death at their answers. There is little to inherit from my mother. She took our stepfather's entire fortune and used it to buy a pension for her last partner, the art painter Rudolf Führmann. For 50,000 DM, that was quite a chunk of money back then. Rudolf had gotten a stomachache when they wanted to go together to Paris, where he had lived in exile for so many years. The stomachache turned out to be stomach cancer — and Rudolf went to his grave and not to Paris with my mother. This was a great misfortune for all of us, because we thought that before Rudolf's death our mother would be happy once again, after her first husband hanged himself and the second one wanted to leave her for another woman. Didn't she deserve to be happy with Rudolf? But after one-and-a half years of happiness, the six months of misfortune came, and everything was over like a bad dream. And I thought, oh God, not again such a terrible despair like after the death of Dad. At that time, I brought her to Lausanne, and she screamed and sobbed every day because her husband wanted to leave her for another woman — and she wasn't even younger than my mother. But after Rudolf's death, mom remained remarkably calm: "He loved me to the end, and that is a great consolation," she said to me, "but Dad betrayed me for years with that other one."

Remo's mother had a daughter from her first marriage whom she never saw again after the divorce.

"She's entitled to your house," I said to Remo. "A child is a child."

"No," he contradicted me. "The house is from our father, and not from hers."

"The law doesn't care," I said to Remo.

And his mother said: "I've thought about that too, we have to trick her."

And mother Glück invited her unknown daughter to Bunte and said after the visit: "Well, she's not very pretty, elle n'est pas très belle." She offered her a settlement and the old, bent crone — she was only fifty years old, younger than I am now — accepted the sum with thanks and thank God, disappeared again. What must the despised daughter have thought of the fine-city mother, with the thick rings on her hands, the fur collar on her neck, and the many valuable pieces of furniture in the large dark apartment? Maybe the same as I, the despised future daughter-in-law: "Who does she think she is?" A maid who became a farmer's wife and who called Remo and me to dinner every day in the tone of a general, although she would have preferred to serve me rat poison instead of beef roulades.

After Remo had finally finished his dissertation, he took a position as an archivist at the Swiss National Library. And his mother went to her hometown for six weeks, where she had an apartment in her sister's house. I stayed with Remo in Bern — and now it turned out that I had taken the wrong course of studies: instead of studying German and French literature, I should have taken courses in housekeeping. My knowledge of French proved to be completely useless when I stood at the stove and didn't know how to prepare a sauce. Or how to fry an omelet. Or how to bread Wiener Schnitzel. I could only brown the veal sausages and serve them with burnt onions.

On the fourth day, Remo yelled indignantly: "What kind of muck is this? And if I put my shoes in this corner, it means they need to be shined!" I had not looked for shoes in the dark corner. I don't even shine my own shoes, after all. I had to get up at seven in the morning, although Remo only gulped a cup of coffee while standing up.

"Can't I sleep a bit longer?" I asked him like a frightened child: "The day is so long, sitting around here waiting for you."

"No, you get up with me!" he ordered: "I'll make sure you're no better off than I am!" In the evening I wanted to talk about Gottfried Keller's *Green Henry*, but he interrupted me angrily: "I can't stand your semi-literary blather anymore; how many times do I have to tell you!"

The next Sunday, we went to Neuchatel by train, a beautiful trip through a beautiful country but, unfortunately, we hardly spoke to each other, because I didn't want to tire him out with my semi-literary blather. He didn't tell me anything about his work in the state library, but it must have upset him tremendously, because he was so angry at me that he had to make sure that I was no better off than he was. In a small restaurant, he yelled at me: "When will you finally finish your studies? I want to see money!" That's when I knew that I not only had to be able to cook and shine shoes and iron, but that I also had to go and earn money. Right away I felt exhausted from the ground up: I'll never be able to do that, I thought. That's too much work for me. I need rest. Back in Bern, I packed my suitcase and took the streetcar to the train station. Remo was after me like the devil, who suddenly turned into my angel and protector on the train track: "Please come back. I didn't mean it!" But no sooner was I back in the dark apartment, he had meant it like that, after all.

"When I come home, the food must be on the table," he demanded in his mother's tone. But you could only demand literary knowledge from me; other than that, I understood nothing of practical life. Sometimes I ask myself nowadays: why didn't you take a cooking course and take lessons in Swiss German? Those who had already learned English and French and Latin should not find Swiss German impossible. Nor should the breading of a pork chop be impossible. But I didn't want to study home economics, but rather literature and history, and my mother had always said to me: "Learn something, so you can leave whenever your situation becomes unbearable." And life in Bern became more unbearable every day and I thought, learn something so that you can leave any time. And I learned, so I could go and not have to stay. For five years, I had been the beloved woman and now, from one day to the next — just because I wore the thin golden ring on my finger — I was the unskilled cook and cleaning lady. And I thought of Anne Boleyn, who had been courted fervently by Henry VIII for seven years and had been beheaded as his wife because she had failed in her duty to bear him a son.

Under no circumstances will I let myself be beheaded here, I thought angrily, and called my friend Katja in Lausanne. She said: "Why don't you come over here, Larry is already waiting for you. We always have dinner together in the dormitory in the evening." And I saw Katja and her fiancé Henri and Larry drinking cheap wine at dinner and Larry was singing along with his beautiful dark voice: "Love and marriage, love and marriage, go together like a horse and carriage."

But my carriage just wouldn't fit Remo's horse. Either my carriage was too fragile, or Remo's horse was too powerful. And every day, Remo's horse, which at the beginning had been such an elegant racehorse, turned more and more into a heavily built farm horse, while my carriage visibly lost its shine and glory in his eyes.

Yesterday afternoon, I went to Richard's office and told him that we three children would have to give up our mother's apartment. To my amazement, he started to go berserk like I have never heard him go berserk before: "This was my bachelor apartment, which I had specially fitted with built-in closets and all the trimmings!" But that was thirty years ago now, I thought rebelliously. "I want it back in its old condition!" he ranted on: "You probably think you can get up and leave quiet-like because we are family! But family or no family, I know that you are the owners of these three houses at the market square 'Am Sand'!" What do our houses have to do with this? I asked myself.

If my mother seemed to have been punished for her life as the wife of a high Nazi by the quick death of her husbands, her sister — my beloved Aunt Käthe — was punished because her second husband is taking his sweet time to die, and one must fear that he will survive her. Although he, the architect uncle Horst, looks much older than she does, he is five years younger than her, and is determined to make her life a living hell. He, too, must have sworn to himself that she must not be better off than he is, and he aggravates her pathological sense of tidiness as often as he can, with ties, shirts, and socks that are deliberately thrown down on the floor. And he bounces his overturned leg tirelessly in her presence, even though he knows exactly how much she hates unnecessary movements in others — except in herself.

"Stop it, Horst!" she shouted every Sunday during our visits, because he either teetered with his feet or rubbed his nose excitedly with his index finger and thumb. Most of the time, he kept silent when in the presence of his incessantly chatting wife and put on a face that looked as well-behaved and simple as the bulbous-nose faces of the comedian Loriot's male comic figures. But this bourgeois face was as sly as they come. After the death of our stepfather, he reported us to the building authorities, because the firewalls of our houses on 'Am Sand' supposedly were not thick enough — and if my lawyer brother hadn't been able to convince the officials of the opposite, we would have had to sell the houses, since the cost of the walls supposedly would have been as enormous as an annual income — and how would I pay for my studies in Switzerland then? Surely, our uncle Horst, who had become rich, was already counting his fortune at home, in order to be able to buy the houses from us at a low price, and was happily rubbing his hands and nose, because through this family prank would acquire a possession he had long since been eyeing covetously. And now you see it, now you don't, the houses would be his! Commercial buildings in the best location in Lüneburg, three hundred years old, with magnificently preserved ancient gables. And in our family for over a hundred years. And wasn't his family also our family? Well, then everything remained in the family! After my brother Max had convinced the building authorities that we would not need a new firewall for another two hundred years, he wrote a letter to his uncle, which a lawyer should never write, or he would be doing something wrong, as my mother thought, after her brother-in-law showed her the infamous letter.

And it was no wonder that our family broke apart because of this letter: "Uncle Horst is family, after all," my mother defended him.

"But Mom, he was the first to forget himself and reported us," I contradicted her, "he's a pig!"

"Pig, or no pig," my mother said, "family is family." What I didn't know for a long time was that my mother had allied herself with Uncle Horst against her sister Käthe — she couldn't forget that Käthe had once said to her mother: "I have always envied my sister, but now it's my turn!"

So, at that time, the giant box in Prague, and later, in Oldenburg, the beautiful villa near the Dobbenteich lake and her fine second husband, the senior government official, who had studied. Uncle Horst, on the other hand, had only gone to engineering school, not to university, and he was therefore not allowed to call himself a graduate architect, only an architect, which brushed my aunt the wrong way. And my uncle, too. And in Oldenburg, our garden bordered on many other gardens, which made it into a kind of park, while my aunt looked out from her balcony onto a cemetery and saw the cross on the grave of our war-crimes father every day, a sight

The Dobbenteich lakes in Oldenburg from the
air. The villa is in the foreground left.

that was certainly unpleasant for her. The war-crimes father had also studied, even law, albeit the wrong one, and Aunt Käthe's first husband had only completed an apprenticeship as a salesclerk. And our dad, Selig, had become a war criminal only after the war had been lost; during the war, he seemed at times to be an actual war hero with half a dozen awards on his chest.

"Might is right," my American husband Larry often says: if Hitler had won the war, Mr. Selig might still be our family hero today, not our family murderer, and my mother would not have had to throw away his Knight's Cross into my grandparents' outhouse. And in the photos, he would not have been cut out of the picture whenever he wore his sleek SS uniform.

After Richard went berserk because of his beautiful built-in closets in the bachelor apartment, I called Max. And he immediately calmed me down and said: "Of course, we'll have the apartment painted and repaired, don't worry, I'll take care of it." What luck that I have this lawyer brother: he's as practical as I am artistic. And without him I would not be able to cope with the situation.

Aunt Käthe just called me and invited me to dinner. I haven't been to her house in an evening for years — even though I was there so often during my youth. But since my mother can no longer stand her sister Käthe, and blood is no longer blood but bile; I was hardly allowed to visit her anymore when I was in Lüneburg.

"Come home soon and don't stay there until dinner," she ordered me when I went to my aunt's house. And I didn't need to say hello to her, either.

86

The two strokes have affected my mother's bladder; she now has to go potty every fifteen minutes. She refuses to have a catheter inserted: "You get infections from it," she stuttered.

So I get the heavy pot despite my back problem and push it under her butt, or a nurse will do it, but the nurses here get angrier every day when I call for them. They all seem to argue among themselves and also with the deaf-mute and smoking doctor. When you have lived in the States for a long time and are used to the easy-going Americans, this eternal back and forth wears you down. In Germany, they always say that the friendliness of the Americans is superficial — but I reply: the Americans treat each other in a friendly way in superficial dealings, that's something completely different. And the Germans would do well to copy some of this kind of superficiality from them. Especially here in the hospital this is apparent again: yesterday, I was with the deaf-mute and chain-smoking doctor, whom I could hardly see because of all the dark-gray smoke in the air. At first, she praised my book of poems, which I gave her a few days ago to get a little respect from her. Suddenly, she got terribly upset and started screaming: "Purple nights, purple nights! What kind of horrible color is that? Why purple?" And I didn't know at all why purple is a hideous color. I was thinking of irises and the color of the night when a burning candle is lit, nothing more.

In the evening, I asked my mother's neighbor what was wrong with the color purple, and she laughed and said: "I think it's the favorite color of women who love women." And I thought: oh well, you never stop learning! But do you have to shout like that when you teach someone something? You never stop learning. Or you forget it again and have to learn it time and again. Isn't the saying always: beauty fades while knowledge remains? But that is not true; knowledge, too, fades— and even before death. Into one ear and out the other, gone again from the mind.

The third engagement of Remo and me took place in Bern in the presence of — and actually for — his brother Jean who had resolutely rejected me for five years, on the grounds that my eyes would not laugh if my mouth did. What offended him was that I knew, of course, that he had slept with my girlfriend Cornelia in Bonn when he was subletting with her, while his wife, in the States with the child, waited for the news that he had finally found an apartment for the family in postwar Germany, which was short of housing. At least I believe her that he did sleep with her, because Cornelia was proud of every man in her bed and never thought that the English proverb "A gentleman enjoys and is silent" also applied to women. She liked to talk about her lovers everywhere, at a time when it was not yet fashionable to have many of them — and so she was a kind of pioneer of sexual intercourse in our generation, while we poor, cuddly girls lived with the fear of being publicly labeled a 'mattress', if it turned out that we had slept with more than two men.

"Never admit to more than two," the mother of a girlfriend counseled us, when she provided her with sex ed much too late. "You must still claim only two on your deathbed!" — and my friend Helga and I intended to be true to our word for the rest of our lives. Even my sister-in-law, Astrid, the doctor of internal medicine, threatened her daughter, my beloved niece Rieke, with the word 'mattress' for more than two lovers — and that was a whole generation later. But Cornelia had hurried proudly from mattress to mattress without becoming a mattress in her own eyes — and I had always been a little envious of her numerous variations on musical beds, while Remo had forgotten to read the enlightenment book *The Art of Love Play* in his parents' library and therefore lacked foreplay and main play — he actually only knew the afterplay with a cigarette or two — which is why I sometimes wondered why mankind made such a big thing about something as fleeting as sexual intercourse.

Jean gave me two simple, but noble wine glasses for the engagement: one for Remo and one for me. There should be no guests in our house. One of them broke when I moved to the States, meaning, half of my Swiss engagement gifts. The other half stands protected in my glass cupboard next to the most important of all family heirlooms: the old Hutschenreuther porcelain set for twenty, now only for fifteen or so, from my grandmother and the gold-plated brooch from my favorite friend Friederike and the Meissen porcelain vases from my mother, who rescued them from the war.

For dinner at Aunt Käthe's, we — my once so beloved cousin Anni, her half-sister Karin, her father Uncle Horst, the aunt and I — sat around the far too small dining table in the tiny corner dining area of the house, to which the architect uncle had added a lot of space at the back and upstairs; only the space for eating was still missing, guests were not intended to be here either. As always, my aunt was the only one who spoke, and we listened more or less attentively to what she had to say about her latest trip to Venice — although we had all been in Venice in the meantime, including me and my mother several years ago — and my aunt couldn't invent any news; one would have noticed right away that she was imagining things.

To bring the conversation to something more interesting than boring travel reports, my cousin Anni said unexpectedly:

Hutschenreuther porcellain set

"Why is it always so empty in Rosie and Richard's store and so full next door?"

"I can tell you why," it came out of me, because my mother was not sitting next to me and stepping with her foot on mine. I stopped, confused.

"Well, let's hear it," my aunt Käthe said, curious. And she turned her brown eyes, which were beautiful even in old age, towards me.

"Well," I said, embarrassed, "I happen to know that."

"Out with it!" ordered my aunt, who, like all members of the family, loved gossip above everything.

"A cab driver told me that!"

"So, Well, what?" the aunt wanted to know, restlessly and fearful that I might fall into silence. And Uncle Horst turned his most well-behaved comedian-Loriot-face toward me.

"Rosie is supposedly so brusque and arrogant to the customers, he said, that nobody in Lüneburg wants to buy anything from them!" The well-behaved comedian-Loriot-face changed to a cheerful smile. You could no longer call that a well-behaved thing. I looked at the face, embarrassed — it looked down at its shoes with a smile, as if it were looking for a piece of sausage there.

"I hope you won't tell anyone else," I stuttered embarrassedly. "Make sure you don't. Richard and Rosie must not find out." But knowledge is power. But what you don't want to know, you kill off. Just like in earlier times, when the messengers of bad news were killed. And uncle Horst continued to study his shoes and had that dangerous grin on his otherwise well-behaved comedian-Loriot-face. And I foresaw betrayal: "What Gorda is talking about you, Rosie, you should find out, well, that's outrageous ..." Absolutely not that, I thought. And I said, once more, while looking at the family pig: "You won't betray me, right?" Aunt Käthe quickly started talking again about her trip to Venice and the next to Florence — and so nobody had to swear to anything.

Where did Rosie get her self-confidence from? I often asked myself. I had had a stepfather who had studied at the university, a real gentleman — and her own stepfather is a cross-eyed, unskilled worker who always talked about the lady neighbor in the nursing home with whom he wanted to have sex, without having any knowledge of what's what and what's not. And I listened to him in bewilderment during his visit, and looked at Rosie to see if she was ashamed of him, but she looked quite untouched at her beautiful glass of wine in her well-groomed hand with her long fingernails that were painted pink. My mother had gone to high school, even if only up to the first sets of graduating exams, and she read Proust or Thomas Mann when the cleaning lady came to us, while Rosie's mother had to go cleaning herself and found no time to read. And the store where Rosie had trained to be a saleswoman was located in the houses that belonged to my brothers and me. And I had been in California as a German exchange student when I was sixteen, and spoke fluent American English and also French, because I had studied for five years in French-speaking Switzerland because of Remo — and yet, Rosie served me the steak with the delicious herb butter and homemade bread with the panache of a daughter from a good family. I, however, was and remained the Cinderella child who was beaten up by her mother during her schoolwork, and one day — that was at the cursed puberty age of thirteen — she smacked the reason for her rejection of me around my ears: "You have always reminded me of my mother-in-law, and I couldn't stand her!"

And when I protested by saying — "I didn't wish to be born, you could have aborted me, after all!" — she screeched self-righteously: "You with your malicious tongue!" But whose tongue had been vindictive now? And Rosie's mother must not have had such a bitter tongue and heavy hand as my mother, whom I couldn't please all my life. When I finally had my doctor's cap, she said, to my amazement: "As I get older, I admire practical people like Rosie more and more; that is a capable woman, she painted her own kitchen sky-blue last week herself!"

"But mom," I said, "I may have two left hands when painting kitchen walls, but I inherited enough money to be able to afford a painter."

But my mother was not to be put off: "It's not the same; the kitchen will never be painted as beautifully sky-blue as Rosie's."

"Then it will be painted pink, instead," I shouted angrily.

And my mother yelled at me: "Why do you always get so angry every time I praise Rosie? She just happens to be my ideal of a practical woman!" And because Rosie's painting skills counted more for my mother than my doctor's cap, I told Aunt Käthe and the family pig, Uncle Horst, that Rosie was so brusque and arrogant in the store that nobody wanted to buy from her. I was angry at my mother and at Rosie, even though she had done nothing to me. And that's why you beat the dog when you want to beat the man. But it's always the same anger, a clever psychologist and writer explained to me once: you just beat someone or something up where you can without being punished and not where you perhaps might want to.

Our houses in Lüneburg are under a curse, there is no doubt in my mind. The curse must have already been on the houses when our unknown paternal grandfather acquired them. One day, he climbed on the roof to inspect it and fell off and broke his neck. He left his young widow with a seven-year-old son, our unknown war-criminal father. This only son was born in the unlucky year of 1907, because that way he was twenty-six years old and had just finished his law studies when the Austrian devil — but do devils even have a nationality? — came to power in Germany in 1933, due to the stupidity of the old von Hindenburg, and then immediately abolished the good old law. And according to the new law, the unknown father had to beat and murder, and murder with gas — and perhaps he, too, would have preferred to exercise a peace-loving law peacefully, as a judge or lawyer or senior government official in a state under the rule of law, where law was law and not murder and manslaughter against whoever didn't suit the regime. Perhaps he was not a sadist, as one American friend said: All Nazis would have been sadists and would have enjoyed hanging and shooting the socialists, the communists, the homosexuals, and the Jews and Slavs. So many sadists in a country not all that large, did they really exist? In any case, our war-criminal father, who had to hang himself from a bed sheet in the British prison of Wuppertal in 1946 in order not to be hanged in Nuremberg, proved in any case the curse that was on our houses. They came to us, the three half-orphans of war criminal, from our grandmother — his mother — and that must have outraged the other members of the family: the children with the murderer's blood in their veins should not be allowed to inherit, unless something fishy was going on there. And yet, the three of us inherited, because with Hitler's death the Allied Forces had abolished family liability — and we three little ones were considered innocent of his war crimes. But despite that, the curse of the evil deed still weighed on us. Hence the secret envy in the family, and the resentment because of the unjust inheritance at a time when most people in Germany had nothing.

I was studying in Lausanne when I arrived in Lüneburg one morning on the night train, and the old, precious city center was ablaze with a fire. A huge flame rose up into the sky. That same afternoon, I learned from my mother that it was our houses that had been set on fire by some envious person — hopefully not a jealous person in the family nursing a grudge. The tenant of our houses had transformed them from a three-hundred-year-old crumbling building into a brand new, well-run menswear store — only the gables shaped like stairs had to look as old and noble as if never restored. One day, to his misfortune, the only son of our tenant, who worked in the store, travelled with his wife and two of the three children to Cortina d'Ampezzo in October. They never returned from that trip. For months the father waited for his son and daughter-in-law and grandchildren, who had disappeared and remained disappeared in Cortina d'Ampezzo. Even on television, he begged for news of his family who had been kidnapped or murdered. The whole of Germany was heartbroken when it saw the poor man crying publicly on TV, and we, the heirs of misfortune, cried with him. In spring, during the snow melt, the four bodies were found lying under a huge copper beech tree. During a storm, the family had taken refuge under the tree, which now resembled a half-burned ruin, a ruined tree felled by heaven itself.

After that, the business, which had flourished until then, went steadily downhill. C&A, Karstadt, and other cheap department stores began to steal its customers. Nor did he have a lucky hand in the careful selection of goods which, under these conditions, would have had to rise to a higher class of quality, which any real businessman would have known. He, however, left everything as it was. And nothing was as it once had been. Then, he finally gave up and left the ruin of his business to a

Arrow points to tree struck by lightning that killed a
family of four from Oldenburg in Cortina d'Apezzo
after they sought shelter under the tree.

new owner who knew how to renovate the menswear store. He turned it into a ladies' and children's clothing store for the elevated social circles and again the business flourished and never stopped growing and prospering with time, just like the beautiful beech tree in Cortina d'Ampezzo once upon a time.

Until lightning struck it again. This time, the city fathers had been wise enough to rid the traffic-laden and congested city center of the annoying air-contaminating cars. Unfortunately, they also freed the shopping streets from the thousands of customers from the rural areas, because in their city wisdom, they had forgotten to arrange for parking spaces. And so the stores were empty just like the streets, holes instead of displays were to be seen everywhere and the huge signs with the threatening sentence on them: "For Rent!" Soon it would be "For Sale," we feared. But our clever lawyer brother found a tenant who owned three hundred excellent shoe stores all over Germany — and we thought we were saved forever.

But a new storm was already brewing: all over the city center, new shoe stores were opening; there was no escape from them, and the shipping of shoes was taking on increasingly threatening forms. People no longer shopped in the city, but by catalog, thus saving themselves the long journeys and the annoying parking lot fights and fees. And for thirty years now, one part of the family has not been talking to the other part, because family pig Horst and my smart, but irascible lawyer brother have been responsible for the family dispute that has transformed our family association from a flourishing, towering castle into a ruin struck by lightning. And here I am, sitting alone in the hospital with my mother who has suffered a stroke, and nobody comes to comfort me.

But it is not only our houses at 'Am Sande' that seem to be under a curse, but also the souls and bodies of our family.

Maybe the roofer grandfather and buyer of the houses at the beginning of the twentieth century threw himself off the roof in a depression and didn't just fall. And the brother of our grandmother, our mother's mother, put a bullet in his head because he had borrowed money from a cash account he was managing for a gentlemen's club, and he had failed to put the money back in time as he must have certainly planned to do. And our grandmother is said to have regularly gone into the basement with a rope over her shoulder with the words: "Now I am going to hang myself!" And maybe this was not a joke of hers, but she really meant it. And all her life, my aunt raced from the coffee table to the toilet and back again, many times a day, because she was plagued by mysterious stomach cramps and diarrhea (you don't talk about such things!), until she didn't want to live anymore.

"I don't want to live anymore, Gorda, really, I don't want to anymore," she exclaimed again and again, and her beautiful face, which remained astonishingly young, was disfigured by a crying fit. Yet, she loved to travel around the globe and marched back and forth for hours every day during the cherry blossom time in the Altes Land region near Hamburg or on the beach walking paths of the island of Sylt in the North Sea. But she always headed to the bathroom in between. From bathroom to bathroom, with me always following her. Because, from the age of seventeen on, this mysterious family disease with stomach cramps and visits to the bathroom also caught hold of me at completely inappropriate times. Even my brother Heiner ran back and forth constantly, leading me to wonder whether he was affected, too. And when I read in Peter Rühmkorf's autobiography *The Years You Know* that he, too, had inexplicable stomach and intestinal problems that started

Peter Rühmkorf in 2004

when he was seventeen, I thought in amazement, such a genius and yet always running to the toilet.

And when my little nephew Tristan was born, he got the first stomach cramps soon after birth and had great difficulty breathing and had to be taken to the intensive care unit. And this happened several times, until the doctors told the unhappy mother not to feed him wheat and milk. Yet another attack of this kind and one had to fear for one's sanity. And my second nephew — Felix, the lucky one — ceased growing after two years and wanted to become Oskar, the drummer from the novel *The Tin Drum* by Günter Grass. But my mother, his grandmother, who loved him very much, braced herself against it with all her strength and went with the boy from doctor to doctor, until finally someone had the idea that he might be lacking the thyroid hormones necessary for growth. And had he not been treated in time, his spirit would have taken the way to heaven while his body would have been pointlessly staying here on Earth. And today, Tristan sits motionlessly in a wheelchair and his mother has to push the cigarette between his lips and give him his beloved espresso, which he cannot get enough of. And one day, the paralysis will take hold of his lungs and the disease is unstoppable, although some people get incredibly old with it. But not Tristan. And Felix' bride threw herself off the roof of a tall building on an October 12, while my niece and I were traveling to Palermo, following in Goethe's footsteps.

Well, every other child in our family is under the family curse because our unknown, biological father was a war criminal accused of shooting prisoners based on Hitler's last order, which was: "There will be no prisoners taken!" But the order was against the Geneva Conventions, of which

Hitler must not have known anything, as he was issuing kill orders so straightforwardly and cheerfully. And Mr. Selig was away from Adolf Eichmann, one of the major organizers of the Holocaust, so that he didn't have to gas Jews. He had reported to the front, primarily to die a heroic death against the enemies of his beloved Fatherland. There, in the Ukraine, he was allowed to shoot prisoners and partisans instead. Unfortunately, he didn't die then, and so he had to hang himself in the British prison to avoid being hanged. The gassing of Jews, on the other hand, was something completely new on the face of the earth and was therefore not mentioned in the Geneva Conventions. That is why the American and the British troops didn't look for the men around Eichmann and they lived on happily, even though they no longer had to kill. Maybe they were quite relieved, and the killing and gassing had not been put into their cradle, either? Maybe it weighed rather heavily on their hearts, if they had not turned to stone in time. Evil is not banal, it is mysterious.

In the meantime, I had gone to visit Friederike. Her sweet rabbits are all gone, long ago, she says, and she has bought cows called Galloways from Scotland in their stead.

"What do you want with these huge creatures?" I asked her in horror. "Who would trade rabbits for cows?"

"They are terrifically easy to maintain, they don't need stables in winter, and they eat everything on the meadows evenly, like a lawnmower, so that no undergrowth grows on the pasture. Sheep love only the fine, delicate grasses and they spurn the gnarled remains, so I have gotten rid of Werner's sheep."

"Did he have sheep?" I asked stupidly, because I couldn't remember them at all.

"That's because you never listen," said Friederike. "Of course he had sheep, and they are really hard to look after. In the winter, they need stables and must be shorn, which is a terrible nuisance, and they need a vet to help birth their lambs. The Scottish Galloways are still so healthy that they don't require any obstetric help: their calves fall between their hind legs right in the field. Meaning, they are pure marvels of nature." How practical, I thought. It's a pity that Friederike and I didn't become Galloways, but rather particularly complicated female human beings who consequently couldn't have children without tremendous obstetric help. So, we decided to make sure we wouldn't need help.

Suddenly, I remembered that Friederike had once become pregnant during her marriage to her first husband, the rude Rüdiger, who rightly carried his name, because he often treated the delicate Friederike in a very rude manner. But she was forty years old at the time and wanted to get away from Rüdiger and not carry his child in her arms. When the doctor told her on the phone that she was indeed not sick but pregnant, she fainted in horror. Then I can no longer get away from him, she thought, I'll be stuck with him! Just not that! And she had the sticky stuff removed, so that she could go about fresh and free and go into a more beautiful, more harmonious life than that with the male dog Rüdiger. Now, that was her life with Werner. The new life with the Galloways and without the sweet, but useless rabbits. We went to the fields every day with buckets of feed and Friederike exclaimed: "Aren't they sweet? Aren't they cute?" But I don't think cows are sweet or cute, I thinks cats are sweet and cute. Wherever I see any, I suffer from a compulsion to pet them and start to shout: "Aren't they sweet, aren't they cute?"

Obviously Friederike no longer loves what we loved together before: no longer rabbits and cats and dogs, but rather big, fat, clumsy, and slightly stupid-looking creatures, which — at some point — are eaten up like a huge box of chocolates: so that's where their meat supplies, their steaks and sausages, stood on the pastures and no dearly beloved lap and love animals like my precious and petted little kitty cats. I was supposed to pet the evening roast and admire it right there on the pasture. I couldn't do that, honestly. I was hardly able to raise my hand; I let it drop again when Friederike looked away. Also, now she no longer reads the books I send her so that we can discuss them together, but the ones that Werner buys for her as cheaply as possible on the Internet: English historical and aristocratic hams that don't interest me in the least. She discusses them with him at the breakfast table in the morning. Meanwhile, I was dressing, when I heard her chirping in the kitchen, but never his beautiful, male voice (the shepherd has a beautiful voice, indeed).

"Did you hear how we talked together in the kitchen?" she asked me about it afterward: "Yes, this is how we talk about the books he buys for me — so please don't send me any more in the future!"

"And he reads the books too?" I asked Friederike.

"Oh no, he doesn't need to do that, that's why he has me," she replied to my amazement. And I remembered Peter Rühmkorf, who once said to me that he no longer reads, that he lets people read; namely, that his wife Eva does that for him. He supposedly had no time to read when writing his books, and reading other people's things distracted him anyway and was an enormous strain on him. Why should Friederike and Werner discuss books other than those of the genius Peter Rühmkorf and his wife Eva, the Minister of

Culture? However, when I want to talk to Larry about the books I'm reading just then, he yells at me regularly: "Please, no lectures!" or: "I'm reading something myself right now, don't bother me!"

"What are you reading that is interesting?" I ask him often and plead with him. "Why don't you tell me what's on your mind?"

"You wouldn't be interested," he rejects me brusquely or claims he wants to listen to the news right now.

Or he says: "Shut up, I want to sleep!" And with his eyes open! Knowledge is power, Larry often says, which is probably why he doesn't want to share his knowledge with other people, even including me. So, if Larry heard on the radio in the morning that a Russian nuclear bomb was on its way to Chicago, he wouldn't let me know about it — and I would have to pass into eternity without lamentations nor quick prayers. An unpleasant thought.

One morning — Friederike and Werner had disappeared with the feed buckets in the field — Werner's daughter Brigitte from the first marriage stood at the door and asked about the dog, a collie, with which she wanted to take a walk.

"He is in the field with Friederike and her father," I answered. Then she came in for a cup of tea and said: "What is Friederike doing in my parents' house? She has no business here. We hate her for it!"

I had advised Friederike not to move into the beautiful thatched-roofed house located by a lake, because Werner had lived there with his first family.

"You don't do that, it's in bad taste," I said to her. But Friederike countered that Werner wanted it that way. And her connection should not fail because of a house, such as it did with her colleague, Benno, who had also loved Friederike, but remained stuck to the possession of the house and didn't find the strength to scrape away the annoying sticky stuff.

"Now the poor man lives in one half of the big house," said Friederike and laughed bitterly, "and his wife in the other. This way, they never have to see each other! And that's what you call staying together! That's what he got from the fact that he found the house more important than his love for me!"

Werner had bought the house in his name, although his first wife had always generated income, by working as a teacher. But since she innocently left all financial matters to him, he could do whatever he wanted with the finances. And so he made a possible separation from her possible, by assigning possession of the property to himself early on. At the time, there was no second wife and no escape aid in his life, Friederike assured me. In a similar way, many years ago, he had bought an apartment for his poor widowed mother as a precautionary measure and, as swift as he was, he put only himself in as heir and not the baffled first wife. And when her mother-in-law finally died, only her son inherited and not she, the mother of his children, from whom he had — thank God — obtained a divorce in the meantime.

Werner, the handsome man, is a sly one, handsome and manly with a beautiful voice and with two sly ears on his head, from whom one can learn a lot. Unfortunately, he looks a bit like the young Remo, with his broad shoulders and regular features on his face, which resemble those of Pierce Brosnan, the most beautiful of all top movie stars. And yet, I detest Werner, because he stole my best girlfriend from me. At night, I woke up in the reed-thatched house and felt godforsaken and miserable in the world. Without a girlfriend, without Remo, without a mother. Even though the deaf and dumb doctor, who always smokes, recently shouted at me that

I shouldn't make such a fuss, that my mother had a strong heart and could still live for a long time. But what good is a mother who can no longer speak? Or if she did, it was mostly contradictions that came out of her mouth. And a girlfriend who is no longer allowed to read Virginia Woolf or books about the Bloomsbury Group, because Werner might think we were lesbian or bisexual like they were back then, and that we were keeping horrible secrets from him. Yet, the secret of our, until then wonderful, relationship was the endless conversation between us, the conversation Remo denied me after the late engagement, and Larry from the beginning of our marriage. Finally, I spoke on paper, although I should have done it on a stage in a foreign play rather than in my own home and always in my own tragic comedy. And now Friederike wanted to play the main character in her own play and no longer be some supporting actress in the novel by the unknown writer Gorda Selig-Go-to-Hell.

The second engagement with Remo took place in Gunten at Lake Thun on September 29. Mother Glück came with her old, long-time friend Eugen, who had meanwhile moved into her eight-room apartment. And I came under the protection of Mom and Dad, and both of them dressed up expensively for the occasion, talking charmingly, and laughing, as one does only for important people. Mother Glück appeared to be delighted with them and forgave me my miserable and superfluous existence. And Remo and I strolled wordlessly, and without touching each other, along Lake Thun under low hanging black clouds. A harsh evil wind blew in, announcing winter and the end of a great love.

In the meantime, I had lain in Larry's arms a few times, seeking comfort, and desperately asking myself whether I really wanted to spend my life in a giant American metropolis of the

Lake Thun as seen from Gunten on September 29

twentieth century or in the well-preserved nineteenth-century German-speaking Switzerland, as a cleaning lady, cook, mother of future screaming Swiss brats, in short, the house slave and prisoner of a man whose equal, smart, funny, constantly reading and studying lover I had once been. How low had I sunk! A white-faced, melancholic-looking, so-called bride wrapped in sorrowful black, on whom only the engagement ring shimmered golden — nothing else, especially not the future. We had not talked to each other for a long time. What was there left to say?

"Do you even want me anymore? That pile of love ashes into which you incinerated me? You don't want me anymore, not even in bed, where you can't get it done and over fast enough until you can finally smoke once again and pour a big glass of whiskey into yourself." Without alcohol he couldn't get a word across those grumpy, spoiled lips anymore. Now, the alcohol had to replace love, the embers of fire, the shining light of the sun in August. And I was desperately looking for warmth in the wrong arms in the wrong city. That couldn't end well. Man proposes, God disposes. Or the devil. The dark clothes for the engagement in Gunten, the dark grey skirt with the black velvet jacket over it, the deep burgundy red blouse and the mousy-grey long coat came in very handy when we buried mother Glück a quarter of a year later.

In Bern, Remo drove the love out of me with his daily yelling "I'll make sure that you're no better off than I am," while mother Glück began to drink excessively in Büsingen, where she shared a house with her sister. During a telephone conversation, she had overheard that the unmarried sister's will would be completely in favor of their brother, and from then on, she drowned her rage first in champagne, but then she began to pour some brownish stuff down her throat.

"What kind of drink is this?" I asked myself, "Tea, maybe?" and I went into the kitchen to do the dishes and saw the bottle of cognac sitting next to the closet: mother Glück had forgotten to push it back into its dark corner. As it turned out, she therefore got drunk out of rage over the unjust will. And Remo got drunk because he was disgusted. Nowadays, I think it was disgust of marriage. Out of fear and disgust of a marriage like that of his parents, because from the very beginning the young couple lived together with their father's old mother, who hated her daughter-in-law from the country, who had divorced at an early age, because she had taken her only son away from her. This means that Grandma Glück had hated mother Glück just as much as she hated me, the Miss Selig (which means 'Blessed' in German) and future Mrs. Glück which, unfortunately, means 'Fortune' in German. Misfortune was everywhere, wherever I looked. This is how you pass on not only the houses, the pieces of furniture and the jewelry, but also your anger and your hatred and disgust with marriage. And the love for the bottle, for the many beautifully shaped bottles of champagne, wine, and cognac and whiskey and gin, and the deliciously hot grappa to go with raclette. And you drink until all love is buried, until only the love for alcohol remains. And for the cigarettes, afterwards.

I continued to love Remo for another five years, when he was already married and father of three children, and I was living separated from Larry. For three months, he had threatened to beat me up if I didn't get home from the university by 9:00 pm at the latest.

"One more word and I'll hit you!" he called it. Finally, I said the word, "you asshole," and he hit me. He beat me black and blue, and the next day I went to a divorce lawyer and showed him my black-and-blue spots and he said: "He's allowed to do it once. But once more and he's a habitual thug. Then you'll get a divorce right away." In those days, there was no such thing as the pragmatic no-fault divorce. You still had to beat and shoot and cheat or drink yourself unconscious before you could get divorced. In the evening, I went home and told Larry: "Get out of here or you'll get a divorce!"

So Larry rented the apartment next door in our high-rise building and moved out with all the junk he had accumulated in no time at all. Because Larry not only liked to drink, he also was a passionate collector, the kind of person who can't throw away magazines, who creates piles of newspapers, his archive, as he calls it. And stacks of books he buys up in thrift stores and takes them upstairs from the laundry room where housemates had put them, happy to be rid of them. And as Larry collects cameras with all the accessories, he soon had about thirty of them, and he collects floppy disks, of which we have hundreds, and ten radios, some for overseas and some don't even need electricity, they're important for survival after World War III, he says, and he collects medicine books, oldest and older and newest editions, and he collects *Newsweek* and *Life* magazines and, especially, coasters and cans. One time, when I arrived back from Germany, he had set up a whole pyramid of beer cans in the living room. He said that, due to my absence, he had been forced to drink them out of desperation. He thought I would laugh about that. Because, in Lausanne, I had been famous for my sunny sense of humor. But I wasn't laughing, I was screaming in desperation: "Get rid of them! Or I'm leaving again right now!"

Larry had praised his father to me in Lausanne, saying that we should get along splendidly, that we both had such a wonderful sense of humor. When the father picked me up at the airport on my first arrival in Chicago, he felt he had to tell me: "Tell me honestly, why did you marry Larry? You could have had any man you wanted." Is he crazy, I wondered, or is my hearing malfunctioning? But I had heard right, because the father kept on with his strange humorous remarks like the following: "Larry, why don't you fly to Vegas with me? They have the most beautiful whores there." Or: "Frieda says Larry has to be gay, otherwise he wouldn't let his wife go to Germany so often!" And years later in front of the whole family: "My son has popcorn balls; he can't make children with them!" Even then, Larry still laughed. But I haven't done so for a long time. My sense of humor became less and less sunny every year, and more and more black like the famous little evening dress.

Once, during dinner, when his father said to me: "I, too, could have married a woman with money, but that was a question of power for me" — and while doing so he crushed an imaginary ant on the dining room table with his right thumb, or was it the woman with money? — I could only remain bitterly silent. Larry laughed and laughed, just as Remo had always laughed at his brother Jean's jokes. And here I sat, in Chicago, and heard Remo's laughter again from Larry's mouth. And I endured it, until I could no longer take it, and travelled to my mother in Germany.

Why does my best girlfriend do this to me? Leaving me alone with my books and my writing? Didn't I write everything for her? Didn't I go to her house a couple of times every year to read to her the latest poems and stories, to see her lovely face laugh and hear from her mouth: "That's beautifully said, Gorda." She liked to refer to my 'heroine' as her little pocket philosopher. "Doesn't one always write for an ideal reader, for the one who understands and loves everything, but also complains about everything that doesn't fit, that has gone astray in tone, in tact, and in the goodness of heart? Because all this goes into writing:

The knowledge about mankind and the knowledge of the tone in which it must be described. One discordant note, and you stand there naked as a writer in your rage, in your spitefulness, your vindictiveness, all of which has no place on paper, unless you describe a monster. But I don't want to describe monsters here — I leave that to the biographers of Hitler and Stalin, Pol Pot and Mao and what they were all called and are still called today: the murderers with the honest everyday faces. And their hearts are a huge murderer's pit, a concentration camp, a gulag, a gas oven ... Awesome on the outside and an awful devil on the inside.

I want to write here with love; I loved every one of my girlfriends, they were all replacements for my beloved lost cousin Anni, the first one I loved so much. I had to love her so fiercely because I couldn't love a mother who beat me while I was doing my schoolwork. And without love, humans die, both not so great ones and great ones. And the not-so-great person in me continued to love the many girlfriends, one like the other, and everywhere I found in them the warmth that was missing at home.

But the most beloved of all friends was Friederike, until Werner came into her life and threatened to take her away from me. But how can a man take your girlfriend if she doesn't want him to do that? And so I have to accept that Friederike wants to leave me for Werner and the cows and the books that he buys for her cheaply on the Internet, so that I don't have to send her any more for the joint bookshelf, as Friederike used to call it.

And here I stand in a storm that is threatening my friendship without a raincoat and without an umbrella, and with shoes made of cardboard, which threatened to dissolve in the downpour. And I didn't even know that I was wearing cardboard on my feet. Friederike's love for me was made of cardboard and dissolved into nothingness in Werner's rain of emotions: now she only wants to read to him the books provided by him for him and watch Galloway cows giving easily birth to calves, and no longer wants to be the very important obstetrician for my novels, which were brought forth with great effort and pain. All of this is worth nothing to her anymore next to the so-called love of Werner.

But haven't I always noticed that she not only enjoyed my writing, but that it hurt her as well? While, in the beginning, it was still said: "Oh God, everybody wants to come see me, because I am the best friend of such a talented woman. Always this fuss about your poems, Gorda, excuse me if I sometimes get fed up with it!" She had not allowed a young woman to visit us, because she also wrote poems and wanted to talk about poetry. "Please, no more poetry," she had said to her on the phone, as if she meant to say: No mangy dogs in my house! And hadn't she constantly been looking for an 'artistic niche'? For a while, she made clay bowls, which she painted herself, very delicately and beautifully. And then she started to take pictures — and it was clear to all of us that she was a born photographer, her photos looked like impressionistic paintings, while Larry bought thirty and more cameras, but never rightly photographed anything, because he lacked the artistic eye to accompany his technical expertise. For a while, it seemed that Friederike was satisfied with her artistic niche, photography, but from one month to the next, she stopped taking them, and now she wanted to translate from Dutch, and did that and was satisfied to be a translator for a while, but then she began to study computers and threw herself into the art of technical thinking with a passion with which she did everything for a while, to fight the growing feeling of inferiority that I, as a poet, instilled in her without intending to.

For all I wanted was her happiness and satisfaction when I read to her the latest poems over tea in the garden. I needed her praise to be able to write. But she needed the praise of other people to be able to stand beside me. That was the tragedy of our friendship. My love for her was therefore worth nothing next to the love of a man who was beautiful and masculine, but who had no sense for literature and art, who was a lonely human wolf among his flock of sheep because he couldn't bear the company of people. Only that of my best girlfriend. Unfortunately. And Friederike has already bought a house in Scotland, where she will move with him and her Scottish cows, which she wants to give a life worthy of animals before they are destined for steaks and roasts, even though she is far from being ready for retirement.

"Why are you already planning now what you can only do in many years to come?" I asked Friederike.

"Oh, that won't take that long," she replied.

"And how do you plan on doing that?"

"Just like my colleague Franziska, who claimed she had to take care of her demented mother — and instead moved to Portugal with her boyfriend, and her brother had to look after the sick woman by himself. There are a lot of tricks and ways out," said Friederike with satisfaction. And I had to think of my friend Cornelia who, even after twenty years of teaching, quit her profession so she could retire and devote herself entirely to her hobbies, which were world travel and reading. And she did so to her heart's content, even though she had taken early retirement because of a serious stomach disease that didn't allow her to exhaust herself physically, what with the daily shouting in front of her snotty students. In contrast to that, the running around in the most beautiful cities in Europe didn't affect her at all. Since retiring, she had been to Rome about twenty times, and if there is one city that is heavenly beautiful, but also hellishly exhausting, it is Rome, which is congested by millions of cars and tourists.

And, hopefully, my beloved Friederike will not soon get a mysterious stomach disease that makes it impossible for her to prepare unwilling creatures for the seriousness of life, and she too will set out to escape to Scotland instead of caring for her mother who is slowly crumbling to dust. Friederike wants to have Werner all to herself, away from all childhood attachments. He is supposed to be totally dependent on her in his frailty of age; she wants to be allowed to push the bedpan under his butt and change his sweaty sheets and heat the bouillon for his weak stomach and push the Galloway roast cut into small pieces between his remaining teeth while the sauce drips from the corners of his mouth, as it does now with my mother. And, if she's lucky, he'll even lose the memory of his two children from the so shamefully abandoned, eternally tennis-playing first wife who used to be his childhood sweetheart. And she also seems to have been preparing herself financially for this early retirement for a long time. Her sister told me on the phone, when I wanted to talk to Friederike who was visiting her mother at that time, that she's pursuing her mother's money like the devil a soul.

"Friederike went to the bank with my mother to get money."

"Why," I asked, astounded: "Does Friederike have money problems?"

"I don't think so," the sister said: "But she always wants to have large amounts of money from my mother; we don't know what she needs it for. It's as if she's hoarding it for bad times!" But Friederike wasn't hoarding for bad times, but for beautiful ones in Scotland; only the sister doesn't know that, yet. In general, the two rarely speak to each other. Friederike says her sister is jealous of her and criticizes her for that, if possible, all day long.

"There are people who are born jealous," she says. But Friederike's sister is ten years older than her — and had always been quite close to her mother, until her little sister wanted to push herself into this relationship by giving birth, by constantly whining and constantly suffering from illnesses.

"She was such a small, pale, and skinny thing! She almost didn't make it," explained the sister. And maybe the little sister had been jealous of the big one from the beginning and not the other way around. In earlier times, Friederike spoke of this sister with great respect. She earned a doctorate in chemistry summa cum laude. And a priest wanted to change his vocation because of her, in order to be able to marry her, but she couldn't accept such a great sacrifice from him; he would not have forgiven her later. And she built herself a beautiful house very close to her beloved mother; she actually designed it herself; an architect couldn't have done it better. And the furniture: like a dreamy English castle! Then the two charming children, as highly intelligent as her sister and certainly Nobel Prize candidates, both the little one in chemistry and the big one in physics. And Friederike had to be so annoyed because her mother always talked about her sister and the two beloved grandchildren as if she no longer existed. The mother even wanted to bequeath part of her property to her grandchildren, which Friederike saw as an attack on her inheritance rights. And she threatened mother and sister with the lawyer in the case of this dastardly form of expropriation.

"You'll still get plenty", the mother said to her younger daughter, but in vain: Friederike wanted to disappear to Scotland to retire early, and for that she needed a lot of money, her mother's money. And she had promised Werner to bequeath

Some of Friederike's Galloway cows in Scotland

her entire inheritance to his children, so that he wouldn't have to suffer so much from feelings of guilt, the poor man, because he left his wife and children behind penniless.

"Well, yes, if your mother agrees," I said to Friederike, astounded. "Surely, she wants her inheritance to go to her grandchildren and not to other people's children!" Friederike only laughed for a moment and spoke of the magnificent Galloways, her own 'children', whom she wants to raise to be happy cows before slaughtering them. Hopefully, they will appreciate that, I thought, slightly cynically, but I didn't say anything. Is my beloved Friederike not as altruistic, after all, as I thought? Haven't I always seen an angel without wings in her? Didn't she always speak lovingly of all kinds of people? Isn't the saying always: "And met these lovely people on such and such journey?" Or: "The letter carrier is such a lovely person." Or: "The butcher around the corner is so charming and gives me extra bones for the dog." Everywhere charming people converge around Friederike, while us poor average citizens saw envy and resentment and greed for money swimming in their sea of love. Either Friederike is blind to faults, or we are wearing the wrong glasses.

And am I not whining here in the diary like at a wailing wall, to console myself that the most beloved people have left me for what I write, although I write to be loved by them? Didn't Richard read to Rosie from my first book of poems in my presence in the tone of: That is totally hilarious here!

"Listen to this, Rosie:"

> Unsatisfied love is like a lurking, frazzled tiger.
> And jumps out at you in the night and
> in the morning you look eaten up

"Eaten up, that's so funny! Rosie, do listen now!"

> Unsatisfied love is like a pit
> in the bed and you fall into it more
> broken down than dead and
> in the morning, you look dissipated

"Dissipated, Rosie, what a joke!"

> Unsatisfied love is like a speeding bullet
> In the chest aiming for you
> And in the morning, you look shot

"I'm laughing so hard I'll pee my pants! You look shot, such a sentimental nonsense, — of course, Gorda, you had to pay for the publishing yourself, otherwise this crap would not have been published!" I thought the ass was thinking that the memory of our love, which lasted two weeks, was killing me nightly. How wrong he is! And hadn't he also threatened once: "If you write anything negative about me, I'll sue you!" Just like Friederike.

At my first reading in Lüneburg, Rosie and Richard sat in the fifth row and slept the sleep of the just who didn't need to peddle their own silly stuff somewhere. And after the reading, they had to go home immediately, instead of having another glass of wine with me as usual. They probably wanted to howl with laughter at me in the safety of their own four walls. And my own mother never showed up at any of my readings, because she allegedly didn't want to experience how I defiled myself in public from top to bottom with bad luck, with the bad luck of the no-goods, me, who couldn't even heat water, let alone boil eggs in it. And my once-so-much-loved brother Max and his wife Astrid avoided my events from the very beginning, where I only wanted to draw all love and attention to myself again, as my sister-in-law realized early on when I was joking around with her children whom I loved so much, which the children thought was great. However, Astrid didn't. She never just joked around. She worked hard and earned more with her work than her husband, the lawyer. I, however, was a work-shy, good-for-nothing family clown, who stood on stage to get attention for such stupid stuff as my poems, because who reads such moronic things today anymore? Just a few poets who want to see if the competition can do something better or not. My great first love, my cousin Anni, also didn't show up at these events. I'm sure, she thinks I won't go there, she gives me complexes like Rosie, the bird of paradise.

Altogether, the whole writing process began under the unlucky star of envy and resentment. We, Lore, Christoph, and I wanted to write, rather than do a doctorate at a university so that we could teach later. That's why we started to write early on and read what we had written to each other, a tiny group of 47, with only three poets and six patiently listening fellow students. Eventually, we all received doctorates, and Lore and Christoph taught at the university, as expected, only I continued to write instead of teach, because the cursed houses in Lüneburg allowed me to express my despair in all solitude. And the lonelier I became, the more I wrote, because I hated loneliness and should have rather become an actress than a poet. Actors rarely act alone, but writing is best done in exile or in a prison cell.

A student asked me, after a reading, if I had ever thought of suicide. That student is dangerously bright, I thought, bright and very perceptive. And I told of snapshots of the feeling, whereby one feeling is constantly being replaced by another, so in the morning "I want to die" and at noon "I'm so looking forward to lunch" and in the afternoon "how I'm dead tired" and in the evening the little happiness from the champagne bottle; then the Valium sleep, interrupted by many nightmares. When I sent Lore my first published book, it came back unopened, without a word of explanation. I guess it was supposed to mean: "Don't brag here like that!" And I never heard from Christoph again. And yet, these two had been my first readers! I had been writing for them for years! And hadn't Professor Sigrid Kellenter of the fine Union College, once owned by Henry James' father, published a tender essay about me? Yes, hadn't I been her 'subject' until her retirement? Then she disappeared without leaving a forwarding address and here I thought we had become friends. How can you detest a poet whose poetry you love? Doesn't that mean that you also love the person who wrote the poems? Obviously not. And didn't my childhood love Hans write me an indignant letter about my essay about my twenty-year friendship with Peter Rühmkorf? As if he was interested in that! Wouldn't I consider myself to be above boasting about my relationship with a so-called celebrity? He hated this kind of literary gossip. The recently published letters of Ingeborg Bachmann to Paul Celan, too, transformed the readers into despicable voyeurs of such exposures.

After a reading of my work in Berlin in front of Hans and his younger, very handsome lover Nikolaus, Nick accused me of having insulted him all evening, because I had spoken of my childhood love (which was a long, long time ago!) for Hans without mentioning him even once. And, finally, I was supposed to accept that Hans was gay — as if I hadn't already done so a quarter of a century ago! And, from now on, he wouldn't read my books anymore: "You don't have to send them to me anymore, at all!"

The secretary of a famous journalist and writer wrote to me that my poems were very beautiful — but for heaven's sake, I should not send any more books: "We're buried in this stuff!" My products seem to dirty the homes of the recipients of my presents, as if I had sent them piglets and not books of poetry. Any box of chocolates would make people happier! And everybody reads and hates books and doesn't buy them anymore, because the walls are already full of them.

One day, a young doctoral student wrote to me that she had discovered poems of mine in a literary magazine and found them so beautiful that she would like to translate them into English. "May I?" She was allowed to. And she translated and translated and wrote me the most wonderful letters of comfort about the beauty of my unsuccessful poems. Until, one day, I heard nothing more from her anymore. What had happened? We had planned to publish a joint book of poems with her translations. When I met her by chance years later and asked her why she had disappeared into nothingness, she explained that she had to take care of her own career. In addition, she had thought at the time that I was a Jewess, and as a non-Jewish person I didn't belong in her field of work. And, today, Jane Austen is her field of work, my beloved Jane Austen — she, too, not a Jewess — who was hardly noticed during her lifetime. When I gave a reading to a group of literature-obsessed Americans, featuring the young doctoral student's translations, there were perhaps five brave old women sitting there, but when my translator introduced Jane Austen, the house was packed. I am looking forward to my posthumous fame!

Once, I danced for a whole evening with a highly sensitive newspaper man who confessed to me: he would never want to marry a poetess, he had sworn that to himself. As if being a poet meant that one had an infectious disease; and in the end, he, too, would write poems instead of his well-paid articles for the weekly magazine *Der Spiegel*. My love during puberty, Jan, recently wrote to me again for the first time, although I had sent my books to him for twenty years. "I like to read them, they are written amusingly, but too exhibitionistic for my taste." And he had no use for poetry, anyway. So I wrote to him that a well-known critic had told me that my last 'love book' hadn't turned out well because I was too inhibited, sexually speaking. The reason being that, at the same time, a young author's book was published, in which she describes sex with her own husband in pornographic glory and accuracy, so that people all over Germany felt like trying it again with their old husband — or they stopped reading because they had already left the chapter on sex behind, as well as the chapter on fasting and losing weight.

The expression 'losing weight' reminds me of a class reunion in Norway, at my old friend Doris' house, where I had visited her aunt and grandmother before at the age of fourteen. During the first evening we were sitting around a long table for dinner, when one of my former classmates — she had been a very silent, beautiful child, and is now the mother of three sons — said to me: "Well, you've put on quite a few pounds since we last saw you!" I hadn't come to the class reunions, so we hadn't seen each other for many years, because my old friend Ortrud had written to me after one of the reunions: "They all don't know what to do with you." And since she was a psychologist, there must be something to that sentence. Well, then you don't, I thought. And I wrote to her: "They were jealous of me because I was the best in German class." Even though I had only been second best; the first best was Doris, at least in her opinion. But when the class reunion in Norway took place at the house of my old friend Doris, I couldn't resist and flew in from the States. After my excess weight and how to get rid of it had been discussed at length ("you must never eat more than three potatoes in the evening"), I finally said: "Stop talking about my weight and count the wrinkles on your faces instead!" I didn't make a good impression with this sentence, because everyone looked at me, the ball of fat, in indignation instead of looking for their mirrors.

In the hotel, at breakfast, I sat across from Ortrud who had been smart enough to warn me that the class couldn't handle me. She had also sent me a Christmas card several years ago, which showed a pretty winter forest in the front and inside was written in her own hand, right under Merry Christmas: "I don't want to have anything more to do with you. Please, heed my wishes!" I had answered her in the same tone: "Why don't you come visit me in Chicago sometime? I'll show you the city and spoil you! Please, heed my wishes!" But she stuck to her own Christmas wishes and not mine. And didn't come. And didn't write to me anymore. And never told me, what I had done to incur her wrath. I finally learned the reason in Norway.

"Tell me, why did you send me that awful Christmas card that arrived exactly on December 24 and ruined my holiday? It was as if someone had put an explosive device under my tree!"

"You wrote in your novel that I was underexposed," she said gruffly.

"What? I'm supposed to have written that?" No wonder that you are angry at me! But wait a minute, that was completely different, so, I'll have to read that and see if ..." Thank God I had brought Doris the novel as a guest gift, and no sooner was I holding it in my hand than I was leafing through it until I found the nasty passage: "Thea is entirely unlit," it said, not underexposed. Ortrud was lying in Doris' large, beautifully manicured garden in the sun, which rarely shines in Norway, when I sat down on the grass with her and read the passage to her:

"It says unilluminated, not underexposed," I emphasized.

"What do you mean by that: perform unilluminated?" asked Ortrud suspiciously, still offended.

"Well, what I am telling you here is, after all, that some of us aspired to the stages of life, so Sigrid planned to play the transverse flute there, and Cornelia hoped to show her art, and I longed to portray Gretchen and Queen Elizabeth and Lady Macbeth. As you can see, we poor, weak people needed the limelight to be happy. Today, the ghastly expression 'stage hogs' would be used for us. But you, happy Ortrud, you didn't need all that, you were happy just to be there in the dark, unlit auditorium, clapping. 'Unilluminated' means unilluminated by the limelight, of course, not by flashes of intelligence."

"Oh, I see," said Ortrud dryly, "now I understand the passage. And I thought you meant that I was slightly stupid."

"But how can I have meant that, Ortrud? You were such an intelligent, good student!"

"But don't forget, I once got held back," Ortrud confessed, still full of shame after so many years. The wounds of childhood never heal.

"Who among us didn't get held back, Ortrud? For example, I got held back myself a year after my year as an exchange student in California. And Cornelia, who also got held back, later wrote a brilliant doctoral thesis. And Thomas Mann never made it through high school, he was too brilliant for that, and the great poet Peter Rühmkorf couldn't finish his studies because a professor in Hamburg first wanted to teach him how to write a decent sentence. Germany has rightly forgotten the professor's name, but never that of Peter Rühmkorf." That's when Ortrud finally smiled in Doris' Norwegian garden, with the smile I would have liked to see on her face while reading my novel. She was not the only one who had taken offense to my writing. My old classmate Helga said bitterly: "You made fun of our class in your novel!"

"Made fun of?" I asked indignantly: "I wasn't making fun of you!"

And Doris said sternly: "I won't read the book anyway; I can't stand your prose. But your poems are very beautiful." In the novel I had described that our friendship had ended because Doris had built a wall of silence around herself. And from then on, I stuck to the cheerful Cornelia, who, like me, always read and liked to talk, what we called 'chatting' in those days.

"How could you leave me for such a girlfriend?" Doris asked me in Marseille, where she had moved to after marrying a Frenchman. "A girlfriend with a wart above her upper lip!"

"She had it removed long ago!" I replied angrily, because I hated it when women judged their own kind like men, namely by warts above the upper lip, by hooked noses and unattractive glasses, whose wearers were called 'four eyes', while in men glasses only enhanced their intelligent charm. "Don't talk to me about such ridiculous outward appearances! Do rather talk about a woman's character instead!" But, most likely, Doris didn't like Cornelia's character back then, either. And now she didn't like my prose.

After many years, I gave two readings to my old school class — each of them eager, intelligent, and ambitious. Then these poor creatures, maltreated by me during puberty with my poetry lectures, had to listen once again to poems from my mouth which, this time, I had partly written myself. An imposition, I admit it. During my lecture on love and marriage poems by Goethe, Heine, and Selig, one of the teachers present (she had always been one of the most amiable as a student) shouted, after I had talked about Goethe's amazingly numerous love poems: "We all know those already! And now it's your turn and Heine's! How long is this here supposed to last?" The organizer in Düsseldorf had indicated a wrong time on the posters: Instead of 5:00 p.m., my reading was supposed to start at 8:00 p.m. in the evening. We read this in amazement on the notice on the institute door, when we arrived punctually at 5:00 p.m. And so we sat down for three hours in a nearby restaurant — and when I finally raised my poetry voice at eight in the evening, everyone was digesting and needed a post-meal nap. For this reason they went to bed quickly and, as if liberated after the reading, no one had found the time for a word of praise. And after the reading in Oldenburg, Cornelia and I broke up; although, for years she had sent me the most beautiful letters about my books — and without such letters I would have poisoned or shot myself or drunk myself to death a long time ago like Hemingway and Scott Fitzgerald and Sylvia Plath.

It had been our twentyfifth class reunion, an anniversary year, so to speak. The evening before the celebration, Cornelia announced: "Do you all know what wonderful plans I have for tomorrow? I am going to listen to *The Magic Flute* at the opera, just imagine, I got the last ticket." As if she wanted to say: You donkeys can celebrate the twentyfifth together in a nice restaurant. I, however, will celebrate it with Mozart! As if there are no operas to be heard and seen every day somewhere in Berlin, where she has been living for a long time — and they are better staged than here in the provinces. Unfortunately, that made me angry. And, furiously, I stormed up to her like a bull to the red cloth.

"Really, I don't have to come to Oldenburg to listen to *The Magic Flute* or whatever. We have an excellent opera house in Chicago! I experienced Pavarotti and Placido Domingo there!" My objection made Cornelia so bitter that, after my reading two evenings later, she wanted to leave immediately with her friends:

"We're not staying here," she said sharply, "we're going to eat in town!"

"But I want to celebrate with you," I protested, offended. And ordered them to stay. They stayed, but they were upset. After dinner, at a Greek restaurant, Cornelia sat down next to me in the empty seat and said, to my astonishment:

"Why did you actually dye your hair so blonde? It's hard to recognize you anymore?"

"Because they are white," I replied, as calmly as possible.

"So, what?" Cornelia said: "Why don't you do like I do," and she reached into her curls that had turned gray, which had once been such a pretty shade of brown.

"I just want to stay a little bit attractive. You've probably given up already," I heard myself say. Cornelia flinched — from anger or from pain — and pulled away, as if I had held the removed wart above her upper lip under her nose, which wasn't the most beautiful, either; even though I hated it when women complained about women's physical deficiencies. And now I had done it myself! Besides, in Doris' blooming garden in Norway, Cornelia pointed out to me once again that she had not only slept with my great love Remo, but also with his much older brother. And this brother hated me for his surely not sole infidelity and, therefore, didn't want Remo and me to marry. I could have betrayed him to his wife. That is how, in Norway, old wounds opened up in me and secretly bled through the whole class reunion. You slut,

I thought angrily — and yet, I hadn't gotten through life without sluttiness myself.

It got to be interesting in Norway, when we began to talk about our fathers, for the first time about these war-damaged or dead fathers. Cornelia who, until then, had always said that her family had been 'on the opposite side' in the so-called Third Reich (like almost all my acquaintances claimed), unpacked with the words: "He worked as a doctor in Berlin for a boss who participated in the euthanasia program! And after the lost war, he abandoned my mother with four children. You cannot imagine how poor we were back then. My old stepfather, the captain, saved us. But I think my mother only married him for financial reasons. He was never really a father to me."

And Herta told us that her mother also remarried after her father died in the war and had a child by her stepfather. "Then they loved only my brother and not me, or so it seemed to me, at least."

And Roswitha told us that her architect father had become very old, that is, ninety-four, and had denied all his life that he had heard anything about the murder of Jews in the Third Reich. "At the same time, he worked for Albert Speer in Berlin, just imagine that. And we know today that Speer was not as ignorant and innocent as he claimed in Nuremberg, and would have deserved to die on the rope, just like the other Nazi criminals. The man was saved by his lying, innocent-looking face! And when I became pregnant before the end of my studies by my boyfriend, whom I married immediately, he cut off my tuition fees. And many years later, my family found out that at the same time he had impregnated another woman, for whose child he now had to pay alimony. And as a punishment, he ceased paying my tuition fee!"

What a great story, we said appreciatively. But mine was even better: And I talked about Gustav Adolf Friedrich Suhr's collaboration with Eichmann, which only lasted one year. Then came his murdering on the Russian front, albeit on orders from above, and the shooting of the French prisoners of war as an execution of Hitler's last order. And his suicide by means of a bed sheet in an English prison. Thank God I found out about all this only as an older woman, how could I have lived with it as a young person? And so Roswitha lamented about her father's denial, and I thanked heaven for my mother's silence.

We asked Doris about her German father and how he was able to marry a Norwegian woman, whether he had been a German officer in occupied Norway? In those days, it was a disgrace for a Norwegian woman to have a child by a German occupying officer. But Doris maintained that her parents had married before the war, and that she was born in Bremerhaven, not in Norway. No one demanded to see her passport.

And Cornelia found herself a substitute father when she was twenty. He was married, but not really married, and had no children, and Cornelia became his daughter, but at the same time also his lover. And her biological, criminal father dared to fight against it. "But that doesn't work with me, I tell you!" The old lover, however, bequeathed his entire fortune to her in the end. "A big house and a whole lot of money," Cornelia said with satisfaction. "And he died in my arms," as if that would make her his widow and not the other woman.

Remo didn't die in my arms. I always keep thinking that I should have stayed with him until his miserable death of cancer, I don't even know which one. I left and left the most loved thing in my life: Remo and the Swiss literature and the German language and Switzerland with its mountains and lakes and its elegant French, and right next to it France and Italy, the most wonderful art museum in the world, and — oh God — how could I leave all that for a then dirty mega city on Lake Michigan, far and wide no mountain and no castle and no flowering geraniums in front of the windows with the green painted wooden shutters.

I never fully recovered from the shock of this liberation. Yes, I was liberated from Remo's shouting when I ordered bread or wine for myself from the waiter, because as a man he had to do it himself and I was supposed to play the little docile gray mouse that takes the pieces of cheese from his hand, even though I hate cheese. And in a yellow costume and with freshly washed hair, I no longer look like a gray mouse, rather more like a smashing, fluttering bee on its way to the yellow sea of canola blooms. The years with Remo went by, and I moved ever more freely through the Swiss regions and was able to buy the sausage and the bread myself, even pay for it myself — but as soon as he was by my side, I was supposed to play the inhibited, insecure, obedient child that he had to guide and feed and put down so that it would finally grow up after a hundred years of his guidance. When the students took to the streets in Germany to rage against the American war in Vietnam and their German Nazi fathers, I sat in Remo's ancient, intact city and raged against the millennia-long dictatorship of man over woman.

"I won't put up with that anymore!" I shouted. Or: "But that's not how I imagine marriage to be!" And: "Just who do you think you are? My father? I am not playing second fiddle, just because I am a woman. I've learned just as much as you have, and isn't that why you loved me once?"

But he wanted to tear out the hair of the little gray mouse at his side hair by hair, until it turned into a naked mouse in front of the eyes of the whole world, and in front of his and hers, too.

He took from me what makes me me. My laughter, my tenderness, my ability to be happy, my compassion, my ability to help, my animalism, my radiance; he squashed every appearance of all this until it didn't come up again. "But why does someone do that, I don't understand ...?" writes Ingeborg Bachmann in *The Book of Franza*.

"Yes, why do men do that?

"I don't know what you're complaining about," Remo said: "After all, I give you the freedom to read the books you want to read!"

When I first visited Remo, the railway station of Bern was manageably small. Over time, it grew into a giant train station, as if Bern had become a modern American giant city. And when I left Remo, it was enormously large and was stretching out in all directions: Like the soul cancer in the love of Remo and me that destroyed it.

But never completely. I never stopped loving Remo, nor Bern, nor Switzerland. Like a disease from which one cannot recover, like malaria or multiple sclerosis or the tuberculosis patients in *The Magic Mountain*. I remained lovesick for Remo all my life and didn't want to recover, not from the belief in an ideal marriage, in which husband and wife read to each other from the books they are currently holding in their hands: "Listen to the interesting stuff I found here," she says. And he: "Wow, how amazing, I didn't know that. And did you know that Hermann Hesse was always ill and often lived in sanatoriums, with his stays being paid for by rich patrons? He writes in one of his letters: Today, it took me three hours to digest a few tablespoons of gruel." That sounds like Celiac Disease, I would have said, if Remo and I had remained who we once were: two equally literature-obsessed people chatting wonderfully with each other, and no speechless idiots like Remo, the fiancé, or Larry, the husband, who simply cuts me off with his favorite sentence: "Shut up! Shut up!"

In the first years after our separation, Remo and I met once a year at the Schweizerhof restaurant in Bern. He invited me to a five-course meal and brought me books as a gift, as he used to do when he delighted me with them every time I visited. The great happiness that was Remo had become my great misfortune — but once a year we would pretend that I hadn't left, and the prince wouldn't have turned into an ugly frog that you could throw at the wall as much as you wanted: he always remained an ugly frog.

The more years went by, the more modest the restaurants became, and the courses of the meals diminished noticeably, because Remo now carried a significant belly in front of him and had five mouths to feed at home, those of the three little ones and those of the parents. Whenever I thought of his offspring, I always saw three hugely opened bird beaks and red throats in my mind. I didn't want to see pictures of the children — and neither of his wife, of whom my friend Hanni had told me that she didn't look like anything, which pleased me and angered him, because I was stupid enough to repeat her words to him. In the end we only ate a bratwurst with French fries and lightly burnt onions at the Mövenpick fast food restaurant, that's how little I was worth to him. When I asked him if he could remember that he once told me: "You wouldn't believe how much I loved your face, that mixture of tenderness and austerity," he couldn't remember anymore. That is the reason why I preferred not to tell him that Goethe wrote the same thing about his beloved sister Cornelia in *Poetry and Truth*.

It would not have interested him anymore. Just as our family owned the houses in Lüneburg, the Glück family owned two tall buildings glued together in the most beautiful Swiss style, which a grandfather, whom Reno didn't know, had purchased a long time ago. That had been, as in our case, over a hundred years ago. Remo and his mother lived in an eight-room apartment, filled with antiques; the floor was covered with old Persian carpets in bright red and blue, the walls were full of originals by Swiss painters which had been collected by father and grandfather. Also in the vacation apartment near Lake Constance: everywhere pictures and precious furniture and carpets. The cupboards full of Rosenthal crockery and delicate wine and champagne glasses, silver in abundance, embroidered linen tablecloths and bed linen of the most solid kind, which lasted for a century and more.

Had I been many years older, my heart would have rejoiced at the sight of all these things. But at twenty, my heart had no sense for earthly goods and thought the display cases with the family silver, the teapots and sugar bowls and fruit bowls were "old stuff" and didn't want to live in the past of family happiness, but in my own present and future with modern, newly bought armchairs and sofas without the green plush and the tassels on the lampshades. Everything had to be chosen and paid for by myself.

Paying for it now was difficult, when Larry and I tried to set up our first apartment in Chicago: Larry's father got us the chairs from old bars, those beautifully curved Bentwood chairs that you see so often in the pictures of the impressionists. Timelessly tasteful and practical, they were built for bars and restaurants and nightclubs. I still love them today. My mother repainted them when I visited Chicago while outside the first Siberian winter was raging. High mountains of snow on the

Interior of mother Glück's eight-room apartment near Lake Constance

roadsides, and hurricane-like storms sweeping across the lake directly from Canada. Radio and television warned us to stay inside, if possible. In the uncomfortable 'inside', on the other hand, there was tropical heat fit for monkeys — where does this expression actually come from? — and my mother was wearing a sleeveless light green summer dress when she first painted the chairs in black, after sanding them down with her own hands. How did she know that you sand the chairs before you paint them? Unfortunately, I didn't ask her that. Too bad, now I would like to know. Did she learn this in the miserable post-war period, when nobody in Germany had anything substantial, in contrast to the people in rich, war-free Switzerland? And what was she thinking when I left the eight-room apartment with all the antiques and silver chandeliers for this shabby two-room apartment full of cockroaches in the refrigerator and the view of a Jewish temple as a daily reminder of the murder of the Jews in the Third Reich? Her distraught owner's heart must have cried at the sight of the poverty in my new home with the prints of my beloved Impressionists on the walls, the cheap white garden table in the tiny dinette corner and the rickety brown armchair in front of the old TV that Larry's parents had given to us along with the tattered sheets. But she didn't say anything. Silence was something she was born with or brought up with in the Third Reich. She seldom spoke about the magnificent villa in Prague in the ambassador district. Probably out of shame.

Back then, all buildings in the States were heated to a too-high temperature in the winter and cooled to a too-low temperature in the summer. We wore cardigans in the cold movie theaters in the hottest July weather and, in winter, thick wool coats over light summer dresses. Oil-rich America had no fear, yet, of a future without oil. That came much later. I had to give away all my winter sweaters to all my German girlfriends, because I would have gotten a heat stroke in Chicago in them. But in my mind, I still see myself in an orange mohair sweater that Remo once found so pretty. In Chicago's huge department stores, salesgirls wore white summer blouses with black skirts. And customers held their heavy winter coats in their arms. That was annoying and I didn't like to go shopping, but now I had to do it tirelessly to buy cheap knives and forks, glasses, crockery, sheets, tablecloths, a vacuum cleaner, buckets, a shovel, floor cloths and brushes, all items that were in abundance in Bern and which I had ignored in indifference. Now I had to be careful of expenses and pay for the items with the little money we had.

So I learned the value of everyday things the hard way: slowly and with a lot of effort, we scrimped and saved up the money for the most necessary things; well, we didn't take it from the food budget, but rather took it from the money for shoes and clothes and purses. I went to the cheapest department store to buy clothes, and yet, in Lausanne, I had owned beautiful cashmere coats and expensive pant suits made of the finest wool. Good-bye, Mrs. Swiss Affluence. Greetings, Mrs. Poverty in the States.

But I was young and believed in the future in a big white Southern Colonial Antebellum mansion, with large columns on either side of the front door, which Larry had promised me as a student. In the first year of his hospital training, Larry had to work every other night and, of course, also during the day. I almost always sat alone in the hot apartment with the cockroaches, and from noon on I got drunk on cheap whiskey in front of the TV, where I liked to watch an endless series. It was called 'All My Children', and there was a beautiful Erica in it, who was still beautiful after a dozen or more affairs, relationships, marriages, and divorces, and so the love carousel could continue to spin. Erica was always scheming, losing, and conquering — and I was allowed to imagine that I, too, would continue to love and lose and conquer for a long time, that this, here, was not the last station of my life, only the second of an infinite number, because nothing was as it had been in Switzerland. All friends had disappeared like the cockroaches when I opened the door of the refrigerator; there were no protective mountains east of the lake, which is as big as an ocean. I could no longer go to my mother's house while sleeping on the night train, but now I was wide awake, sitting for hours in the narrow seat of the expensive plane, where, on the right and left, you had to fight with your elbows for the support of your arms.

If nothing is the way it was, do you then still love the man in a foreign place with foreign relatives and a foreign literature and history? And the husband is no longer the man he had been as a student in Switzerland, no longer loving and attentive and all ears for your sufferings and joys, only brusque and uncommunicative and angry about the poorly paid slave job at the hospital. But because he cannot punish them, he punishes you and your life with him — just as Remo punished you in Bern for the end of his wonderful vacation time as a doctoral student. He, too, didn't want to get up at seven in the morning, and go to bed at eleven in the evening, only to be fresh again the next morning, to be where he didn't want to be, and to do a job that didn't suit him, namely the library work; after all, he was a born author who, even though he had not written anything yet, would most certainly do so if he found the time for it. That's why Remo lost his best years while fighting for the correctness of the footnotes that his articles on Hesse or Rilke required of him.

And Larry was like a born heir to a huge fortune; he didn't need a job to be happy. Unfortunately, his parents were not wealthy and would leave him very little, and even that was a long time off. So he lost his best years in a bread-and-butter job, which, at the moment, gave him only bread, but no cold cuts on it and no house with white columns in front of the door. Only a used car.

To protect myself from Larry's anger and from loneliness, I went back to university and did what I had always done: I continued to study German literature, this time in the English-speaking United States and not something new, like theater studies and acting would have been, which would have been just the right thing for a person beaten up in childhood, who only becomes alive and is pain-free on stage, and who, without the daily applause or encouragement, thinks she is ugly and brainless and superfluous.

I lost Larry the first year in Chicago the same way I lost Remo: to the job that sucked all strength and all kindness and all mobility out of him, so that I lived only with an empty shell, a shell that wanted to fill itself with beer and whiskey and wine and schnapps. And I drank along with him, as much as I could stomach, without having to throw up the next morning. But Remo and Larry never had to throw up and could keep on drinking when the glass was already falling out of my hand. Back then, many glasses broke. Glasses and luck. Today, we drink from sturdy plastic glasses so that we don't have to pick up the broken pieces of glass from the floor. Now, we would have plenty of money for precious things made of glass, but as a civil servant's daughter, I was afraid of fragile things all my life, because as a child I broke one of the crystal champagne glasses on New Year's Eve that Mom and Dad bought after the war. Later, one after the other, nine of the twenty soup plates made of Hutschenreuther porcelain — heirlooms of our once rich grandmother — slipped out of my hands. You never forget something like that, and after that, prefer to eat out of a tin bowl rather than from Meissen porcelain. A rich girlfriend once asked me: why do you offer your guests the wine in these simple glasses and yet you have such beautiful ones in your glass cabinet? At the time, I was ashamed like that clumsy child back then and lowered my eyes and didn't say anything, but now I'm telling it as it is.

In Bern I had buried a mother-in-law who didn't like me, and for years I suffered from this rejection. Lucky me, I now had two new parents-in-law in the States, who enjoyed taking me into their lives with open arms and hearts. Every weekend, we were invited by them to a banquet. It's a pity that I didn't have my mother-in-law write down her recipes so that later I could feed her son with the food he was used to. Because, in the beginning, love may focus on the eyes, but later, the way to a man's heart is through his stomach, as everyone knows. Only I didn't know that, and my generation of female university students, who all didn't want to be like their mothers, they also didn't think much of cooking and baking and ironing and mending. Only of food that was supposed to get to and be on the dining table by itself in a wonderful way, but which it didn't, to our amazement.

On the days, when Larry wasn't eating at the hospital, I put a fried steak, a baked potato with butter and sour cream, and a salad on the table in front of him and thought: There is no better way to eat. But after a year of eating steak and potatoes, Larry went on a rampage like I knew them from Remo:

"What kind of muck is this? I can't stand baked potatoes anymore! Why don't you make some pasta here?"

"Because I don't like pasta."

"Why don't you like pasta?"

"Pasta makes you fat," I said, and thought of Friederike, whose saying "cooking makes work and makes you fat," had become a mantra among us friends. Who would want to do the work if the result made us fat? We weren't allowed to look like cooks with huge breasts and bellies and buttocks under our aprons. We were supposed to look like the pencil-thin mannequins who, based on the pictures, lived only on air and fun. Audrey Hepburn was our idol, not Marilyn Monroe. The men probably wanted to have Marilyn Monroe in bed, but Audrey Hepburn in the theater at their side. At least, that's what we thought. And we fasted until we were pencil thin. And ate no noodles and no bread and, very rarely, a bite of our beloved baked potato. How could Larry not love potatoes? I asked myself, starved, and bought cookbooks with recipes full of noodles and rice and whole cups of butter and cream, all of which I was not allowed to eat, in order to live up to my ideal pencil-thin line in the landscape.

It was then that I began to cook for two different people: for one who ate what he liked, and one who never got what she wanted. And we rarely ate together, so that I didn't have to look with envy at his filled plate and think: that plate contains my calories for the whole day! In my mind, I was counting calories and not the money, which we didn't have anyway, but my Swiss mother-in-law had it and she took her fat body without shame to the nearest restaurant.

Larry's parents loved Christmas so much that they wrapped their whole living room furniture in gold and silver. The beige sofa was threaded with many shiny golden threads, as were the armchairs and the window curtains. The lampshades, on the other hand, shimmered like silver and all around the huge mirror in the dining area, there was a baroque frame shining golden and silver. The only thing that was missing was the tree and we could have sung "Silent Night, Holy Night" all year long. That's how much Christmas was around us. Even the names of my parents-in-law were a perfect fit for the Christmas image: their names were Mary and Joseph, just like the parents of the dear baby Jesus. And Larry was their baby Jesus, for he was born on December 24. If Larry's parents had been Mexican, they would most likely have named their child Jesus. But this was not common among the Poles, who called their children Edward or Lawrence or Richard, because they wanted to have names like the WASPs in the States, like the White Anglo-Saxon Protestants. As Poles, however, they were Catholics, a minority almost despised in North America at the time, and not like the Germans, who were proud to belong to the actual Christian church and not the version later invented by Luther, which was invalid to them. In America, on the other hand, the Catholic faith seemed to be something 'absurd', something that had strayed from the right path, and the right one here was the Protestant one. It was rumored that they were in bondage to the Pope and not to the President, and that they prayed not to Christ, but to the numerous saints, and, above all, to Mary, the Mother of God, who didn't play a role for us Protestants anymore. We didn't need to worship a woman and mother.

Mary and Joseph and Larry and his sister Magdalene were excessively Catholic, I thought, coming myself from the Protestant north of Germany. Remo's Switzerland, too, was influenced by the Protestantism of Zwingli and Calvin. All of us had already quit going to church regularly a long time ago. We had left such 'fanatical' times behind us. In Larry's family, on the other hand, at bedtime, they prayed loudly on their knees in front of the bed. "Desdemona, did you pray at night?" always came to my mind when I saw father-in-law

Joseph kneeling on his knees in the bedroom, and next to him his Polish Mary or a Desdemona or Mary, Queen of Scots. In our marriage, Larry no longer prayed loudly on his knees, but silently, in his favorite armchair. When he stared at nothing in particular, with glassy eyes, I knew: now he is praying for us. And I kept my mouth shut. Until he opened his again and asked: "What's for supper, today? Hopefully, no baked potato?"

Right at the beginning of the marriage, he had forbidden me to speak to him on the weekend morning at eight or eight-thirty or nine or nine thirty, because then he listened to the news on the radio and had to remain undisturbed, because, at any time, WW III could break out, for which we waited daily, with the desperation of those condemned to death. Actually, we were all condemned to death from the beginning, but man doesn't want to admit this and lives on, apparently senselessly, because he should, actually, immediately put an end to the game with this final outcome.

Larry's sister Magdalene had studied pharmacy like her husband, but she didn't take the last exam for fear of failure. She didn't want to take the exam before that either, that's how strong her fear of failing was, but her father had personally picked her up at the dormitory and drove her to the exam, against her will. Later she didn't board an airplane for fear of flying and didn't see anything of the world for fear of traveling. But, at home, she ruled like a female pope, who was showing the husband and the children how things were to be on earth. She also wanted to show the German sister-in-law the right way to the right religion, but she protested in a Lutheran way and argued, where there was nothing to argue about.

"Don't you believe in transubstantiation, after all?" she yelled out, once. I had to look it up in the encyclopedia at home to see what kind of Christian miracle that was. I see, it meant that one ate human flesh like the cannibals and drank human blood without vomiting, but not me, I continued to drink wine as wine and ate bread as bread or, at most, as a symbol, if at all. Mother and father and the girlfriends, none of them had spoken of God in Germany, except in a slightly derogatory way, as if speaking of a ghost, which no one had ever seen, and which one preferred not to believe in, or else it might begin to haunt you. For us, faith was something like being mentally unwell, one should rather concentrate on what was right in front of one's nose, that is, homework or setting the table for dinner than the unprovable, like the meaning of life or the deus ex machina, which only existed on the theater stage, anyway. In real life, chance reigned without rhyme or reason, which didn't bother us at all; to us, the belief in a hell, in which one had to stew for one's evil deeds, seemed much worse, because then all Nazis would have had to prepare themselves for an eternity with the devil and his hell brood — and who would wish such a bad end without end for his parents?

Before Larry and I lived in Chicago, mom and dad had rushed up every weekend to see Magdalene and her husband Patrick, to enjoy the three grandchildren. And along the way, the father-in-law would teach his son-in-law how to clean the toaster and the car engine and how the TV would work better. Meanwhile, Mom cleaned up her daughter's 'mess' ("where does she get it from? She doesn't get it from me"). She preferred her own chaos to her mother's order and went through life dirt-blind, thereby saving herself a lot of work. You could learn a lot from her. "If you have to clean up first to receive guests, then you don't want to have visitors anymore," she concluded logically, preferring guests to cleaning. After all, nobody complained, either. Because Magdalene was well-read and eager to talk and discuss, just as her brother loved iron-clad or golden silence. And I liked to talk like Magdalene; we argued happily for many hours, because she was never offended, and neither was I. We picked up the thread of the argument again, where we had dropped it during the last conversation. I would have lived much better with Magdalene than with Larry, but biology wanted me to live with her silent brother. My brother-in-law Patrick also liked to talk about his wife's catholic rules with a lot of humor, so no sex without marriage and no sex without children and no sex unless absolutely necessary. And for whom was sex absolutely necessary? Maybe it was like that with animals, but after all, we were human beings and had the choice between good and evil. Between being human and being an animal.

And, without a doubt, women were the better humans, because they didn't need war and sex like the men, I mean, who has ever heard of a Russian army of women taking over a city like Berlin and then raping all the men or nailing them to the wall or killing them in any other way? Are there brothels where women stand in line like the men did in WWII?

Fighting and sex, that belongs naturally together for the men, as sex and having children does for the women. After seven births in ten years, even the bravest woman no longer has any desire for sex, just like Mrs. von Stein, who asked her doctor to raise an objection with her husband so that she would be spared further pregnancies. No wonder she didn't want to sleep with her beloved Goethe. Just a little 'petting', as they call it in the States.

"There's no such thing," my mother objected. "Of course they slept together!"

But I didn't agree with her: "Put yourself in that time. You were married as a very young girl, as a child-wife to such an old guy and forced to have sex through the sacrament of marriage — how dare they speak of the sacrament if it was rape? And after the rape came the swollen body and the agony of a dangerous birth and then again and again and again and again, no, thank you very much for the sex of yesteryear!"

"But Christiane Vulpius was completely different!" my mother interjected. That was true. "Christiane, as a child of poor parents, voluntarily laid down in the fragrant grass at twenty-three, as an old maid so to speak, for the beautiful, rich, and still young Goethe, and not at fifteen, after a forced marriage for dynastic or financial reasons, in a marital crypt. We women are living in happy times by comparison!" With the pill, and marriage for love, and no love after marriage, but that was our own fault.

"One must work on a happy marriage," my mother said to me. "So shut your mouth when he's angry and don't open it again until he has eaten and burped." Or belched, as Luther called it: "Why don't you belch and fart? Didn't you like it?" We laughed heartily at this saying of our beloved founder of religion at school, just as we laughed a lot at that time, as if we had known that later there wouldn't be as much to laugh about anymore. That is why my best school friend named her daughter after me: because we were so funny, and she wanted to have as much fun with her daughter as she had had with me. She succeeded in that. Until she got breast cancer and a hip surgery, which is when she told me that she was so afraid that she would never be able to laugh again like she did when she was in school, before the Abitur, the final high school exam.

"Do you remember how we used to laugh about everything and anything?" Of course I remembered: we laughed to stock up on laughter. Just like when you pick apples in the fall and put them on wooden boards in the basement cellar as a vitamin-rich supply for the winter. Laughter was an absolutely necessary vitamin for survival, and if you couldn't laugh in the present, you thought of the past when we did so every day and didn't even know that we were laughing for the future, when there might not be anything left to laugh about. May the Lord preserve our laughter!

I have just received a letter from my sister-in-law, the beloved Oldenburg lady, who is such a wonderful cook, saying that she and my brother Heiner will not visit me again before Christmas, even though I am sitting here with my mother in the hospital, and I am despairing because she can no longer speak. And how I would love to argue with her again, anything but this, this forced, desperate muteness and the horror in her face, disfigured by excessive smoking. Susanne, where are you and where is our happy laughter from back then? I really need your visit right now! Or a visit from Hilde and Heiner. But Hilde writes that Heiner has pneumonia again, and she would have to look after her own family, and I did only ever travel around and had a good time in life, while she had to take care of the household with the cooking spoon in her hand.

That is true. But my traveling around had often not been a sign of luck, but of misfortune. When Larry was drunk and sleeping on the living room carpet again, every night, I would pack my suitcase and fly home to my mother during the summer holiday. And then, when my mother contradicted every sentence I said ("that just can't be true"), I packed my unpacked suitcase again and travelled to my girlfriends, even though my mother always said: "Go to your cousin's: blood is thicker than water." But with blood you can't laugh — with water, always. On the beach in Wilhelmshaven, on the edge of the Wümme river, or in a café on the Aare River in Switzerland. Or I went to a health spa, because, over time, I got severe back pain from sitting so much. You can't read and study while walking. The whole learning process was a misfortune for the body, and I would have preferred to run dramatically back and forth on stage waving my arms; I would have been spared years of back and neck pain and the tiresome gymnastics that Larry prescribed and supervised me on when I got lazy; and I got lazy regularly. At the health spa in Oberstaufen, they wrapped us in hideous wet wraps at five o'clock in the morning, which became red-hot, and in the morning, at noon, and in the evening, we were given a cup of grated carrots for expensive money, and in the afternoon, we walked through the beautiful foothill region of the Alps, without really seeing them. After twelve days of this physical torture, one was guaranteed to be free of back pain and without belly-fat and one had been bored to death, unless, in the meantime, one had made a connection with a companion at the spa, which all patients did with each other, except those who had real ailments, such as incontinence or bladder pain or pangs of conscience, which have no place in such a spa.

Once, such a beautiful companion wanted to drive me in the car through the sunny parts of the country, which I would have liked to do, because walking was an ordeal with the many blisters on my feet. But you shouldn't praise the day before the evening, my mother always said to me, and after such a wonderful day in the car of the spa companion the discussion of the evening would start, and with it came the first sip of wine mixed with a lot of water that was accompanying the plate with the grated carrots:

"Why not? What's the big deal?"

I actually wanted to get away from Larry and his boozing, but I was afraid of change. Better the old misfortune than a new one, because Remo and Larry had turned me into an incorrigible pessimist, a kind of Gustave Flaubert who wrote to George Sand: "I'm afraid of life," and that's why he lived with his mama and preferred to write and look for the *mot juste*, rather than the right woman, because he was convinced she didn't exist. Not even after the death of his mother. "Marry at last!" wrote the successful author George Sand, who was fit to live and write (she wrote thirty pages a day!): "Every person needs company!" But this wonderful writer needed only the blank page and the pen in his hand, and he invented worlds that generations after him had to study: Madame Bovary and her many affairs, for which she finally poisoned herself, guiltily and dutifully. Just not that, I thought; then rather no more erotic pleasures, only the books and the back pain and a health spa cure to treat them every once in a while.

For a while, I traveled through the States with a girlfriend, but she always contradicted me like my mother did, and after a fortnight of the most unusual desert regions filled with contradiction (the cloud there is not bluish, but gray), I and my patience were completely shredded, and I longed for my silent Larry, who only said "shut up" once in a while, but contradicted me much less. For that he would have had to listen, which he usually didn't do until he started to suffer from hearing loss. Since then, to my surprise, he has suddenly started to ask me:

"What did you say? That horse is crazy?"

But, of course, I hadn't said that, but rather: "That divorce is crazy," but he was already no longer interested in the divorce of our best friends.

"You only have to be interested in what concerns you," he advised me. "That's what I did, and I did it well."

"But didn't your Christ say to take care of mankind? Love your neighbor as you love yourself; that's in the Bible, isn't it?"

"Yes." Larry agreed with me. "And I am a neighbor to myself. Don't worry about things that are none of your business."

For a long time, the most pleasant journeys had been with Friederike, who fled from her first husband, the rude Rüdiger, just as I fled from Larry. Friederike didn't remind me of my mother at all; on the contrary, she was always very attentive and comforting and encouraging at the same time, and loved everything I wrote. Well, not everything; she objected every once in a while, when absolutely necessary, and because of this objection, I believed her when she said: "How wonderful, Gorda, Schopenhauer couldn't have written it any better," and then we laughed. And laughing together is still the best proof of friendship. You and I, we belong together, we can talk and laugh and read and travel and keep quiet. And neither one of us has to prove themselves, being better than the other, being more beautiful, knowing more, and being able to do something that the other can't. It is as it is, and the Lord above, if he exists, can look down proudly on his creation without having to be ashamed.

Friederike and I were living proof that girlfriends can love each other without being belligerent or jealous of each other because of men. Until we were separated because of the men, that is, because of Werner, and now she loves the mooing of the cows more than the voice of a pocket-Schopenhauer, the grouchy sage, from the mouth of her old friend Gorda. And so, friendship can't do anything against sex, which comes first, and then comes morality and friendship with a woman and traveling around and hours of phone calls, because one is so lonely in marriage and yet was once so happy, in the beginning. Because of the sex.

One day, Magdalene gave me a book about life after death, written by a woman who claimed to be a kind of secretary for a secluded spirit who had the kindness to dictate to her what mankind has always wanted to know: telling us what the afterlife looks like. And this dictating spirit made every conceivable effort to enlighten us that there would be no peace and quiet after death; instead, it would go on and on with learning and relearning and rethinking and re-feeling. And one would have to suffer what one had done to others, to feel the grief one had caused, in full ignorance of one's own cruelty. All dead Nazis would have to endure the horror and the sorrow and all the horror of their Jewish and gentile victims, so that they would never again hate and throw stones and give out beatings and spread poisonous gas, as during the times when the devil himself was on earth. And he didn't limp at all, only Goebbels did, and he was a lower-level devil next to his master, the chief devil, whose name was Hitler.

It is so difficult to recognize evil in time, because it likes to appear in the garb of the saint, as savior and leader, and Old Man Stalin and Old Man Mao, or as a kind, pious priest who gropes the little boys and sticks his fingers into the tiny openings of the girls, that are meant for later use. They want to put their feelers out, they say; that's what Nancy's first husband said when he wanted to teach his little daughter what life has in store. But she told her mother, and that was the end of putting out his feelers.

I read Magdalene's book of the afterlife like one of the fairytale books I loved so much in my childhood. There, too, was a lot of beautiful and bad and possible and wrong things in it. And, perhaps, it was true that there was an afterlife, for thousands of years mankind had believed in it — only not in modern times, at least not in Germany, because we now believed in mathematics and the sciences and had thrown away the fairy tale books like toys from our childhood days. Mankind had grown up and lived and murdered in an adult manner with the help of brilliant technology that the inventive human spirit had provided us: we could quickly turn everything on and get it over with, vacuuming, spin-drying the laundry, washing the dishes, and laying the cities in ruins in no time at all. Oh beautiful, fast world!

When I wanted to read another book of fairy tales by the secretary of the departed spirit, Magdalene protested that I should let it be.

"But why? You were so excited about the hereafter and really looking forward to it, you said to me."

"Oh, you know, my priest thinks that this is the devil's stuff, and I should rather not read such things, he would already describe to me what it would be like in the hereafter, and the Catholic person didn't need to know more than what the church prescribes." Disappointed that I no longer had Magdalene at my side when I read, I bought another book, and another one and stayed with these fairy tale books for adults who want to comfort us with the assurance that there really is a cosmos with a sense of order and that it is not all coincidence what happens on earth. And when you meet someone you haven't seen for years, but the night before you dreamed of this meeting, heaven wants to convince you: this cannot be a coincidence! But Larry believes in the LORD in heaven and in chance on earth and mathematics and the sciences.

He often says to me: "You, always with your strange occurrences. It's all coincidence!"

"And there is no such thing as fate, huh?" I asked him.

"Fate, fate," he muttered and continued to read in his book.

"Just what is it that you are reading that has you so fascinated?" And I grabbed the book just as he was trying to hide it from me. It was *The Prince* by Machiavelli. So, I looked through the book, and I said to him: "Are you reading this masterpiece as a marriage counselor? The woman, the conquered land, and you, the ruling tyrant?" Didn't Larry always say to me: "I am the Lord" — meaning the Lord in our marriage? Or the captain on the sinking ship? Then again, the commander of the troops in North Africa, a kind of General McRommel, the desert fox? He prefers to wear the beige of the desert sand and the camouflage color dark green, as if he would have to prove his leadership qualities for WW III. Until then, he liked to roar around on the military training area called 'our marriage'. He hated military service, because he was supposed to learn to obey and was not allowed to issue commands.

Larry has always had only one friend in life, and that friend was his main window to the world. In Lausanne, the window's name was called Arnaud, and in Chicago, Andrew.

"What a coincidence, both first names of your only friends begin with an A, in German: *Ausnahme*, meaning exception, probably!"

"Just don't give me any more of your stupid coincidences," Larry said to that.

Arnaud had the beautiful name of Baron Westenfels, in German: *Freiherr von Westenfels*. "You can forget the nobility title," Arnaud said. "It's only small nobility and very recent."

"Where does it come from?" I asked him: "Something like that is incredibly interesting!"

But Larry only said: "You don't ask something like that!"

I protested: "There's no shame in being ennobled, is there? Go ahead, tell us: was it a disgrace?"

"No, back then, it was even a great honor," Arnaud said modestly: "My great-grandfather had been the tutor of Crown Prince Rudolf of Austria who, however, brought shame to the giant Catholic empire with his suicide and the murder of the young Countess. The profession of my great-grandfather was professor of geology at the University of Vienna. But as tutor to the Crown Prince, he had only him as a student."

"That is so fascinating," I said, "It's as if you read it in a history book or in the magazine *Die Bunte* with its aristocratic weddings and aristocratic scandals. Crown Prince Rudolf, that is a special case, like that of Ludwig the Second of Bavaria with his suicide in Lake Starnberg — or was it murder? The two of them were also related through Sissi, the depressed, beautiful Empress of Austria and Princess of Bavaria. And how did it come to the nobility?"

"All tutors of the Crown Prince were ennobled," said Arnaud: "It's like you reaching into a pot of gold dust and some of it sticks to your finger."

In any case, no gold dust had gotten stuck on Larry and me. I was a murderer's child and stood under a curse, so I had to take care of the poor and the losers of the world, and Larry often drank instead of studying and absolutely wanted to become a loser, which I tried with all my might to prevent him from doing. Arnaud, however, studied full of energy and intelligence towards a remarkable career, and many years later I read in a book about Crown Prince Rudolf by a German historian in Vienna that her professor, Baron Arnaud von Westenfels of the University of Basel, had left the diaries of his great-grandfather, the tutor, to her, and she quotes from them tirelessly, enriching her historical work, which reads like a crime novel, with many details. "That's who you want to marry?" Arnaud said to me just before our wedding, when Larry walked in front of us, staggering with happiness and beer, and still became our best man, together with my friend Katja, who lent me her precious hooded wedding coat made of Brussels lace: there was no need for me to buy an expensive white dress, which you only wear once in a lifetime anyway,

Empress Elisabeth of Austria in Courtly Gala Dress with
Diamond Stars, by Franz Xaver Winterhalter (1865)

and then never again, and which then rots in the closet for years, waiting for the eternal return.

We had no money for something like that. The money was spent for the expensive wedding ring made of very thin white gold. During its purchase, I was thinking desperately about the other gold ring which I had purchased with Remo three years ago, the ring that brought me nothing but despair because it turned the loving Remo into the loveless, future husband. Into a man which one should better not marry if one didn't want to sink down into the morass of a children-cooking-church.

I thought: "Hopefully, this white-golden ring will bring me luck." I'm not talking about Remo-type luck, no, just Larry-type luck. But maybe men give us these rings to finally be able to let themselves go and become what they really think they are: OUR MASTERS! The ring as a ring through the woman's nose and not a ring around her loving heart. Men mostly refuse to wear a wedding ring. Remo and Larry certainly did.

At the wedding dinner at the Mövenpick hotel of Lausanne, I started puking and then continued puking at night in the student apartment where I slept with my mother, who left the next morning, so we could save the money for the hotel. Just as from now on we had to save money always and everywhere. I didn't know, however, that Larry would have saved even if he had a million in the bank, so strong was the saving gene of his parents and grandparents and Polish great-grandparents in his blood. His ancestors had saved since Adam and Eve; they had to save, because Poland had always been a poor country and wealth could only be found among the top ten hundred.

My throwing up on my wedding night with Mother in the next bed was the result of tonsillitis. Larry, a newly graduated doctor, prescribed salt water for me to gargle with, but I said he didn't have to study so long for that advice and made him get me antibiotics at the pharmacy. "Tell them you're a doctor," I ordered him. Then he went to the pharmacy with his brand-new diploma from the University of Lausanne and pulled it out in front of the stunned employees as if it were a weapon and demanded antibiotics. Upon seeing the huge diploma, they didn't hesitate either, just laughed out loud, which offended him very much, and he got the wonder drug of the twentieth century, which soon put an end to my tonsillitis. Thus began my semi-self-inflicted career as a guinea pig for antibiotics, which Larry stuck in my mouth every time I coughed, summer and winter and for weeks on end. For the frequent bladder infections and the treatment of a tick bite for nine months, because the red circle with the tick bites on the left upper thigh would not disappear. After that, I couldn't get out of the bathroom because of all the stomach cramps, and I couldn't eat any more and lay with my friend Herta, who loved to cook, on the red sofa fitted to the orange carpet with a hot water bottle on my sick, bloated belly.

And nobody knew what was wrong with me. Especially not Larry, just like all other doctors in America. My new disease was called irritable bowel syndrome, and it was affecting millions of people at the time, especially women who were married to a doctor, like me, or had a doctor for a brother, or like my beloved aunt who goes to the doctor once a week: after all, you never know if you're still healthy. And who is healthy, after all? She, too, suffered from daily diarrhea, and when we saw each other, which was seldom enough, we spoke covertly, as we thought of nothing else, until Uncle Horst shouted:

"Now I've had enough!" Then my aunt would tell me about her last trip to Rome, or Venice, or Paris.

Once, Larry and I flew to Paris with his only friend in Chicago, whose name was now Andrew instead of Arnaud.

Many, many years ago, Andy's young sister, who must have been quite picturesque — given that Andy was also beautiful in his Irish way — flew to Florence with her two girlfriends. There, a racing driver loaded the three girls into his sportscar and, on the way from Florence to the beautiful Tuscan countryside, crashed them all into a wall and to their deaths. Only one of the girls survived, unfortunately not Andy's sister. On the night of her death, she appeared to him at his bedside, even though Andy doesn't believe in his Catholic god and doesn't believe in ghosts and life after death. And only such people can be believed when they report ghostly apparitions; the faithful believers only imagine such things.

Andy's parents got rigid with pain and died soon after, and Andy's brother got an incurable brain tumor, so that Andy inherited from parents and siblings and became financially independent and now only has to take care of his inheritance, the many apartments that he manages and paints and repairs and has cleaned when new tenants come. Otherwise, he can get drunk, at his leisure, and preferably with my Larry who, unfortunately, is prevented by his strenuous work from incessantly consuming beer and schnapps.

It is thus that I flew to Paris with these two fidgety drunkards, where I had been many times before — also with Larry — so we both knew exactly how to use the Metro and at what times it was better to take the bus or walk. In addition, we spoke French and thought we were the perfect tourist guides for a newbie like Andy in Paris. Until then, I wanted to believe I was also something of a good friend to him, but the trip to Paris taught me otherwise. From the start, Andy got annoyed when I spoke to the waiter in French or to the young French woman who showed us Versailles. He thought my language skills were me showing off. I was not to show off to him here, so I finally shut my French beak, while he made contact with the environment with Larry. And that contact consisted of him disappearing as fast as he could into the next pub and beckoning Larry to follow him. And he followed obediently, as if Andy were not his friend but his father, whom Andy actually resembled. And I had become the third wheel on the Parisian bicycle and thus completely superfluous. While Larry dropped his friend Arnaud for me in Lausanne, he dropped me for Andy, and thus I knew what I had already understood with Remo: a wife is not a mistress and may not claim any rights other than marital ones. Work and drinking buddy and bars and beer and schnapps are more important than her, the deposed queen of the heart. In order to play a queen again, one had to conquer a new heart. And if you were unlucky, it was the heart of your best friend's husband.

I met Maurice and Aurora right at the beginning of my stay in Chicago: he was the French consul, and he and his wife represented the French culture in our vast, at that time unkempt metropolis. I loved them passionately for that, and when I was at their house, I was visiting France and not a normal married couple with two children. For the first three years in Chicago, when I wasn't in college speaking German, I spoke French exclusively, and Larry was hard to have a conversation with, as he slept at home, exhausted, or frequented a bar with Andy because of his low-paying slave labor at the hospital (patience, patience, patience, I told myself often: one of these days I'll be rewarded for that!).

Aurora had been given the pretty name 'the Dawn', because her family came from the Berry area like Aurore Dupin, also called George Sand who grew up in Nohant Castle with her grandmother and lived there until her death, although the castle, like all the inheritance, belonged to her husband after her divorce, as everything did in those days always belonged to the husband, including the children, if there were any. George Sand was a great-grand niece of the war-hero Maurice, Comte de Saxony (Moritz von Sachsen), who had been an out-of-wedlock son of Augustus II (who was, at the same time, also king of Poland) and his mistress, the Swedish countess Aurora of Königsmarck. How romantic! I would have loved to have descended from such a family, too, and not from a war criminal father who shot prisoners in Toulouse dead on Hitler's orders.

In Paris, I had once visited the Musée de la Vie Romantique, dedicated to George Sand, and I had read, with enthusiasm, a book about the life of this amazing woman, who was all woman and — at the same time — a little man, and who is, still now, a celebrity in the land of the Castle of Nohant, which I had always wanted to visit. There, many girls were named Aurora, like my French friend in Chicago, "so don't be surprised by that," she said to me. She had magnificent thick red hair, red as the dawn, and I have never seen more beautiful red hair, not even in the movies. And her husband, whose name happened to be Maurice, like Maurice of Saxony, was as handsome as a god in France, but as *I* imagine one to be, and not like Louis XIV. The writer George Sand had many lovers, a scandal in her day, including quite famous ones like Alfred de Musset and the terminally ill Chopin, who certainly was too ill to play the man in bed and at home. Even Aurora, my friend, sometimes seemed as if she might have had many lovers. When she was sober, she behaved like a fine countess, and when she had been drinking, like a merry courtesan. She always drank a gin and tonic before dinner, which consisted of a large glass of gin with a drop of tonic in it. It often took her a long time to stir the dressing into the salad and distribute the napkins for dinner and put the bowls on the table, so much did she sway back and forth, which always reminded me of drunken Larry in Lausanne.

"Actually, why do I have I so many drunks and drinkers in my life?" I sometimes asked myself in despair. "Because they are more interesting than the non-drinkers," replied my friend Marianne, whose husband also liked to raise one or two to his lips, making him a speaking prodigy with his long monologues on all sorts of fields of knowledge that you never knew existed. And I loved these know-it-alls.

Aurora had named her children Solange and Maurice like those of the famous writer who could write thirty pages a day, slept very few hours and always had guests around her at the chateau. And every six months she hurried to Paris, where she held a reception for the intellectual elite at her place, for example for Heinrich Heine, about whom I wanted to write my doctoral thesis, if I ever were to make it that far, because the head of the German Studies Department in Chicago had given me hardly any credit for my Swiss studies and thus forced me to take my master's degree a second time. Which is the reason why I was to have to study for two more years, until a giant exam, which easily consumed half a year, and finally, finally, one was allowed to get down to the dissertation when one already had no desire to do so anymore at all. And writing the dissertation took another three to seven years. After that, I was an old woman, too old to have children. But without that doctorate, I would never get over the beatings I had taken in my childhood, would never get over the certainty of being as dumb as a post. And I never would be able to shoo away the black fog around my soul that so often settled over me and threatened to suffocate me.

George Sand, in any case, had no fog in her brain and still wrote and writes in the afterlife her thirty pages and more a day, while I have trouble forcing two or three pages onto paper without interruption. She was a born writer, while I was an unborn one at the time. I loved Aurora and Maurice de Merteuil and their two children, Solange, and Maurice le petit. And how I loved them! They were my surrogate family, the substitute for my mama and my aunt and my beloved cousin and my brothers and the German Christmas and Easter celebrations and the birthday parties with girlfriends and the crusty rolls in the morning and the sandwich with minced smoked pork and beef sausage in the evening.

When I was at the Merteuil's house, I knew I hadn't been wrong about marrying Larry and not Remo: in the friends' huge apartment, with a view of the lake, which from the window looks as large as an ocean without a shore, there were antiques from the countries where they had lived, for example from Bangkok and India; there were oriental carpets on the floor and real silk carpets hanging on the walls and pleasing natural landscapes that resembled those of the Impressionists. What did I care about my poverty when Aurora and Maurice forgave me for the junk in my apartment! I was in seventh French heaven when my friend handed me her bouillabaisse or the plate of 'Choucroute Alsacienne' that she had cooked in my honor. It wasn't until Chicago that I spoke fluent French — in Lausanne, I stuttered until the end. But love for this family had loosened my tongue, and I spoke with the language of love, as if I had been born with it, to the astonishment of my friends, who had never seen such a tongue-tied German with a sense of humor, for the Germans were, after all, known for their lack of humor, as they had proven for all time during WWI and WWII with explosives and tanks and bombs and poison gas.

Interior of the Merteuils' apartment along the lake shore in Chicago

And here sat such a member of this despised group of people, amusing the representatives of France in their own highly civilized language. The Merteuils were almost as delighted with me as I was with them, and I had the presumptuousness then to claim "Je suis drôle en trois langues," I am funny in three languages, which I would not dare do today. I am glad if I am still funny in one, and every day I am losing more of my wit, the more my limbs ache and my knees fail me.

Unfortunately, I realized with time, that I loved Maurice more than anything, that is, more than Aurora and Solange and Maurice, le petit. One night we started making out when the kids were in bed, me with Maurice and Aurora with Larry. I guess we thought, what the heck, they're moving back to France soon anyway, and then they'll be transferred to a foreign country. But misfortune would have it that they were sent back to Chicago because no replacement consul could be found who felt like putting up with the Roman humid heat in the summer and the Siberian winter with the hurricane-like storms and the daily murders on our streets. And while Aurora and Larry didn't retain any memory of their smooching, Maurice and I had caught the "smallpox of the heart" (Heinrich Heine): and from then on, we were lusting after each other, instead of looking at each other calmly and harmlessly.

We thought only of kissing. And said: "Tu veux encore un morceau de pain?" (Do you want another piece of bread?) and meant "Donne-moi un baiser." (Give me a kiss). And he poured me the wine with the words: "Tu aimes ce petit vin rouge?" (Do you like this little red wine?) And meant: "Tu aimes encore ma bouche?" (Do you still like my mouth?) And I thought "Oui, je l'aime encore (Yes, I still love it)". When I downed the wine, I drank his blood. I became a vampire before his eyes and, unfortunately, also before those of Larry, who noticed more and more that I loved another and no longer him; he who had become a stranger to me because of his murderous teaching schedule.

The heart is a vulture's heart and always picks at some carrion and eats where it can. No wonder the Catholic Church has declared marriage a sacrament, it is precisely to keep the vulture in us in check, the rapacious boar in the pen, and the wild wolf behind bars in the zoo. And Aurora also noticed that something was wrong with her husband, because he was sleeping with her again, as she told me, and he hadn't done that for two years when he fell in love with a singer who was starring in a leading role in the musical *Jaques Brel is alive and living in Paris* in Chicago. I heard her once, too. Unforgotten the song: "Ne me quitte pas! (Don't leave me) Ne me quitte pas!" making us all cry.

At that time back then, Aurora started drinking and then boozing, so Maurice couldn't leave his two beloved children with a sick mother, and so he stayed where he belonged and as his duty as a Protestant pastor's son dictated. And then I came, and sucked his blood like the French red wine and became funny like a comedienne in his own language, because I wanted to rob his mind with laughter. And how much fun we had! We laughed until we couldn't laugh anymore because of sadness. You can see that in the Christmas photos from that time: all six of us looking grimly into the picture, with the look of "Ne me quitte pas! Ne me quitte pas!"

Où sont les neiges d'antan? (Where is the snow of yesteryear?) And the loved ones, where are they now, and the laughter, and the young skin, and the swallowed sobs: Ne me quitte pas! Ne me quitte pas! Everything, everything has left me!

Three years later, Aurora and Maurice moved to Atlanta to his new job. How frequently did I fly to Atlanta because of them, where the family no longer lived in an apartment, but in a beautiful house in the suburbs of the city with a garden and a swimming pool. Everywhere the blooming bushes, tulips, daffodils, and hyacinths already in March, while we had to wait until the end of May for spring and summer. That's three months of joie de vivre that Chicago weather robs us of every year. No wonder then that we became grouchy and drunkards, having affairs all over just to have some fun. Maurice, on the other hand, felt happy in his paradise garden with apple tree and pool and the warm Southern climate that was similar to that of the French Provence, which was his home.

Aurora, out of habit, continued to drink her glass of gin with a drop of tonic in it as an aperitif, slurring her words in front of the astonished guests, who were used to the proper behavior of Southern ladies, as seen in the movie *Gone with the Wind*, but not the funny stories of a buzzed French 'courtesan'. Maurice had to wipe the smile off his face when, at the frequent receptions, his wife sobbed away in the evenings on the stairs of the house or lay asleep like a child on the terrace. "They are the talk of the town," one of the ladies whispered in my ear.

The children began to protect their mother and put her to bed as fast as they could. Solange and Maurice le petit have hated alcohol all their lives, proving that the apple can fall far from the tree. Once I was visiting the family I loved so much for New Year's, and there, to my amazement, was a little blonde sitting on Maurice's lap all evening long. "Poor Sandra," Aurora told me the next day, "she lost her husband. Imagine, he poisoned himself because she kicked him out. He was a gambler, you know, and that's why I told Maurice to take care of her."

And now he was taking care of the pretty young widow of a suicide victim, at his wife's request. But men should only be advised to take care of old, ugly widows. Maurice never stopped caring for Sandra, he still does, twenty plus years later, because Sandra said to him that his wife's alcoholism was not his problem, but hers, just as she was not to blame for her husband's gambling addiction. He would have to give Aurora a choice: go to Alcoholics Anonymous or "get out." That's what's called 'tough love' in America, and that's why she did it that way with her husband who, unfortunately, then poisoned himself, which was not foreseen in the tough-love program. However, Aurora didn't take her husband's threat seriously and thought that a glass of gin and tonic couldn't be called alcoholism.

In the end, not Aurora, but Maurice left and moved into the poor widow's house as a sub-tenant, so to speak. And Aurora tried to poison herself with sleeping pills like Sandra's husband, but the children found their mother in time, and she was saved at the hospital. Thank God. After that she went to AA, unfortunately too late for Maurice, who in the meantime married tough-love Sandra, who taught him that he should quit the diplomatic service and look for a job in the States, because she had no desire to move somewhere where she didn't know the language. And she wouldn't learn French either, he should improve his English; that could be expected of him after so many years in the States. So the proud Frenchman had to speak English, which he had never liked to do.

One day, he called me from Atlanta and said: "Sandra et moi, nous avons rien en commun (Sandra and I, we have nothing in common). Do you want to meet me somewhere in France, wherever you want?"

That's when I yelled: "Fous le camp — get lost or I'll kill you! Don't you dare show your face here!"

Because he had told Aurora that she had been so stupid not to notice that her best friend had been after him. Aurora had noticed, of course, but had forgiven me because she had also been in love with a friend of Maurice's for a long time and knew that loving hearts are vulture hearts; they pick where they can and don't let anything be dictated to them and tear themselves apart if they don't get what they want. That's the beast in us that the Catholic Church and Magdalene have always warned about.

Years later, Aurora married an American architect, whom she met at Alcoholics Anonymous. She said to me: "You have to go there if you are looking for a man, you find the greatest guys there, all newly divorced! A virtual marriage institute!" And the architect loved the French language and culture, as I did, and traveled to Paris with Aurora as often as he could. After all, you don't just fall in love with a person, you love everything around them; in Remo I loved beautiful Switzerland, innocent of the crimes of the Third Reich, and in Larry I loved the year I had spent as an exchange student in California, the best year of my life! Young and exuberant and celebrated by classmates like a star or a star that had fallen into their midst.

I had been the first exchange student at Placentia in Orange County, and a teacher told me a few decades later: "Gigi (because they called me Gigi, they didn't like the name Gorda), we never had such fun again as with you!" That one year in California should have shown me the way to the stage as a comedienne or actress, but instead I fell in love with Remo and wanted to wash his socks for life and become well-behaved and bourgeois because of all my love for him. That couldn't turn out well.

In Atlanta I woke up one morning feeling terrified, as if a second Civil War were threatening the city. Aurora and I were still sitting around the breakfast table with the kids when Maurice came back with the car and told us that a tornado had swept through the city and suburbs in the early morning hours. The downed trees blocked the roads, so he couldn't get to his office downtown. Curious, we looked through the side streets: there, mighty trees, torn out with their roots, lay felled. One of them had even fallen on the garage of some friends and crushed two of their cars. Thank God, not the family. We had escaped the damage!

Three weeks later, on January 13, Chicago was hit by a snowstorm that began quite innocently, like in the Christmas carol *Softly Falleth the Snow*. I was sitting in my friend Margarete's wing chair for afternoon coffee, cozy and warm, looking out at the snow falling outside the window, which put us in a festive post-Christmas mood. Margarete had put on a record with songs by Schumann (and lyrics by Heine), and we ate the cookies and gingerbread left over from Christmas and lit the candles as the sun disappeared behind the opposite wall of houses. Instead of doing that, we should have been listening to the news!

"I'm going now," I said to Margaret much too late, looking for my thick brown leather coat — a Christmas gift from my mother — with a large hood that was not a fashion fad in Chicago but an essential winter protection. I foolishly waited an hour for the bus, until I finally realized, frozen and covered in snow, that no bus was coming and struggled my way to the subway. There were already thousands of people there, whose cars were stuck in the snow and who, like me, had only one thought: getting home as quickly as possible, before it's too late! I left the subway again, and made my way to our high-

The suburban street in Atlanta after the
tornado hit early in the morning

rise building, with a wild, hurricane-like wind coming at me from the lake. The snow mountain was almost up to my chest, when I saw Larry sitting in the armchair in our little first floor apartment, as if all were still right with the world. "And I'm dying out here in the snow!" I thought angrily: "Shouldn't he come out and save me?"

Our mayor was blamed for the snowfall, because they claimed the city should have been better prepared. We got a woman as mayor, an extraordinary event, since women had no place in politics, business, or science until then. This is how I learned to fear not only the vulture inside my chest, but also the weather outside. And to listen to the news before I went out of the house.

My second surrogate family consisted of a German woman and an American man, as with me and Larry, except that Herta's husband Rex also spoke German and Larry spoke only French. I had met Herta at the university where she had enrolled because her body refused to get pregnant a second time as planned. "You need to distract yourself," the gynecologist had advised her, and the studies distracted Herta so successfully that she couldn't quite rejoice when she did get pregnant, because now she had developed the burning ambition to get her master's degree.

At that time, studies in the States hardly resembled those in Germany and Switzerland. American educators felt that young students needed to be guided along as they had been in grammar school or high school and thought nothing of academic freedom and loafing around in the city's cafés. Right at the beginning of the semester, we were assigned the lists of tasks and books, and we read and studied without looking to the right or to the left, from morning till night. And if you hadn't found a partner by then, you wouldn't find one, since there was no time for that. Also, not even for growing up, since that had to have been completed by then.

Herta and Rex had obviously managed to do that, because Rex had been working for the government as a tax investigator for years, and Herta was the mother of a daughter and a gardener and an excellent cook, all in one. Only I had always been a student and nothing else. And for me, nothing seemed to suit me but reading and learning, and I often wondered how one would become a housewife if one had not had any lessons in it. No lessons in cooking and cleaning and gardening and mothering: it's as if we were expected to sing Desdemona on the opera stage, without years of vocal training.

Some of us were not able to do that, and I was one of those failures. This is why I admired women like Aurora and Herta all the more; women who cooked with their left hand and with their right conjured up a wonderful garden of flowers and vegetables and herbs from a wilderness around their house. I, on the other hand, had two left hands when it came to cleaning and cooking and ironing; and two right hands when it came to turning the pages of a book. And a dangerous vulture in my chest because Larry was never home. During the day, Herta was a caring, humorous friend to me, with whom I could have stolen books if I had had a disposition to do so. I ate the tastiest chicken legs of my life on her terrace: seasoned with lots of garlic and rosemary and with lemon juice poured over them. And the most delicious cakes for dessert, of which I asked for the recipes, but didn't follow them.

And except for Friederike, no one was able to comfort me as she did; and I needed a lot of comfort, since I had grown up without a protective mental skin under my mother's hard look at my appearance, which reminded her so unpleasantly of the unloved mother-in-law.

Unfortunately, like Aurora, Herta turned into a slurring alcoholic in the course of the evening, with an irresistible urge to vomit out all her delicacies in the bathroom. Then the next morning, astonished, she said to me on the phone: "I must be allergic to alcohol, I didn't drink anything!" But while Aurora remained the Countess de Merteuil, Herta's drunken shrieks took on a vulgar air that made me more and more melancholic as the years went by. "What do I have for a girlfriend?" I thought in despair. When she had had enough to drink, Herta began to lament about her years as a refugee child in a Bavarian village, where she was housed in a barracks compound with many other refugees from the German eastern territories, now part of Poland. These Protestant refugees were utterly despised by the extremely Catholic original population, as if they alone had started and lost the war and not the rich Bavarian farmers on their estates that were untouched by war. Herta suffered from this contempt now as she did on day one, the wounds never healed, and the alcohol sprinkled salt into them. I mourned with her for years and held her hand and tried to comfort her with the words: "But it's not your fault that you were poor refugees and had to live in a tiny apartment in a barrack. Your father had been a respected carpenter in Silesia, with a house and garden and beautiful furniture that he made himself. That's something! He was an artist!"

"But," sobbed Herta, "we were the last dirt in the eyes of those horrid Bavarian farmers, I tell you, the scum of society and Protestant to boot, so without the right faith. All Catholics are hypocrites, they go to confession on Sunday, and on Monday they sin again. They had very wicked hearts: for two eggs, my mother had to slave for a day in the field, or for a few potatoes thrown at her feet, those scumbags!"

Her dancing-lesson partner had been one of the most sought-after boys in the village, the son of a wealthy shoe merchant, but when he picked her up in his father's limousine for the final ball, he had the driver stop one street away so that he wouldn't know where she was coming from. From the refugee barracks. The stupid Bavarian driver was more important to him than she, his dancing-lesson partner; the beautiful, blond girl from Silesia who was attending high school!

Later I found Herta's anger and hatred of the rich and proud reflected in the life story of the author Ulla Hahn who, as the child of an unskilled worker and a cleaning woman, felt humiliated by her home, but who didn't hate the Catholics — for she herself was Catholic — but the tall blond daughters of bourgeois society, the ones "with the fur on their coat collars." Now then, I myself belonged to this class hated by her, but cannot remember any fur collars, only sometimes velvet; yes, we had velvet back then. The times had been far too poor to put fur on the collars of the daughters. And I remember well that some of us no longer had a father. Having a father was a good fortune in those days, even our stepfather, who saved my brothers and me from the fate of growing up as orphans of a war criminal. And who protected us from the contempt of society, which no longer remembered having run with or ahead or behind in the Third Reich. Because all of a sudden, the survivors had all been "against it."

Herta and Rex and Larry and I spent all the feasts and suffered all the cares together, the Christmas and Easter celebrations, the birthdays and Thanksgiving, when Herta baked a huge turkey like a real American, and the days, when the whole family had to spend it with me, when their chimney was clogged, and they were almost poisoned. Herta came to Wisconsin when she was young and went to high school like I did, but not as an exchange student with the American Field Service, but as a guest of her mother's American pen pal who taught biology there. This 'pen pal' had initially been nothing more than an address sent to Herta's mother from the Relief Service so that she would make contact with someone in the States who was willing to support the starving family of a hated people with care packages. Countless Germans were gifted with these care packages full of rice and noodles, coffee, condensed milk, and chocolate bars, as if Santa Claus himself lived overseas in what was once a hostile country. After the war, the Americans seemed like angels who delivered us from evil in human form, and it was only during the Vietnam War that they turned back into devils for the young. Unfortunately.

The American biology teacher became something like an adoptive mother for Herta, and she was also allowed to go to the nearby college after graduating from high school at the expense of the unmarried woman who thus came to have a daughter. That made them both happy.

At college, Herta met her American husband Rex, who had previously completed four years of military service and for whom the government paid for his studies in return. His family would not have been able to do it; he came 'from a modest background', as my mother put it. His father had been a letter carrier, and Rex was the first in the family to go to college. Rex, too, would have liked to become a letter carrier, but Herta took charge of his life and demanded that the intelligent man, who was somewhat lacking in drive, finish his studies, otherwise she would not marry him. That put an end to his dream of getting through life with as little effort as possible. Herta herself had been driven to work by her mother with the words: "You're as lazy as your Uncle Erich, now get on with it!" And Herta did and did and didn't stop doing until she had completed her master's degree in German literature and then even the courses leading up to her doctorate. All this in addition to her exhausting work in the household and the two children, for whose care she had her mother come from Germany. Now it was not the daughter but the mother who was punished: "Mom, why don't you sew on a button properly!" Or: "What are you mending here, these are ancient socks to be thrown away!" The mother couldn't do anything right for the daughter, and the old woman quietly grumbled to herself while darning and sewing and ironing from dawn to dusk.

Later, Herta taught German and Spanish at a high school, a nerve-wracking job since, by that time, many of the students were latchkey kids and had developed neuroses of all kinds, such as the familiar ADD (now ADHD): Attention-Deficit Disorder. At the beginning of the school year, Herta received a list with the names of the students and their respective illnesses — and there was hardly anyone who was not under the influence of medication, which greatly reduced their ability to concentrate. Herta had to crack the whip to drive the bunch of students unwilling to learn forward in their subject matter.

Every year, Larry and she and the children traveled to Europe for recreation. They visited the entire continent in rental cars of all kinds, and although I imagined these trips with the old mother and small children to be very exhausting, they seemed to be a fountain of youth for Herta and Rex. Maybe then his wife didn't drink so much, and Rex didn't have to placate her in the evening for her drunken monologues on the subject of the despised Protestant refugee child from the refugee barracks in the Catholic Bavarian village near Kulmbach. The two of them always showed us their slides quite happily, and we commented

El Greco's *Madonna*, painted by the author >

together on the often blurry pictures with sentences like: "Here the heads are missing, did you lose them on the way?" Or: "The same dress again? I thought we were watching a fashion show!" This is how Larry and I managed to suffer through the slide presentation evenings, which we dreaded when at the houses of other people. Nothing is more boring than the travelogues and travel poems of untalented travel writers. Even Goethe's *Italian Journey* is no exception to this. Larry and I preferred not to show our photos of Paris, since everyone has seen the city anyway. Now all the pictures are in boxes in the back of the closet, waiting in vain to be seen.

Despite all her successes, Herta always remained a bit of a barrack child and reacted sensitively to remarks that she perceived as insults. Once, in Kulmbach, an old classmate from high school asked her what she was doing in America? Herta answered proudly: "I'm a high school teacher!"

"How can you be a high school teacher without an Abitur high school diploma?" the woman thoughtlessly asked.

"Who says I don't have a high school diploma?" Herta shouted angrily. "Of course, I graduated from high school in the States and went to college!"

"But didn't you have to drop out of high school in Germany?" asked the puzzled woman.

"Not at all!" Herta yelled, even more incensed: "I went to America of my own free will. I was not forced to do anything!" However, at that time, Herta had been in danger of flunking and having to repeat a year. And that's why she went to America. And now, she suffered forever, thinking that she might not have made it through high school in Bavaria. This wound, too, didn't want to heal, just like the barracks-child wound. When her best German friend, Martha, once wrongly improved her American pronunciation ("that is not called Wustershire sauce, but W o r c e s t e r s h i r e sauce"), she threw a fit of rage that ended the friendship. Only those with an eye for mental wounds understood her agitation. Martha didn't understand anything. And was angry.

During the course of my studies, I went to a psychologist employed at our university to help students like me, in order not to become a drunkard from grief like Aurora and Herta. At first I became a comedienne out of embarrassment, and Dr. Sacks laughed at me, happy not to have to listen to whining for once. So I amused him for months, until he said sternly to me: "To the point, Gorda, what's on your mind?" That's when we talked about Larry and his boozing and how he had changed as a husband who now shook his fist at my chin, while we were shopping, with the words: "Have you gone crazy, spending so much money!" so that I could no longer go shopping with him. And no more going to the movies as I used to do in Lausanne. In the middle of the movie *The Great Gatsby*, he had jumped up and run out. "My ass hurts," he called it, and he would never go to a movie with me again. After the subject of Larry, we talked about my great love for Remo and how he had changed when he bought me the engagement ring and acted like a tyrannical husband, even before we were married.

Then we got to the main subject and talked about my mother and that I had been an unwanted and unloved child who reminded my mother of her mother-in-law because I had a strong chin like her, and that she could never have liked that ugly woman. And because she thought that, in me, she had a second stubborn, stupid child (the first was my brother Heiner), she did my schoolwork with me for six years, that is, she threatened and beat me until I became really stubborn and stupid, because I was not able to think and calculate because of fear. During all of my childhood, I always had but one thought on my mind: "I can't wait to get away from this woman!"

I spent most of my time at my friend Karin Niedermayer's who lived next door and had two siblings with whom I played cards and where I ate the delicious honey cake that their dear mother baked for us. At Mrs. Niedermayer's, I was not stupid and stubborn and frightened, as I was at home. As frightened as my brother Heiner, who also ran away from our mother at an early age and fled to his friend Hans', where he was taken in and loved like a third son. Only our oldest brother, Max, escaped the fate of being an unloved child. That is why he didn't suffer from depression from an early age like Heiner and I and was the best at a school of three thousand children.

When I began to tell Dr. Sacks about my mother, I thought I loved her so much that I wrote her a letter telling her how attached I was to her and that I couldn't imagine life without her, that is, I would have to die without her being around. This sentimental letter came back after a year, why, I don't know anymore. I had probably forgotten to write the city on the envelope. Back then, at that time, I wrote a poem for her called 'Mother and Daughter', for which she gave me a beautiful cameo with a Bacchus on it, surrounded by grapes and decorated with sapphires.

Mother and Daughter

Homecoming and miracles
The old puddings bloom again
Feeling secure in the fragrance
Of vanilla sauce on hot apple pie

I dig down into your
Honey bun
I'll lie down in your
Minced-meat sausage roll

Mom, come, we'll celebrate childhood
Oh, please yell at me again
Say: she's too stupid
Then you do it yourself

I'll play fourteen
And you'll play yourself

Tell me about politics
While I ponder about eternity

Which you hate so heartily
Realism against symbolism
On the couch and on the chair
In front of the old TV movie with Willy Fritsch

In the hand the
Undamaged umbilical cord
Your youth delights me
When Zarah sings:
Tomorrow we'll play sisters!

Unfortunately, later — after undergoing psychoanalysis for a long time — I wrote her a second letter, which was not returned. In it, I described her continuous yelling and beatings during schoolwork, which did turn me into a frightened person whose brain disappeared during exams. And that because of her, I would have to study all my life, because otherwise I would be afraid of remaining a stupid, stubborn child; and only if I had passed all the exams in the world would I perhaps forgive myself for having interrupted my studies for a year; back then, when I asked myself what all the messing around and sitting around in the cafés in Tübingen and Freiburg was actually about, nothing would come of it, especially not a teacher or a Ph.D. which I mockingly called a doctor-who-cannot-do-a-lot-of things. And so I studied all my life without having much fun or joy in myself and without being able to cook and bake and iron — I wouldn't even have dared to get my driver's license; I was still practicing driving for fear of failing the test.

I would be a cowardly little mouse when Larry yelled at me. At the same time that he supposedly said he couldn't stand cowardly little mice, he wanted a woman who would stand up to him. But where should my opposition come from? My mother never allowed me to fight back — even today; if she raised her hand, I would flinch in fear. And why she had separated me from my aunt and grandmother and my beloved cousin when I was five, back when she married our stepfather, I don't know. She had destroyed the poor child and made her unfit for life, and now I was sitting here with Dr. Sacks, so that he could straighten me out a bit. He told me that I had a hunched-over gait, with hanging shoulders, and that he could see from that that a person had been mistreated in childhood. I would be in therapy to learn to walk with an upright posture, and that would take years. What others learned in childhood, I would have to do as an adult, and I couldn't even describe how sad it looked inside me: that's why I played the clown in the family, just like Heiner, so that I wouldn't have to whine. A chin that is shaped too strong and a tiny heart-shaped mouth and then the whining on top of that, then really no one would be able to love me. She would be responsible for my messed-up life. She alone — and not me.

My mother never forgave me for this letter, just as she never forgave me for the first novel, in which I describe her as a widow distraught by the war, who beats the little girl because she has no one else to beat, and who only wanted one child and got three — and who gave her two youngest children the feeling of being unwanted guests — which she, unfortunately, couldn't simply turn away. From then on, I couldn't say a word to my mother without her feeling the urge to prove me wrong.

One of her favorite phrases was: "That can't be true." Or: "But I don't remember that." Or: "What stories you're making up again! Such silly stuff! Of course, I never said: You remind me of my mother-in-law, and I didn't like her. Such nonsense would never cross my lips! It's true that I didn't like my mother-in-law — but nobody did; that wasn't my problem, only hers!"

My mother lies in bed as if unconscious, and I write here that sometimes I hated her, although I loved her very much, and that I couldn't live without her. What this has taught me is to endure a turmoil of anger and tenderness that others would not have endured. They would have disappeared into a new life like my brash girlfriend Cornelia did, who opened her heart and arms (and everything else), and there was always someone to share the mattress with her without becoming a mattress in her own eyes. I, on the other hand, lived with my shame and my guilt and my cowardly cowering and my self-doubt that took away my ability to say "no" and "no more" and "screw you" and "I'm leaving now and I'm never coming back!" However, I did say "I'm leaving now," numerous times though, but I still came back like a beaten slave whimpering before his master and tyrant: "Please, please, forgive me for my rebelliousness!"

There are even girlfriends who have asked me why my husband allowed me to write and publish and let me travel to Germany every year where I gave lectures and readings.

"He doesn't have to allow me anything!" I answered defiantly. "He doesn't ask me what he should and shouldn't do, either!" But in truth, I let myself be ordered around in order to have my peace. No sooner had Larry finished his endless and poorly paid training as an internist than he told me that he needed to recover from all the drudgery, and money meant nothing to him anyway. Therefore, he had decided to work only a few days a week and otherwise devote himself to his hobbies. He said he had just started a moderately paid job in a private clinic.

So there was no reward for four years of toil and agony; Larry was relaxing with Andy in a depressingly dark bar with his favorite hobby: drinking beer and schnapps and eating hamburgers that the German bar owner knew how to prepare for her guests. Larry should have married this bar owner, she would have had her fun with him, and not me, who was sitting at home with my textbooks on the history of German language and literature and Gothic grammar. We had to learn Gothic because some lucky person had found a copy of a Gothic Bible in a monastery — and now it seemed imperative to the universities of the world to burden us students of the German language and literature with the knowledge of Gothic. Yet, in that language you could only read the Bible and nothing else. After all, there was fascinating literature in Latin, as there was in Greek. But this Gothic Bible stood all alone by itself — and for it we learned grammar, week after week, in order to read a text in the original, which already existed in German, English, French, Italian, Latin, Greek, and, and, and.

All of this lost time in my life I could have learned to sew like an Italian, cook like a Frenchwoman and keep order like a German. I could have become a practical being, just as my mother in her old age wished for her daughter to be, a Rosie who knows how to paint her kitchen blue and serve the delicious herb butter with the rosy steak and the homemade bread with the crunchy crust to go with it, a Rosie who is untouched by completely useless knowledge, the burden of which is almost threatening to crush me.

For, where is the Remo of the early days of our love, who would be happy to talk to me about my endless studies, about Gothic and the Luther Bible and Middle High German, which is so similar to Swiss German? I continued to study for a man who no longer existed, whom I had left, and who had shut me up before with the words, "I can't stand your semi-literary prattle anymore." And now Larry did it with his favorite phrase: "Shut up!" Shut up or Zip it or Be quiet, however you want to translate those two expressive words!

My mother wanted a practical Rosie; Remo wanted a children-cooking-church-cleaning lady, and Larry wanted to be left alone at home or go boozing with Andy, undisturbed.

And where should I go to? "Quo vadis?" I asked myself and moved on to the next book.

Without flipping the cover over the mud of my life: after all, here, I'm writing down what I shouldn't talk about.

This morning I dreamed of Remo. He says: "Come on" to a woman I don't know, whom he wants to marry, and then the two of them walk away into the darkness. I try to call him, but I don't know his number, neither the one from the library, nor the one from Rosenweg 18. I am desperate, I want to remind him of our love: don't marry her, you love me …

Since my separation from Remo so many years ago, I suffer this nightmare separation at night in many variations. From this I have made a narrative that I have called *Exorcising the Devil*.

Exorcising the Devil

Everyone has their way of tempting fate, even in the form of depicting the devil in a painting, in order better to kill him.

The devil comes in the most beautiful form and calls himself this-time-it-will-work. He lacks nothing to make your heart big and ready to live in. You build him a fluffy nest, a splendidly furnished king's room: And you say, come, my fate, move into me, all is prepared for an excellent beginning. Then he comes down from hell, to pay the honor of his visit to your king's room. And while the others are checking over the earth's texture, abolishing jungles, constructing temporary bridges, turning cartwheels, snaking cables, you keep the door open to your beautiful devil day and night. For he lacks nothing to make you ready for him to live in you; you, who could never possess enough corners, a pointed bay chin and sad gray curtains over the non-existent splendor. But he, the most glorious of all devils, brings light into your darkened chambers, and you immediately hang lustful paintings on the walls for him: a Zeus as a golden rain, who is blessing a well-prepared Danae, or was it the longing Io? Oh no, he robbed her helpfully, or lay as a swan in her immaculate lap, and then the powerfully shaped Europa with the dainty bull and dahlias and asters on his head, and everybody hums and sings the song of the most beautiful of the devils in the form of a god.

Truly, nothing is lacking for him, so that you throw out the folding bed, and you prepare the place of his retreat with damask and a canopy, and little angels look down teasingly from the stucco into the midst of the miracles set up: oh, how well, how pained I'll be, when I think of my king's room, which for so long has not seen the honor of his visit. How I stand there, dusty and broken, the gold lacquer off, the pictures crooked, and my courage on shaky legs. Where to put the junk, when my devil moves into a fresh chamber? And you don't know how to check over the earth's texture, how to skin leopards, how to straighten river edges — just always this urge to be a nest, a cave, a womb, and a lock.

So I went to tempt fate, even in the form of depicting the devil in a painting, in order to better kill him. It's best to do it at night, because you're most likely to hit him with your eyes closed. You dream him away, for years; you dream him out of the king's room, and while you're already typing at noon and cleaning and teaching like all the other basic normal creatures, you are the night witch, wielding the counter-spell, year after year; so fifteen years can go by, if the devil was the right one, the first one, the eternal one, the unspeakable one ...

First, you have to hex him back, to be able to cast him out forever and ever. You dream him to you; he, who dwells in strange rooms, looks at strange, lustful paintings, who caresses his devil's brood. Or you dream yourself to him, to the city, where he appeared to you for the first time in the form of this-time-it-will-work. It is an unknown city, never seen but fully felt, just always his, and you wander through the déjà senti and look for him, all your hither and thither, without which you can no longer dream, or you rush into some kind of hermitage and push telephone buttons, but his number has changed, or your fingers have fallen off. You push buttonless discs, and you scream into the ether: Hello, it's me, the one you held as forever-love for so many years, I seek your scalding fire — and it can go on for a year or two that way: during the day, you love a, current, local one, cook for him and write comforting aphorisms, and at night you lie down as always in the unconquered bed and continue with the haste that summons the only one to take possession again of what has been prepared for him. But, without your wild assistance nothing happens; so you get on trains and drive off, and you are always on the road and never there, but now it works on the phone despite the fingers that have fallen off, yes, he laughs, do come to my office, but then the wheels slip and the direction is wrong, and this goes on for a few months or years, and in the meantime, you are pulling out the first gray hairs from your eyelashes, and the local, current here-and-now-one says: you are no longer the youngest one, either. That is how you know that you have to hurry, otherwise you'll reach him on the wrong side of the fountain of youth. So you dream longer, you already sleep away eleven hours in one piece, that makes two dreams or more per night, and now you are at his house or castle and you roam around it like a lost cat that no one is looking for; you look up into the room, the lusty chamber where he celebrates his current local one, but you always stand there and become eye and nerve, night after night, to avoid no pain in any respect — and that can consume half a year or more in that manner. You lose all strength for the day and the typing and the partying, you long for a bed to dream away your life's sentence, you now stand at his door and ring the bell shamelessly. He comes out and beckons, you can't skulk around here, shoo shoo, away with you, so at least he waves at you, even though he slips away again; there are the precious seconds or nights in the walking around the block, shoo shoo, away with you, he is with you and not with her, and you tell him — but we're already fifty dreams away — but you've always loved me and how dare you love this person — and he laughs in understanding — but you're already twenty dreams away — and he takes you in his arms somewhere in his house, I think it's her house, but she's just been scared away — and now you've been sleeping for fourteen hours straight through, and you say to the day-man, I'm sick, I have to have a check-up to see if I have a brain tumor or addiction to dreams, but you know you don't want to get well at all, so you cleverly burn the bridges to work and normality on all sides by stating that: "I have a mysterious illness," and you plunge into the nights as if into a fresh bath, from which you rise exhausted by the heat and ill well-feeling, for now you meet him nightly at his house, in his apartment, at his office, and so you do it devilishly — and thus summer and winter move in and out — and you say to him, it's time to part from her, you see that I'm the only one — but he avoids such directness, he offends her with kisses and let me, we have everything, but everything is not enough for her, she wants him with skin and devil's hair and goat's leg, all the beloved mischief should come over her daily and nightly.

What do you mean here, to gain experience from pain? That's the last thing we want, to learn from pain, come here, you, my sweet cup of hemlock — and you can do that for a hundred dreams, a fight between you and the devil, and you and the — or whatever the other one is called, you chase him to the lawyer; the papers have been ordered and signed, where are the stamps, you didn't put any stamps on them, here is the most important one, the last of the letters, now finally do go to her and tell her there's no coming back, or I'll do it for you, that's what you dream close to twenty awful times, that you'll shout her away with the flaming words that light up her path: He has always loved only me-me-me, and they protrude like swords from your chest, from her chest and from yours — and so your best years pass, which are the worst for you, because you can dream and rage so full of strength, open up the memories again that are so youthfully fresh.

Until the night comes, then you have reached it, now twelve years have already passed dreaming, and he says, she is gone with the children, and you ask him, strangely sobered, where has she gone to? And you sense her in strange chambers, and you know yourself as a kindred spirit, and you think of her gently from now on, and no longer full of raging swords, more like a beloved deceased cousin to whom you write posthumous letters, you become all tender-eyed and never stop asking about her when you enter her wide-open spaces.

It all goes like clockwork now; he sends off the most bitter letters without batting an eye. You talk intimately and without any pressing desire, and the nights become shorter and the sighs smoother, and the current local here-and-now-one is happy about your recovery and says that the diet is good for you, the doctor was right after all, and you complain that if I had but gone to him sooner, I could have gained years that I wasted in bed, suffering. I don't know why I accept illnesses so passively, as fate and punishment and addiction, and not as a metabolic disorder. But the main thing is that I'm better now, and that goes on for close to thirty dreams; you peacefully sort out his chaos, and you also meet her once again in her house, where she picks up memories; you greet her calmly and not triumphantly, like a Nike without head and arm, you humbly take the pictures from the wall; what does she really want with these photo shots of her old god? And you forbid yourself any thought of the past and live completely in the here and now, during the day and also at night, these are your best years, unfortunately so short — finally the time has come; for this you have turned fifteen years of your life into night, when he tells you everything is finished and done, move in with me. And you float to your mother's house — in the last of those dreams, of course — and you tell her, dangerously uneasy: this time it will work. I'm going to be very lonely from now on, mother, do you hear me? She nods and nods. I will be very lonely, mother. Come, let's go dance …

You wake up, screaming. And you take action: out with the king's trash, down with Zeus and his she-devils; at last, you erect pyres for your failure, make room for me and my loneliness; I want to sleep dreamlessly and want to wake up dreamlessly, to search the earth's texture, to slay seals, to set up rockets, to devastate jungles, to break bridges, to rob ships, to sink countries.

There is a mild knock at the door, and you change noticeably when you catch sight of the dainty bull from the sky.

Oh, my God, how shall I receive you? Europa utters suddenly against her better knowledge.

And he does you the honor of his visit in the barest of all rooms.

That is how gracious the devil is in his many forms.

The Great German Chief Devil appeared in the guise of a rather slight, brown-haired, and brown-eyed Austrian and not in the guise of a blond, broad-shouldered Aryan hero. I thought everyone knew that, but I was wrong. I had just given a reading at the Varnhagen Society ("Gorda Selig, a reincarnation of Rahel Varnhagen") when I said to one of the gentlemen present: "After all, Hitler was an Austrian!" The man addressed, a Mr. Lemming, replied in an agitated voice: "But, actually, he was a German. Properly German in character, I mean!" "But this German was an Austrian," I insisted. "He was born on the border of Germany and Austria, so he was practically a

German," the gentleman said as persistently as I did. "But he was born and raised as an Austrian! Surely a German would never have thought of invading Prague and declare: All of this here belongs to us now!" "That can be explained historically," said the gentleman angrily: "Czechoslovakia had been part of Austria-Hungary for centuries, after all." Hearing himself say Austria-Hungary, he became confused and changed the delicate subject.

"Why aren't you actually represented on Wikipedia? You don't want to announce how old you are, admit it! What year were you born?!"

I had never lied before when asked about my age. In general, I didn't like to lie, and therefore only did when it was absolutely necessary for survival. And I had not bothered with a Wikipedia biography. "I was born in 1943!" I said curtly. The gentleman hurried home to the computer and wrote a partly invented and partly eulogistic biography of me, in which I was born in August 1943 and not in March, and was actually called Klothilde, a name I have always hated, and not Gorda, so he took away my distinctive or peculiar first name and gave me the one for the shithouse (loo in a nutshell), and then he wrote down what I had confessed to him under twelve seals of secrecy: "She is the daughter of the war criminal Adolf Suhr ..." Thus the world learned what I was in reality: an impostor who tried to blame the poor Austrians for Hitler's crimes because her father had been a German Nazi war-criminal pig. And I had thought the man liked me. Now I thought, he can just kiss my ass.

My second attempt to explain to the world that Hitler had been an Austrian failed just as much as the first. This time, Martin Walser, the famous writer, was my adversary. In Chicago, he read from his book *A Gushing Fountain*, in which he portrays the Austrians as Hitler's pitiful victims. Gorda Selig was ridden by a little sub-devil when she raised her finger and lectured the Big Man that Hitler simply 'brought home' his countrymen, and whether he had never heard that Hitler's family came from the poor Austrian hinterland. He had been born in Braunau and gone to school in Linz, and then he had lived for years in Vienna, where he developed his political ideas that disgust us today. Didn't he ever read Brigitte Hamann's book *Hitler's Vienna*? One could expect historical knowledge from such a great writer as him. Someone would have claimed that if the Austrians were raped by Hitler, it was for their own orgasmic pleasure and joy.

The Great Man stuck his tongue out at me while blah-blah-blahing as if I were a naughty child and not a well-dressed elderly lady with knee and back pain. And he played the angry ZEUS and THUNDERER: Blahblahblah blahblahblah blahblahblah!

A murmur went through the hall, and I heard a young girl whispering behind me: "What does that have to do with the novel?" "Shh," said a male voice. And now I really got going, in German and in English: "Hitler had to learn High German with the help of an actor, otherwise he would have declared war on the world in his comfortable Austrian dialect, which, of course, would have been less convincing to the North German Aryans in Berlin. Hindenburg derided the brown Adolf as a 'Bohemian corporal', unfortunately in vain. Because nine months later, Hindenburg appointed Hitler Chancellor of the Germans, although his party had won only thirty-seven percent of the vote. A historical scandal!" Thereafter, no one spoke to me at the reception: I was the contagious leper among healthy people, the leper who belonged on a devil's island with deformed people like myself.

Thereupon I wrote, desperately, a poem regarding the diary (1933-1945) of Viktor Klemperer:

Reading the Diary of Viktor Klemperer.

> Now I live in his diary
> In the Third and no longer in the Fourth or Fifth Reich
> With my Polish husband
> Who, at that time, worked as a slave laborer in this factory
> Zeiss-Ikon, or something like that
> Without me, he would have worked every day
>
> And the Austrian devil squats in Berlin like a giant octopus
> And he stretches out his thousand disgusting arms
> To grab us, they are called SS and Gestapo and Reichswehr
> And some of them are even strangely friendly while doing so
>
> And if it weren't always for those tender Aryan gestures
> Like a bit of extra sausage or a bit of forbidden vegetables
> Wrapped in the rare newsprint
> I would cowardly close this sacred diary
> Before my guilty gentile eyes

For this poem (and several others), I received a poetry prize in the States, about which I couldn't rejoice, for it came accompanied by a letter from the president of the German Society, telling me that I had received the prize without his approval: I didn't deserve it! I thought, the man meant

I couldn't write poetry, and in my reply letter, I quoted the famous North German proverb: "What is one man's trash, is another man's treasure. With greetings from the Chicago trash." He immediately replied that he had revoked my prize because I had impudently called Hitler an Austrian. And he was — as everyone knows — actually a German. No, I wrote back, he was an Austrian, born in Austria of Austrian parents and raised in Austria. That made him an Austrian. "But he left for Munich so early," wrote the wise gentleman. "Twenty-three years old is not early, he would have had to move to Germany at five years of age, at the latest." "But the Austrian military rejected him after all." "If you are rejected by the military, it still doesn't mean that you lose your citizenship."

This old gentleman, an Austrian professor of German studies from Vienna, didn't want to help carry the collective guilt of the Germans. I understood that well. I also didn't want to be guilty of the crimes of my war-criminal father. And that's why I often said: "He is not my father." My stepfather was my father. He fed me and raised me. You have to earn the word father first. A little bit of semen doesn't make a man with soul, character, talents, and intelligence, or no intelligence and no character.

And thus Hitler became a native German, and I became a virgin birth.

After Remo, Larry, and my mother, Dr. Sacks and I discussed my unknown so-called father, or sperm donor, as I called him.

"I determine for myself who my father is," I kept telling Dr. Sacks. "And Adolf S. is not my father" and wanted to speak of my stepfather. But Dr. Sacks insisted on the speck of semen that provided me, on the path of life, with my strong chin, the narrow lips, the protruding left ear, and the bent little finger on the right hand. And, in addition to the collective guilt of the Germans, that special one, due to his war-crimes in Toulouse 1944/45, when he carried out the last will of Hitler and executed the prisoners of war there.

"Please, I don't want to talk about that," I begged Dr. Sacks.

"Yes, you do," he said, "that's precisely why we have to do it."

"I don't even know what he did in Prague," I said in despair.

"Why don't you ask your mother?"

"She says she doesn't know, either, that he was not allowed to talk about it. He had to swear an oath to keep his mouth shut — but she most certainly didn't want to know, either. In their huge house in the finest area of Prague, where the palaces of the envoys are. That's where she spent the best years of her life. I mean, the best, as far as her body was concerned. As for her soul, I don't know. She always used to say that we lived on a volcano, and that it could spit fire any day now and bury us under its lava. We lived in a town like Pompeii before the catastrophe, and not in the golden city that all of Europe raved about. Try living in Pompeii for years and you know: red today, dead tomorrow. Burned to a pile of ashes. We were surviving in a crematorium, she said. Hitler would have made all of Germany into a crematorium, after all."

"And your father?" asked Dr. Sacks.

"What do you mean, father?" I snapped at him or myself: "I'm telling you, he's not my father!"

"So your non-father, where was he back then?"

"He was back in Berlin, and then from 1942 at the Russian front."

"How did he get there?"

"He already reported to the front at the beginning of the war."

"Why is that? Wasn't it more peaceful in Prague or Berlin?"

"He didn't want to do what he had to do," my mother said, and that's why he enlisted for the front. But what he actually had to do, I don't know." And I started sobbing and reached for a Kleenex to dry my face. From then on, every time I went to see him, I sobbed and used his Kleenex.

This went on for a few months, until Dr. Sacks said: "Now I finally understand why so many young Germans go to Israel and help build the country on the kibbutz, it was always a mystery to me."

"They're working off their guilt," I said, "their German collective guilt, which is really the parents' guilt. That's a kind of debt from ancient times, and our children and grandchildren will still have to work it off. Right down to the third and fourth generation, as the Bible says. What surprises me is that the Russians don't suffer from any collective guilt because of Stalin's gruesome crimes. I mean, Stalin's daughter, Svetlana, can live peacefully with us in the States and no one is outraged and says: Throw the daughter of the devil, Stalin, out. Just imagine if Hitler's daughter lived in Chicago! There would be an incredible weeping and wailing in the newspapers: The devil's spawn is polluting our beautiful, free, innocent country! They would shoot her in the street like fair game, I think. She would not live long. And I would be happy about it. And, actually, I should be glad if someone shot me!"

"Well, I've had enough of this!" Dr. Sacks exclaimed angrily: "You are not guilty of your father's crimes!"

"He's not my father!" I objected stubbornly.

"So, you are not guilty for the unfortunate S., God have mercy on his soul, one might say. But let's leave that sorry chapter. And don't whine about it like that here, you're not guilty, Gorda! I hereby declare you innocent and an honorary

Jewess for writing your doctoral thesis on Heinrich Heine, my favorite poet, and for wanting to dedicate your life to his works. In the future, I'll see you lecturing on Heinrich Heine at universities and Goethe Institutes around the world. About Heine and anti-Semitism in his time, and about Rahel Varnhagen and her despair as a Jewess, and about the famous Jewish salons in Berlin."

And then he asked me if I was good in bed.

The pain started in my neck and flowed from my shoulders down my arms. Larry hung me on a hook on the bathroom door. At the hospital, the physical therapist put me in a stretching bed. That helped, but as soon as I was out in the fresh air, the pain returned. I wanted to go buy a stretching bed.

Larry said: "You're nuts, that costs a lot of money." Instead, we bought an expensive special bed that could be made softer and harder. I was on the soft Protestant half and Larry was on the hard Catholic half. But my Protestant half was never soft enough for me.

"You're a real princess on the pea," Larry said sullenly, "one can never please you!" I bought an air mattress with a pump at a sporting goods store in Munich; I was overtired, because I hadn't been able to get a wink of sleep in the hotel bed that night and was afraid my bones would break from the concrete I seemed to be lying on. Finally, finally I was sleeping again! After months of insomnia. And Larry's growing anger: "You're doing this on purpose! You're just trying to ruin my vacation!"

By now the pain had penetrated to my thighs and knees. I stiffened and roared in agony. Larry read all the articles in the professional journals on the new civilization disease that I and many others, especially hysterical women, had developed to drive their husbands crazy.

"I think you have fibromyalgia," he finally said.

"What kind of disease is that?"

"You have pain all over, we don't know where it comes from."

"How come the doctors don't know?"

"Well, do you think we know everything? We don't know anything about the black holes in the universe, either."

"What do black holes have to do with my pain?"

"Now, stop talking nonsense and take an antidepressant, it will relax your muscles and reduce the pain." I dutifully took the drug and prayed for a miracle.

From then on, I traveled around Europe with the air mattress and the pump. My friends' husbands had to pump air into the mattress in the evening, and at night I slept like a baby. My suitcase was half full of the big rubber animal, and on my back, I carried the air pump in my backpack. My hosts thought I was coming with a roomy suitcase full of ravishing clothes, instead I came with the bare necessities: a pair of black pants, a white blouse, a gray sweater, a pair of slippers and the practical cotton underwear in stripes. The rest of the space in the suitcase was taken up by the rubber contraption. Now I slept well, but I traveled poorly. Loaded like a luggage mule.

"Can't you pack better than that?" a friend asked me, the kind who always knows everything better: "I'll have to show you how to do it sometime." But when she showed me, it turned out that I was traveling with a hospital, with a heating pad, a neck bolster, rubber contraption and an air pump and the many bottles full of painkillers, and not with a suitcase of clothes. My beautiful clothes, they hung in the closet, at home. Who cares about looks anymore, when your body has turned into an instrument of torture, as if by some evil spell.

"I am under a curse," I said to my astonished girlfriends.

"You are prattling nonsense," they said, trying to comfort me.

"Yes, I am," I said, "because my unknown sperm donor executed partisans and prisoners of war."

"You're not seriously going to shoulder the sins of your father, are you?"

"Yes, yes, I am."

"Now you've really gone crazy!" the husband of my friend Reinhild, in whom I had seen the ideal man for me and all my girlfriends until then, said indignantly. From then on, thank God, I saw him less idealized, and I no longer suffered so much when I visited Reinhild and saw her walking hand in hand with him in front of me. Larry and I hadn't walked like that for a long time — not since Lausanne. Hand in hand. Soul on soul. Word by word.

And a small miracle happened. The pains receded. Even during the day. Not completely, but in such a way that from now on I was able to no longer think of suicide, but of the black holes in the universe and why we existed at all, since we were destroying the planet so murderously and selfishly. And each other. Homo homini lupus est (man is a wolf). There is nothing new under the sun, only that God is dead, as Nietzsche recognized, and he had to be dead, because otherwise he would not have permitted the gassing of millions of people. He would have intervened with thunder and lightning and volcanic eruptions and earthquakes and snowstorms; he had many means at his disposal, for example the great deluge, of which the Old Testament tells so impressively, almost as impressively as a modern thriller or an action movie.

"The good Lord, he doesn't sleep," my mother used to say, "because he doesn't exist."

But Larry says he does exist. And goes to church every Sunday to pray. Or Saturday evening, so he can sleep in on Sunday morning. He goes to pray for all of us. For us, who sleep or sit in front of the TV and hear about the wars and the executions around the world on the news. Because we don't want to miss anything. Before it's over with all of us.

After Remo, Larry, my mother, and the sperm donor and war-criminal S., Dr. Sacks and I discussed my seemingly passionate, infantile love for my cousin Anni, who had to substitute for my mother's love and missing sisters. Until I sought that which is called love in men. With men, who themselves didn't know what love was. Except for their mama.

I told Dr. Sacks how beautiful my little cousin was, with her brownish skin and thick blond hair, her forget-me-not-blue eyes under straight aligned black brows in a face grown so regular and symmetrical that mine looked like a wild growth by comparison. I might have hated this cousin in puberty, when we chose the pimply boys as the heroes of our hearts, and when nothing counted anymore, no talent for painting, no intelligence in math, no A in the German essay: only the texture of the face and the latest in fashion regarding clothes with which we covered our mostly skinny post-war bodies. We transformed ourselves from child-women into the most enchanting flowers possible, trying to attract bees with our display apparatuses, and nothing else. We hung up our brains at home when we went to dance lessons. And we learned to put up a smile like Venus-come-out, so that the corners of our mouths would not point sadly downward. Downwards, where there were no dance class partners. There, where you had to stay seated when it came to dancing. And when it came to dancing, we didn't ask for long whether the other person could dance or not, the main thing was that there was one, because alone — without a partner — one wasn't worth a tired penny and wanted to hang oneself on a nail at home, where the brain was already hanging and impatiently waiting for our return.

As soon as the brain was back in my head and no longer hanging on the nail, I took out my diary and wrote my pubescent despair down, so it was gone from my heart: Dear diary, today I sat on the waiting bench, and no one came to dance with me. Just don't think that I'm going to kill myself now. Things have to get much worse than that; so if no one comes the next time and the time after that and the time after that, I don't guarantee anything. But sometimes I also rejoice in the diary: today someone told me I was cute, just don't ask me what his name was, Klaus or something. And then he wanted to take me home, but I preferred to walk with Doris. Maybe he wanted to kiss me at the front door, well, anything but that …

Almost all my girlfriends were beautiful, like my cousin Anni. That was certainly no coincidence. Anni's beauty marked me forever: I only wanted to look at beautiful girls' faces, and Dr. Sacks asked me if I had ever thought about possibly being a lesbian. No, I hadn't thought of that. But the following night, I dreamed that I was hugging my beloved Anni, almost like a man hugs a girl and not like a sister does it. From then on, Dr. Sacks and I wondered if I was a lesbian. Because I was clearly having trouble with orgasm. So, where sex was concerned, I was clearly one that belonged to the slow troop. But otherwise, I was mostly part of the quick one. After that, we wasted months poking around in my sexual morass to see if there were any lesbian skeletons there or not. We didn't find any. But I received the last proposal of my life from a woman who asked me what I thought about lesbian love? "Unfortunately," I said, "nothing at all." Yet, in a dream, I had embraced my cousin like a man, and given that, you don't say nothing, nothing at all. This woman, the questioner, whom I liked very much and wanted to have as a friend in my life, has not forgiven me and doesn't want to talk to me and no longer comes to the German book club that I run in Chicago. And I got terribly angry at myself and swore that next time, I'd answer smarter by saying: "Who knows for sure," or something like that. Because even Freud says we don't know for sure. Man proposes, God disposes, and suddenly, from one month to the next, you leave your husband and children and live with a woman and her three dogs, you, who has always only loved cats. That is how some of us have gone to the dogs already.

And Dr. Sacks asked me again if I was good in bed. That's none of his business, I thought angrily. And remained eloquently silent. He then explained that as a psychologist he had to know how good I was in bed, because that showed him whether I was an adult or not. Only adults have orgasms, he said. Children merely groped each other. And some people would never get out of the groping age. Just like others always say NO when you ask them to do something, much like two-year-olds, they just said NO, too. And all compulsive NO-sayers have actually remained two-year-old children and would never get out of that pitiful age. And still others couldn't part with a worn-out cent, as if they still lived in post-war Europe and not in rich America and with many millions of dollars put on the side. Those all lived in the past and still wore the hairstyles they wore back in their dance-class days when they were just show apparatuses and not human beings with brains and talents and an A in their German essay. Or a C.

I didn't like telling Dr. Sacks that I had, unfortunately, only slept with two men so far, and two sexual experiments would not yield a statistically convincing result. I would first have to sleep around a bit like my great role model in matters of sex, my friend Cornelia, who — for example — would have slept with dozens of men ...

"I don't want to hear anything about Cornelia right now," Dr. Sacks decided to continue the treatment session. "Tell me about yourself!"

"There's not much to tell."

"Start with number one."

"Remo is number one, you know that!"

"So, how was Remo in bed?"

Yeah, what should I call it? "Quick, quick, you might say. As if he actually wanted to do something else, write his doctoral thesis or read an important book on the subject of Conrad Ferdinand Meyer as a literary critic." It all went quickly and was over in a flash. Hardly begun, already finished. Brevity is the spice of life, was his motto when it came to coitus, while afterwards he couldn't smoke enough cigarettes, I sometimes counted five. Yet, the doctor had told him to stop with that poisonous stuff.

"Stop talking about smoking afterwards," Dr. Sacks said: "Talk about the sex before that, instead."

"There's not much to tell," I said.

"But something must have taken place," Dr. Sacks asked incredulously, "or was he impotent?"

"Well, no, not exactly."

"He had an erection?"

"Yes, he had one."

"And then?"

"He would be erect and go in and come right back out, as if he hadn't found what he was looking for inside. Often, I didn't even notice that he had already been inside. I only noticed it by Remo's moans."

"And you, did you also moan?"

"What was there to moan about? I wondered."

"Why did you wonder?"

"Because I couldn't stop thinking about Hans, my childhood-and-class sweetheart, Hans."

"But you said you never slept with him."

"Yes, that's right, we didn't sleep together, we caressed and kissed for hours instead of sleeping with each other and smoking."

"And how did you feel about that?"

"I felt it was wonderful!"

"And did you never want to sleep with him?"

"That's the strange thing: no."

"And why not?"

"I was afraid of getting pregnant. I really wanted to go to university and study."

"And Hans, he didn't want to sleep with you either?"

"Well, yes, he wanted to."

"And how long did you do that?"

"Did what?"

"The making out."

"Well, for about a year and a half."

"And you really didn't...?"

"No."

"No one's going to believe you, Gorda."

"Nobody needs to."

"But I want to know the truth, I can't help you without the truth."

"The truth is, I didn't need the sex, the making out was enough for me."

"What do you mean, enough?"

"I was in all the love-cloud sevens of the world, I was way up high, shot up like a rocket when making out, and the rest of the night I was floating up there and not in my bed. "That was just my body down there."

"So you had a mental orgasm?"

"Yes, you could call it that."

"And Hans, in which heaven was he?"

"He wasn't in any heaven; he was in a hell, and he was getting madder and madder."

"And what did he do?"

"Once, he beat me."

"And how did you react to that?"

"My rocket raced even faster to the moon and then to the sun! I never experienced anything like that again. That was so crazy!"

"Are you saying that you have to be hit to have an orgasm?"

"You're saying that, not me!"

"But you have to ask yourself what this experience means for your life. Do you want to be raped, perhaps?"

"Maybe," I said, suddenly feeling dead tired. "I'll have to think about that."

"Okay," Dr. Sacks said, "come back in a week when you've thought about it. That's enough for today."

To the Psychologist

> Sometimes a father to me, sometimes a priest you
> And suddenly also my super-id
> What yesterday was still absolution
> Today, the brown eyes torment
> By being heavy and scrutinizing me.
>
> The questions remain up in the air
> I'm begging for a judgement

But you are looking heavily melancholic
Just like a thousand years ago already
The magic sphinx from old books.

I run towards you like my god
I climb around on you
And I search for a gap into the soul
You, however, are looking so melancholic and cold
And are letting me crawl to and fro.

Your silence guarantees me an
Answer that I am destined to find
And for years, my ways
Follow the wisdom of your great
Brown eyes between eruptions of anger.

Yes, for years, yet, I'm telling you
For all future, all time
A monologue down into the grave
You god of this world who has become a sphinx
You father to me, you super-id above me.

Forever is enough, I thought angrily, and didn't go to Dr. Sacks for three months.

"Don't ever do that again," he said, when I finally appeared at his office in the fall. "Where have you been for so long?"

"In Germany and Switzerland."

"Did you see Remo again?"

"Of course, I never go to Switzerland without seeing Remo again."

"Is that the only reason you go to Switzerland?"

"Well, I also have four girlfriends there that I visit."

"The dearest of my four girlfriends in Switzerland has always been my Hanni, because it was quietest with her. Sonja had had three children and Eva two, and the little children screamed and raged through the mothers' house and lives as if they had brought twenty into the world, and not just two or three. I thought, that's more than anyone can put up with and left again two days later. And decided to stay longer when the children were grown up. Hanni, however, had only had one child at present, because she actually had two. But with eleven years between them, it seemed as if she only had one. And such an only child is the dream of all mothers: it plays calmly with dolls or cars and no other child throws a tantrum:

"Want that, want that!! Susi wants to have that!"

"Give the doll to your little sister, right away!" Sonja then shouted, because she needed her well-deserved rest.

But then, the littlest one whined: "Want that, want that!! "Mary wants that!!" And Sonja had to yell again:

"Quiet, quiet, aren't there enough dolls here for the three of you?! I count about twenty dolls in the room!" But each of them always wanted the doll that her sister was holding. If it was in the corner, no one wanted it anymore. It was like in dance class: if you sat too long in the corner or on the waiting bench, nobody wanted you anymore. Then you were an unappreciated doll that belonged in the trash can of life, where everything ugly and unloved can be found. And who of us wants to end up in the dustbin of life?

But with Hanni, no child cried "want that, want that," because they already had everything. And the sister, who was eleven years older, seemed to be a little second mother for little Gottlieb, and not a jealous sister. The truth is that Hanni had had three children, the second of whom was stillborn after nine months. "And it was also a little son, just imagine," Hanni said with a face contorted by pain.

She hadn't been able to get over this dead son for the longest time: "Carry a child around inside you for nine months, and then it's born — and birth is something awful, no matter what they tell you about it — and you think it's about to lie in your arms and scream with the joy of life, and you're so terribly happy about this tiny screamer — instead you get the tray shoved in front of your fat belly with the disgusting hospital food on it, which you are certain to not be able to get down. You won't be able to eat for a long time, and you'll get skinny as a rail, and soon you'll look ten years older with grief, because you have nothing in your arms and no little son to feed and kiss."

"Do you mean to say that you would not have felt such grief over a dead daughter?"

"Oh, what do I know, but it was a little son, and I already had a daughter, after all. And Karl-Hansi wanted to have a son, like any real man. And I failed and didn't give him one!"

"But it wasn't your fault' And you were only twenty-eight years old. Why didn't you get another one right away but wait until forty instead?"

"I had no courage left after the great disappointment. I thought I was under a curse, and the next child would also turn into a figment of my imagination."

"I don't understand that: you had given birth to a healthy child. The odds were in your favor. However, Goethe's mistress Christiane had four dead children after August was born, all of them stillborn or died right after birth. She must also have thought she was cursed, or she was happy about it because she wasn't married, after all, and unmarried pregnant women were put in jail as whores if they didn't want to name the father. Those were still hard times!"

"What did her children die of, then?"

"With Goethe and Christiane, the rhesus factor probably didn't fit, she would have needed a blood transfusion, an unknown cure back then. In contrast, how good we have it today!"

"Giving birth to a dead son was the worst experience of my life, Gorda. Up until then, everything had been going well: Abitur [high school diploma] and training as a consular secretary, four years in Paris, and I married the love of my life, Karl-Hansi, a Swiss from the beautiful Emmental valley, even if his parents didn't want me as their daughter-in-law. Yet, I grew up in a mansion, and his parents were poor people, and their house was tiny."

"Much like my mother-in-law, Mrs. Glück. "But why didn't Karl-Hansi's parents want you in the family? You were Swiss, weren't you?"

"Since I grew up in Germany and not in Switzerland, I am an expatriate Swiss; even if I have a red Swiss passport, that was not considered good enough. I should have been from their village, there was such a girl, she went to the village school with Karl-Hansi."

"And I lost the great love of my life and Switzerland with all its lakes and mountains on top of it!" I lamented for the hundredth time.

For years, Hanni was my dearest wailing wall, my Kleenex, and my female Dr. Sacks. She helped me get over the horror I felt when I first landed in Chicago by plane and the security police led me into a bare room like a criminal, where one of the policewomen patted me down from my collar to my brassiere and pant legs. What were they looking for? Maybe gold? But then I remembered the narcotics that the young people in America loved, which they smoked as hashish or snorted as cocaine and injected into their arms as a liquid to forget the horrible Vietnam War in the Far East, where the Yanks had no business, just like the French who had left with their tails between their legs.

As far as I am concerned, my friend Angelica, who gave birth to a sick child at the age of twenty-three, is a miracle of a woman. No, at first it was healthy and then the small body suddenly cramped up and the doctor said she must get to the hospital immediately. There they did many tests, and then the doctor explained that her child would become autistic, that is, it would have little contact with the environment and live as if behind a wall. And the young couple should undergo a test so that the medical team could decide whether to keep the child or send it to an institution. It was decided that the parents were too young and immature to raise such a child, and that it belonged in an institution staffed with professionals who would know what to do and what not to do. These are the kind of children Hitler would have killed, and where my American sister Nancy has been working the night shift as a nurse for years already. She took me with her once, and there were babies like this sitting everywhere, drooling babies that weren't babies anymore at all and were, maybe, fifteen years old already, I think I'm going crazy, and I escaped to the cafeteria for a coffee. I couldn't get the food down.

"But the little ones are quite cute, aren't they," Nancy said to me. "Don't make such a fuss." Yes, if it had been that easy!

Angelika and Tom kept the child.

"I'm a pastor's daughter! Who do they think I am! And my Tom studied to become a pastor. There simply couldn't be a better home for such a child! What impudence!"

"How did you ever have the courage to have another child?" I asked her meekly. "Weren't you afraid of being under a curse and having a second sick child?"

"No, never!" said Angelica again, beaming: "I knew I was born under a lucky star, that's what my parents always told me!" The loving pastor's family had referred to her as "our sunshine" from an early age, because the sun rose in her face even when it was snowing and storming outside. And in her parents' lives, it had snowed and stormed hard when her mother was ambushed and raped — probably raped — by Russian soldiers while fleeing from the German eastern territories:

"Because, of course, they never told us the truth. We children had to guess, because they suddenly fell silent. Then we knew: something terrible has happened. We always lived in fear of a war and in fear of the Russians. The Russians, they were the worst. But the Russians and Poles claimed that the Germans had been the worst."

"How did your parents have the courage to bring another child into this terrible world after the war?" I asked Angelika, because even in peacetimes, I had not mustered the strength to do so. Yet, Dr. Sacks had always tried to persuade me: "Have a child at last, Gorda! Every woman needs a child, at least one. Just like your cat, she should have a litter before you sterilize her."

The cat didn't have a litter before we had her spayed and I didn't have a child. I seemed to be sterile by nature. Or was it fear that made me infertile?

"Maybe you're not sleeping with each other enough?" Dr. Sacks probed more deeply. "How often are you doing it?"

"Well, about once or twice a month"

"Once or twice a month? Well then, nothing can come of that. Why so rarely?"

"Well, when we have a fight, Larry doesn't talk to me for a week or two. And then, of course, I don't feel like sleeping with him. And when we talk with each other again, we have another fight right away, and Larry grumbles for two more weeks. So we don't get to talking and we don't get around to having a child. Only to arguing."

"And it was the same in Lausanne?"

"Of course not!"

"It was nice having sex with him there?"

"Yes."

"Yes, and?"

"What else is there to say? Great is great and says it all."

"And now it's not great anymore?"

"No. How can sex be great when Larry shakes his fist at me while I'm shopping or throws a tantrum because I can't cook and he's sick of steak and potatoes. I could eat those every day!"

"Yeah, well, then finally learn how to cook!"

"I'm already learning the German Middle Ages and Romantic literature and language history; I don't have time for a cooking class!"

"Why don't you finally sleep with him? You really could do that!" Dr. Sacks said sternly, as if I didn't want to sleep with him, either.

"I want to, but then he'll yell around again: where did you put the papers, I put them here on the table yesterday? That's a disgrace, that you just put my papers wherever you want!"

"But the table is for eating," I hissed. "The table is for eating — it's not a repository for your goddamn papers!"

"Goddamn papers, those were our statements for the month!"

"And then he yelled for a long time, and you don't want to sleep with a man like that. He can kiss my ass! I might as well have married Remo then!"

Larry and the author in Lausanne, Switzerland

"No wonder, if you don't get around to having a child. And you only have a few years left, Gorda. Don't be like that!"

My beloved cousin Anni, too, had a stillborn son, who was already eight months old, a real baby with ten little fingers and toes and everything.

"He was a little doll," my mother said, and he had to be buried at a proper funeral with a priest and all.

"That was a sad day," Mum told me: "You can consider yourself glad you weren't there." And my mother suffered for my cousin, who wanted a second child as passionately as my mother had only wanted one. Thus everyone wishes for something different. And what is one person's planned child is another person's doom. Or it is a reminder of the unloved mother-in-law.

And I have had only cats, no children. I have had three cats, one as cute as the other, and none obeyed, each was headstrong like Larry and me, and they let themselves be served like my husband at the beginning of our marriage and me today, because everything in me is full of pain. My cats were a great happiness, just like the men at the beginning of any love affair, and a comfort in the Siberian loneliness of the Chicago winter, when you don't go out because of the cold and for fear of the snowstorms. And in the summer, you also stay indoors because the Roman heat is full of moisture from the lake and makes the clothes stick to the body. It is only a few days at the end of May and in the month of September that one can walk outside in the park. Otherwise, you walk around the park with your eyes when you drive by in the car, or you sit by the window and think, if only I could be out there. But the temperature points to 92 °F heat or -13 °F cold. You become a groundhog and soon lose your love for the fresh air as it sweeps across the lake or flat land at hurricane speeds.

For me, my cats replaced the missing nature, just like the few potted plants and trees in the pictures by Rudolf Führmann on the walls and the roses and asters in the beautiful glass vases that Katja brought me from the part of Poland that used to be Silesia and the land of her ancestors.

Hormones

My cat squirmed and screamed
And rolled around like a
Trembling muff

Based on that, I believed that love
After all, it was a matter of
Hormones and not as
Promising joy as I
Dreamed at fourteen

Now it lies castrated
Tenderly mewing in
My arm and again
It serves as a maxim:

The day will come —
That sterilized one — when
Life doesn't disturb
You anymore when
Reading peacefully

My first cat was a common street cat, and we slept tenderly together in bed until I couldn't sleep anymore due to sniffles and sneezes, nor Larry from the noise I made, and it was banished

Drawing of the author by Rudolf Führmann

to the kitchen at night, to his annoyance, and I thought I was under a curse, I wasn't even allowed to love a cat. Now I was sleeping again at night, but during the day, my lungs would tighten up if he lay on the German book or on my lap and I petted him. Before I would suffocate on the asthma, I went to a specialist who did a test on me and determined that I was allergic to animal dander and house dust and eggs and chicken meat and pepper and pineapple and chocolate, just about everything I ate and liked. For three years, he gave me shots for the allergies, because there was no way I was going to give up my feline child, as he suggested. Child is child. And Larry got me pills and eye drops and skin ointments, and I came to appreciate a husband who was a doctor, and he bought by the dozens — the Kleenex containers that were in every corner of our apartment, on the lamp tables next to the bed, on the refrigerator, on the windowsills, and in the bathrooms. I used up five boxes every week. For years, my nose was sore, and my eyes were red. I had unsightly rashes on my hands and arms. But true love passes every test by fire, and I needed a cat because I had lost my cousin, Remo, Switzerland, and Larry's love, which he seemed to have lost in the hospital. Because there he had to remain cool at the sight of the dying and the dead. There, emotion is not of much use, my friend Katja, the internist, had told me.

"Even when dissecting the corpses, you have to learn to cut cold-bloodedly, otherwise you can drop out of your studies right away."

"And the best doctors are people without feeling?" I asked Katja timidly: "Is that why Larry has turned so icy inside? But he starts crying at the silliest and most sentimental movies!"

"There you are," Katja said to me triumphantly. "He has split himself into two people, one who feels and one who doesn't. The one who doesn't feel brings home the money, don't forget that, and the other one, after all, can watch kitsch movies like Lassie and cry." I promised myself not to forget that, when Larry said, for example: "Leave me alone with your little aches and pains, if you die, I'll notice!" Once I showed him a black spot on the tip of my nose that had previously been a harmless freckle. Larry inspected it under his magnifying glass and exclaimed excitedly: "You actually have a melanoma there!" A melanoma? That was something horrible and deadly, I had previously thought. But then, why was Larry so pleased? It was just the ice-cold researcher in Larry who could rejoice over his wife's deadly skin cancer. He was looking at my nose as a doctor and not at the screen as a feeling human being. Thank God the spot wasn't melanoma. Just white skin cancer.

Symbiosis

My husband and I
Work together:
He is a doctor
And I am always sick

My cat, unlike Larry, never split itself into two beings, one that loved me and one that showed me its ice-cold butt when I was in bed with the flu. On the contrary, he lay against my sick body and looked at me questioningly with his touching cat eyes: "Don't you have the strength to get up and open a can of tuna for me after all?" "Of course, my darling," I replied and staggered into the kitchen to feed my fat child. If I'm asked lovingly, I'll do anything. Just don't scream at me. Or put your fist under my chin. One day, Larry read in a doctor's magazine that cat owners who are allergic to their pets, should get Abyssinian cats, they had the least problems with them. The spit must be different that they use to clean themselves all day long, less harsh, and therefore better for sensitive people like me.

When my first kitten died, I was visiting my mother in Germany and screaming on the phone with grief because my little animal had to die without me. I sent black-bordered bereavement cards to all my friends with cats, because they knew what I had lost: my child. Others might have laughed or pretended as if they knew that it is possible to love a pet like a human child. Only dog lovers still understood me. Friederike, with her three dogs, received a bereavement card and immediately called me and invited me to her place. And I went to see her in Rosenthal, where she lived with her husband, the rude Rüdiger, very close to Worpswede. We went there every day, to think of Rilke and Clara, who had been abandoned by him, and of the great painter Paula Becker, who died giving birth to her child by Otto Modersohn. Here is where our beloved dead had walked, and there is where they had drunk tea and painted their pictures. Back then, Friederike and I wanted to set up an artists' village, or at least an artists' retirement home, where the residents didn't have to be artists at all, just love paintings and the other four Bs: Bach, Beethoven, Brahms, and books. And they should be able to listen when someone does a reading. And dispense comfort when someone needed comforting. And praise where praise was needed. It was supposed to be something like a sanatorium for unwell souls, because most artists were unwell in their souls and most non-artists too, and not just in their bodies. No one can say which of the two is actually worse. Did the sorrow for the dead cat come first and then my nasty asthma attack in a Worpswede café, and had I, of course, forgotten my asthma spray, or was it the other way around?

Friederike's three dogs, two Scotties and a dachshund, lay at our feet and looked at us in love, as if they knew what we were talking about, about Friederike's rude Rüdiger and I about Larry's two souls in his chest, the ice-cold one and the sentimental one, and that it is the ice-cold one that brings the money home, that I as a wife should never forget. And I'm sure that Rüdiger had two souls in his chest, but Friederike no longer noticed the sentimental one. He obviously only showed it in the office, because his colleagues held him in high esteem and were constantly calling him for advice. But Friederike was advised to get the advice she needed from her girlfriends. He couldn't and would not advise her. And when she told him she had fallen in love with her boss, he said after a long pause of silence: "Just don't think I can give you advice. You have to decide for yourself. But what is to become of us now?"

"I don't know that either," Friederike said cautiously. Then he suggested to her, God knows, that they could continue their marriage as a threesome, and everything would stay the same; he hardly ever slept with her anymore anyway. And that he found her boss acceptable.

"Imagine, Gorda, he wanted to have a three-way marriage with us!"

"They did it in Bloomsbury, you remember, the painter Dora Carrington, the writer Lytton Strachey, and the husband of Carrington, what was his name again, who was also Lytton Strachey's lover?"

"Just how did they manage it?" asked Friederike with deepest admiration.

"Well, it didn't last forever, either: Carrington's husband left with another woman, and Carrington had to deal with the fact that Lytton slept with young men, and when he died, she shot herself; she had had enough."

After my beloved alley-cat Kitty, I got my first Pumi, an Abyssinian who looked like a monkey and which we named Puma, so he would grow big and strong like a wild cat. Which he didn't grow into, thank heavens. But he was able to watch TV, from the first day on, when he went for the bull in *Carmen on Ice* with Katarina Witt and Brian Boitano. From an early age on, he loved to watch the animal movies I got for him, especially the cries of birds, and his head would turn back and forth, as the foals and lambs galloped and jumped around. *Animal Babies in Spring* was his favorite program, and he couldn't watch it often enough. I, too, watched it over and over again, delighting in how well he could follow the animals' movements on the screen with his eyes. And while doing so, I ate vanilla ice cream with cognac over it, even though it gave me a stomachache, but first the pleasure and then the punishment. Even the *Youth*, the German Art Nouveau magazine, was a pleasure followed by a punishment. These little lambs jumped around in the spring meadows as if there were only sunshine and butterflies and buttercups in their lives. And bang they got a knock on the head and were sold as roast lamb and eaten as leg of lamb. Roast lamb had always been Friederike's favorite food. Petted first, and then eaten with appetite. My angelic Friederike always adhered to this rule of life for humans and pets.

Reminder

My cat lies on the dining room table
Like a badly turned-out
Sunday roast

And reminds me daily
That it is time
To become a vegetarian.

Friederike came from the countryside, and her mother had kept chickens and ducks and a donkey, on which she had ridden in her childhood. She doesn't remember what happened to him. "Definitely not a stupid married donkey, like most men!" she said with a laugh.

Back then, a huge oil painting was hanging in Friederike's living room. It was a good copy of Murillo's *Boys Playing Dice*. In the evenings, I sat opposite the painting and drank a few glasses of wine with my best female friend.

"Where did you actually get this painting?" I asked her one day.

"From my wealthy aunt, with a warm hand, because she is still alive. But in the nursing home — and there she had no place for the huge picture. First, I thought, what an old museum ham and wanted to sell it, but now I love it so much that I couldn't part with it anymore. Do you see the dog on the front left, looking pleadingly at the standing boy who has the piece of bread in his mouth: his gaze asks: "Can't you give me a piece of it? God, aren't the animals touching — and in a moment you give them some of the food, and if it's the last piece of bread."

"Unless they're lambs, in which case you eat them," I added with a laugh. "This picture has played an important part in my life, Friederike, have I ever told you that?"

"No, not that I know of. And how did that come about?"

"We had to write an essay about this picture in high school in Oldenburg, I think we were about fifteen years old, a ghastly age where you are made up of nothing but

Murillo, *Boys Playing Dice*

inferiorities and sensitivities. The teacher hung a large print of it on the blackboard at the front of the classroom with the words: "Now write down spontaneously how this picture affects you!" "I thought, well, now I'll be spontaneous and not think twice and write my joy from my heart. Unfortunately, not from the brain. And that was a mistake, as it soon turned out."

"Why?"

"The German teacher gave us back the spontaneous essays a week later with the words: Gorda, read yours!" I thought, then it must be good, maybe an A. What a joy! I was weak in English, French, and math, so I needed the consolation of being good at German. So I eagerly began to read out my essay. At least, eagerly at first. Because, soon after that, my classmates started shrieking with laughter, holding their stomachs, and slapping their thighs, as they say. I can't think of any better expressions right now, excuse the clichés, of course I would delete them in a novel. So, they laughed themselves to death or alive while I stood at the pole of shame, because I was a stupid and stubborn child who had to be beaten up by the mother while doing schoolwork so that she would learn to think before spontaneously spouting stupid stuff on paper. THEY HATE ME, those were my thoughts and feelings. My God, I am a person to be hated. Why do I attract their hatred? And still, I like them. Well, not all of them, but most of them ... I was the only one standing in the classroom, the jubilant classmates were casually rocking on their chairs. A wall of horror and fear surrounded me. Then the teacher found her lost voice again and said: "Sit down!" And continued: "So, do be quiet and listen, I gave her a B for this." Again, the peals of laughter went through the classroom.

"An impertinence!" exclaimed one of my tormentors.

"Yup," said the teacher, realizing she had made a mistake: "She deserves a B-minus, because the essay is good but contains some mistakes." There was no end to the indignant shrieking.

"You can go out to the courtyard now!" ordered our usually admired German teacher, when she had her fill of being in a room with a bunch of girls screaming STONE HER: STONE HER!"

"Why did they hate you so much?" asked me Friederike, who by now had compassionately put her right hand on my left.

"Because I was good at reciting poems and good at interpreting them! I was an actress and didn't know it and had to learn in German class that I had an unusual gift. Talent is called 'gift' in English, while the German term 'Gift' means poison. And such a talent is gift and poison at the same time, for which you are loved and hated by those who are envious. And those who are envious are everywhere in the world, in very large numbers. They exist so that you don't become complacent and don't think highly of yourself. They bring you back down to earth, and the fact is that a talent that is not recognized is a curse, a poison, and there's no mercy from above. Part of being an actress is having an audience that rejoices and applauds you, and my classmates didn't want to applaud and admire, they wanted to stone me. That's why I left for America when I was sixteen, as an exchange student to California, and didn't return to them afterwards, but went to another school, one with co-education, which was something new here at the time, as you know, but common in the States. "I never wanted to be stoned by them again, do you understand that?"

"Yes, I understand that well," said Friederike with tears in her big blue round eyes. "And have you never been stoned again?"

"Yes, I have, I think, because when I was at the class reunion in Norway, I took blows for the book I had published in the meantime. I supposedly defamed the class in it!"

"But you didn't do that at all!" said Friederike, astonished.

"What I described wasn't all pomp and circumstance — and if you didn't put a halo on the characters in your books, then their idols will attack you and scream STONE HER! I once wrote a story called *After the performance, the artist may be stoned.* There, such a stoning took place after I did a reading. My childhood love Hans and his lover threw stones at me. Believe me, you never forget something like that. You know that Hans later only loved men."

After the performance, the artist may be stoned. When she read that Robert Frost had recited his poetry before an audience of thousands, tears pearled on her eyelashes. She was now soon to be forty-eight years old, and she had rarely attracted more than twenty listeners, usually fewer, once three in a shamefully large performance hall. In Hamburg, there were exactly ten, nine of whom were acquaintances, so they counted for only half, and less than half if one considered that she had sent out at least thirty invitations to so-called friends. Nine of them, after all, had taken the trouble to trudge here from the dry TV armchair through puddles and sleet, she thought, while she read aloud with an intensity as if the bare room with a fireplace — which is said to have once belonged to a brothel, as Hans had mockingly told her before the reading began — were packed beyond standing room only. She had learned that in the course of the last lean seven years. The fat years didn't come anyway, and she moved almost with relief from the poems to the prose, which inevitably provoked laughter; she had already tried that in Lauenbrück, Stade, and Celle. The poems, on the other hand, were received with cringes, in Celle full of anger; what am I actually annoying people with, she had asked herself. "But that's not my image of Celle at all," one person present said indignantly: "Remnants of the Middle Ages, after all, they're everywhere!" With the merriment of a drowning woman, she had called out, but please, laughter is allowed, and as if on cue, the two in the front row giggled. Finally, loudly, the pitiful rest.

Hans and Stefan sat separately, as if they didn't belong together. Stefan had frowned dismissively, as Gorda recited her hymn to her childhood love, the childhood love that Hans had awakened in her over thirty years ago. In those days, he had possessed exuberant silky hair on his beautiful head and the now strange-seeming inclination to women's bosoms and women's buttocks. None of that had remained with him. Or, he was already then inclined to the present, in which case he had never desired Gorda, which was not possible, so much had they desired each other. Never again, in her life, had she so desired a man she had rejected, and the more she rejected him, the more they desired each other. What man would be so wise to go through such an ordeal again, the very slow first caress and strangulation of lust? Nevertheless, there was something shameful about the fact that Hans no longer desired women today. After me, Hans has never been able to love a woman again, Gorda used to say in so-called jest: I cured him of that. And thought, what a strange quack I am. And I wrote hymns to the youthful love in rhythms and in prose and recited them with the intensity as if the love had never died. As if she were still alive today — like in a fairy tale.

No one laughed at her prose in Hamburg. At least not Hans and Stefan. And yet, she had said to Hans on the phone: "It certainly won't be boring, I promise you." Now Hans and Stefan proved to her that there was nothing to laugh about in her texts. Hadn't someone been giggling there? Yes, of course, Dolores and her husband did, but their giggling didn't seem contagious today. Hans and Stefan seemed to be brooding into the far distance; their mutual acquaintance, Helene, sat with both hands pressed tragically to her forehead, the corners of her mouth drooping plaintively; her childhood friend Cornelia picked nervously at a paper handkerchief, making crumbs by twirling the paper, as if she had just given up smoking and was looking for therapy for bored fingers. Her new husband — it was the fourth, if you included her lifelong passion for a much older, otherwise married principal, but actually she was in love for the first time now, she had recently said to Gorda — the new man didn't wrinkle any of his forehead and cheeks that would signal his immoderate dissatisfaction. The happiness with Cornelia was obviously still too young to leave any traces on his face.

Gorda read as if betrayed and sold. No, like as if betrayed and unsold. As unsold as her books of poetry and the only novel she had managed to finish so far. Thank God, an hour is short, especially when you are around fifty; she added another three minutes, full of joy that there would be a closing word and a bottle of consolation wine in a moment. She had certainly only been allowed to read here because she hardly demanded a fee for it, as she had done in Stade and Celle. She rose gratefully, but no one clapped, not even Dolores and her husband. Cornelia excused herself with exhaustion: "I'll see you tomorrow," and she left, without having spoken a bitterly needed balmy word of friendship. The new man reached his hand out to her in full discontent. Gorda stood as if wiped away.

All too loudly, she called out: "There is a pub here in the house!" whereupon she seized her coat and hurriedly preceded the little troop, which followed her willingly, willingly at last. To her right sat Helene and Stefan, to her left Hans and an unknown playwright whom Gorda had spoken to very briefly — say twenty minutes — at a literary symposium. She was all the more pleased that he had come to her reading. Karin and Heiner, Friederike, Uwe, Nelly, all had stayed away, claiming a cough, appointments, deadlines, late shifts, but this unknown man, this man whose name she didn't even know, he was there as if she wasn't about to turn fifty, but thirty-five. She introduced Hans and Stefan with the words: "These two here are filmmakers!" Yet, Stefan was the filmmaker, and Hans was advising him on it. Hans earned his bread, which was probably moderately buttered, by teaching piano.

"Study something solid," she had said to him, when he graduated from high school with the Abitur: "Dentistry, you don't have to work long days, you still earn good money, and you can play the piano as much as you want in your spare time." Instead, he had studied piano performance and taught piano performance; though, of course, he wanted to be a pianist, like all the other piano teachers.

"My parents never taught me that I would have to earn my own living someday," he had said to Gorda a few years ago, as if you didn't know that on your own. Although Gorda didn't have to earn her living at all, and her parents hadn't taught her that, either. She studied in three different countries with the goal of becoming a simultaneous interpreter, and by the age of thirty-three, she established a hereditary — albeit limited — financial independence. So do what you always wanted to do, write, her husband said to her, and she wrote, without being able to write, the first four years filling many notebooks. By the fifth year, the first beginnings of style were showing. "You are using too many adjectives," the editor of a literary magazine had told her, so Gorda knew what Cocteau meant when he wrote to a young poet: Cultivate your faults, they are your style. Gorda decided to take care of her adjectives. Hans spoke overeagerly — or so it seemed to Gorda — to the unknown playwright. She was rid of both of them. Strange, she thought, I give a reading, and afterwards they turn their silent backs on me. So she said, turning to the right, to Helene: "What a jaunty hat you're wearing, dear Helene." Helene was wearing a man's hat, her husband's hat, as she now announced. Since the man had been dead for many years, the hat had to be quite old.

"How chic," Gorda said, "men's fashion à la Marlene Dietrich is in again right now." And she thought: poor, poor Helene, still wearing his hat. "She is suffering from depression at the moment," Hans had said to her on the phone. Helene is seeking protection under her dead husband's hat, just as I put on the ring today that Elke once gave me, when it seemed that our friendship couldn't be lost, she thought. I have always sought protection in friendship: protection from love, protection from homelessness, protection from myself. But where do I seek protection when protection leaves me?

"I don't even know what city I would move to if you died before me," Gorda had said to her husband: "There's no way I'm staying here abroad!" If he came home ten minutes late, she thought: Now I'm a widow. Where am I going to move to now? And she counted her beloved ones in Lauenbrück, in Hamburg, and in Stade. Beloved ones everywhere, but nowhere love. Friendship as a protective wall against the fall into the iciest lovelessness. That is why she held on so tenaciously to her friendships. As long as there is Friederike and Nelly, Leonore, and Hans and Stefan, that's how long I can't fall for the lovelessness of the world.

Gorda signed a book of poems for Helene, who had asked her to do so.

"But you don't look like that at all," Helene said when she noticed the photo on the back: "Here, you look like you have blooming lips!" Gorda was painfully aware that her mouth had turned out too small, too small even for a time that loved small mouths. And hers had always loved big ones. Heaven must have had something in mind, to give me such a tiny mouth in such a big-mouth era, she had written in her novel, which was a novel of development: the development was to lead to blooming lips. Once again, Helene repeated, as if she suspected deafness in Gorda: Blooming lips! Stefan, who had looked over to Hans, irritated, a Hans who spoke ever more eagerly to the unknown visitor, said: "Gorda is not pretty, but who wants to be pretty? Do you want to look pretty, Gorda?" Gorda would have liked to look pretty. At their first meeting with Stefan, he had said to Hans: "That's how I imagine the Callas to be." Callas wasn't pretty, but she was beautiful.

"Your face is hard," Stefan said, "the narrow cheeks and strong chin are to blame." He made a face, as if he were cutting himself on the hardness of her face.

"Hans did always say that I was attractive. Attractive and pretty." Gorda smiled contentedly, as if Hans had not said that thirty years ago, but yesterday. "Why, actually, is my appearance being discussed here?" she thought grimly, got up and went to the bathroom, where she dusted her shining nose and traced her lips, so that at least she had lips, even if not blooming ones. When she returned, she was back in an oh-let's-be-finally-nice mood. My God, she had given a reading to her friends in Hamburg, I mean Hamburg, that's not Stade or Celle.

Helene said, turning to Stefan: "She has beautiful hair." In the tone of: Well, she's not pretty, but at least she has beautiful hair.

"I think I have something more than beautiful hair!" Gorda snapped, and she looked sternly at Helene's bulging belly. No deceased man's hat could cover that.

"Well, she's stated her pieces with aplomb," Helene said magnanimously to Stefan. At last, the conversation turned from her unsatisfactory exterior to her interior. Gorda clearly trusted her insides more than her outsides. Stefan seemed to disagree with Helene's comment. His handsome face — and his face was clearly handsome — expressed displeasure. Anger. The inability to be able to agree with her.

"Where did you meet that man, anyway?" asked Stefan. "On the train?"

"No, at a literary symposium, just very briefly. The one on the train is someone else." Again, Stefan looked angrily at Hans. Gorda heard Hans talking about their ambition. For years, that had been his favorite topic. "You're so ambitious," he used to say. Because she had the ambition of wanting to be a humiliated, unknown, suicidal poet. A poet who pined for a bit of praise and publication. Suddenly, Helene called out irritably: "Tell me, Hans, are you talking about me all the time?"

"And about me?" asked Gorda, now also irritated.

"Have you been listening to me?" Hans seemed more arrogant than bashful: "I said, there are three people sitting there, Gorda, Stefan and Helene, all suffering from depression. I don't know anything like that. I never suffer from depression." Hans stretched his head infinitely superior, because he never suffered from something as ridiculous as depression. Gorda was eager to exorcise this superiority from him.

"I suppose pure happiness has eaten the hair off your head." Her tone was sharp, all too sharp. The unknown playwright said: "What kind of tactless remark is that!" He is already completely under his influence, thought Gorda and was tempted to tell him to keep out of it; but didn't say it. And she regretted having introduced Hans to him not as a piano teacher, but as a filmmaker. He probably wants to sell him one of his pieces. And throws himself at Hans. Now Stefan, who also suffers from depression, suggested a place to eat. That was a good moment to bury the battle axe and start the evening anew, in renewed friendship.

The air was pre-Christmassy fresh and smelled sharply of even more rain. Helene suddenly didn't want to go out to dinner anymore and said goodbye by doffing her memory hat. A few minutes later, they were sitting in a diner. Stefan to the right, Hans to the left of her. Hans was talking again to the unknown man. He was still talking about the depressions and ambitions of others but, actually, about his own modesty, which had led him to become a piano teacher instead of a pianist. That was enough for Gorda

"Yes, I have the ambition to be able to write as well as I can," she declared fiercely.

"I think, you're arguing because the novel hasn't been published yet," the stranger said. Gorda thought this explanation to be absurd.

"It's only a matter of time," Hans countered.

"And you, Hans, were lazy and untalented in school, as I well remember." And meant: Don't tell me about your modesty. In fact, she had written the Abitur papers for him, although he was already cheating on her with a Spanish girl at the time. Hans always had to spread jealousy around him.

"How tactless," said the stranger.

"You keep out of this!" snarled Gorda: "I've known the man for over thirty years." Why does he actually make me so angry? she asked herself. The best thing about Hans is his good taste in being friends with me and Stefan! Gorda moved closer to

Stefan. She seemed to have forgotten his nasty remarks about her chin and mouth. Stefan, however, was not pleased with Gorda's approach. Her words that Hans was lazy and untalented had offended him, you could see it on his face. Gorda regretted calling Hans lazy and untalented.

"Maybe I'll write down what happened here," Gorda said. Because she herself didn't know what had happened here.

"But would that be objective?" interjected the stranger.

"Only God is objective," exclaimed Gorda against the restaurant noise. Hans again spoke objectively to the playwright, probably about the depression and ambition of others and how he was not lazy and untalented at all.

"Hans has no feelings for you at all," Stefan said to Gorda, smiling courteously. I hope he doesn't have any, because I don't have any for him either, she said:

"For you, neither. He's cold as a fish, he once said to me." She knew that Hans loved and respected Stefan in his own way. And didn't she respect Stefan, too?

"You have to come to terms with the fact that Hans is gay," Stefan said. Gorda had known for over twenty years that Hans was homosexual — she had always hated the word gay. So she didn't have to come to terms with it at all, because she had already come to terms with it over twenty years ago, and there was nothing to come to terms with. Instead of saying, yes, do you think I want something from Hans, she said: "I haven't seen a man in Hans for decades. More precisely, since our history back then." Stefan winced, as if she had said: Hans is not a man at all — for anyone.

"I'm more of a human than a sexual being," Gorda corrected herself.

"You are like a mother to us," Stefan continued in a sweet voice, "because you are so much older than we are."

"How can I be a mother to you when I'm two years younger than Hans and only nine years older than you!" He wants to make me his mother! Gorda boiled with scorn.

"You haven't paid any attention to my feelings all evening!" cried gentle Stefan at the top of his lungs.

"You don't listen at all when I tell you something! Helene, too, has noticed that already! Yes, that's why she left. Helene and others, as well. It has already been noticed everywhere. Everywhere!! Everywhere!!!" Stefan's beautiful eyes were red from screaming.

"I've had enough of this," declared Gorda "I don't want anything more to do with you."

"On the contrary, tomorrow you'll call again!" Stefan continued yelling.

"He wants you to leave now," Hans said in a lecturing tone. What can he actually want from me?" Gorda thought. Moderate yourself, she said to herself, although she would have preferred to slap him. And left. At the door she turned around and heard herself shouting:

"And it's all your fault. You there, what's your name, anyway?"

Even the death of the first Pumi was also a kind of stoning for me, although now the stones came from 'up there'. He has decamped to my bathroom, where he first slept as a kitten in the soft stuffed suitcase that had been his cradle. He would later politely knock on the door when I was inside: "May I come in and be with you?" And, of course, he was allowed. Only Larry and our guests were not allowed in there; the bathroom was my sanctuary, where I could be naked and ugly without having to feel ashamed. I turned away from the mirror to avoid looking at the ravages of age, the growing belly and the full breasts that had once been small and apple-shaped, back when Remo had said to me: "Naked, you look like a beautiful boy." The beautiful naked boy had become a full-blooded woman, a type that Larry loved, who had grown up with Marylin Monroe and Jean Mansfield as idols of the movie world, and who saw in Audrey Hepburn, whom we women loved, a repulsive skeleton, her face could be as adorable as it wanted. And, he admitted, it was enchanting. Once, he had even stood behind her in line at a Lausanne department store.

In the bathroom, Pumi had often sat in the warm bathtub when the water drained from my bath, as if waiting for the Nile to return.

Father Nile

The ancestors of my cat
They are from Egypt
And loved the Nile
If I lie in the bath
My cat sees
His father, the Nile
And says: Father Nile
Don't leave
Taps with his paw
Checking the place
Where the Nile flows
In and out
Of my house
Out of pharaoh's house
And still he waits for hours
My cat in the tub

For the return of the Nile
His father in the house

He was an old Egyptian and belonged to the Nile and the desert. And was a sacred animal to the Egyptians, as much as he was a loved one to me. And what we love is sacred to us. Later, Pumi played in the filled sink with three bright yellow rubber ducks, which I had received as a 'white-elephant' gift. In America, 'white elephant' is the name given to gifts that people find superfluous and give away because they would otherwise throw them away. And the three rubber ducks had belonged to the two sons of my friend Elke, but they were grown up now and played with the toys for grown-ups, with real cars and twenty-year-old girl dolls. Pumi joyously hit the rubber ducks and was happy, when they swam back and forth, just as Elke's two little boys had once had fun with them in the bathtub. There are such pretty drawings by Loriot, with old men's children in the bath water and the same rubber ducks. We never stop being children. Especially not in the tub. When I told Elke about the fun my Pumi had with her ducks to make her happy, she looked sad. And I knew she was grieving for her sons, who no longer were her children, but had become desirable men for other women.

"What an injustice," a wise friend said to me, who is a psychologist: "You raise them and have all the work with them, the nasty diaper changing and the perpetual feeding, and then some young woman comes along and takes them away from you, when they've just become interesting and report on their studies and are no longer constantly screaming 'want that, want that', or asking a hundred annoying questions like: How does the grass come out of the ground? Or: Who lit the sun on fire? And: Is snow a frozen cloud?"

Herren im Bad (*Men taking a Bath*) by Loriot. Left Dr. Klöbner, right Müller-Lüdenscheidt, and in the foreground, left, the rubber duck.

One day, our beloved Pumi got diarrhea and lost weight and became as thin as Audrey Hepburn, he who had once been nice and plump, though he never liked to eat, I must say. Nothing was good enough for him. He was like Larry in that way: the two of them were always bitching about food, Pumi about the canned contents of the best kind, and Larry about my vegetable soups, which I cooked at regular intervals, so that he could get something green in his stomach and fiber in his gut. After all, he could live exclusively on chips, pizza, hamburgers, hot dogs, and donuts. Poison, nothing but poison for the body. At the end, Pumi moved from his favorite place on our red living room sofa to my bathroom, and I put a soft mat under his belly, on which he shook with fear and pain; I don't know, he couldn't tell me what he was suffering from. And I suffered with him more and more every day until Larry said, you have to put him down.

"Not me! You do it yourself!" I said in horror. But Larry had to work the day-and-night shift, when I could no longer bear the suffering of my pet child and put him in his carrier and took a cab to the vet. I didn't have a driver's license, after all. At the vet, my terminally ill little animal revived and curiously looked around at his brothers and sisters in the waiting room, and I thought, surely you can't let such a living creature be injected to death? But then it was my turn, or rather my Pumi's turn. And he was put on a mat in the death room and looked around again with interest — and finally he lay there as if asleep, as if a healthy animal were sleeping there and not a sick little one. I screamed loudly in pain, and the vet said: "I'll go now and leave you alone with him, so you can say goodbye to him properly. Have a good cry, it will do you good!" She didn't know that I get migraines from crying and lying in bed for days with the windows blacked out and earplugs in my ears. And now I live forever with this memory that I had my kitten injected to death, and I understand why Goethe never wanted to be present when someone died. Not even when his poor Christiane died, who must have screamed for days and nights in agony. He didn't go to see her, not even when she died. He explained that he had a photographic memory (of course, the word didn't exist at that time) and would keep the last impression in his head like a true-to-life painting, and that his Christiane would die for him every day until his own death, and he couldn't stand that. So, I can understand if he stayed away from everything that meant dying and death and burial. He also didn't attend the funeral of his beloved spiritual brother Schiller. Later he sent his son August to the funerals and to the birthday celebrations he disliked — he himself was sick in bed. Or at least he claimed to be. That was Goethe's migraine day.

I never went to funerals, either, until my motherly friend Georgina told me that you have to do that, Gorda, it is proper and a great comfort for the relatives. Her partner had just been buried. He had thrown himself out of a skyscraper window at age ninety; he was a psychiatrist, my God, he must have been desperate. Georgina gets up for breakfast and doesn't find him in the apartment, but the kitchen window is, strangely, open. She looks down and sees something lying down there, that was her beloved life companion, a heap of clothes and flesh, someone who had once been a clever, fine man. So, one can believe in the right to take one's own life in a more civilized way with an injection given by a loving doctor, like the veterinarian gave to my beloved Pumi. After all, we would not push our little animals out of the skyscraper window when their time came. I was told later that, at the funeral of Georgina's husband, his twin was present: ninety years old, also a psychiatrist and the spitting image of his brother, so they say: A double. A living ghost.

I had told Georgina that, two weeks before the famous date, 9/11/2001 (nine-eleven, the Yanks call it, because they first designate the month and then the day) I had had a vision while waking up: the black shadow of a man was jumping off the top of a skyscraper. I stared in horror at this horror dream image and went over to Larry, who was having breakfast in our dark little dining area and told him about the vision. As usual, he laughed ironically and said: "That's pure coincidence, it has no meaning at all, forget it." Although he is the one who firmly believes in God's existence and thus should consider visions and premonitions to be likely. Instead, it is I, the baptized Protestant, educated as an atheist, who believes not only in coincidence, but even in something as crazy as fate.

"Why should you, of all people, have visions and premonitions?" Larry asked me angrily: "Why not me?"

"Maybe because you believe in The One Upstairs, and I need tutoring from HIM." On September 11, 2001, my beloved niece Rieke from Hamburg was visiting me in Chicago — and the day began like a beautiful, slightly autumnal summer day with a long walk in the park by the lake, which is as big as an ocean. To my amazement, when we both returned, Larry opened the door and laughed maniacally, as if his mind had left him, and he yelled incessantly: "Television! Airplane! Television!!"

I yelled at him: "What are you still doing here, you should be at work by now?" because his maniacal laughter struck me as sinister. And with my rebuke, our world would be fine again. But it wasn't, and never would be again. We hurried in front of the television in the bedroom and remained frozen in silence: there, the first plane flew into the tower of the World

Trade Center and then the second into the other tower. And we thought: Are we watching a horror movie? This can't be true. When the first skyscraper collapsed, we noticed all the little human dolls throwing themselves out of the windows.

"My vision! My vision" I yelled: "That's just like in my vision!"

"Stop it with your visions!" my niece said dryly: "Otherwise they'll think you're crazy!" Rieke has studied biology and believes in no miracles on earth and in nature, because everything has been explained by Darwin and his theory of evolution once and for all, and one must be already a believing dinosaur, if one considers something like higher intelligence to be possible. In any case, she didn't want to be related to any believing dinosaur. Since her grandfather was already a war criminal and had worked with the Nazis, which suggested that he had not been in his right mind either.

"Now this rich country finally knows what it means to be hit by earthquakes and volcanic eruptions like the poor people in India," Rieke said. She had lived among India's poor for six months and knew what she was talking about.

"But earthquakes and volcanic eruptions are natural events and not actually evil," I countered. "This here is an attack on America by evil people. War has been declared on all of us in the West. By unknown enemies. Which is what makes it so ghastly. Who hates us so much that they are getting pilots to steer harmless passenger planes into the Twin Towers? All those innocent people who had to die!" David and Goliath, Samson, and Delilah, I thought. The little ones murder the strong giant with cunning and guile. In the twenty-first century, war will be waged with cunning and trickery and terrorism.

That same afternoon, we went to my friend Ute, the wife of the German consul Engelhard, to have lunch in the city. We still hoped that our world had remained the same and that we would not have to suffer any disturbing consequences. To eat lunch in the city belonged to the normal world. But downtown was cordoned off by police who obviously feared an attack on Chicago's largest tower, the Sears Tower. So we turned back and ate at Ute's house, watching it happen from far away, as if in a movie. This can't be all true, we thought. All of America thought that. I told Georgina about my pre-9/11 vision, and she laughed out loud: "What kind of stories are you telling there?" Because like her Jewish psychiatrist husband, she didn't believe in any God, since that's who would have prevented the Holocaust.

"The Holocaust is proof positive that there is no God," she said to me. "And don't tell nonsense like the one about your vision! Otherwise, they'll think you're crazy!" A short time later, her husband threw himself out of the kitchen window of their high-rise building. Soon thereafter, Georgina began to have memory problems and would call me from morning to night. And I tried to write, through the constant ringing of the phone, and didn't answer the phone. And in the evenings, Larry would yell angrily: "What kind of dorky girlfriends do you have, let the hysterical woman call somewhere else. Under no circumstances are you answering!" And I didn't answer the phone. The last thing I heard from her was the tender-sounding, pleading sentence:

"Gorda, do you hear me? Do you hear me? Pick up the phone!" And then she didn't call again and lay in bed demented for a few more years. I cried when I heard she had died. That's how ashamed I was not to have responded to her call for help. And hopefully, there is no God up there to punish me for it. And out of shame, I didn't go to her funeral, either.

On September 11, I said to Rieke, call your parents. They are worried. She tried but didn't get through. All of Europe called us to find out if the American relatives were still alive. What always amazed me was that my sister-in-law Astrid didn't call us to ask if her child was all right or if she happened to have traveled to New York to the World Trade Center. It remains a mystery to me: how can a woman like Astrid, an intelligent, much-read doctor (her favorite work is also mine: Thomas Mann's *Joseph and His Brothers*), reject me for a lifetime due to the fact that, on the first day we met, I went out into the garden and sat down in a deck chair from which I couldn't get my butt up, as she wrote to me. I mean, the butt was only twenty-two years old, after all, and my brother had held his fist under our stepfather's chin in the hallway with the words: "If you don't accept her either, you won't see me again!" And he was a coward and was so afraid that he didn't tell her the truth. Then he would have had to admit that, shortly before, he was going to marry another girl, and she would certainly have loved us and was charming, as my uncle said to me: "You won't be able to keep up with her, Gorda! You're nothing compared to that!" Nevertheless, my little charm brought me a lot of misfortune in life. For example, there was the party at my rich friend Elke's house. Her husband wanted to separate from her, the second he had become rich and that out of pure luck, because he had bet on an inventor whose invention had struck like lightning in the oak of Cortina d'Ampezzo. He came to the feast of his wife, who would soon be his divorced wife, and talked to me, and I answered in a friendly manner, as my mother taught me. Then Elke said: "Gorda, would you please come with me, I have to tell you something!" And she said: "Would you please go; my friends want to talk to me and not to you." So I grabbed my coat and left. Pelted with dirt like Pitch Mary in the fairy tale of Mother Holle.

A few months later, I went out with her and her architect and his lover, and because I wanted to cheer Elke up, I got funny out of silliness — and the two gay men found me funny and said: "Where did you get this funny woman? How come we only got to know her now? We must meet again soon!" Then Elke got a face as if she were drinking vinegar and not expensive Bordeaux paid for by her. Unfortunately, a week after that, the two of us — Elke and I, together with a group of women — were traveling around Austria, my beloved Austria, to Lake Attersee and Lake Wörthersee and whatever all those gorgeous lakes are called that I visited with my parents and my beloved cousin Anni in my early youth. And I wanted to thank my generous hosts by becoming a funny noodle, and they were all happy about the funny noodle from America. Only Elke was not happy and always shouted: "Do I have to hear that again? Can't you stop with your nonsense! Shut up already!" And yet, years ago, with nothing but her blonde beauty, she had hooked a handsome Jewish man who left her a huge fortune in the divorce, and still she did begrudge me my 'charm', because her husband had told her at the parting that she was a boring woman. Now I was an enemy in her eyes, because I was not boring, the woman who had stolen her man with her penetrating wit, although it was not me at all, but a doctor. To err is human, a wise man once said about such confusions.

And so, charm and wit can attract misfortune and enmity, and not just love and attention, as my sister-in-law Astrid accused me of: "You want to attract all the love and attention to you!" And the envious and jealous of the world don't allow that. But hadn't I also been jealous of the great beauty of my friend Annina, whom I call Aviva in my narrative?

Aviva

I would like to paint a portrait of her — not so much because of the portrait, but to get her out of my mind. There she lies like a dark mist, and sometimes, like a picture from a thousand-and-one nights. Today mist, tomorrow again the most beautiful woman, Helena, miraculous creature, ideal image of every man who doesn't love men, of which there are so many here. It must be admitted, without envy — and how often the envy of the others infected me again, just when I believed to have overcome it once and for all — when God created this woman, he was in a most excellent mood, the genius who wants to show once and for all what he is actually capable of, if he only intends to create perfection. In other words: The great artist-in-chief had just finished a hard day of tedious variations on the theme of perfection — a hump here, a crooked nose there — when the holy hour of rest came, and he created Aviva.

He gave her the greatest soulful, melancholy-looking eyes — as little heart as she possessed, so much soul was in those eyes — with eyelids that seemed chiseled and were carefully brushed by her each morning until she resembled a Greek statue from which the paint had not come off. Ah, Greek statue, her profile was Egyptian, Nefertiti awoke in her little nose and unforgettably her cheekbones swung up to most beautiful roundness, to then interestingly move inwards, giving her the elegiac look so coveted today. The mouth would have to be called as being almost too small for an age that loves beaded lips — but it held to dimensions that even in the second half of the twentieth century made one yearn for unique shaping. These lips had a teaching effect, so to speak: Look, this is what a mouth should look like, not like yours. Pain poured onto the faces of women and young girls who had just been laughing, and a tenderly addicted type of grin onto those of men because of this face, which always seemed equally perfect when seen from the front, the half side, and the profile. But it was not only this face that left the most painful scars and that had a depressive or exhilarating effect on the hearts of her friends, if they possessed any at all, in the narrowest sense. She actually had an hourglass figure, although, at first glance — in evening dress — she appeared skinny. What a thin person she is, I had thought when I saw her for the first time ten years ago, after her beauty had been described to me in bright colors. Nothing makes the painter so beauty-blind as the exaggerated praise bestowed on an oil painting painted by someone else's hand: I saw only a long stick, excessively smeared, nothing in front, nothing behind, and gathered in the middle with roses; no, it was a bunch of violets that held her dress together. With the best will in the world, I couldn't detect any beauty. A giant pony fell down to her snub nose, very little appeared underneath; this was supposed to be a face? A perfect one at that? Either I'm crazy or the others are, I thought, feeling slightly distressed at the effort it was taking me to endure the general madness of the world. If I had never seen Aviva again, this one image of her would have remained with me: a thin tall woman with dark blond hair in a blue dress dances with an even thinner, even taller man with gray hair where he has some, and he hugs her until you can't believe anymore that they are married, although I thought so at first: Aha, that's Aviva and her husband Dietrich. Tell me, Karin, isn't that Aviva's husband? I ask an acquaintance who should know. Oh no, she smiles mischievously. And this smile, a little wise, a little mischievous, I have never forgotten; I myself have often smiled like that, when I answered a woman, oh no, that is not her husband — while one could have said exactly the same, that is also her husband, but that is not proper in our wicked society.

So, God must have kneaded the clay dumpling that used to be Aviva in the middle, which left a real wasp waist — it didn't need a corset and strings to be tiny. Really, I never saw a waist like that again. When a woman is narrow from top to bottom, and thus has a narrow waist, then it's no wonder. But Aviva possessed a pair of pronounced shoulders, the back ran pointedly from two sides to the center of the body as if trying to form a triangle, just before the sides collided, they swung back out into the world as hips, like Indian goddesses, then came a round butt that could tease even heterosexual women into pinching it, though perhaps more out of annoyance than admiration. The bikini legs appeared round in the thighs and fragile in the calves. Since she always stumbled along on insanely high heels, the sight of her made one think stencil-like of a filly or of a Chinese woman whose bound feet can only do a dance-like tripping-along. The great supreme artist, however, must have thought when he completed Aviva that this creature was too perfect for an imperfect world, and he gave her three faint points to remind her of her decomposability in a most sobering and wholesome way: she possessed a dark-haired mustache on her lovely upper lip, thin single hairs on her flower head, and varicose veins stretched along her ravishingly shaped knees. Aviva, however, knew how to transform even these weaknesses into almost-virtues, pushing the thought of her humanity, with all the grunginess that goes with it, as far away from her as possible. She bleached the mustache skin-colored until it gave her only a kitten-soft appearance, she washed the hair daily and knew how to drape it so skillfully that it actually looked to be full, and in summer, a brown complexion completely hid the evil blue veins, and strong silk stockings did the same service in winter.

A woman is born who is as beautiful as Helena — into a quite ordinary family, which doesn't even know what happens to them when they see the gasping, red-faced creature for the first time. Well, all newborn babies are ugly — or beautiful, as you prefer. The "Well, you sweet little one" later became "My God, is your daughter beautiful," and the shaking of the maternal face to go with it, implying: Shh, be quiet, otherwise she will become vain. But the shaking didn't help, nor was the mother always there, you can't say to the whole world: Stop it, you're driving my daughter crazy. So much praise is not good. She is driving us crazy. Aviva soon learned that people looked around at her wherever she walked, lay, or stood. Even quite prosaic, money-grabbing friends of the parents exclaimed in amazement with a hint of lyricism in their voices: "It is true! Aviva, you are beautiful like the bright morning!" And the girlfriends at school mysteriously withdrew from her under the most comical pretexts, although Aviva was clearly lovable.

She had physically developed into a woman at fourteen, fifteen, and all the magic was at work that can be so healing and so disastrous, first for the good of her own soul, then for that of others. Aviva must have stood in front of the mirror one day — at least that's how I imagine it — and thought the following: My eyes are the most beautiful eyes I have ever seen. My nose is perfectly small, my mouth could be bigger, but a little lipstick will help it along. My teeth (at this, she pulls her lips away with the index finger and thumb of her right hand) couldn't be better. My profile is gorgeous, I could fall in love with my cheekbones ... etc. ... etc. And indeed, Aviva fell in love with God's work of art

250

— only, unfortunately, she forgot that she was not the creator of all these body wonders, but she said: Mine, mine, mine, absolutely all day long, and when you say "mine" so much, you think you are talking about yourself.

Although Aviva certainly had intelligence and talents she could have developed, cultivating and maintaining her beauty was easier and more effective than any Chopin etude, no matter how delightfully it was played. How many people could play the piano perfectly — and how rare is true physical beauty. Now and then, Aviva sat at the piano as a very young woman, the image must have been heartbreaking for a person with a heart that could be torn apart by beauty — but I don't think anyone around Aviva was that receptive to her charisma at the time.

She had since married, or rather, her parents had given their indecisive daughter away to a much older man, who they hoped had all the maturity their daughter lacked. These loving, good-natured, persuasive, simple people had marveled at the child prodigy God had placed in their cradle a little anxiously. To compensate for all the praise of her beauty so lavishly bestowed on Aviva by those around her, her parents held back on any good word, never mentioned her beauty or only in a slightly derogatory way ("Aviva, stop admiring yourself"), tried to urge her to play the piano and study ("Aviva, only an educated person is a human being"), and believed they could combat their daughter's increasingly apparent character flaw — her excessive vanity — with severity and persistent criticism. Unfortunately, the parents were mistaken in their choice of remedies: Aviva longed for praise from mom and dad; the astonished exclamations of strangers did little to help her; she wanted to hear from her father: Child, how beautiful you are! But he carefully kept his mouth shut. Aviva adorned herself, washed her hair, smiled adorably, looked like a dazzling work of nature, but Dad remained silent. The anxious, carping behavior of her parents unsettled Aviva and drove her to spend her life soliciting praise wherever she could. "Daddy, aren't I beautiful after all?" was her moving question to the world, as well as other people's musings from morning to night: "Why am I even alive? What's it all about?"

Her husband, the so much older, ill-tempered Mr. Dietrich, took the role of the parents also in terms of refusing to praise and addiction to criticism, and now it went all day: "Aviva is only interested in unimportant things like fashion, Aviva is so horribly vain. Aviva never reads. I can't discuss anything with Aviva."

"This criticism from her parents and husband developed another trait in Aviva, that of lie, lie, and always deny. "No, I like reading a lot, I'm not interested in fashion at all, look, I've had this skirt for a long time, really, I don't like shopping very much. I only have classic things, things that you can wear for a long time, and I only buy on sale, I'm not crazy like other women who spend a fortune, this skirt used to cost 500 dollars, I got it for only 250, that's incredibly cheap for a real designer skirt, look, this workmanship, all these seams, so 250 is a give-away for a skirt like this, a real work of art. Dietrich is always making scenes regarding money, but my God, I'm not a whore with extra income, Dietrich, I always say, do you want me to go out hustling in the street, so I can be decently dressed? I can't go naked, after all."

On the daily trips to the city, where I had to run errands, she sprinkled me with such speeches — and she rummaged through the racks of clothes for new exquisite pieces for her magnificent body.

When I saw Aviva for the second time — it was on the yacht of a ship owner, namely the very dancer, the long, thin one from the first encounter — she was wearing very tight white pants in the hot summer evening air, a red Chinese silk blouse that hung down to her hips, and around her famous waist she had pulled a snake belt studded with cubic zirconia eyes, which flashed in the evening light, glowing poisonously. Good Lord, she was so beautiful. And so eager for affirmation. A young man I had met just recently, was sitting next to her, was staring at her as if in disbelief, and held onto her arm and kept saying "Aviva, Aviva, Aviva" over and over, as if the name were some magic formula. When she got up and started mincing around — while doing so, she also waved her sweet bottom quite unnecessarily — saliva flowed from the corners of his mouth. I'm not exaggerating, I have hardly ever seen anything so revolting, my heart clenched in disgust; I hated him and her and thought: "Stop admiring this stupid broad. Don't you see that she's gone crazy? She's insane with vanity." Then I looked to the right and suddenly saw a knife in the hand of the shipowner, the long skinny one, who was waving it — was he cooking or what was he doing?" — and moving his lips while doing so. His face was remarkably ashen, he was always waving that big knife like a madman, and now I heard him muttering between his teeth: I'll kill him, I'll kill her. He must be crazy, I thought, even more disillusioned, that stupid cow Aviva must have turned his head, the men all have a screw loose. Don't they see how immature this woman is? Then I caught sight of her husband, and he looked so indifferent, so tired of his tripping wife that was swaying her butt to and fro, that my world was all right again. I sat down with him and said: "Dietrich, don't you care at all about your wife?"

"Oh, Aviva has enough worshippers, after all, as always. I don't need to make any effort, then."

"And you are not jealous?"

"When you've been married to a beauty for so long, all you can do is laugh at the nonsense. Just take a look at that ridiculous young man and that crazy host, the shipowner. Such a silly fellow, it's a real hoot." On the way home — after I had finally persuaded the young man to accompany me — I said to him: "Tom, be careful with Aviva." And he just laughed:

"Why, that Dietrich fellow doesn't care about her at all." That's when the knife flashed before my eyes, and I kept my mouth shut. If he doesn't want to understand, then he doesn't. The shipowner also had his wife on the yacht — and it sounds really like a novel when I say now that she was the ugliest woman I have ever seen, black-haired from top to bottom, i.e., she was hairy everywhere where there should have been naked skin, a bird's nose in her scrawny face, receding chin and protruding ears — so, the great supreme artist must have created her as proof of his eccentricity in the sense of: see, it can also go like this and like this and like this. While women instinctively hated Aviva (the stupid cow, she was commonly referred to — not only in my mind), they pitied the tall black shipowner's wife, without bothering to first check the circumstances. Maybe she punished her husband with mental cruelty, maybe she wore the pants behind closed doors, even whipped him, all this hardly interested the female audience. It saw only an insanely ugly woman and an old rich peacock infatuated with Aviva.

A week after the party on the yacht, I got a call from Tom: "Guess what, I got a call from that stupid shipowner, he threatened to kill me if I approached Aviva again. We have a nice relationship that you must not disturb, he said. So, they're having an affair?"

I was getting all hot all over, and I thought careful, careful, don't put your foot in it, here. "I can't say that either, how would I know. In any case, I'd keep my distance from Aviva."

"I couldn't disagree more. The guy is not her husband, after all. Who does he think he is? He has the nerve to threaten me."

Well, that's not enough for him, yet, I thought, he needs a few blows to the neck, that will open his eyes. It's weird how some people have such a difficult time to understand how things are and go through the world with blinders on. Time went by, I didn't hear from Tom anymore; I moved next to the house where Aviva lived and saw her every day, got used to her discourses about: "No, I'm not interested in fashion at all", and lost the inner defense against so much hypocrisy, because never ever again will I see a woman with so many gorgeous clothes, a walking fashion magazine with a thousand accessories made of turtle, rhinestones, and silk. Her shoes by Italian footwear artists were gorgeously multicolored and fashioned in delicate leather; one day she had to clean out the closets because the bedroom was to be painted, and probably a hundred pairs of such ravishing creations came to light. I, whose splayed feet with fallen arches, who require insoles, plus a shoe size that is rarely made for women (I would have to go to the men's department to be able to shop carefree), I then, who am grateful if I get hold of a single pair in a season that is not too roughly made, I stared with immense envy at these sweet little rainbow-colored leather creations, and I prayed silently: Please, God, let this cup of jealousy pass me by; but it's just unfair that this stupid cow has so many shoes, and I have to go to the university ball with the old gold pumps, which are completely ragged and old-fashioned, because I couldn't find a suitable pair despite weeks of searching.

"Could you give me a hand carrying out the skirts and blouses?" asked Aviva into my sullen meditations.

"Yes, of course, where do you want them?"

"On the couch in the living room, the closets are getting repainted too, you know." We lugged and lugged. There was no end to the lugging. There must have been many dozens of silk blouses, uncounted skirts, sweaters, pants, and dresses. In addition, there were the belts, bags, Hermès scarves, the fashion adornments a jet-set princess. I took refuge in the humor that laughs anyway, and I saw the huge pile of clothes that had cost someone a fortune (whether it was the shipowner or Dietrich, it actually doesn't matter) as a sacrificial offering for Aviva's beauty: "A beautiful woman must adorn herself in a special way. To him who has much, more is given, that is an old worldly wisdom — and I just have big feet, a not exactly delicate waist and skin that is much too pale, to say nothing of the rest." But my ordeal wasn't over yet. Suddenly, Aviva is holding a large box in her arms; it is covered by Chinese carving work, strikingly set with semi-precious stones.

"What's that?" I ask, dumbfounded after all the afternoon's amazement.

"It's my jewelry box," Aviva replies mysteriously. Why is that a secret, I think irritably?

"Let me see your jewelry."

"Oh, you already know it."

"Please, Aviva, I love looking at jewelry." Then Aviva can hardly wait until I sit next to her on a spot of the sofa that had remained vacant (she was just being coy, I think), she opens the box — and my jaw drops. There it sparkles out so impudently, I still think today, I should rather not have looked inside.

"Where did this gorgeous bracelet come from?" I'm holding a wide bangle set in hand, with thousands — or so it seems to me — of diamonds. Aviva smiles like the Sphinx.

"From my parents," she says with downcast eyes, which is how she always looks when she lies.

"And this pin?" Pin is a silly word for a large beetle whose body is made of a beautiful sapphire and the wings are made of moving parts set with pearls. Aviva continues to smile.

"And this necklace?"

"That's from China. It's old jewelry from the seventeenth century. It might as well be in a museum." I see huge yellow stones in incredibly old settings.

"Aviva," I say, "where did that come from?" Thinking: Surely Dietrich — a bank employee in a moderately high position — can't pay for something like that. Then I see the flashing knife of the shipowner in front of me, and I lower the necklace. It makes a clacking noise, falling on many other brooches, bracelets, rings, earrings, chains, loose stones. I have lost the desire to admire. I feel stifled and want to go home.

"Why don't you stay for dinner?" Aviva says, as endearingly as ever. "There's curried rice, quite delicious."

"No, no," I lie: "I forgot that I am waiting for an important phone call, and I still have to write a letter." I quickly go into the bedroom (I hope she doesn't stop me), where my coat is lying, ah, there it is, and what is that that's lying there? A photo, I know that one, it can't be true ... I hear Aviva approaching, automatically put the photo in the pocket of the coat, nervously put the coat on, when Aviva is already standing next to me, smiling adorably, swearing: "The curried rice is a blast. Please do stay."

"I can't, unfortunately," I stammer, and with a bye, I flee from the most beautiful woman I've ever known. And the most enervating one. A year later, I moved to another city and lost touch with Aviva. But I had friends who associated with her. That's when I got this letter one day:

Do you still remember Aviva, the stupid cow? And the shipowner, the tall thin one with the few gray hairs on the back of his head, such a jealous old peacock? You remember, he had an ugly, black-haired wife, and to make up for it, he loved the most beautiful woman in town. I always wondered, how, as a young man, he came to have his own witch, because he had an ardent love for everything beautiful, one has to admit that, despite his silliness; I mean, his parties were among the most beautiful there were, beautiful apartment, magnificent paintings, silver candelabras everywhere, Chinese carpets and wall-mounted closets. In general, he loved everything Chinese. And, without question, he loved Aviva, who could rival any beautiful Chinese (Greek, Egyptian, witch) woman. On his yacht, they found this young man, the guy named Tom you used to go out with (but you didn't like him, if I remember correctly), stabbed to death. A big kitchen knife in his heart. There were still cleaned and cut-up vegetables lying around in the kitchen; you know the ship owner liked to cook, and, by the way he cooked well. Aviva also got hurt some, but not dangerously so. The shipowner is in custody, and this is our Trojan War ...

The photo, my God, I must still have it, the one I found on Aviva's bed. Which coat was I wearing back then? The dark blue one, yes, I must still have it somewhere, in the mirrored closet, for sure. It must be back there, I have it here — and, in the pocket, I find the crumpled photo of Tom, young and sweet and smiling endlessly stupidly, as if he were worshipping Aviva at that point in time. The night on the yacht comes up in my memory, Aviva wearing a Chinese silk blouse and the wickedly glistening belt snakes (attention, attention), the stupidity of the men fighting each other over a silly cow. When will they finally fight over the smartest woman in the world? I ask myself angrily. Then, in my mind, I climb up to the deck, oh yes, there had been a couple standing there, hand in hand, this time it was a married couple. A very unhappy one. Their young son had been dying of leukemia for two years. He finally died the following year. And the couple fathered another child to replace him. How can anyone want to replace a child? She had difficulties giving birth. The child didn't get enough oxygen. The mother had breast cancer, was operated too late; a few years later, she was also dead.

My God, I thought, murder and manslaughter and terrible disease, the seeds of which are all contained on this unlucky yacht. And the couple had been such a cute couple, rich, happy … And Aviva so pretty. I wonder if the great artist-in-chief is envious like his poor creatures?

"What kind of tall tales are you telling about me?" Annina had said to me." "They're not tall tales," I explained. "They're fantasy stories. And from fantasy stories comes literature."

When I picked up the second Pumi from the pet shop, we had just had a huge fight in our German culture club in Chicago. In Germany, people always wonder why, after thirty years and more abroad, I can still speak German, even almost flawlessly and without an accent. It is because I speak only German in Chicago. My husband is American and doesn't speak German, but he is lazy and prefers to do crossword puzzles instead of talking to me. He doesn't want to talk to anyone. Only to his best friend. So I talk on the phone with my German girlfriends, go to American theaters with German girlfriends, and then to dinner amidst German conversations. And I run a German book club that forces me to read German novels, even though

I would much rather read American and English biographies and histories like *Marie Antoinette* and *Catherine the Great*, and I wouldn't have read novels for a long time, especially German ones, if it weren't for this book club that keeps me to the grindstone regarding the German language. And so, even today, I speak German better than English, and English better than French, and not like my Norwegian friend Doris, who speaks German, French, Norwegian and English, but says of herself: all fluently, but none quite right.

So, there was this huge row in our German cultural club, because one group wanted to move away from our old English looking clubhouse into a mighty high-rise building, where it took us half an hour to get through the parking garage. At the entrance, we had to show our IDs for security and had to have our handbags rummaged through like at the airport, which no woman loves. You might have a purse full of tampons at that time. Or you might have packed a second pair of underwear, just in case of diarrhea. The elevator took us to the fortyfifth floor, with ears popping, and then you needed to walk for a quarter hour to reach the bathroom. And another quarter hour back. And when you came back, you had missed half the lecture. With that being the case, you could stay right outside and have a cigarette, if you were a smoker. Smoking was not allowed in our old English clubhouse, which was a nuisance to the wife of the German consul at the time, and that's why she pushed for the move, which we non-smokers detested, since most of us had long since given up smoking. Instead, we drank. With relish.

I remember very well that the board met for a situation meeting, where we yelled at each other without restraint and not ladylike, decorated with our jewelry as if they were first-class medals and wrapped in the very finest of fabrics: we yelled six against six and the president, the thirteenth as if at the Holy Communion of the founder of our religion and of our peacemaker, the president listened with closed ears, because she wanted to move and the arguments of the non-smokers didn't count with her: that we were too old for such a high-rise, that the parking garage was too big, that the time in the elevator was too long for the short span of time we had left in life, and that the way to the bathroom was a virtual day trip and therefore unreasonable.

From this unforgettable board meeting, Larry picked me up in the car, and we drove to the only pet store in town where there were supposed to be Pumi-like kittens, as the young man on the phone assured me: "Yes, come on, there are plenty of them here!" We then walked through rows of poor pitiful creatures, all crying out for mommy and daddy. I wouldn't want to experience a visit like that to a pet store again. The young man — the owner of the store — showed us two Pumi-kittens, one with an infected eye. We should have taken the healthy animal, of course. Instead, we took a poor, desperate little animal that had been sitting trapped in a cage for five months with a sick red eye. No one would have bought it anymore and maybe it would have been put to sleep like my beloved Pumi. The owner, his name was Harry, took him out of the cage and said: "Take a look at this beautiful animal here, you can get it for a mere $500, normally it's $700. A bargain! An absolute bargain!" The cat, who was to become our Pumi II, suddenly started purring as if the dreadful Harry were his dear daddy, and my mother cat's heart began to pound loudly, and I pounced: "We'll take him!" We paid Harry the money, in cash, on the counter. And I snatched the animal from his arm and put it in our carrying cage, and Larry and I hurried to our car as if they were trying to snatch a treasure from us.

He also ended up being our treasure for ten and a half years. And the veterinarian said: "What, the breeder gives such a noble animal to a pet shop, that's an impertinence! Give me the phone number of that Harry or what's his name, that case must be investigated." But we didn't want an investigation, we just wanted to have Pumi II's sick eye treated.

"What a bleeding heart you are," Larry said to me. But secretly, his heart was bleeding too, and that's why he ran so fast to the car with Pumi II.

And how a human being treats his animal, that's how he treats his children. Mass murderers like to murder pets in childhood and skin hamsters alive to practice for later, when they have bigger plans. As a child, Adolf Hitler probably crushed bugs and earthworms with passion (he loved his shepherd dogs idolatrously), and Stalin, as a small boy, most likely twisted the necks of the beloved cats and dogs of his neighbors secretly. One knows that practice makes perfect, even where murder is concerned.

Actually, I had wanted to write my doctoral thesis on Heine's motif of eating. But in the middle of the preparations, I found out that a doctoral student at Princeton was already writing about that. I was so distraught that I lay in bed for weeks and wanted to die, because I no longer had the strength to go to the library to find, among thousands of titles on Heine, the one that didn't exist yet. Then *The Women in Heine's Work* was the non-existent title. Which, of course, already existed, but with the subtitle *Female Cliché Figures in Heine's Work*. I wanted to prove that Heine's female characters are not clichés, but lively and funny, seductive, and perhaps a bit aggressive, but mostly erotically appealing women or even whores, the ones with the golden hearts, see Venus in the Tannhäuser ballad. How man looks at us when he desires us.

Because, otherwise, he looks right past us and doesn't notice us at all. I read that in something by a Turkish writer, whose name I have forgotten: Either the woman is young and pretty and desirable, or she is invisible to the man. That's as if she were wearing a burqa over her head and featuring the chubby body of a matron. That's why, with aging, we women don't find the idea of a burqa so outlandish: then you don't have to wash and lay your hair and paint your face before going for a walk around town. You hang the black sack over your body and look with interest out of the eye slits at the colorful world outside. And while you think: What does she look like? What a hideous outfit! The woman you are looking at cannot form any derogatory judgment about you, because what can such a black walking coffin tell you about the taste of the woman it contains?

When I laid in bed in such despair, wondering if I could ever again go to the library of our university, which I had loved until then, the beautiful Annina called me and suggested: "Come, let's take tennis lessons, it will distract you and be good for the figure." Tennis, I thought snootily, such a sport for rich women who have nothing to do but hit a ball over a net with a racket. Always back and forth. Stupid activity. I'd rather read my book about the numerous mistresses of Louis the Fourteenth. But suddenly, the full moon rose in my spiritual night: That is your salvation! Get up and walk to the tennis lesson with the beautiful Annina at your side. Bat the balls over the net and right back at her so they whizz around her ears! She who can do that is normal and fit to live life and, in the evenings, cooks the vegetable soup with cured pork spareribs for the husband and the three kids without batting an eyelash and without longingly looking over to the book detailing the true reasons for WWI.

"All right," I said to Annina. I got up, put the sweaty body under the shower, washed my greasy hair, blow-dried it into some sort of a hairstyle and made up the eyes, lifeless with grief, with a dark pencil, and drew red lines around the nondescript mouth. Dot, dot comma, dash, smiley face in a flash, we called it in childhood. In the city, I bought a short tennis dress in light blue, a pair of opaque sports knickers, the racket, and the balls to go with it. I also had to get light blue shoes and socks. I looked like a tennis queen at last. So I introduced myself with Annina to the teacher in a huge, cold gymnasium, and she smiled delightedly and called us 'honey' and gave us the feeling that she had been waiting just for us. The way you are rarely greeted in Europe. Unless you are a movie star. Then the teacher showed us what an art it is to hit the ball with the racket in the right way, how to stand and how not to stand. And how to jump around quickly to get the opponent's ball to their own side, but as far away from them as possible. It was like the rules of conversation for educated, witty people. Ball followed ball, blow followed blow, joke followed joke. Suddenly I felt like I was among people of word and wit. And I was no longer a waddling duck in the chicken yard at all, I belonged; tennis was the ideal sport for a woman who loved intellectual combat; tennis was competition and elegance and victory and defeat in the tennis dress that showed off the long legs and butt so beautifully, when you had one. Annina and I were both beautiful playing tennis. Unfortunately, Annina was more beautiful than I was. And I looked enviously at her noble movements, as if she were dancing in a tennis ballet and not playing in a cold, ugly gym. And Annina knew exactly how gracefully she was floating along. And she wiggled her bottom where there was nothing to wiggle and waved her arms impudently, as if she

were a prima donna in Swan Lake and not a housewife with a
stable full of children.

I paled with envy: How she is acting up again, I thought
with anger. And I would have loved to snatch the racket out of
her hand and hit her on the ideally shaped head. Thank God,
Annina decided to drop out after the second course — and
I stayed with the training for many more weeks, until I was
me again and not a candidate for suicide, and my heart not a
pit for murder, but "small and pure, none shall dwell in it but
Jesus alone," oh no, Heinrich Heine. Now I could go back
to the library to study the titles of the books about Heine, to
find the one that didn't exist, yet. For weeks, I lived patiently
in the library and often had to kneel down to be able to look
at the books on the lower rows, but my tennis-steeled body
did it effortlessly, and I didn't groan or moan. A healthy mind
in a healthy body: at last I knew what the sentence meant,
which before had seemed 'contestable' (a favorite word of our
German teacher).

It was on the day when I sat with my friend Margarete, and
we sang Christmas carols in January and ate gingerbread hearts,
and outside the snow fell silently and quietly and abundantly,
until it brought down the roof of the ugly gymnasium, that
I experienced for the first time how that which is tender and
gentle could destroy the great and strong, if only it appeared in
immense quantities. The blizzard swept our mayor from office
and brought a woman to his desk for the first time — and for
me, it put an early end to my career as an ace tennis player.
The gym hall was not rebuilt until a year later, and by then I
had lost interest in the sport, living only with Heine and his
scholarly fans who had written book after book about him.

I felt the same way about jogging, which was supposed to
be so healthy for the lazy body, the old Adam, the flabby sack.

At my mother's in Lüneburg, I ran every day in the woods that surrounded her apartment and felt enormously healthy and normal, until I felt a twinge in my left, slightly skinny thigh and cried out loudly in the deserted woods "Ouch!" which, of course, no one heard. When I looked inside my tracksuit pants, I found a bright red spot with a dark red dot inside on the skin where the bug had bitten me. Only, I didn't know which one. Also, I found no trace of it, it had bolted from my clothes right after doing its dastardly deed. Later, Larry told me that it was an allergy, when the stain would not go away. But I had a migraine every day and, finally, went to a doctor who was not my husband and didn't have personal reasons for his diagnoses such as that of 'hysteria'. The other internist diagnosed that I had Lyme disease, a newly discovered illness caused by tick bites. And I was to take antibiotics until the spot was gone. Or I would get rheumatism, meningitis, lose my mind, and be paralyzed in a wheelchair. Terrified, I took the antibiotics — and was still taking them nine months later, because the spot wouldn't go away. Larry kept insisting I had an allergic reaction and not Lyme disease, but I was terrified of the wheelchair and the rheumatism and life without sanity. And got such stomach pains and diarrhea that I no longer found the daily need to eat a joy, but a punishment. Punished three times a day. For hours on end. Larry, on the other hand, rejoiced in my stomach pains and diarrhea and said: "You see, at least this way you won't get fat!" That was true, but strangely enough, I didn't get thin either, as one might have expected under the circumstances: No harm without benefit, as the saying goes, after all. The only thing I never did again was to go jogging. Heaven had shown me: that sport is not for you. As the snowfall had proven to me: thou shalt give up playing tennis! Sport is a kick — in the bucket.

Unfortunately, I also no longer dared to go biking in the summer, because there are no restrooms in Chicago's mile-long park by the lake. American women seem to have male bladders, and not only do they have a desirable masculine self-confidence, but they all go to the bathroom only once a day like Larry, who considers me and my regular trips to the restroom ridiculous.

"Think about something else," he used to say. "Then you also won't have any pain."

"You're out of your mind!" I yelled indignantly: "If you have bladder pain, you can't think about anything else!" He only has the bladder in his head and an eye for the restaurants, where you could stop in order to become a peaceable person again. Americans also have no sense of tourist cafés, like they have them everywhere in Germany and always restaurants or cafés where you can stop and have a coffee and eat a piece of Black Forest cake or apple pie with cream on top. Then a visit to the usually well-kept restroom. I think the Yanks don't eat cake in the afternoon, because they love a hearty country feast for breakfast with scrambled eggs and fried potatoes and bacon and sausages and the sticky pancakes soaked in syrup. A lumberjack is full for the whole day after this kind of breakfast and doesn't want to eat again until evening. Such real men don't need cafés in the woods. And no restrooms. This is a land of pioneers who, with ax in hand, first had to cut their way through the jungles of America. Unfortunately, most of today's men are no longer lumberjacks, but their taste for country breakfasts has stayed with them. They are sitting in offices with one thousand calories in their bellies from a single meal in the morning. And for lunch, a quick hamburger, and their beloved fries. And in the evening, of course, a huge steak with a baked potato and sour cream on top. And the whole country wonders why it has become fat.

Interior of German café with a broad offering of cakes

And I'll have to eat something right away, that's how hungry this part has made me …

Unfortunately, not only can't I ride a bicycle because of the lack of restrooms, but I can't drive a car, either. Even though I used to be able to, and ninety-nine percent of Americans can as soon as they are sixteen years of age. And rightly so, because America is a huge country with huge distances and huge metropolitan areas. It seems underpopulated compared to Europe. Israelis could move to our most glorious areas with ease and not have to live a life of daily fighting and war and assassinations of their people, for which we pity them, in front of TV cameras. I had gotten my driver's license right when I came to Chicago, had also enjoyed driving on the interstate to Florida, on our belated honeymoon trip to St. Augustine. But as I drove out of our garage in Chicago, I timidly stepped on the gas three times, because I was terrified of city traffic. Larry, who was sitting next to me, started yelling like my mother would if I got only a 'satisfactory' on a school assignment, and the child in me broke down nervously. So, unfortunately, I gave up the steering wheel to Larry, and he steered me through life. The way he wanted to. Now, I was dependent on rides when Larry was at work. Since everybody drove, someone always took me to the numerous luncheons, and I could have a few glasses of wine, unlike the driver. A huge advantage. So far so good. Unfortunately, for many years, I had to ride with a woman who had inherited my mother's spirit of contradiction and who tirelessly contradicted me, without pausing to allow me to contradict. Instead of keeping my mouth shut now, like any sensible person, I felt obliged to entertain the driver — let's call her Ortrud — with my funny stories in gratitude for her services at the wheel. However, these stories brought Ortrud into a frenzy of contradiction that was inexplicable to me, and she interrupted my stream of speech with sentences like these: "Why are you telling me this? I don't even know these people. You've told me this before. You are repeating yourself. Would have, would have, could have, could have, all useless reasoning, you can't change the past anyway!" She had dozens of these phrases at the ready. And I continued to talk politely, politely, I thought, and she contradicted me more and more rudely, almost roughly, without me giving myself permission to give her a verbal slap. Just as she didn't give me a punch in the mouth, which I probably deserved. In the end, we hated each other, and continued to pretend to be chummy friends on the trips to the funniest luncheons. I thanked heaven when Ortrud gave up driving and sold the car. And vowed to keep my mouth shut in the future when on car trips. Didn't my mother say to me already years ago: "You talk too much. I can't stand that much talking at my age!" Or she said: "Why are you sitting here in silence and are grumpy when you come home from your round trips?"

"I've noticed that, too, Mommy," I confessed to her and to myself: "I think, I get manic with joy with my girlfriends and then talk too much. And when I'm here again, with you, after a short time I fall into a deep hole and can't get a word out because of despair."

"Oh, I see," my mother said, and now she understood why I was talking too much in the first place and telling nothing at all in the second. The fault was mine and not hers.

For seven years, the MVA sent me thank-you letters for my perfect driving because I never got any traffic tickets. But in the eighth year, the people at the MVA required me to retake the written exam. I didn't go, and now I'm forever part of the one percent of the population that isn't allowed to drive. And instead of a driver's license, I show people at the airport on domestic flights a replacement paper for fools like me who can't even drive and get drunk at luncheons while the driver sips from her water glass. And I talk too much, and she politely keeps quiet or says: "Shut up for a minute, I need to focus on the traffic." Quite like Larry. One of us was on a trip in a minibus that had an accident that killed three women. I didn't go on the bus because I couldn't find a ride to the suburb where the trip was leaving from. So not being able to drive is, at times, beneficial and saved my life at least once. Besides, my mother can't drive either, neither can her sister. It runs in our family: our weak nerves are no match for traffic.

The dean of the German department wanted me to write my doctorate on Wieland, and I secretly laughed at this absurd suggestion: Wieland, who is that? I thought cheekily. Then my further life and learning taught me otherwise. Wieland was a witty poet and a writer who wrote much and well, and was, not by chance, the prince educator at the Weimar court and a good friend of my great dead love, of Goethe himself. And when, after the fall of the Berlin Wall in 1989, I began to travel annually to the spiritual capital of Germany, back then a nest of six thousand inhabitants, rather than to the huge French metropolis of Paris, I also went to his estate of Oßmannstedt and, to my amazement, stood not only in front of his grave on a bank of the Ilm River, but also at that of a young sister of Bettina Brentano, Sophie. The girl, at the age of twenty-two, had been, for a short time, the muse of the aging man Wieland, and lived happily in the bosom of his numerous family, and when she died, she was buried next to him. The young muse next to the old man. Just as the aged men imagine the ideal world to be, a paradise full of beautiful virgins. There are no old muses in paradise and in literary history, only old, nagging mothers-in-law.

When I attended Professor Lee Brian Jenkings' Heine seminar, I knew immediately: Heine was going to be my doctoral topic. It was as if I fell in love with him a second time. The first time, it was in my youth, when I went to the island of Fehmarn with my friend Cornelia. Years later, I loved his wit, his sarcasm, his humor and self-mockery and his tender, romantic heart again. Didn't I also unite all these opposite qualities in me? Or was it presumptuous to assume that? Writing about him would enlighten me on this point and perhaps instill humility in me, like my mother's cane in childhood. Pride comes before the fall. I wanted to write about Heine, but not, actually, for Lee B. Jenkings. He was a highly intelligent Germanist, writing elegantly in English, but afflicted with an unattractive illness, that of timidity. It was so extremely pronounced in him, the like of which I have never again experienced. He was hardly able to look his conversation partner in the eye, he whispered, yes, he stuttered even when speaking to himself and stepped backwards when one approached him. A crablike nature in a housing fit for a crab. His wife, also a Germanist, had already left him long ago. And his girlfriend, a young student, had been stabbed dead by a pipe sticking out of a bus as they both waited together at the bus stop. Just imagine: The much older man in love, side by side with the young girl who loves him, whom he wants to protect with his presence, and there she is stabbed to death by a pipe that should not exist. No wonder that he became whimsical and held seminars on ghostly apparitions in literature for years. I thought he was out of his mind when I heard that he participated in spiritualist séances, because he wanted to connect with his dead lover. I wrote about Rilke in one of his spirit seminars, and couldn't decide whether the spirits haunting his work were meant seriously by the author or conjured up just for fun. For this reason, Jenkings wouldn't give an A to me, who until then, had only received As, a perfect record, as they call it in the States. I should have made up my mind, he claimed. That's when I so intensely described my despair over the spookiness in Rilke's writing that he forgave me my wishy-washy attitude and made the reluctant decision to give me an A. How was I to know that he firmly believed in ghosts?

And Rilke, as well. He is said to have claimed that his French poems were dictated to him by a ghost who sat in a corner of his room. The ghost may have been a good spirit, but he was a bad poet, and Rilke's French poems aren't worth anything, according to the French Romance scholars. When, at readings of the PEN Club in the dreamlike Feuchtwanger Villa Aurora near Los Angeles, I was asked by the female director whether I also wrote poems in English, I told her about Rilke and his ghost and that such a gifted apparition had never appeared to me and that I therefore wrote only in German. Poetry comes from the darkest corners — and in English, I have not developed such a corner, even after more than thirty years of living in the United States. My morass consists of droned-out German cultural heritage. And doesn't writing poetry mean standing firmly with both feet anchored in the cultural mud and doing extraction work without complaining about the unpaid dirty work?

However, I knew Lee B. Jenkings well, because my friend Margaret had left her husband for him, a rich, good-looking engineer, and thus her beautiful house in Crystal Lake for this shy eccentric who also happened to be a professor of German studies who, however, had once celebrated great successes with his lectures in English on the works of Hermann Hesse. Five hundred or more students rushed to join him in the auditorium when he spoke about the favorite writer of American youth back then: about *Demian* and *Steppenwolf* and *Narcissus and Goldmund* and whatever the names of all the bestsellers are. I never had liked Hesse. Most likely, because I read him too late in life. You have to be eighteen, nineteen, twenty when you read him, or you'll never read him. Or only reluctantly. You consider him a little ridiculous with his longing for India, as if there weren't millions and millions of poor people there, and unrealistic regarding his fantasies of self-realization, and find his *Glass Bead Game* boring enough to fall asleep. Because the famous editor of Suhrkamp, the Great Unseld, had written his doctoral thesis on Hesse, I thought in my youthful cockiness that I couldn't admire him — and when I was introduced to Unseld at a literary meeting in the States by his friend Paul Nizon, I said cockily: "I wrote my doctoral thesis on Heinrich Heine," implying to him that his Hesse was no good compared to my Heine. He looked past me, dumbfounded, since he had written his doctoral thesis half a century ago and was writing his two-hundredth work on Goethe, perhaps with the help of some poorly fed Suhrkamp slaves, it was rumored behind his powerful back. Then I remembered: I once wanted to write my doctoral thesis on Hesse, too — but I wanted to tear his work up in the wittiest possible way.

At the university I had written about *Demian* in a literature seminar called 'Literary Evaluation'. The topic of my paper was *Kitsch or Art in Hesse's Work*. And I reckoned it was kitsch and enthusiastically lingered for many pages on this investigation, noticing for the first time that anger made me creative, that my arrogance loosened my tongue, and that rage drove my pen forward rapidly. So, with the help of rage and haughtiness, I wanted to write the doctoral thesis, in a hurry, since I was already a perpetual student anyway, due to the many changes between universities and countries. But Dr. Shaw put the brakes on my unhealthy zeal and informed me, that there was already a stack of papers on the subject of 'Kitsch in Hesse's work'. So I should rather write about 'Art in Heine's work'. Wherein, to be frank, there was also a lot of kitsch. His *Book of Songs* is dripping with it like the pancakes soaked in syrup available for breakfast in the States. But in his work, there is also a lot of wit, sarcasm, irony, and even self-mockery. A very rare virtue in German poets.

For a while, I drank beer in a student pub with Margarete, — who was probably approaching fifty at that time — and old Lee Jenkings, in the evenings, after the ghost seminar, and we ate a pizza with it. I didn't understand what Margaret wanted from this chubby, awkward man: she was slim and tall and curly blond like the Lorelei, admittedly a somewhat aged one. But you could still see what a beauty she must have been in her youth. Once, she showed me an old photo of herself, on which she was as a beauty queen from some one-horse town in Kansas. A woman like a movie star of the nineteen-thirties. At that time, she was married to her first husband, whom she had left for her engineer. And now she was itching for Lee B. Jenkings. Why him, of all men, whom no female had wanted for a long time? Who attended spiritualist sessions and consorted with the spirit of his dead lover — much as the mad Strindberg had consorted with the spirit of his divorced wife, even though she was still alive.

"Tell me, what do you see in Lee?" I asked her back then, during the great snowfall, in her miserable room where she now lived instead of her stately house in Crystal Lake.

"I love his intelligence," she replied dreamily. That was true, he was intelligent. But you also love a man's body, and not just his mind? And what did she want to do with this elderly, fatty body that had never exercised?

"I don't want to do anything with him," said Margarete.

"So, a pure intercourse of the spirits?" I asked her ironically.

"I need my rest," she said then.

"Rest from what?"

"Please, stop asking!" replied Margaret, agonized.

"Rest from what?" I didn't give up.

And suddenly she yelled out: "Rest from intercourse!" I was really frightened by the coarse word sexual intercourse from the mouth of the so well-groomed, well-behaved bourgeois woman, who nevertheless looked like an earlier blond-haired Lorelei on her cliff above the river Rhine.

"Yes, who did something to you in bed, you poor child?"

"My husband!"

"Which husband, exactly?"

"My current husband, of course?"

"The engineer?"

"Yes, who else?"

"And how did he do that?" I suddenly felt like Dr. Sacks, who also tormented me with his questions about sex in marriage. Then Margit finally told me the reason: "He wanted to make love to me every night. It was like Desdemona's night prayer."

"Every night, really?" And I thought of my friend Lilo, who had told me she needed it a few times a day, and her husband could only do it three times a week. And now, she was constantly lusting after him. That would be an unbearable state!

"Margarete, why didn't you tell him that it was too much for you?"

"Because, he said, he actually needed it twice a night, but to spare me, he would do, well, you know what I mean, to the bathroom, to spare me the second time. He considered himself to be such a considerate man!"

"How decent of him," I said dryly.

"You wouldn't believe how I dreaded going to bed! Because of that coitus out of a sense of duty. First you make the man's drink, then you serve him the well-cooked dinner, wash the dishes for him, and then naked into bed for the night shift. He always wanted me to sleep naked, even though I hated it. He thought I was so beautiful naked. I often watched TV for hours in the evening to avoid having to do my duty. But in vain. No sooner was I in bed than I felt his hand on my stomach."

"Ah, your beautiful flat belly," he used to say. "How I love it!"

"Poor Margarete," I said. And thought to myself: How many women would like to have such a potent man — and there the poor man ended up with the wrong one. And, usually, the wrong one wants the wrong one. So that we can whine about it here in the valley of tears. And not play the harp at angelic heights. What devil is playing this game of misfortune with us?

"And how is it with Lee in bed?" I asked Margit, as if I were Dr. Sacks.

"Oh, he can't do it right," said Margarete happily.

"Why can't he?"

"Well, yes, he can't get it up or not quite up."

"And for him you separated from your husband?" I asked, horrified. "That can't be true, then you'll soon be lusting after him like my friend Lilo does after her husband! What are you guys doing together in bed, singing choral music?"

"Well, there are other ways!"

"What are they?"

"Don't play dumb!" Margarete said sternly. "I'm sure you know what else can be done!" And suddenly, I thought of my cat, Pumi, who always went between my legs during my gymnastics and wanted to lick me until I threw him out of the room. And suddenly I felt sick, and I didn't want to know anything, so the old Lee and the aged Lorelei, I didn't have to imagine that; I wanted to scare away this image as soon as possible.

"You can't possibly want to marry him, do you?" I asked Margarete indignantly.

"Who's talking about marrying? He doesn't want me, at all!"

"He doesn't want you?" I said, stunned into disbelief: "Lee doesn't want such a beautiful woman as you? He should give his right arm for you!"

"Yes, imagine, that's what I thought, too. But then I found the diary of his dead girlfriend in his house, and with it the solution to the riddle."

Now I was getting really curious. "What does it say?"

"It says that Lee wanted her when she didn't want him, and when she wanted him, he didn't want her."

"A real ballet dance of I-want-I-don't-want, how hilarious!" I laughed out loud imagining it: The awkward Lee as Baryshnikov in a modern ballet of back-and-forth. To-and-fro-and-to-and-fro, that's actually the primal movement of all procreation, I remembered, and I didn't feel like laughing anymore, because I also had my difficulties with the to-and-fro-and-to-and-fro of life.

"And what are you going to do now?" I asked Margarete, curious again.

"I just won't call him. And already, he's calling. I claim I have an appointment and don't say with whom. And there he is already, at the door, he, who the week before claimed he had to sit for weeks to work on his essay on the ghostly apparitions in the work of Justinus Kerner. And if he's still playing hard to get and acting difficult, I'll call my husband and take him to the movies and tell Lee the next day how it was with him in bed."

"But you don't want to go to bed with your husband!"

"But Lee doesn't know where I was, and beggars can't be choosers! Lee has already sent me a large bouquet of red roses in desperation!"

"The diary of the poor stabbed, dead student — her ghost, in a way — is like an instruction manual on how to handle difficult men," I said pensively. With Remo, such an instruction manual would have been extremely useful to me: always disappearing and reappearing, letting the phone ring and not answering it, barely answering the letters, and not waiting at the train station as agreed, and making up excuses and having lies ready like Marcel Proust's Odette. Making oneself scarce, although in reality, one would like to crash in on the man. At the time of my great love in Switzerland, I had done everything wrong with my obedience and punctuality. And Margarete did everything right to conquer the wrong man for the rest of her life. Because he was wrong for her and she for him. I didn't doubt that at all. And I thought of *The Prince* by Machiavelli, which is also such a useful book regarding the battle strategy of life. Stalin is said to have had it on his bedside table, and Churchill and Roosevelt and Napoleon and Bismarck, too. And my husband uses it as a marriage guide.

I met the famous Bernese writer, Paul Nizon, at a literary conference in St. Louis. In the huge hotel lobby, to my surprise, a porter rushed up to me with the words: "What a precious diamond ring you're wearing!" A behavior that would be inappropriate in Chicago, since otherwise the guest would suspect he was encountering a jewel thief who was taking the precaution of inquiring about the value of the loot. No sooner had I enlightened the porter as to the triviality of the ring, which consisted of an abundance of tiny stones rather than a single valuable diamond, that the next surprise awaited me. A short-legged man with the aged features of a former playboy (his father was Russian!), introduced himself to me with the words: "Vous m' impressionnez — You impress me!" What woman is not impressed by such a sentence! In addition, I was also in the awkward years of transition that turns once attractive women into matrons — and I wasn't sure if I was still attractive or already a matron. He politely introduced himself to me, but his name meant nothing to me, much like Peter Rühmkorf's at the time from the mouth of his friend Lee B. Jenkings. Paul Nizon, on the other hand, was the good friend of the Great Unseld, the king of all publishers in Germany. And it is better for an author in search of a publisher to meet a great publisher than a great poet. Even a great critic, like Marcel Reich-Ranicki, would have been better for me than a Peter Rühmkorf, who was known for his numerous affairs and in whose praise of a woman's poetry one saw a thank-you for hanky-panky — although I knew that with my 'absolute ear for poetry' (as Rühmkorf had called it) his judgment is far superior to that of the overly powerful critic.

So it was through Paul Nizon that I met Germany's greatest publisher, whom I should have met years ago, namely when he met his future wife Ulla, the black-haired actress and Lorelei, and fell under her spell, which tempted him to leave his wife and children to follow the lure of a late love. A romantic in the shape of a sturdy peasant, that made him attractive to me, and

I forgave him his doctoral thesis on kitsch-as-art-Hesse. When he asked me my name, I introduced myself with an old joke of mine:

"Selig (Blessed), as in Blessed are the poor in spirit!" He looked puzzled, as if he didn't know the Bible; also, self-irony seemed to be foreign to him. While getting this slightly confused look, Paul Nizon laughed uproariously, and his heartfelt appreciation of my native wit (where does that expression actually come from? My mother has no sense of wit) turned me, for the rest of the days, into a clown fooling around. And Paul Nizon always laughed, only never his best friend, the king of Suhrkamp. Meaning, the wrong person laughed. In this, the poor great publisher resembled Hesse, who was not fond of witty wordplay and such bad habits. They belonged to people like the poor Jew and outsider Heine. And I resembled Heine in that and was funny and an outsider among all these glorious Suhrkamp authors. Or I thought I resembled him in my presumptuousness. It was only the presence of Paul Nizon that protected me from Unseld's wrath, I think, when I had the impudence (what devil was riding me?) to tell him that my former Swiss fiancé had met his wife Ulla and, when asked if she was really as beautiful as in the photographs, replied to me: "Yes, she is beautiful, but with her forty years, she's also no longer the youngest!"

Couldn't find a younger one, that's what it meant. Yet, he found whatever he was looking for in all places. Back then, in St. Louis, it was a very pretty, also black curly professor, who, out of caution, wore wide-meshed fishnet stockings with her short skirt to give herself a slutty look, certainly because the men should not notice how intelligent she was. The Lorelei belongs naked on her rock, not as a professor in a classroom. After dinner, the two of them — the Suhrkamp king and his chosen princess of the night — sat in the bare dining room for a long time as we, the common folk, wearily thought about going to bed. Paul Nizon politely asked me if I wanted to share his hotel bed, but I wouldn't and couldn't because, as usual, I was tormented by back pain and a headache and bladder pain and again could only sleep with my heating pad. He forgave my indisposition and as an old husband was used to such grief. And I thought, a little sadly, of my friend Cornelia, who was ready under any circumstances to give the men the pleasure they wanted, and who didn't take long to act as if she lived in a bygone age when, as a woman, one had to defend one's virtue to the point of suicide (like Lessing's poor Emilia Galotti). I, on the other hand, was incapable of enjoying the freedoms of my century. The son of a friend once told me: "You yourself have to fight for all your freedoms. Every gift that is given for nothing is given for nothing if the recipient doesn't know what to do with the gift!"

"I wonder if he caught on to me?" I thought and looked at him scrutinizingly. But by then he was already talking about something else. I was the only clown among the always serious and thoughtful-looking Suhrkamp authors, and Paul Nizon laughed as heartily at me when I couldn't get a smile out of the Unseld-Siegfried. I must have reminded him daily that he had neither wit nor drollery and sometimes it seemed to his fellow human beings like he was inhibited despite his considerable number of publications, so that one wondered where he found the time to even appear at literary conventions like those in St. Louis. Shouldn't he be busy day and night with his research? A man in his study room. What was he doing here?

Paul Nizon told me in St. Louis about his 'amour fou', his then Lorelei and now wife, for whom he had left his wife and mother of several children. He, too, a victim of his late love. He, too, a romantic.

"She was my daughter's age," he told me proudly, reminding me of Max Frisch's book *Homo Faber*, in which the father accidentally sleeps with his own daughter. Men seem to have a longing to sleep with their own daughter. With their daughters or even with their granddaughters. The young girl as a fountain of youth for the old man. She gives him back his strength, his muscles, the hair on his head and his fallen-out teeth. Now he can bite and kiss again. And all this without witchcraft, just by the perfection of her young body.

"And what does the 'amour fou' do?" I asked Paul Nizon. Brought down to earth, he said: "Well, we live in a normal marriage, as marriages go; unfortunately, there is a young son." Seems like one should never try to marry Isolde, I thought, since amour fou only exists outside of marriage.

"Marriage is the death of passion," I said to him, and he looked glum.

"I have never written so well and so quickly as I did in those days of amour fou," he confessed to me. "The sentences came as if by themselves, I couldn't write them down fast enough, where otherwise it sometimes comes to a standstill."

The bible says: "Those whose hearts are full, find that their mouths are overflowing." And I knew exactly; he was once more looking for an amour fou and not as a romantic, but to be able to write better. And he considered me a possible object of his desire, because he didn't know that I was already in menopause. And a Lorelei still has, of course, her period. And therefore, her nights. On the last day, Paul Nizon told me that I had sometimes narrowly slid alongside the precipice with my cheeky jokes.

"That's a risk any comedian has to take," I explained to him, "the audience is virtually just waiting for them to break their neck. Yes, they wish for his death as punishment for his arrogant cockiness and their own stubbornness." We parted as 'good friends' and thought, we would never see each other again. But then I was invited to Paris by the Maison Heinrich Heine, a kind of Goethe Institute on the grounds of the University of Paris, to give a lecture in French on women in Heinrich Heine's poetry, my dissertation topic. Paul Nizon showed up on time for the lecture, and afterwards, the three of us — Larry was there, too — waited in the Metro station for the subway, and Paul Nizon lectured me in German, even though he knew that my husband didn't know that language, that the old man and the young woman made the ideal image of a couple. So, he still hadn't found a new amour fou and was living, just as back then in St. Louis, with his wife who was of the same age as his daughter, except that now she no longer had the magic power to inspire him in his writing, and he had to pull everything out of his own sleeve of brilliant ideas. That, of course, was much more tedious. Many years later, in Chicago, I happened to see his number in my phone book and called him in Paris. He was surprised to hear from me, no doubt. He was divorced from his amour fou, he told me, and the little boy from those days was already studying at university.

"Why did you get divorced?" I asked him curiously, and somewhat gloatingly.

He said: "The age difference was too big." But, of course, it wasn't the age difference that had caused them to separate, it was the fact that you are supposed to let your Lorelei, your muse, sit on her rock and not lock her in the marriage bed. Steak and potatoes every day, who has an appetite for that? Unfortunately, I then told him that my biological father had hanged himself as a war criminal. He listened to me with interest and asked many questions. Then he wrote me a long letter, to which I didn't answer quickly, because our apartment had to be repaired. When I called him again, he was obviously offended. When I said: "If I had lived in the Third Reich ...", he interrupted me:

"But you lived in the Third Reich!" And wanted to rub my old age in my face with this sentence.

"No," I replied, "I was just vegetating back then, I was a drooling worm." He didn't like the answer and he had to get off the phone quickly. Silly me, I sent him my book *The German Exchange Student: A Love Story*.

That's when he wrote me a caustic letter: "Your book is below my level in terms of content, thought, and language. For that reason, I soon got rid of it (he probably meant: put it away). And don't be so ... clingy in the future." Clingy, I thought, the former potential object of his desire, a possible amour fou and fuel for his writing. And now I was just old and clingy. The glue on which ridiculous fly legs got trapped, but not a great Suhrkamp writer like him. With the greatest interest, I read his book about his amour fou, *The Year of Love*. But all we learned about the amour fou was that he had spent a passionate night with her, and that the young woman had then left for the States. In the book, he lived off the memory of this 'good fuck', as the magic night would have been called in the States. And he went regularly to the brothel in order to be able to remember her better. And the painful separation from his once beloved wife also took up a mere half page. *The Year Without Love* should have been the title of the book, I thought indignantly. Instead of writing about his grief and passion, he described Paris in all its familiar details, even though by now everybody and their neighbor had been to the city. And detailed accounts of the world out there have seemed somewhat superfluous and tedious ever since the invention of photography and film. When I visited Paris again, I sent him a postcard signed "the diffident Gorda Selig, brittle, not clingy." And didn't call him.

The Russian émigré Nina Berberova writes in her fascinating autobiography, which I read in the French original (*C'est moi qui souligne*) — she lived for a long time in Paris and in the States — that the greatest difference between the European intelligentsia and the American would be that the Americans didn't take themselves so seriously. How true!

I can boast all I want about my native wit from my mother, — or father — or my own wittiness: the fact remains that I have not become a comedian, but a German writer in the English-speaking States, thus something completely out of place, and my verbal fireworks don't count anyway, only the ones on paper, and those were rejected by the Suhrkamp king when Remo sent him my manuscript. Even though he had just sent me his thick volume on Goethe's publishers. Written in the most beautiful Germanic language — by him? By the smart Suhrkamp slaves? Who did the years of preparatory work, who studied the hundreds of publications on the subject of Goethe's publishers? Did he? He, who had the time to travel, to love (he couldn't live without love, he once said), to divorce, and who lovingly cared for his authors with their mimosa-like souls? "All Lies and deception," Robert Gernhardt calls one of his witty, clever stories, yet he never became a Suhrkamp author. Those with wit usually ended up at the Rowohlt publishing house.

Siegfried Unseld dedicated the book about Goethe's publishers to me in handwriting: In three different writing styles! Did he unite three spirits in himself? Three lives? Three truths? They say that his son hated him after his parents got divorced. I saw Unseld's son in Klagenfurt. He wanted to sit with me, but again, the devil rode me, and I said to him:

"No, stay where you are. You are too young, too beautiful and too rich for me!" He looked offended and stayed where he was. Why was he offended? I surely was no longer a Lorelei, with her days and nights. Rühmkorf laughed out loud when I told him about the Unseld son's strange reaction: "I, too, would have liked to hear that from the mouth of a woman. You are too young, too beautiful and too rich!" Who wouldn't?

Everything I didn't achieve was achieved by Ulla Hahn, whom I met at Radio Bremen at the time. And her boss, Dr. Helmut Lamprecht, thought I was more talented than she was. But in Germany, people only know Ulla Hahn and not me. A meaningless life? Here I am, sitting in the hospital room at the bedside of my mother, who is lying in a deathlike state, and I am asking myself about the meaning of my life. The meaning of any life. Ora et labora, pray and work, was Luther's answer. Was it Luther at all? What do I know for sure after so many years of learning? I already don't know today what I read yesterday. I write in a race against death. Fighting against death with love. With the love for my mother, for Anni, for Friederike, for Remo, and for Larry. Even though I sometimes seemed to hate them. In the beginning, there was love. In the past, writers were revered and celebrated like saints; today, people tell of their shabby character.

"What a terrible person, this Günter Grass," an acquaintance said to me recently. The terrible human being and the wonderful work, how does that go together? In the German book club I run in Chicago, so that I don't have to read American or English history books and autobiographies all the time, my old college friend Elga insists that we should only talk about the authors' works, the less we heard about their horrible private lives, the better. Yet Germanists are constantly examining the lives and works of authors at the same time. They must have a screw loose.

Envy is as the evil shadow side of admiration. The evil view of the one who can do what one would like to be able to do. Mozart and Salieri, the unforgettable play by Peter Shaffer. As soon as I saw it, I knew that a modern playwright had hit the mark, into the black heart of envy. Into the heart of us all. Who has not envied from the bottom of the heart? What can you do against it, the evil envy? You begin to love the envied one. There is no remedy for the great merits of another, other than love, said the great Goethe, who was fiercely envied because of his prominent and well-paid position as Weimar's first minister, friend of the duke and poet-king of Germany. A son of a wealthy family! How the wonderful, but poor and sick Schiller envied him at times! And especially his childhood friend Herder! But even the great Goethe only wanted to be loved and not envied!

Love as a means of rescue

Benn and Brecht couldn't
Hold a candle to me
(they were too dead for that)
But the living Rühmkorf
Told me the pure truth
When we were dining together on fish,

Using the comforting words
Cheer up, girl
Hardly anyone understands poetry

But yours has a tone all its own
And only your skin is as smooth
As that of a child's bottom

Against the great merits of another
There are no means of rescue other than love
Was said by the great Goethe
Who wrote humbly
"Love me"
At the end of his letters

And thus I loved them all:
Goethe and Grass
Heine, Lyngi and Hölderlin
And also Hahn and Kirsch
(No pantheon without the ladies)

"Love me"
Is written invisibly at the end
Of all great poetry

Standoffishness has troubled me all my life, in a time when
a woman's standoffish nature seemed repulsive, not attractive
anymore, as in earlier centuries.

"And why do you always say no?" Dr. Sacks asked me one
day, "when you could say yes with ease?"

"I don't want to talk about that," I replied.

"But that's exactly why we have to talk about that," Dr.
Sacks insisted.

"No, I don't think so," I countered. "At least not today."

"Well, next time then." Maybe, I thought: or the time after
that, after that or maybe after that. Or never.

In Switzerland, we wrote the class papers without the professor's guidance. Afterwards, we listened with humble faces to his criticism, which told us why we had taken the wrong course again. It was only at the end of our studies that we found out how we should have studied and written. In contrast, in the States, we were taught, from the beginning, how to look around in the library, how to master the secondary literature, and how to become 'scholars' of the subject and not remain dilettantes all our lives.

When I wrote my doctoral thesis on Heine, I took out my seminar book on *Bibliography and Method* and learned again how to grasp the vast field of knowledge about such an important poet. And only then did I start reading and taking notes on index cards. And, in a year and a half, I had finished the work, which for some doctoral students needed seven years or more. Acting stupidly, I told Dr. Lorbe in her unforgettable Art Nouveau class about my rapid approach, and she said disgruntledly: "Yes, how is that possible in a year and a half?" Surely, she had spent three times that amount of time, and now I was making her feel slow 'getting it', or whatever else the term we used in my school days was supposed to mean. She must have thought, "I'll show her!" And since she was on my doctoral committee (it always consisted of five professors), she had the opportunity to do that. She sent the paper back to me with the words: "That's neither here nor there in your intellectual vegetable garden! Get your intellectual vegetable garden in order first!"

I was as shattered as I had been in Lausanne, when Professor Stauffacher's young assistant proved to me that I was no better than she was, although she had erroneously assumed so, at first. And I would only get a pitiful 'C' for the work that Remo had found so excellent. Humiliated and exhausted, I read through the thesis again and didn't know where to start, since everything seemed in perfect order. A professor said that I should have sent the manuscript in perfect condition, since such a first version virtually demanded the reader's criticism. Now, I had been advised by the dean to send a kind of draft, to send the finished manuscript seemed pretentious, as if I imagined that I couldn't make mistakes. That advice had clearly been the wrong one.

Desperate, I passed the thesis to a secretary, who typed it a second time, this time with headings to the various parts, which had an extremely organizing effect, without my having to change or even remove a word. Dr. Lorbe was delighted with the rewrite, which I didn't submit until a year later, so as to give the impression that I had gone through a long, hard time of rewriting. And so I was allowed to successfully defend my thesis that the women in Heine's work were original dancing and philandering figures and not just ice-cold young girls who sat naked on their hard rock like the Lorelei and brought about the downfall of the skippers with their magic song.

After the examination, Dr. MacGlathery said to me, to the doctoral student who had been rejected and humiliated for a year: "You are a wonderful person, very honest, very funny and deep, very deep." And when a publisher wanted to publish the work and asked MacGlathery what he thought of it ("But the truth please"), he said: "Like her poetry, her dissertation has a touch of genius." Thus, within a year, I was transformed from a woman with no sense of order into a genius Dr. Poet. Only in America could there be such metamorphoses! In Switzerland, I was and remained the ugly frog that you could throw against the wall twenty times without it turning into a clever princess. The saying there was: Once a frog, always a frog.

The creepy emperor Wilhelm the Second is said to have said that he could learn through praise alone, and that his educator knew only criticism. Unfortunately, that's how it is for me, too: constant criticism takes away my strength to continue. That is why Friederike was so extremely important for me at the beginning of my life as a writer. She put her hand on mine and said most lovingly: "You said that beautifully, keep it up." And I kept it up. For years, just for her. And when Werner came into her life and took her away from me, he also took away the portion of praise I needed to write. Sometimes, I was silent on paper for a long time. Like after Remo yelled at me, when he had read my second manuscript of a novel: "You should never have given this to me! With every page, I thought, what have I done wrong now!"

When I sent my first novel to Dr. Lorbe, she wrote me the following letter, for the graduate student whose vegetable garden was once full of cabbage and turnips.

Dear Gorda,
Because I'm so enthusiastic about it, I'm going to jump right in: I think your book is wonderful! At the moment I can't think of any book I've read in recent years that I've absorbed with such enthusiasm and fascination as your *Mephisto*. I put it down in between only hesitantly, and took it up again with excitement, and I couldn't get away from it.
First of all, therefore, I would like to congratulate you from the bottom of my heart on this beautiful volume. Surely you have already received many positive and admiring reviews and opinions about it, and I am incredibly happy for you …
Of course, I have asked myself in between, again and again: "How did Gorda do it?" Everything is flowing

along like this, seemingly effortlessly and as if it were a matter of course, and at the same time one realizes the abundance and richness of the content one is confronted with here. Just <u>how</u> you could manage all this is a mystery to me — the richness of the remembered impressions; your immense literary and the cultural (self-evident) knowledge, i.e., education, at the same time a certain lack of inhibition, great naturalness — organizing principle: the chronology, the progressing of life itself. In addition, the whole historical background — war (and even before), post-war period, the beginning of the economic miracle, the cultural life in Germany, especially: school life, the situation of the young people born into and growing up in that, who come to life as convincing independent personalities through your apt descriptive remarks in the book, seemingly made only in passing. And against this backdrop, the American year. Which intertwines all this, and even the most seemingly trivial things become important, take on a 'higher' value.

I believe, Gorda, that you have succeeded to write this work "as if from one cast" above all, so perfectly, through your very special, <u>original style</u>, which you, so it seems to me (I would have to re-read the book critically regarding this!) hold from beginning to end. <u>Whatever</u> you talk about, so well-known, familiar, because it has been — in part, experienced by the readers themselves, sounds fresh and new due to your stylistic processing. Clichés are unmasked. And your sentences — sometimes they are not complete at all — often capture foreground and background in one breath, yet this is not 'proclaimed' solemnly, but appears in a <u>skillful</u> lightness for which one could envy you (note the subjunctive!!).

I believe, Gorda, that with this book you have succeeded in doing something very important, which, to date, many have tried in vain or have accomplished with only partial success:

<u>This</u> is what the postwar period in Germany looked like.

<u>This</u> is how people lived, reacted, etc.,

and <u>this</u> is how young people (here, from the educated class) experienced themselves and their immediate and more distant environment,

they have integrated themselves or have resisted,

they have become critical.

and have experienced their fates in rudimentary beginnings or already in a concentrated manner.

Maybe you only (sorry!) wanted to write personal experiences from your chest, but just through the pointedly personal aspect of it, the situations and people achieve general validity.

The young Gorda becomes almost (I am careful, as you can see) the manifestation of the educated, thoughtful, sometimes a little crazy, headstrong, immensely serious, and so sympathetic young Germans of that time (I don't mean that patriotically, not at all), at the same time full of desires, feelings and above all: humor. It's not for nothing that Heine already appears there.

I must close now, dear Gorda — I have tried to put my impressions down on paper for you. I'm sure I've

forgotten or overlooked a lot of what is also important
in your book — I hope you'll forgive me for that. But
I want you to know: my praise is sincere — from the
bottom of my heart, I am happy for you and hope that
you are also happy about your book.
Thank you very much for sending me your book —
with all good wishes and many greetings.
Yours, Ruth Lorbe

(Dr. Ruth Lorbe, Professor Emeritus of modern German
literature at the University of Illinois, Urbana-Champaign, on
February 18, 2001)

Was she trying to make up for what she had done to me then
by rejecting my dissertation? I look back at scathing reviews
and high praise and wonder: How does that fit together? How
does it fit together that I married a man who has read only one
novel in his life and leaves the talking to the parrots — while
he silently reads Machiavelli's *Prince* to know how to win the
marriage war? How does it fit together that I love children but
didn't want to have any? That I find cooking tedious, but love
good food? That my dream is a backyard garden — but remained
a dream because I stayed in an apartment on the twenty-second
floor of a Chicago high-rise? With a tiny balcony, but a view
of the lake and park. How does it fit together that I was raised
atheist and pray at night for the preservation of my loved ones?
How is it possible that I love a mother who beat me up in
childhood? How does it fit together that I sometimes seem to
be dumber than a rock and sometimes as smart as Einstein?
How does it fit together that I never want to die and think
about suicide every day? Why do we want to be young again
and yet we were often extremely unhappy in our youth? Why

do we want to live as long as possible, even though old age is a punishment with hip and knee surgeries and Parkinson's and Alzheimer's?

Questions upon questions and silence upon silence from the-one-above, who may not even exist. Don't I often say I would have liked to have had a sister? But I had my beloved cousin Anni, whom I unfortunately lost at the age of five, because the adults separated us when my mother moved to Hanover with the new stepfather and me, but the brothers stayed with Anni and grandma and grandpa and the beloved aunt. Every day, I cried for all of them, but especially for my Anni. Inwardly, outwardly I was not allowed to show anything. Otherwise, my mother would call me a crybaby.

How could one do such a thing to the pathologically sensitive child I once was? Because the adults at that time didn't know that children are pathologically sensitive and therefore never forget what is done to them in the first seven or eight years of their life. Besides, so much had been done to the parents by WWII (even by WWI) that they didn't consider the feelings of children worth paying attention to: first and foremost they had to focus on themselves and their survival, and only then on the children's souls, if at all. And how could it be otherwise? I loved Anni with a passion until I was sixteen and came to California as an exchange student. There I found a new sister; this was Nancy, the daughter of the surrogate family, with whom I went to school every day. We called ourselves 'foster sisters'. And remained so all our lives! Nancy had a sister, ten years older than me, with whom I spent Christmas many years later, along with Nancy and her mom. And who said one day: "Gorda came as an exchange-student into our family, and never left us again!" While doing so, she laughed bitterly and derisively. At least it seemed that way to me. "My God, she has been jealous of me," I thought, startled, but I understood her well. Wouldn't I have been jealous of a 'new girl' in the family, the girl from the country that just fourteen years earlier had fought the States in World War II? And since she was ten years older than we were, she remembered well those days and the news on the radio. For Nancy and me, on the other hand, World War II was something of a horrific tale. You had heard about it but could hardly believe in it. And in the meantime, the evil enemy had become America's closest ally.

Nancy and I got along well from the beginning. She was the first whose English I understood. The important thing was that neither of us were great beauties. We were merely 'good looking', how good, we didn't know at the time. But it was important that one of us didn't outshine the other with her beauty. Because, unfortunately, the strongest bonds of friendship between young girls are shaken by nothing more than outward appearances, because the boys who, from then on, dominated our minds and hearts, went by the features and figure alone. After all, what else should they go by at first sight? The only astonishing thing is that we girls considered the judgment of these pubescent boys to be the judgment of God, and we felt like little gray mice at any rebuff from one of these god boys, who himself could be as ugly and pimply as he wanted. Each of them was a Paris to us, handing the golden apple of discord to the fairest. And it was always about 'The Fairest One' in all the stories and poems and novels of the man's world. Never about the smartest, wittiest, most talented one, no, only the face counted. The mask we wore underneath for our appearance. The costume in which we hid ourselves.

While we girls saw through each other to the bottom of the soul, the adored youngsters saw the size and color of the eyes, the texture of the skin, the shape of the nose and the curve or otherwise non-curve of the lips. We looked at the essentials when we looked at each other, the boys, never at the non-important ones. For this reason, it was so important to Nancy and me that neither of us was the Beautiful Helen herself, just an Elizabeth Bennett in *Pride and Prejudice* or a Josephine in *Little Women*. Jane and Meg were the 'Beauties' in the novels. Therefore, we weren't beauties, but we also didn't have humps on our backs and pimples on our faces, and we didn't wear glasses. "Boys never make passes at girls who wear glasses," Nancy often said, and quickly put her reading glasses away at school. Thank goodness I didn't need any, just sunglasses in sunny California, but they didn't count and didn't make me a 'four-eyes' or an 'old maiden'.

We were both later successful in the marriage market — as required — and Nancy married a fellow student at twenty-two. And so did I, many years after that, when Nancy already had two children. Whom Larry and I visited in his second year of training in Northern California, where Nancy moved after her marriage to Richard, then still called Rick. Nancy, like her sister, became a registered nurse, a very prestigious profession in the States, with a long period of study and good pay. Rick tried his luck as a realtor, but rather listlessly, for he had really wanted to be an actor and was always talking about his student role in 'The Visit of the Old Lady'. Unfortunately, he hadn't gotten an engagement yet, but he tried hard to get one, and every time he got turned down, he drank heavily and had to spend the next few days in bed. In the end, he was drunk more often than sober, and it was only when he was drunk that he could be happy, like so many artists before him. He found little time for selling houses. But thank goodness, Nancy had a good position at the hospital in Sonoma, and she often worked overtime, so the family didn't starve, and Rick could drink his six-pack, his six cans of comfort beer, every night. And eventually, the money they saved was even enough for a tiny bungalow. The furniture in it came from the Salvation Army and seemed to be damaged all over, which I noticed with amazement, because I had not yet learned that young American couples save first for their own homes and not for furniture. In Germany, on the other hand, no one was thinking of buying a house at the time, but new furniture was purchased immediately. Americans were working for future prosperity; Germans wanted a nice home. I was so shocked by the pitifulness of Nancy's home furnishings that I insisted on leaving quickly; I couldn't bear the sight of this 'slum', I explained to Larry. He didn't know what I was talking about. And Nancy didn't understand the haste with which we sped away in our rental car.

"I never want to go there again," I told Larry. "Don't they call people like that white trash? Anti-social elements?" But Larry already wasn't listening to me, because he had been wearing mental ear protectors since the beginning of his strenuous training at the hospital. When I saw Nancy and Rick again ten years later, we were celebrating the first class reunion in Southern California. It was very exciting for me to see the classmates again with whom I had spent the best year of my life. And I thought, everyone would rush up to me and hug me and be happy because I could be there, the German exchange student from back then. But no one rushed up to me and no one hugged me. I had to go up to the old classmates and greet them one by one — and I realized they didn't see me as a 'star' from the past; I was just one among many, a woman who had married an American. Nothing special. After all, I wasn't. And Larry wasn't there, so I sat around and was happy when one of the men danced with me. One of them was the one I'd fought with all evening at the drive-in theater that night back then because I didn't like his bad breath, and he apologized to me for pushing so hard for a kiss, and I forgave him and myself for acting like a hysteric who thought she was about to be raped. The poor man must have always lived in fear that a 'rapist' lived in him. And another dancer came, he had been such a thin, shy little boy back in the day, whom we had not paid any attention to at all, and suddenly he turned out to be a great dancer and conversationalist. And our class valedictorian and speaker was drinking like a professional drunkard with a beautiful Italian-looking mistress at his side, because he had just left his wife and four children. Rumor had it that his company was about to go bankrupt, and we had thought him the most promising of us. And the most beautiful lady, who had once been his high school sweetheart, was still the most beautiful, but had a mentally handicapped child in a home and had already been divorced twice. She shone as young and as sweet as a cherry blossom, and that was her name, Cherry, that you knew she would soon be a bride again, time and again. She was born to be a bride forever. Like the Lorelei on her rock on the banks of the Rhine River. She sings and plays the harp and lets her golden jewelry flash in the sun, and her long blond hair covers the most magnificent of all bosoms, which never will become sagging breasts. A man's dream of a young woman, a siren, a witch, a whore, a man-eating childwoman! Lulu. Salome. Venus in Venus mountain. And if I hadn't written a doctoral thesis on the poetry of Heinrich Heine, I wouldn't have known all this. I only suspected it.

Writing means to let the hunch become certainty. Everything I didn't know about myself until then came to me while I was writing. For example, that I never stopped loving Remo.

Rick talked at me with the vivacity of a true artist, and Nancy sat silently by, happy about her charming husband. And I chatted with him like with an old friend. That is when he told me he would never have married a woman who was perfectly beautiful and didn't even have a little blemish like a wrinkle in her nose (Nancy) or a scar over her eye (me), so I asked him, slightly annoyed, why he had married Nancy, when in reality I wondered why she had taken to that drunkard and braggart? I hoped he would finally speak of her tireless diligence, of her loyalty, of her practical nature. Instead, he hesitated, looked at me curiously, and said:

"I know what you mean, we don't fit together. But you and I…"

"No," I said, "you belong with Nancy."

"No," he said, "I belong to me!" And I quickly went to the bathroom, in order to put an end to the conversation about who belonged to whom. When I came back out, he was lying in wait for me outside the door, but I walked past him like he was a ghost and not a straying alcoholic husband and father of two children. Later, someone told me under the seal of secrecy that he had tried to have his way with his little girl. Years later, as a young woman, when she asked him for some money, he had none for her. Nancy and Rick had just bought a nice brown wooden house when he left her and flew to Hawaii and no one heard from him ever again. Not even his children. Nor his sister. That happened a lot in California. Now, Nancy wasn't working for four now, but only for three. Unfortunately, she couldn't live without a man. And so she put an ad in the paper that she had a room for rent. In moved a man, whose first name also began with R. His name was Rudi, and he had a lock put on the door of the room, but unfortunately, he didn't pay her the rent. Slick as he was, he hopped instead into bed with Nancy, the nurse with a house and garden who was earning a decent salary. He prayed loudly and fervently in the morning and evening and attended church every Sunday with Nancy. Therefore, she didn't want to continue living in sin and married him, and they swore allegiance to each other, on a Bible, for the rest of their lives. He had already made this Bible oath with two other women, as Nancy learned all too late. He appropriated her credit cards and began making purchases that were not anticipated in the budget, such as two radios, another record player, dozens of records, and cameras.

"Where did you get the money for that?" she asked him, because he couldn't go to work. He suffered from agoraphobia, a disease I had never heard of before. With this fear of wide-open spaces, he couldn't look for work, naturally. Nancy constantly had to drive him to doctors because of his conditions. Unfortunately, it turned out that he was not only a marriage con artist, but also a brawler. Several times, he threatened her with an iron bar in the basement. He wanted to report her son to the police because he had poured sand into the exhaust pipe of his mother's car and into those of many other people. The son began to steal from the school due to his anger at his stepfather, taking money from coat pockets and kept scarves for himself, until the school administration found out and sent him to a school, run by Catholic priests, for boys who were difficult to raise. The poor boy loved this school very much, because of the fatherly teachers, for he longed so much for his own father, who remained missing in Hawaii and was never heard from. I kept having to promise Jeb that we would go to Hawaii together to look for the father — that scoundrel excuse of a father.

Nancy's daughter Jerry was studying in Paris when her mother married the marriage con artist, and she was told by her mother to come back to California immediately because there would be no money for her studies, because that had been claimed by the new man in the house. The relationship between Jerry and Rudi was hate at first sight. She drew the consequences and moved out of the parental home and worked for a rich family as a nanny of the children. So Nancy, once again, provided for three instead of the four. Rudi talked from morning till night about his brilliant investments and asked his wife to empty her pension fund and entrust the money to him, he could invest it for her with great profit. She emptied the fund and the money disappeared into Rudi's room with the lock in front, for which only he had the key. The money didn't reappear.

For many years, I flew out a few days before Christmas to see Mom, who was now widowed, to be with her, Nancy, and her son Jeb. The family lived in the old house, and I slept in the motel nearby. We played canasta every day, a modified family version with few rules, so we could have fun with wine and sandwiches and laugh at each other and not have to pay strict attention to the game. We laughed and drank and ate like never again until late at night. Back then, I filled up with Nancy's lust for life for the whole exhausting year at the university. Once we went dancing, Nancy and I with her friend Joyce and her husband. Afterwards, we ended up at Joyce's house, and her husband went to bed, relieved, when Nancy started talking about her second husband, Rudi. She related all the things he did to her. Rudi had spent two hundred dollars (a lot of money in those days!) on a gift for himself instead of buying the stepson the bicycle for his birthday. Instead, he bought a wristwatch for himself and put it under lock and key in his locked room. When Nancy protested and said, you take that back, he just laughed derisively. Once she got a bill for one thousand dollars from different restaurants, and when she asked him, with whom did you go out so often behind my back, he said snottily, that's none of your business, I don't like interrogations, and I'm still a free man here and can do what I like.

"But not at my expense!" replied Nancy sharply. Or, shall we say, almost sharply.

"What's yours is mine," he declared, "after all, we live in a marital union, not as bachelors! Marriage is sacred!" he preached, and they would spend and purchase everything together, for better or for worse. And he was going through bad times, but he also had brilliant ones behind him, in which he made a lot of money with his investments. After all, he said he knew about this trick that inevitably led to wealth and success, and Nancy should finally trust him and leave the financial management of the marriage to him, that she was overwhelmed with her day-and-night shifts, that she needed a man at her side and in the house who knew how to achieve great wealth in the shortest possible time — and that she had these savings in her account, which hardly increased, but he could quadruple, no, quintuple the amount very quickly, if she would only finally trust him, as one should do in a real marriage. Trust was supposed to be the basic law of a good marriage: Without it, all would be lost from the start. And then Nancy went on breathlessly, as if she were afraid we wouldn't listen to her anymore and she would have to hurry with the rest of the story, he would make her kneel down next to him to beg God for help, that He would finally give her the necessary trust in Rudi: "O Lord, give me the strength to have a true marriage in Thy spirit, and bless this covenant that it may remain with me!"

"Stop it already!" cried Joyce: "I can't hear it any longer, trust, don't make me laugh! I hope you didn't give him your life savings!" But Nancy had done it because she had sworn on the Bible to stand by him always, she by him as he by her, and yet she had been so shamefully abandoned by Rick — by the father of his own children. And she didn't want to be divorced a second time, she wanted to do everything she could to save that sacred marriage. And Joyce said: "This is a conman, a confidence-man, a cheater, you can't give him your credit cards. He's just trying to rip you off! You need to go to a lawyer right now and reclaim the credit cards and put them in your name alone, so they'll be canceled for him!" But Nancy was already not listening and went on: he discovered damage to the house and is now suing the contractor for damages. He's taken away my enjoyment of the house, frankly. He wants us to sell it, he could invest the money incredibly profitably, in no time we would be so rich that none of us would have to work! But I said to him, "no, the house stays for the children, their father left it to me before he disappeared to Hawaii and never came back. I want it to remain my children's house."

"Thank God," Joyce said, "that you didn't get involved in the madness of selling the house. You'd have to be completely stupid to trust that man, and yet you're an intelligent woman with four years of college and training as a nurse." And Nancy told them Rudi had kicked Jeb out because he didn't respect him, and he wouldn't let any stepson treat him with contempt.

"Where does he live now?" asked Nancy, puzzled.

"But you know that, with the Catholic priests at the school home."

"Oh, I thought he was coming home from school in the evening."

"Well, no, Rudi doesn't want to see him with us, he's a thief, he said 'he probably stole the three hundred dollars you're missing from your cash box. Anyway, it wasn't me!'"

"I'm not so sure about that," Joyce said dryly: "You should also have a lockable room in the house where you keep your cash like he does. And you should demand the key to his room — which is actually your room — and check to see what he's up to."

"He's a genius," Nancy said then, to our amazement: "He can turn a one into a three, or a five!"

"I'll take your word for that," I said at last: "But he's not a genius at investing, he's one at twisting facts. He's trying to pull a fast one on you! He's a lying baron, a Baron Munchhausen!" But Nancy had never heard of the Baron, and she went on about how Rudi had already made his mother rich, and his brother, such a selfless man he was, and now finally he would think of himself and make them rich in no time flat! She's beyond help, I thought in the evening, as Nancy flirted with Rudi on the phone:

"Yes, we would be happy if you were here, dearest, so take the next train and come. On the other hand, we'll be with you soon, so it's not worth it. And take care of the cat, she's not allowed out at night. What, she ran away and hasn't come home for three nights already? Say, have you gone crazy, my beloved Nina, well, let's wait and see, usually the animals come back on their own." And-so-on and-so-forth. After five years, Rudi finally disappeared from Nancy's life.

"When he realized he had taken everything but the house, he left me," she told me indignantly. And I had hoped she had kicked him out. After his disappearance, she had called his previous victim, who had once tried to contact her, but Nancy had refused to talk to her, she didn't want to hear about his past life. The woman had tried to warn her about Rudi on the phone: "Watch out, this man is dangerous!" But Nancy indignantly hung up the phone. At the time, Nancy didn't want to be awakened from her dream of love, but now she was prepared to empty the bitter cup of truth to the bottom. The two women spent five hours together and never ran out of material. Rudi was a whole novel. But who wants to read such silly stuff? He had used up the household money for himself. Rudi celebrated his birthday every day. And he always ran around with the Bible in his hand and sayings in his mouth, slaying the hard-working, gullible wives with it. And his great investments disappeared into a secret account or into thin air. Mom, who had changed her will so Rudi couldn't inherit anything, changed it again in favor of Nancy.

"Nancy, Nancy," she had often said to me pained, in anguish: "How can she do that to her children, marry this conman?" I knew no answer to that. And Nancy's daughter Jerry moved back in with her and resumed her studies again, which she had dropped because of Rudi. And she said to her mother: "You ruined my life and brought me back from Paris because of that thug, and now you owe me the cost of my studies." And Nancy was bowed down with guilt and paid it all. Suddenly, out of the blue, the children's father, Rick, who had been assumed to be dead, came forward again, no, actually, it was his new wife who came forward: "Rick is my husband now, and it is time for him to meet with his children." But Jerry didn't want to meet a father who had once run his index finger around in her vagina to prepare her for her future as a married woman. The son, however, departed for Hawaii and lived for a year in the home of his father's second wife, who must have had a motherly nature and took him to her heart from the start. Rick, on the other hand, still drank his six-pack of beer in the evenings and did a little cleaning in the bed-and-breakfast house during the day, because his wife rented out rooms to tourists, of which there are an infinite number in the paradise of Hawaii. He helped where he could, but most of the time, he couldn't because of his stomach aches and headaches. It was his wife who had to do everything, the beds and the cleaning and the breakfast for the guests. But at least now she had a man in the house. Nancy lacked one after Rudi's disappearance, and she again advertised in various magazines that she had a room for rent: For a gentleman. For a gentleman.

"Why do you only rent to men?" I asked Nancy stupidly. "I'd rather live in a house with a woman as a lodger."

"You don't know what you're talking about," Nancy said: "Women are always cooking and making messes in the kitchen. Men, on the other hand, at most heat the coffee water once in a while, nothing else, a tremendous advantage!"

"I see," I said: "You never stop learning!" After all, I had never had lodgers before! "That is, if she just doesn't go back to bed with one of them again because he doesn't pay, I thought suspiciously. And waited for the next Rudi. But for a long time, no one came. In this break between men, Nancy invited me to travel with her to Mexico on a cruise ship. That was the first cruise of my life, and what a cruise it was! Right from the get-go, everything went wrong. I had flown from Chicago to San Francisco, where Nancy picked me up in her car because we wanted to drive together to Los Angeles and from there to the ship. We had hatched this plan years ago when my back was still fresh and young. Now, however, I had had a serious back surgery and was taking codeine pills daily for the pain, which caused me severe stomach pains unless I could lie down. But that was not possible in the small car. And we were not driving on the famous Route 1 alongside the Pacific Ocean, but on the congested interstate. Nancy had to stop every few minutes. Then she took little yellow pills out of a plastic bag.

"What kind of pills are these?" I asked her.

"Oh, some kind of sedative," she said. Hopefully not Valium, I thought. I noticed that she mumbled when she spoke and had to search for words for a long time. Yet, English was her native language, not mine, and I spoke faster than she did. It took many hours longer than planned until we arrived at our hotel on the way, and I could talk to Larry on the phone. He said anxiously: "I just heard on the news that there has been a terrible truck accident just outside L. A. with one dead and many injured. A bridge is on fire. You won't be able to get through."

"This can't be happening!" I exclaimed in horror: "This can't be happening!" But it was true, and we had to stop at a breakfast place where many desperate people were already eating a piece of cake. A friendly man at a neighboring table explained how to get to Los Angeles and we had him show us the same way on the map. It took many hours before we finally ended up in a shabby Los Angeles hotel — but the drive was through gorgeous orchards, flowers, and vineyards, a little Garden of Eden in the vast paradise of California. We listened to old pop songs and felt like we were eighteen again. And like eighty when we lay in bed.

In Mexico, I witnessed a poignant scene: A young mother in rags under a corrugated-iron roof with a baby in her arms, who looked at me firmly with the look: Look here, at my misery, can you bear not to help me? And I went on without helping her. And didn't forget her. I forgot the whole journey through miserable Mexico, but not her. If only I had helped her! Somehow — with a few dollars, that would have been a help. But I saved while traveling and didn't buy anything, while Nancy went into a kind of shopping frenzy and went to the auctions on the ship and finally bought horrible, brown-colored imitations of impressionists for five thousand dollars.

Mexico encounter

On the way back, we wanted to drive the famous Route 1 along the Pacific Ocean, but the police told us we had to get back on the interstate starting in Malibu because a fire had broken out along the shoreline. Through black plumes of smoke, we saw a dark red sun glowing in the sky like a huge fireball in the cosmos. And we could hardly breathe in the car. This is how I imagine the end of all time, I said to Nancy. "But please, not today," she said dryly.

During the whole trip, I read Hape Kerkeling's book *I'm Off Then* (*Ich bin dann mal weg*). So I survived Mexico and wandered in my mind in Spain on the Camino de Santiago. Just as I had read a book in Prague about Colette in Paris during the time of the German occupation. Just as occupied by the Germans as Prague. And my mother in the huge house, and every now and then, this future war criminal would come and give her a child she didn't want. Me, for example. Maybe that's why I was always happiest in books. Away from reality.

Undaunted, Nancy continued to love art and artists. Her first husband had been a wannabe actor and life artist, her second husband a braggart and person who knows how to make the best of things, and her third — his first name also begins with an R, it's Randy — is now finally a real artist, painting with oil paints and not empty words. But, of course, he can't make a living with that. How fortunate that Nancy has such a good job and a house with a large garden around it, which seems like a forest, that's how beautifully she has planted it with trees. She not only has a green thumb, as they say in America, but also a whole green hand, under which every plant thrives. Unfortunately, not the children.

Randy paints like Friederike takes photographs, so realistically, one could take each of his oil paintings for a photograph. Now, Nancy's walls were already hanging full of fake impressionists in brown bowel-movement colors when Randy moved in with a hundred paintings and more, all clamoring for a place in the sun and on the wall. Her house now resembles an art gallery — like my apartment in Chicago. I really liked that when I visited a few years ago. One of the paintings looks like Hawaii, or what I imagine the Desire Island to be like, because I've never been there, although Jeb and I always wanted to go there to look for his birth father. But he miraculously reappeared all on his own. And Jeb has been sitting in a wheelchair for ten years, because he crashed his motorcycle — no matter how much I warned him about that — into a house wall and has to continue living as a paraplegic, whether he wants to or not. And at first, he didn't want to, then he heard a voice in a dream that said: in five years, everything will be fine again. So, he wanted to live again, even if in five years not everything was fine again. He has made great progress in physical therapy and can swing like a monkey from bar to bar, from parallel bar to parallel bar. His upper arms have become muscular. And he is allowed to smoke cannabis for the dreadful pain, but it fogs his brain, and his studies are making only little progress and have been going on for ten years. He now lives with Randy and his mother in the house with the forest around it, and the two men fight for Nancy's love and care and money. Mostly for money. And Randy doesn't want to marry Nancy, but he doesn't have to in California; there's common law marriage without a marriage certificate, and now Nancy owes Randy in case of a breakup. And Randy wants her to sell the house, because then the new house is his, too, if he chips in some money, and he can stay in it if she dies before him.

"I hope you don't do that," I said to Nancy. "You've always wanted your children to have the house, haven't you?"

"Oh, my children!" Nancy said irritably, "they don't respect me. They should finally become independent and live their own lives!" Randy showed us an oil painting of Jasper the dog, which belongs to Jeb, and I asked him if it was painted for Jeb.

"Yes, I thought so at first, but he doesn't respect me, and now the painting belongs to Nancy!" It's all about respect here in the house, I thought. Or about the house? I hadn't met Randy yet — but he was already around — when Nancy and I took another trip together, certainly our last, because from now on she wants to travel only with Randy or not at all. He doesn't have a passport — only his driver's license and that's enough for the States — and therefore he couldn't travel with Nancy to Rome. She had rented an accommodation there through a travel company to which she paid monthly. For the first time in her life, she visited Larry and me in Chicago, and I heard her say to him from the bedroom: "Gorda feels she always has to talk!" She was right about that: I couldn't stand silence with my girlfriends, only with spouses. They are eloquently silent because everything important has been said in the amorous phase (the "acquisition phase", as it was called by Rüdiger, the rude one).

Larry and I didn't even notice the silence between us, unless I wanted to tell him something and he would say in no uncertain terms: "Shut up!" Then I was offended for a while. With Nancy, I talked incessantly because she herself said nothing or had nothing to say, who knows for sure. With Katja, on the other hand, I hardly talked at all because she talked incessantly. I enjoyed that very much because, after evenings with her, I always fell asleep particularly well. Nancy, on the other hand, forced me to speak through her persistent silence. Until I heard her say: "Gorda thinks she always has to talk!" I'll show her, I thought. And kept silent as much as I could during the whole trip. As early as on the plane I read contentedly in my thick book. It was, appropriately enough, Goethe's *Italian Journey*, about which I was soon to give a lecture. Nancy was looking in front of her at her own book of Reader's Digest texts, or she was sleeping. She could sleep with her eyes closed or open. In between, she would take these interesting little yellow pills from a plastic bag and quickly swallow them before I could inquire about their nature.

Having arrived at our accommodations in Rome, I discovered that it was a proper apartment with bedroom, living room, and kitchenette and a large bathroom with a useless anteroom. I had never lived in such a luxury apartment in one of the most expensive big cities in the world. Immediately, the joy of it put me in a talkative mood. Nevertheless, remembering Nancy's words, I unpacked my seven-to-eight things in silence. And at last, I dared to ask her about the yellow pills that apparently did her so much good and made her a completely peaceful, silent woman who could sleep anywhere with her eyes open or closed. I wanted to be like her, and with yellow pills, if need be. Because we had to sleep in one bed, and that's always risky (unless it's your life partner), even if the bed is very big, like ours in Rome. At night in bed, the best friend, through no fault of her own, can turn into an enemy that you wish to hell. Nancy willingly gave me a sachet of the miracle pills; as a nurse, she could easily get her hands on them. "But don't tell Larry about them," was one of the few phrases she managed to muster.

I slept like I was in heaven, although we don't even know if you sleep in heaven or not. Don't they play the harp there and sing sweet melodies to it? Nancy lay next to me — also equipped with a blindfold and earplugs like me — and slept the sleep of the righteous, without moving, on her back, like an Egyptian mummy in a sarcophagus. I, on the other hand, had to turn on my side to disappear into the nothingness of sleep, which I still was able to do back then. Not so today. Today, my hips hurt and prevent me from falling asleep. I woke up in Rome after eight hours of sleep, amazed and completely rested. There was no trace of jet lag, which I usually suffered from for days on end. A miracle, these yellow pills! And the wonderful silence between us, so restful! We sat at the breakfast table like a married couple and ate wordlessly and calmly the sugary breads and drank the delicious black coffee, which deserves the name coffee and is not a brown American filtrate. In the afternoon, we went on the offered tours — and in the morning we both read in books about Rome's treasures and ruins accumulated for many thousands of years. And, at night before bed, I read Goethe's immortal work, his *Italian Journey*, which is one of the great travelogues of the glories of Italy, a work that acted on me like a sleeping pill and greatly enhanced the power of the yellow pills. While Nancy needed two of them in the evening, I only needed one, because the Italian trip helped me find sleep.

What a pity, I thought, that I had learned Latin in my school days and at the university and not Italian, which now would have helped me and Nancy much more to get along in the thicket of the giant city. What a lost time I spent with the dead language, while the living Rome's architecture and art would have opened up to me much more intensively. On our return trip, the customs officer asked us: "Do you speak Italian?"

"No," I answered. "I only speak German, English and French."

"And why no Italian?" he asked, comically exasperated, throwing his hands skyward: "You have to learn Italian!"

He was right, not even the cab drivers of this cosmopolitan city, flooded with tourists from all over the world, spoke a minimum of English. "My teacher very bad," one of them said to me. At least he made me laugh and not despair, like the others. And Remo had not known Modern Greek in Athens, where he had traveled with his best friend Peter, but had studied Ancient Greek for seven years in high school; what a waste of time! But, of course, his brother Jean, who by now had taught Greek and Latin at John Hopkins University for many years, thought otherwise. The knowledge of Greek and Latin would unlock the past for us, and no future worth living would be possible without this knowledge of the past! Once, when I gave a reading at Loyola University in Baltimore, Maryland, I stayed in a nice hotel across the street from Johns Hopkins University. And I walked over to Jean's campus. It was early May, and a lovely, colorful spring garden awaited me, while in Chicago we were still buried in ice and snow. I had called Jean to let him know about my reading. But no one answered, and no one called back. What I didn't know was that he had died on February 17, exactly on his eighty-sixth birthday. And here I did so want to show the man, who had once treated me with such contempt, what I had become, not the mother of Remo's children, his despised cleaner and cook, but a gifted lecturer. As a poet, however, he had already recognized me, because one day — the Gorda devil was riding me again — I sent him my books with warm greetings from the former sister-in-law. He wrote me a magnanimous letter and probably wanted to make up for the wrong he had done to me:

Baltimore, 8th of April 2010

Dear Gorda,
Your new book of poems, *Rescue Means Love*, is a real joy, and I thank you, also on behalf of my wife, most sincerely. Sometimes, you achieve, with very simple means, the most amazing effects, and one retains the impression of a brilliant firework, which sometimes hisses, but always ignites and conjures up the most amazing figures in the sky. You will not soon be imitated by anyone else!
With all good wishes and warm greetings …

Even Remo had not hesitated and celebrated the poems of his former bride, whom he could no longer respect as his future wife, by writing:

Bern, 8th of March 2010

Dear Gorda,
Thank you for *Rescue Means Love*. Once and for all (or however you write that), Peter Rühmkorf has given the accurate judgment of your poems — there is nothing to be taken away from it, and this is confirmed by the texts gathered in this volume. So, no complexes, no auto-skepticism — or just to make a poem out of it …

These letters did me good for a few days. But soon I asked myself again: And where are your children? I gave birth to nothing but stillborn poems, which no one in Germany knows and no one wants to know. I go into eternity empty-handed …

And Ulla Hahn took over the concept from my manuscript, which, at that time, was still called *My soul is called Anne Frank*: Like me, she wrote a novel of development and education in three parts. And when we discussed her book at my book club in Chicago, one of the attendees said: "Sometimes I felt like I was reading your *Mephisto*." "Yes," I said, "she was borrowing from me; is that being called a soul mate or osmosis or something else?" I didn't want to use the ugly word plagiarism. And isn't imitation the highest form of flattery? I wrote her a long letter with all the similarities that couldn't be coincidence ("the best friend Doris, the one with the beautiful clothes!"), but she didn't answer. If I had been Mörike himself, as a poet of German language in America, his poems, his stories, and his wonderful novel *Nolten the Painter* would have been dead to the Germans. Despite this, I must be brave when I think of the fate of my ignored poems. And in my German cultural club in Chicago, they don't appreciate the fact that my name tag has my doctoral degree on it, which has cost me so many years of my life, and it was suggested to me that I shouldn't talk about myself when a professor gave a lecture on Ingeborg Bachmann, that it distracted from Bachmann. The real poetess. And one of my book club members said I talked too much, as if one could give readings and lectures without speaking. Suddenly, I remember that Isaak Dinesen (in Germany her name is Tanja Blixen) was not allowed to talk about her brilliant stories in her parents' house in Denmark, because otherwise, she would cause her sisters inferiority complexes. Her own mother dictated that she does so. Like mine, who said to me: "Don't talk about your many travels in front of the family; they are hard-working people." And she didn't come to my readings so that she wouldn't have to see me embarrass myself in front of the audience. And so I have to hide my knowledge, my stillborn works, my wit, and my quick-wittedness under the cloak of modesty so as not to damage the fragile egos of my friends. Well, what have I spent a lifetime learning and writing for? I ask myself in horror. Definitely not for Larry, who is not interested in people and their novels, only in medicine, mathematics, photography, crossword puzzles, and Sudoku.

"Shut up," he says when I speak of Goethe's love for Mrs. von Stein: "You know, literature means nothing to me."

"This isn't about literature," I say, exasperated: "It's about people."

"People don't interest me either," says Larry, "you do know that. So leave me alone with this literary stuff!"

Sometimes, I think I've spent my life learning and writing only for Remo, he, to whom I sent everything I produced first. Even after our separation, which was never a real separation. Thereafter even more so, because I started writing quite late. And he was enthusiastic about the poems, and even when he was no longer enthusiastic about me as a woman, that is, until after menopause, which brings even the most beautiful Loreleis from their rocks to the stove. And cooking makes work and fat, my beloved Friederike has always said. But she herself has become thinner over the years; I, on the other hand, became fat for two. On our trip to the Loire chateaux, we both ate the same, but she lost five pounds, and I gained five, making a ten-pound difference. Life is not fair. On the Loire trip, I realized for the first time that Friederike was not actually traveling with me for my sake, but because of the men we would meet along the way. Friederike wanted to get away from the rude Rüdiger, like I secretly wanted to get away from Larry. But I always found our friendship bond more important than any man we met along the way: they were all married anyway, or they were gay or otherwise handicapped. With a cane or a walker. Already on the journey at that time I suspected that Friederike would leave me because of a man. In my story I called her Helga.

A Journey to Forget

You always know beforehand what is coming. You just don't want to have known it beforehand. There was, for example, my bus trip with Helga to the castles of the Loire, and we were both in love. She happily so, me unhappily so. Which meant that Helga wrote little letters and cards and looked for stamps and mailboxes in the towns, and always with that penetrating smile of happiness on her face that drives someone who is unhappily in love to devour pastries. I never ate as many pastries as I did then during that crazy trip, and gained weight, even though we walked through the castles from six in the morning until eight at night, sometimes through five a day and the towns to boot. Often, I suffered from an upset stomach and tossed and turned groaning in a church garden, but at the next bakery I bought comfort croissants again. Because I couldn't write cards and letters, I knew that. I would never have eaten more Danishes anymore if I, too, had been allowed to carry my hugs to the post office. And at the dinners, Helga rose before the rest of us to quickly call the man I didn't know, for whom she seemed to live on pure air, while I ate for two, for me and my shame. And my shame and I became more and more visible. Still, there is no better means of getting over a love sickness than such a trip. I recommend twelve days of Loire châteaux to any slightly broken-hearted lover, and in more severe cases another twelve days of Burgundy, followed by three weeks of Provence. After six or seven weeks of such bus tours that make people go out, even Camille would not know Alfredo's name anymore, and finally she would have forgotten her own, which is the surest sign that one is on the path of healing thoughtlessness. But at the beginning of the journey, one doesn't want to be healed at all, one wants to mourn. To stare into the sunflower fields with the exclamation: And to be allowed to admire them with him! To look down into the Loire waters with the knowledge: This is how the happiness of your life flows away ... But the wise tour guide seems to know that he has loaded a bus full of lovesick hearts, and therefore he wisely plans castle upon village and village upon church, so that the mourning travel community hardly finds time to linger and lament. In general, he — who was much younger than most of us — had something therapeutic about him. Every day, we had to change bus seats, always moving one seat ahead, so that no one felt disadvantaged. I would have understood that with children who were five years old, but with children of thirty to forty years and older, that's already a testament to his psychological sensitivity. When you're young, you think people will eventually grow up and not envy each other for bus seats. Only a person who has reached a certain maturity knows that they never will.

One of the passengers always sat by herself and didn't even participate in the dinner conversations. We thought she was particularly heartbroken and was therefore using up her free time licking her wounds, and certainly she needed three more trips to find the strength for saving distractions. But, on the last day, the mute turned to me and said: You know, I make a trip like this every year, and I never talk to people. At first, I did, but there were always arguments on the bus, and I don't have enough time to spend arguing. I had just been talking about an argument I had had the night before. Right at the beginning of the trip, Helga and I, naïve as we were, had sat down with this unknown couple, during coffee breaks in the afternoon and at morning and evening meals. At first, I had chatted with the man because he was a historian, and I had studied history, and he was interested in my book on Frederick the Great, which I always kept in my hand in the unlikely event that there was nothing to look at. But then Helga had latched onto the historian's lips; I think it's instinctive with her. Why talk to a woman, when there is a man nearby, that is her unacknowledged life motto. And even if the man were as toothless as our historian, who was missing a canine tooth on the left and two molars on the right, because he had not found time to have this defect corrected by a dentist. At first, I was not sorry for the historian. In my pain, I had become quite indifferent to the difference between man and woman as discussion partners. So, I turned to the woman with all the courtesy I had paid to the man. While Helga and the historian hurried through stores and alleyways, I sat in cafés with the woman who liked walking less and discussed insignificant things, because the significant matter in my life was a shame to be concealed. Now, this woman had a most tormenting quality for me: She never believed that I wanted to talk harmlessly about God, the world, and the weather, but she always thought that I wanted to lecture her. And there was nothing she hated more than being lectured. She vigorously denied my hints that the weather was beautiful, that the last castle we visited was a miracle of architecture, that the pastries we had just eaten were delicious, and that the coffee had never been brewed so well. No, the weather was too fresh, the castle obstructed, the pastries tough to bite and the coffee the purest liquid garbage. Again and again I offered conversation topics, one more harmless than the other, but nothing helped to cure her of the idea: This woman thinks she knows everything better than I do! And more and more often I thought I was sitting at home with my mother when she was having her 'no' day and I was calling the sky blue and she was calling it gray, and I was finding the happy guessing game sad, and she was finding it entertaining.

And so I sat again like a ten-year-old in front of the castles of the Loire and let a woman lecture me that she didn't want to be lectured. Until I tried to keep my mouth shut completely, but there was a silence between us that offended her strangely, and she asked more and more irritably what was wrong with me. I think I got a stomachache from all the snails, I said despondently, hoping for her pity and a comforting encouragement. You don't get stomach aches from snails, the woman exclaimed, indignant that I wanted to lecture her again. Then I started to get angry at Helga. I mean, she could have taken care of this opposition incarnate every once in a while; she could have stayed in the cafés every so often, and I could have hurried through antiquities with the toothless historian! And what I would never have noticed, if the woman had not always contradicted me so spiritedly, I became more painfully aware of every day: Helga didn't care if I felt bad. Helga didn't see my displeasure standing in the room when she had walked in front of me through the breakfast room door in the morning, in order to sit safely at the historian's side, while I had to put up with the first objection from his wife, unpleasantly and gloomy. You also have to stay with the woman every once in a while, I told her repeatedly, which Helga acknowledged with a reserved mien and even more animated conversation at the historian's side.

To escape this disgusting woman, I began to conversationally approach the tour guide, who wrote a doctoral thesis on the medieval churches of the Provence, which the historian punished with scornful remarks, since he had declared the young man's lectures humbug from the first church and castle tour on. So these were his areas of expertise: history and painting, he explained, and such a greenhorn couldn't make him believe that the painting was from the eighteenth century, that was pure nineteenth. The guide, again, proved his amazing deep-psychological skills by letting the historian mutter critically, cough and giggle caustically, without intervening with an energetic "That's enough!" Or had he been prescribed a course on the treatment of maladjusted travelers? I would have needed such a course, because then I would never have gotten into trouble.

We had to get up at six in the morning and pack our suitcases, because most of the time we spent the night somewhere else in order to be able to cope with the daily workload of five castles and maybe a church or two. Immediately, at the first castle, Helga eyed the visitor troops uneasily, turned around and left the castle hall towards the garden without notifying me in any way. Where is she going? I thought worriedly, but then the gawking stream pulled me into the king's room, which I looked at with pleasure, but without being able to forget Helga's absence. Perhaps she felt sick, I feared, and looked from one of the higher rooms into the park, where my beloved friend — for really, I loved her very much at that time — seemed to be dreaming under a tree of happy embrace, all fours stretched out most healthily and contentedly. And so Helga dreamed away five castles a day, while I suffered hundreds of chambers and halls, bedsteads and chests of drawers, fireplaces, hairy satyrs and artfully spreading nymphs. No wonder, when in the evening, shaken by nerves, I had a hard time enduring the contradiction of the historian's wife, while Helga, in a fresh mood from so much good castle garden air, jokingly agreed with the historian in all things at supper, and the latter visibly recovering from the daily ration of marital contradiction. Oh, how I would have liked to talk to my friend myself instead of to this aimlessly

Interior of Chateau Chenonceau; photo by Dennis Jarvis

325

and indiscriminately denying woman, who didn't let a crumb of conversation fall under the table without emphatically treading on it with her foot. What an angel Helga is in comparison! With her; the sky is blue when you call it blue, the castle beautiful because you found it beautiful, and the book that you gave her is captivating.

But when I told her one more time: "Hey, you, I can't stand that woman anymore," Helga didn't feel compassion and wanted to rush through the breakfast door in front of me again. Then I was seized by a stupid anger that made me run faster than usual; and so it was I who came victoriously through the door and to the side of the ugly man. Helga and the contradictory wife looked a little puzzled, I saw that with satisfaction. And I put up with the morning-coffee-with-croissant, without the shrill accompaniment of the no-but-I'm-not-at-all-of-your-opinion sentences that I detested.

In my satisfaction, I had not paid attention to whether the historian's wife also brought out her hedgehog-like personality in Helga's meekness. It could have been that my brashly presented banalities (ah, that tastes good!) aroused her anger. Helga's mild, almost submissive voice, on the other hand, has paralyzed many a sprightly fighter. If only I had hurried through the dining room doors before her every day, I would have spared myself the final argument! And when I looked at the photos of the castles of the Loire, I would not always have thought of the failed evening but, for example, of the wonderfully furnished state rooms, which in all castles mostly waited in vain for the visit of the high lord and king, so that the buildings evoked the melancholy impression of beautiful, but unhappily loving princesses. Most of the photos are of Helga, and there I stand to the left of the castle with the woman animated by contradiction, and here I stand with her to the right of the castle. One can clearly see on my face that I have just been lectured by her. "No, there I don't agree with you at all," should have escaped as a speech bubble from her mouth. By the way, when looking at the photos, I never knew whether I was looking at Chinon, Ussé, Chambord, or Chenonceau; Helga always had to explain this to me, she who had spent hours sitting in the garden indelibly absorbing the contours of the castles, while I couldn't point out a chest of drawers in the room in question or a fireplace in the corresponding chamber. A hullabaloo of castle rooms and naves reigned in my brain, and an anger at the historian's wife in my heart. And this anger was also directed at Helga, because she refused to talk to a woman when a man was near her. And that's why there was the argument last evening, which could have been avoided effortlessly if Helga had thought about me for once and not always about this principle.

Already in the afternoon I got a nervous heartbeat, because the negationist woman had not missed any opportunity to explain to me my erroneous sensory impressions. Help me, I said one last time, or I'll have a pessimistic outlook. But that didn't help, quite the opposite. Before dinner, I had gone to bed with a migraine suppository and shattered nerves, when Helga spent an hour working with various instruments on her suitcase, which refused to open, instead of asking the porter for help, as I had advised her. Pain-stricken and with uneasy premonitions, I made my way to the dining room, where Helga was already sitting happily chatting at the side of the toothless man — but a man is a man — while his wife, spouting contradictions, invited me to sit next to her. What else could I do but sit next to her? Pull yourself together, I ordered myself, it is the last evening.

"Une bouteille de Chablis," I said to the waiter, as I did every evening, and off went Mrs. Historian: Poor Helga, she really has nothing to laugh about with you. Why, I asked her puzzled, still not grasping the whole extent of this robust stupidity. You don't even let her order her own wine, she said indignantly. Since Helga had personally asked me to take on this onerous task for her, I felt like yelling at the historian's wife. Instead, I indirectly attacked my beloved friend. Well, Helga is also quite lazy, I said, which is probably true in substance, but need not have been brought up here. When, after the usual contradictions, Mrs. Historian, who was in full counterdrive, made the remark: My husband and I said to each other right at the beginning of the trip: We have to support poor Helga, who is under the thumb of her friend, that's when I had had enough.

"No one is under anyone's thumb here," I shouted, "or, if any, I am only under yours: You always think you have to contradict!"

"No!" she objected vehemently, "Actually, I've always been on your side!"

"No!" I said, "You have always contradicted me!"

"No!" she said, "I have defended you more than once!"

"No!" said I, "I only remember that the sky was gray when it was blue to me, and that the castles were obstructed when they were a delight to my eyes!"

"No!" exclaimed the incensed wife, airily, "no, and no again!"

"I don't understand how I put up with you all this trip!" I continued. "Because you don't suffer twelve days of contradiction without wanting to contradict for twelve days."

"No!" cried the wife indignantly.

"No!" cried the husband indignantly.

"No!" cried my inner voice, "Now you stop it!" Then, happily, the couple rose and left the last-dinner table together, freshly united until the next marital contradiction. I was left looking like a victor who had shot himself in the chest. With my self-confidence bleeding out, I stepped up to the bar, where Helga was already sitting next to my friend, the young tour guide, because she said to herself: Why should I talk to a woman when there is a man around? The next day, we drove all the way through from France to Cologne, where we had to change to another bus that took us all the way to our northern German cities. On our connecting bus was a good-looking man in the right years, whom I quizzed about his trip to Brittany while Helga touched up her makeup, as I watched from afar. Then she joined us, steered the conversation into her lines of interest, exchanged addresses with him, and promised information that only she and no one else was capable of giving. This man later wrote Helga a letter, and the two met. There, strangely enough, she asked him about the impression we girlfriends had made on him. He is supposed to have said that I wanted to push Helga into the background. But I don't believe it.

Helga didn't marry the letter recipient from the Loire, who was unknown to me, but another man. From then on, I was not allowed to visit my beloved friend, who had spent two weeks with me every year, for more than twenty-four hours. Probably, because otherwise, I would have pushed her into the background, to my shame.

Just as Nancy now travels with Randy, and Friederike with Herbert, I travel with Hanni, my Swiss girlfriend from the beloved Emmenthal, since Larry no longer wants to travel because of his back pain. Hanni had just moved into a large, light-filled house that her architect husband had built for his family, when he said to me: "Gorda, you are a beautiful woman. I think Hanni had to work way too hard with the move." This reminded me of the time Larry had fallen to his knees in front of a woman, spread his arms and exclaimed: "Oh, you're as beautiful as Angie Dickinson!"

I sat on the sofa next to her and thought, is he nuts? And blushed with shame. Hanni, who was mopping the floor, came shooting up with the mop in her hand and looked at him bitterly. I looked at her and at him — back and forth and again. And thought: Is he crazy? Is he trying to annoy her by praising me? Does he want to ruin our friendship? Hanni, who had once been so beautiful, had become very thin since the move, her cheeks fell in and her skin seemed to have turned gray, like only hair does. The whites of her eyes had turned yellow from the exertion, and her two front teeth should have been repaired long ago, but because of the daily drudgery she hadn't gotten around to going to the dentist yet. I, on the other hand, struggled with the family pounds on my body, starving myself when I wasn't in Emmenthal with Hanni who spoiled me with fried potatoes and fricassee and a Bernese selection of cold cuts and Swiss bread. She herself hardly ate any of it: she only secretly snacked on the bars of Lindt chocolate that I had brought her and her husband as a gift. Hanni was as addicted to sugar as I was addicted to bread and potatoes. I also liked to drink from her pink wine, which she hardly sipped. As a glutton and frequent drinker, I sat in her kitchen, which she had painstakingly wiped clean, and looked refreshed at the mountains of the Bernese Oberland, which could be seen clearly on the edge of the horizon. And I looked forward to our day trips to Lake Thun, which I loved even more than Lake Geneva, because it was narrower and surrounded by high mountains that looked down on it like mighty giants. I must admit I was a little pleased for a moment at the time, because Karl-Hansi thought I was beautiful. To my misfortune, at the expense of his wife, and our friendship.

I had gotten engaged at Lake Thun myself on a 29th of September many, many years ago — and every year Hanni and

I celebrated the canceled engagement — which also caused my heart to be damaged — by laughing derisively: at the lake, about Remo's three Cs (children-cooking-church), and the three Os (Obey-obey-obey); I lamented inwardly about the lost happiness of being allowed to live in glorious Switzerland, at the side of the man who could, as one individual, replace mother and father, brother and cousin. And I had never found a substitute for him: with whom should I talk in the States about Gottfried Keller, Conrad Ferdinand Meyer, and Max Frisch? With my shut-the-mouth Larry?

When I went to Hanni's place a year later — after the visit, during which Karl-Hansi suddenly considered me to be beautiful, although he hadn't paid much attention to me before — she knocked her elbow into his side as I was leaving, so that he winced, and then he stammered out the sentence: "I'm just so happy for Hanni when you come" ... Oh God, I thought, she'd been chewing on that for a whole year, him calling me a beautiful woman. If only he had kept his mouth shut! For a long time, Hanni had been the 'most beautiful woman' in the region, next to whom other women didn't count.

"She was the star in our family," her sister Heidemarie told me, and how terribly she supposedly had been treated by Hanni in her childhood and youth: full of contempt, so condescendingly. And Hanni would never have called her as a young married woman, she never wrote her a letter or a postcard, she wrapped herself in aggressive silence towards every one of her three sisters. For Hanni — the eldest — these three sisters need not have existed. She told me funny stories about the three of them, at which I could laugh heartily, because I didn't know that, one day, I would turn into one of these despised sisters. And I didn't know the three of them and didn't have to be ashamed when I laughed about them. The youngest, Hanni told me, was so stupid, she could only paint Easter eggs or wrap them in self-crocheted lace.

"She has nothing to do at home. Look at her writing," she said, showing me one of those Easter cards with bunnies and colorful eggs on it and the usual texts, like: I wish you a happy Easter with many contemplative hours ... which didn't exist at all, because all the women had to cook and bake all the time like at Christmas time. About the other sister she said: "She has sold herself badly," and wanted to say with it, 'married'. And her current husband was an unemployed bricklayer and would have to drive trucks at night, and so her sister would be alone at night, and when she worked, her husband would be asleep. And her sister, Heidemarie, who was only two years younger than her, had a money mania and only wore the most expensive things, Hermès and Prada, because she believed that that would make her belong to the elite of the country, according to the motto: You are what you wear. And being rich meant being educated, even without education, because she hadn't managed to finish high school and would certainly never read anything other than *Vogue*, and her handwriting would also cast doubt on her intellectual aspirations. But then Karl-Hansi committed suicide — and nothing was the same anymore. I will never forget the fourth of August, when I called her, even though I usually did so only in September to announce my arrival ("Clean up nicely!").

"How are you doing?" I asked her, happy to talk to her.

"Badly," she said in a grave voice entirely foreign to me, "something terrible has happened!" "

"What?" I exclaimed in a panic.

"Karl-Hansi is dead!"

"That can't be!"

"Yes, he drowned. I had to identify him at the morgue at six this morning. My daughter was with me. If it weren't for her, I would have died too."

"Drowned, a grown man?"

"He went for a swim yesterday, at noon, in the heat. And jumped into the Aare River." I remembered that we had once passed a bridge from which exuberantly cheering children jumped into the rushing river and floated all the way to the nearby swimming pool. Unfortunately, Karl-Hansi, who was a fat man over fifty, had also jumped into the river in the sweltering heat and washed up at the swimming pool of his childhood and youth. But no longer as Karl-Hansi, only as a corpse. Later, the autopsy showed that he had suffered a cold shock, his heart had stopped immediately. He had not drowned; no water was found in his lungs. In the Bern morgue, next to Karl-Hansi's body, lay dozens of young people who had drowned on a river trip. They had actually drowned, with water in the lungs. As if it makes a difference how you die in water. But for life insurance purposes, it can make a big difference. Hanni was asked whether Karl-Hansi would have wanted to take his own life. He knew, didn't he, that he had a sick, rather too big, fatty heart? Hanni didn't know that. Whether he had already tried to take his own life before? What would the family say in that case? But the family didn't say anything on the matter, because Hanni would not have received the life insurance money in case of suicide.

"There's no way he ever thought about taking his own life," she swore to the investigating committee. "Never, ever, such a good family man. His family meant more than anything to him on earth," she swore, turning to me: "A father of two doesn't commit suicide; I'm sure it was an accident, Gorda!"

"Yes, it was definitely an accident," I affirmed her words, though I thought: Who can know with such certainty? Hadn't he been strange at the last farewell, saying to me when Hanni was already in the car, starting the engine, because she wanted to drive me to Bern to the station: "After all, you are still a beautiful woman." And he emphasized the "after all" and smiled so strangely, so intensely, as if he had something important to say to me, he, who never said much to me. But this time he wanted to say something, but didn't dare. And I smiled at him with the smile: now say it, out with it! This was my forever farewell to Karl-Hansi, whom I had known as a handsome young man with his thick blond curls above the face of a male angel. This face with the dear smile of his full lips had been inherited by his daughter, who now adorns it like a female angel.

And when he said to Hanni: "Our daughter is the most beautiful girl far and wide," he was actually saying: My face is the most beautiful far and wide. But at that time, he had already covered it with thick cheeks, carried a lot of fat under his chin and an enormous belly in front of him. He, who had once been the most beautiful man in Emmenthal, had married the most beautiful girl, the Swiss expatriate who didn't fit into the valley and had never been accepted by the village population. Her Swiss German enunciation had a slight High German touch because she had grown up in Germany. And the people of Emmenthal didn't like that. Hanni turned away from the villagers, hurt and haughty, and concentrated entirely on her husband and children, saying tersely "Gruezi" when she met a native and passing him by as if he were air to her, but not a good-smelling one. She had lived like that for thirty years; she didn't need friendships in the village, she said to me, her three sisters were enough for her life. When absolutely necessary, she called Heidemarie once in a while, but only very rarely, because she always gave her advice on how to dress and where to buy her clothes, as if a country woman — and Hanni had become a country woman in the course of time, happily working in her vegetable garden and feeding the chickens punctually in the morning and evening — buys from Hermès or Gucci. Instead, Hanni cut her roses in old jeans and baggy sweaters and harvested the cherries in the fall for delicious compote and jam in the winter. She was an all-around contented woman. Up until she wasn't: that was the time when her late-born son Bernd cut ties with her, because he now preferred to play with his school friends rather than spend time with his old mother. And she asked herself, what am I going to do with the rest of my life?

"Maybe you should take an adult education class in Bern?" I suggested to her. "My friend Jutta is learning pottery; she really enjoys it."

But Hanni didn't think much of pottery. "That would make a huge mess," she said angrily, "you'd need a basement room for that, and I don't have one; in our house, that's the office."

"Then take a course in painting with watercolors like my friend Monika," I suggested to her.

"My sister Heidemarie already paints, you know that, and I don't want to get in her way."

"Yes, she paints cats very beautifully, but couldn't you paint dogs or your chickens or the flowers in your flower garden?"

"Please, leave it to me," she said dismissively, and I fell silent, slightly miffed, because Hanni never took advice. But then again, did I take every piece of advice offered? For example, the one to leave Larry, as my friend Elke advised me, when I had just decided to allow him to move back into our shared apartment, after I had advised him to rent the empty neighboring apartment in our high-rise building.

"We're not getting divorced," I had said to him. "Rather, we have a temporary separation. We can figure out what we want to do in the future." And Larry moved all his junk into the apartment next door, filling the living room and the bedrooms, with barely enough room for a comfortable chair, a small dining table, and the overly large television. And I thanked heaven when I had our main apartment, as I now called it, to myself and my clutter, my thousand-plus books, my forty pictures of Rudolf Führmann on the walls (his framed photographs Larry took with him), my record collection, and the many coats and jackets and blazers and pants in the closets. Finally, the middle room also was habitable again for guests who, however, rarely come, since Friederike lives with and travels with her Herbert, and he doesn't want to fly to Chicago because he doesn't want to fly at all with his fear of flying and people. "I can't stand so many people as are crowded on a plane," he says. He has this fear of flying in common with my sister-in-law Astrid — and they both seem so brash and fearless in everyday life, but on a plane, they tremble like aspen leaves — isn't that what they say in Germany, aspen leaves? Now I have been living abroad for so many years and I write in German, although, maybe, I am not able to do it anymore.

After Karl-Hansi's death, Hanni learned from her sister Heidemarie that he had had a sick heart and would have been irredeemably lost without a transplant. Everyone seemed to know this: her daughter, Anneli, and even the innkeeper in the village, only Hanni didn't know. He hadn't told her anything about that. Only lately did he begin to stub out his partially smoked cigarettes in the ashtray or in the potting soil of the pots on the balcony.

"That means he's been trying to quit smoking," Larry said to me, and I told Hanni.

"Oh, I see," she said, despairingly: "and why did he not tell me about it?"

"He didn't want to worry you!" The strangest thing was that he pushed his father up the hill in a wheelchair, as if he were a healthy young man, not a man in his mid-fifties, and with a heart condition to boot.

"Maybe he wanted to lose weight?" I suggested as an explanation.

"But he was eating pasta and meat and sweets as usual — surely no one who wants to lose weight does that?" I remembered saying to him, on the last visit, out of the blue or not quite out of the blue: "You're at risk," when he tried to shove another piece of greasy meat into his mouth.

To my amazement, he put the piece of meat back on the plate and speared a lettuce leaf on his fork instead; he, who couldn't stand to have lettuce or anything green on a plate. He knows that he's at risk, I thought, startled. And where do I get off saying such an ominous phrase to my host? Surely that's not proper! And I wouldn't be thinking about this sentence now if it hadn't been prophetic and Karl-Hansi had died soon after — in the same year. And now we ask ourselves, Hanni and I, whether he planned his suicide or whether it 'happened' to him, that is, only half intentionally. Or whether he really wanted to die? We can no longer ask him, just as I can't ask my biological father whether he repented of what he had done or had to do in the Third Reich before hanging himself from a bed sheet in his cell in the German city of Wuppertal. And I would like to know whether I am the daughter of a repentant man or of a hardened murderer who, in Nuremberg, wanted to avoid his just punishment of hanging by committing suicide.

How advantageous that I only had feline children and not human children with murderer genes. And Larry said he would have married me anyway, even if he had known the truth about me — and he was only glad he didn't go into politics, because the dirt on my stick would have been discovered and I would have been pilloried in public opinion. To be cursed unto the third and fourth generation. Is that only in the Old Testament? Or also in the New?

And Hanni secretly wonders if her children have a man for a father who committed suicide. And when her son stopped working and instead sat sobbing in bed, Anneli, full of fear, had her brother admitted to a clinic so that he couldn't kill himself. But Bernd was not grateful to his sister for this; instead, he wrote her a hateful letter: "How could you do this to me? It's your fault that I got locked up for three days!" Because all people look for the blame somewhere else, except in themselves. Always in a neighbor. Or with the sister. Just like Max and Astrid also blamed me for the rifts in their marriage. Me, who lived far away from them in Chicago. And Max never visited me in Chicago, nor even called me. The sister he was so connected to.

When Hanni sat alone and distraught in her lovely house, I directed all my feelings of friendship toward her. To comfort her, to be by her side, to help her survive. Because she needed help. A lot, a whole lot had been taken from her. She discovered that the house was heavily mortgaged and had to be sold, the life insurance amount was barely enough to help her get through the next year. The lawyer, a family friend, asked her in horror: "Why didn't Karl-Hansi consult with me about the legal situation?

Could I have averted the worst? Why did he allow you to register in the land register, which is a madness under these circumstances? Now you are liable to the bank for his enormously high mortgage."

Karl-Hansi had registered the house in his name; Hanni had not been mentioned anywhere in the papers, until suddenly the people from the bank appeared and made sure that she registered herself in the land register. "In for a penny, in for a pound," was the motto now. Hanni was sitting there with over a million in debts — and was unemployed because, years ago, Karl-Hansi had asked her to stay at home altogether. He wanted that his wife be there only for the house, for him, and for the children. For that, Hanni had given up her tenured position with pension rights at the consulate. And now she cleaned all day for free, when she wasn't cooking dinner, tended the garden, and ironed three shirts a day, which he needed because he sweated so profusely due to his obesity. And he found nothing more disgusting than sitting in a wet shirt during his numerous negotiations with clients. Hanni hardly saw him because of that. And her son went to play with his friends. And Hanni often didn't speak a word to a human being for days, only to the cats. Because in the evenings, Karl-Hansi wanted to relax and not talk to his wife about his clients and their building plans. As soon as he got home, he took the TV remote and turned on the program he loved, sports events, for example, that Hanni couldn't stand. That's why she saw many movies only halfway. A second set would have been a blessing, but then the couple would not only have lived separately during the day, but also watched separately in the evenings. In the long run, the work became too much for Hanni, and she got back pain from all the bending over.

"Say you need help with the cleaning," I said to Hanni.

"You can't do that in the countryside."

"Why not?"

"People here think back pain is a lame excuse."

"It doesn't matter what people think," I contradicted her. "You don't have anything to do with them anyway!" Nevertheless, Hanni was very careful about her reputation in the village and didn't dare hire a cleaning lady. As if I were worried about my reputation in Greenland, even though I have never been there and don't want to go. Hanni was more concerned about her reputation in the village than about her health. I wouldn't keep on talking about Karl-Hansi calling me a beautiful woman if he hadn't destroyed our friendship with that, even if nobody wants to believe that. It is nothing but the truth. To cheer up the desperate Hanni, I asked my friend Katja if we could spend a week in her condo in Southern France, and she said yes and described to us exactly the travel route there. Hanni drove us in her car through Italy — it was a boring, flat piece of Italy — and I was so happy to be on the road with her that I didn't notice that I was talking incessantly. And I also didn't notice that Hanni, who used to chat so lively — so eagerly that Karl-Hansi once said to her, you have to let your guest talk, too — didn't utter a word. Once, she said briefly: "You understand that I am depressed, but surely I will soon be able to feel joy again."

How much my joy of life must have got on her nerves! And I was much happier about her presence than about the boring Italian lowlands. And, out of joy, I talked and talked. And she mourned in silence. The apartment in Vence, unknown to me until then, was large and pretty; it had two bedrooms and a living room with a balcony where you could see the beautiful blue Mediterranean Sea. How wonderfully it glistened! Katja had bought the apartment from her older neighbors when they could no longer travel, and she had taken over everything, the furniture, the beds, the dishes in the kitchen, and the maintenance couple in the building. An ideal arrangement! How I would have loved to own such an apartment! Right next to Vence is the charming old city of St. Paul-de-Vence, where Simone Signoret and Yves Montand lived, as I learned from a biography about him that I was reading at the time. Further below by the sea was the megalopolis of Nice, where I had spent twelve days with Larry a few years back. Larry, however, refused to drive a car in the chaotic traffic of Europe, so we had to rely on taking boring excursions with organized bus companies or walk around Nice on our own. During the travel tour with Larry to Monaco and Cannes it rained cats and dogs — but, for Hanni and me, the sun inevitably shone (when angels travel?). It burned down on the dark blue sea when we enjoyed a big ice cream sundae on the terrace of a café in Monaco, and I talked and talked with happiness and thought: Hanni isn't saying anything, maybe I should keep my mouth shut? My happiness had to get on Hanni's nerves. But, then Hanni began to talk about her two youngest sisters, who had been favored in their father's will. He had left them both a house each, and Heidemarie and her (the two older ones) only money, but not as much money as the houses would have been worth. And the widowed mother would have had the right to live in these houses until her death, but she had gone immediately to an expensive retirement home, where she would have played Skat every day and even found a boyfriend with whom she always drove around in the wonderful Swiss countryside. And by doing so, she further diminished the inheritance of the older sisters. The youngest sister had the audacity to sell her house right away, and the other had taken out a mortgage to buy an apartment in the warm Ticino, where she lived with her husband until their divorce.

"And just imagine, this man, the scoundrel Ferdi, got the apartment after the divorce and now lives there with his second wife like in paradise, on our father's money. That's outrageous!" And here was poor Hanni, sitting in the Café of Monaco, having lost everything, and I had to pay for her sundae and the coffee to go with it, and the admission to the museums, and in the evening I had to pay for the pizzas (because they were the cheapest) in the restaurants of Vence, all of which meant a humiliation of the first degree for her, because she was generous by nature and had never taken advantage of anyone. Now she was forced to 'take advantage' of me. I knew she thought so, and I tried to distract her from her family quarrel with cheerful stories. But she kept coming back to the subject of her younger sisters, who had gotten their father to change his will in their favor during the short time of his serious illness (he had died of colon cancer). And when Heidemarie and Hanni asked their mother why he had done that, the old woman replied: "You already had a house, but the two little ones didn't. Father wanted you all to have one when he died, so he left a house to each of the children. You must understand that. And you were so lucky to be able to choose your own houses, but the little ones had to take what they got."

"Isn't that an outrage, Gorda? Our men worked hard for the houses, but my two little sisters didn't do anything for them, just pretended to be needy, they were good at that, those two slick brats!" And Hanni looked so sullen, as if she were talking to her mother or father and not to me. Her face was wrinkled with anger and worry, and her tired eyes were looking at the concrete floor and not at the beautiful blue sea nearby. I knew that my good mood was misplaced, and yet I was so happy to be on the road with Hanni in the car in Southern France and to drive with her through the mountains behind Vence that I didn't even notice how much of the forestation had been destroyed by the huge summer fires. Hanni, however, pointed her finger at the charred tree stumps: "Look, just like my life!"

Yes, it was terrible what had happened to my once beautiful friend! Hanni either kept silent, or she talked about her greedy sisters and her father's unfair will. She herself hadn't even known about his illness at the time, because she was pregnant with Bernd, and the family didn't want to scare her with the bad news. But maybe the younger sisters didn't want the father to see the pregnant daughter once more and perhaps have doubts about the change of his will. Because they didn't tell Heidemarie either and later claimed that they wanted to spare her the disastrous news in the worst phase of her divorce. That way, the youngest ones had enough time to influence the mother, and she went to her sick husband and put in a word for the little ones, as they were always called, even when they were already overripe young women; and dad let himself be talked into it. And the two older sisters were taken for a ride, as if they were not also their parents' children and not loved by them, a terrible thought. Because sometimes money is not money, and a house is not a house, but rather love or not love.

Our most beautiful drive from Vence was to the magnificent Villa Ephrussi with its amazing gardens, each section of it in a different style of garden: Italian Renaissance, French chateau style, Tuscan style, and planted with Greek olive trees. A magnificent Garden of Eden for an unhappy married couple with the fortunes of the Rothschilds and of the Ephrussi family. And the wife a lesbian. "Hoppe-Hoppe-Gründgens, kriegen keine Kindgens," said the Berliners, witty even during the Third Reich, to such favorably arranged, but ultimately fruitless marriages as that of Marianne Hoppe and Gustav Gründgens. No apple fell from that tree. But so much art in the garden and in the living rooms! I would have liked to walk through the gardens with Hanni, to be able to rejoice aloud about them in front of her. But Hanni wanted to be alone to dwell on her worries. After the garden tour, we ate salmon sandwiches with salads in a small, fine restaurant that was connected to the villa. Now Hanni was talking about her boyfriend, a widower, who didn't allow her to order more than a coffee in a roadside restaurant during their joint tours in the beautiful Swiss countryside; an ice cream or a piece of cake were too expensive for him. And when they were traveling, Hanni would have to pay for half the bottle of wine, even though she hardly drank any of it.

"He's a pathological Scrooge!" she said bitterly, "when I think of my generous Karl-Hansi!" Yes, unfortunately too generous, it ran through my cheeky brain, which never wants to be silent when it should be.

"Why didn't you pay for that piece of cake yourself?" I foolishly asked Hanni, but she was already going on about how he never gave the poor porters any money, "no money, no money," he would have muttered continuously in Mallorca, while she was ashamed of him and secretly pulled out a coin from her little bit of money. With that fabled stinginess, Peter had raised four sons and still managed to afford a small vacation home in Spain.

"You can imagine how he saved the money from the mouths of the children and the wife! He mostly traveled alone, his wife didn't want to go with him when he went to Singapore or to Chile. She certainly must have feared his need to save money at all costs and stayed at home with the children, and they had a nice week without him. And ate Züpfe (white bread with butter) with Anke for breakfast and not mixed-grain bread with margarine."

"Why do you stay with this man?" I asked Hanni, although one should refrain from such critical questions.

"Because he listens to me well, I can tell him all about my sisters and the unjust will and about the many mistakes Karl-Hansi made to be able to build us the house." Oh well, I thought, he spared her the therapy with a psychologist, which she would otherwise have urgently needed to find her peace of mind again. Peter probably listened well on the one hand, but on the other hand he embittered her with his tireless urge not to spend a penny more than necessary. Thus it happened that Peter humiliated Hanni with his stinginess and I humiliated her with my generosity. Surely, she would have liked to get the admission fee for Villa Ephrussi paid by him — and the salmon bread dinner with the salads in the restaurant of the house, but she didn't want to get anything as a present from me and felt humiliated when I took out the wallet without hesitation and put down the bills for both of them. Only a man was allowed to pay for her, not a girlfriend. Those were the old-school rules. So, everything was wrong in her life and only a 'rethinking' could have helped her bear her life. But that thought didn't cross her mind, and I wouldn't dare advise her: accept things as they are. 'The things' were a punishment for her, the daughter from a preeminent family. But Peter had paid a high price for his stinginess: it was not his wife who left him, but his eldest son, his favorite, Ferdinand. Once, when he traveled with his wife to the Spanish condominium, he left his pistol with him ("Why does he have a pistol? I don't know, either."), and Ferdinand shot himself with it without leaving a suicide note or giving any explanation. This was a terrible shock for father and mother, so that from then on they both slept in different rooms so as not to have to deal with the question of guilt at night as well. They finally stopped talking to each other and said only the most necessary things like: "Did you see the bill for the wine? Who actually drinks that much here? I certainly don't!"

And so that's why Peter listened so well to Hanni, because his wife and he hadn't spoken to each other for years before she lapsed at last into complete silence and died. She had struggled with her breast cancer for many years, and I once read that cancer was the disease of hate. I can well imagine that the woman hated stingy Peter after the suicide of her beloved son. The two younger sons, the twins, were unwanted children and only after his money, he said. Besides, he considered them ugly as night. From whom they got that, he didn't know. But he would give them money because he had transferred the down payment for a house to his second beloved son, that is, out of feelings of guilt. Hanni had never seen any of the sons and had no desire to see them. Nor did she want to see photos of them.

"Because of those money-grubbing sons, he won't even buy me an ice cream sundae with my coffee!" she said indignantly. His much younger girlfriend! And certainly, his last! Peter wished that Hanni would move in with him, but she would rather not. He likely would still charge her money for food, although she would surely have to cook and clean and wash for him and mend his socks. He would need a cheap housekeeper, but not a woman like her. What is called love has always been a business, I thought: And she would have to find a job, the insurance money would soon be used up. And her pension would be too small to live and die on.

And Hanni lamented for the hundredth time: "How could I give up my good position at the consulate, a very easy job with pension rights. I must have been insane. But it's all the fault of Karl-Hansi, who wanted me at home." And she told how her employer, the consul, had used her to buy him confectionery for his wife in the winter, even though she was a trained foreign-language correspondent with a high school diploma and an advanced Latin certificate, so she had to march through the slush in the winter with her new red ankle boots, which Karl-Hansi had given her for Christmas, and almost dislocated her foot and ruined the beautiful shoes.

"But then I said to him, no more, you can get the gifts for your wife alone. And I didn't go back. What an impertinence!" But now she'd like that easy, non-tenure-track job with pension eligibility back, and times had changed so much, there was no work for miles around. And there used to be plenty. It was exasperating. She said, she had wanted to go into the private industry. where one earned more than with the government. And I felt quite sorry for her youthful recklessness. But who could have known that her life would turn out this way? Every morning during breakfast in Vence, Heidemarie called to inquire how she was doing. And I was very surprised at the interest of the sister, for whom Hanni rarely found a good word in the past. But the death of Karl-Hansi changed everything. Also the character of Heidemarie.

"My sister paints beautifully, don't you think?" And, of course, I found her cat paintings beautiful, because I loved cats, just like Hanni and Heidemarie did, who owned a black tomcat named Johnny. And the little animals looked lovely in the pictures, just like in real life. I could kiss them, these faces, Hanni said. And while the two not so hostile sisters chatted with each other on the phone as if they were the dearest of friends, I left the breakfast table and our cozy get-together and went into the bathroom to blow-dry and lay down my wet hair, because unfortunately I had to wash my naturally thin

One of Heidemarie's cat paintings

hair each morning to have anything at all on my head. Hanni, on the other hand, only had to wash her beautiful thick and dry hair once a week. What a time saver for reading! On the unfortunate last morning of our vacation week in Vence, I was again sitting at the breakfast table in front of Hanni with soaking wet hair, a woman over fifty with dripping strands of hair on her face, which was naked and bare as nature created it, so by no means a Lorelei, no, rather a mountain woman, but a showered one. I knew that I couldn't win a beauty prize, and yet I had once been Miss Fehmarn [an elected island princess] at age seventeen. But only because I had danced in the style of Isadora Duncan. I noticed how Hanni studied my face as if it were a map showing the way from the south of France to Switzerland, because we didn't want to drive back through the Italian lowlands, but through the magnificent mountains of France.

Suddenly, this sentence escaped Hanni: "You look quite nice, Gorda, but beautiful you are not!" Lord in heaven, I thought, she still hasn't forgotten Karl-Hansi's stupid remark. Thank God, at that moment Heidemarie called, and I disappeared into the bathroom to turn my morning ugliness into a tolerable afternoon facade. Later, when I was on my way back to Switzerland with Hanni, the Gorda devil rode me, and I told her about all the conquests I could have made if only I had wanted to, but I hadn't wanted to. I hinted that I had probably not been a first-class Lorelei beauty like herself, but neither had I been a hunchbacked witch with a hooked nose flying to the Brocken Mountain on her broomstick. Hanni listened in silence. And knew why I was angry and spoke of past and even deceased admirers in my life in all those years when she was plowing and sowing in her garden as a country woman and feeding her chickens and the little parrots in her aviary. And, at that time, Hanni could have had dozens of men, oh, many dozens, hundreds. And I only a dozen. That was the difference between the two of us. But what woman can sleep with hundreds of men? Won't a dozen be enough?

Miffed, Hanni dropped me off at my friend Katja's in Lausanne — and drove on to Bern without thanking me, while I thanked her at length for having driven us so safely through the magnificent regions in her own car. She only pressed her lips together angrily! A short time later, I was already in Chicago, when she told me on the phone about a competition on the subject of 'Am I beautiful?' for which one could win five thousand Swiss francs. She supposedly had sent me the documents for it.

"Surely you have a lot to say on the subject!" and she wanted to burst out laughing about it. She must have laughed like that in her childhood and youth at her little sisters when they peed their pants, I thought. I had changed overnight from a friend into a fourth unloved sister. I listened to Hanni on the phone like a five-year-old who has just been caught by her mother peeing her pants. And I knew Hanni wanted to start a fight with me, since I should finally admit that I had never ever been beautiful, and definitely not as beautiful as she, in any case. That was true, but neither had I been ugly nor diapered wet. And therefore I erased that conversation from my memory. Until I received the pages from the *Berner Zeitung*, the daily newspaper in Bern: five thousand Swiss francs for the winner of the 'Am I beautiful?' competition. That's when the rage awoke in me. And then the Gorda devil rode me. And I wrote a short, literarily insignificant essay, which didn't bring me five thousand Swiss francs, but weeks full of ghastly arguments. And I sent that text to the newspaper and, unfortunately, also to Hanni in a fit of honesty ("One must always tell one another the truth!"). Or was it vindictiveness?

Am I beautiful?

A few years ago, the husband of my very beloved Swiss friend said to me: You are a beautiful woman, Greta. Then he looked at his own and said: Elly has unfortunately had to work too much lately. About which, however, he was right. Six months earlier, he had built her a beautiful and huge house. A dream house that every woman wants, but fortunately hardly any of them get. Elly now had one. I strode full of admiration through the many rooms and thought timidly: Compared to this palace, my apartment in Chicago is a doghouse.

But it is a doghouse with a million-dollar view onto the park and the lake! That view comforts me for everything that has gone wrong in my life. For example, some kind of plastic surgery. I had had to have cancer cells removed from the bridge of my nose, and there was a small hole left from the procedure. What woman wants to have a hole in her nose? I took it to the most expensive plastic surgeon in town. He told me that he would remove it for little money. This tiny procedure then cost $30,000, and instead of the hole, I now have a wide, snake-shaped scar on my nose. Now I know: No plastic surgery for me! I would love to have my breasts reduced, my belly cut away and my lips enlarged. And a whole lot besides that! Because neither from the back nor from the front do I correspond to today's beauty ideal of a beanpole hung with fashionable clothes. Recently, when I leafed through my family album, I found an old photo of my grandmothers: two fat piglets smiling contentedly at the camera. No wonder I have no chance of being thin with genes like that. I've already eaten my daily ration of calories at lunch and still have to have something in the evening, otherwise I'd be drunk after a few glasses of wine. And without wine — and the wonderful view of the lake and park and my cat on my lap — I don't want to live!

My friend Elly was so beautiful in her youth that a schoolmate told her thirty years later that he still owned a photo of her in a cute pink bikini. Back then, she was the ideal embodiment of femininity for him. Even her high school math teacher fell in love with her and tried to seduce her. Until Elly told a false friend about it. Who then told her horrified parents, and they spread it around far and wide in the school alleging that the math teacher was a Casanova and Elly was a seductress. The teacher was fired before he could achieve his goal. Especially as math teachers are known for their dryness and objectivity in all things related to life.

When Dieter built the beautiful house for his beautiful wife, he must not have given any thought to the work created by such a large house with a garden, because he never granted Elly a cleaning lady. Perhaps she never asked him for money for one, either. You can't hire a cleaning lady in a Swiss village, Elly explained to me. That's not proper. You do the cleaning yourself, and that's that. So she cleaned the multi-story house herself, from morning to night, the numerous rooms and bathrooms and the spacious office on the ground floor — and then it was time for the garden.

"Sometimes I'm so exhausted in the evening that I think, how many more years can you take this?" Elly said to me one day. And she looked so emaciated and haggard and wrinkled, as if she smoked thirty cigarettes a day. Yet, Elly never touched any cigarette. It was having to take care of her dream house that cost her her physical strength and her beauty. Is that what her husband meant to say when he called me beautiful and at the same time implied that his wife was worn out? I looked at Elly with horror at the time. I realized how jealous women are of women when it comes to compliments from their own husbands. Elly looked at Dieter full of rage and poked him in the side with her elbow. He then began to stammer and said sheepishly: "I just want to say that I'm happy for Elly when you come, not for me." That afternoon, when Elly got the car out of the garage to take me to the airport, he told me again that I was a beautiful woman, and I thought something was wrong here. Does he want to ruin our friendship? Soon after, I called Elly to thank her for the days spent visiting her. She then said, in a voice that seemed to come from a grave: "Something terrible has happened."

"What? What?" I screamed.

"Dieter drowned, I had to identify him this morning at the morgue in Bern." Then she told me that the day before — on a blazing hot summer day — he had jumped into the ice-cold Aare River to cool off. What his body could easily handle in childhood and adolescence, killed him after many years of stress and hundreds of cigarettes. He went into cold shock and his heart stopped. Not much later, the unhappy Elly found out that her husband had overstretched himself financially and she was ruined. The bank took the house. Elly looked for a job and moved into a small two-bedroom apartment. And there she lives now, with a huge mountain of debt, and the bank is always after her, in case she comes into wealth through an inheritance or remarriage. Why did Elly's husband tell me then that I was a beautiful woman? Were those his words of farewell? Did he know he was going to die? At least his daughter thinks so, because he said goodbye to her with the prophetic words: "I know that I will die soon. Promise me that you will take care of your mother."

I hope no man ever calls me a beautiful woman again. It's bad luck, I think. And the beautiful women don't have it any easier than the not so beautiful ones. They, too, can marry only one man at a time; their children, too, sometimes turn out badly; their husbands, too, lose their jobs; they, too, get sick and old and eventually have to move into a nursing home. The most beautiful of my friends, Aviva, has been taking care of her husband, who has become senile at an early age, for many years already. The doctor says he can still live a long time.

When I then called Hanni — I expected nothing bad — she sobbed and screamed on the phone: "How can you ... an impertinence ... who told you ... you lie, you lie!!!" Then she slammed the phone down. And I stood there dumbfounded with the receiver in my hand, wondering: What now? Who can help me? I first called her daughter and then her sister, Heidemarie. The daughter didn't answer the phone but sent me an incendiary letter to the house.

It is an outrageous impudence of you to use the misfortune of our family to win five thousand Swiss francs. I never thought that you could sink so low. Don't you know what you have done to our mother? You have torn open her barely healed wounds, and now she is lying at home in bed crying and wailing and cannot calm down because her best friend is a traitor. You turn out to be a conscienceless writer, but we know, of course, what baseless, opportunistic natures artists are. And stop being convinced that you are beautiful just because my father called you that. He did that everywhere, even with the ugliest women. He wanted to be charming, nothing else. He even called Lotti beautiful, and you know how horrible that woman looks. The stupid cow also took his words at face value, and even today regularly puts a bouquet of red roses on his grave. I loved my father very much and know what a generous, loving character he had. But all that mattered to him was his family and above all his beloved wife, his Hanneli. You were air for him, believe me.

No longer your Anneli

Now I too had become air, but not good Swiss country air. To justify myself, I wrote Anneli a letter in which I explained to her how I had come to write the essay 'Am I beautiful?' That is, on behalf of her own mother, who had been annoyed that her husband had tactlessly called me beautiful in front of his worn-out, exhausted wife. It would not be my fault, but her mother's and maybe her father's. And I would have had to comfort my friend for three days because her husband had called his own daughter — meaning Anneli — the most beautiful girl far and wide. All things I should have kept to myself. Speech is silver, silence is golden. Anneli wrote back: "I don't want to hear any more about your quarrel. In the future, settle everything between the two of you."

And Heidemarie finally came to the phone — Hanni had also indignantly sent her my essay on the prize competition — and said angrily: "Well, Gorda, didn't you know that the trial for the attempted seduction by the math teacher was a huge scandal at our school? The man was never allowed to teach at a state school again, and my life at the high school was made so difficult because of my scandalous sister that I had to transfer to the Realschule [middle school], and that's why I didn't graduate from high school. It's Hanni's fault. You should never have talked about this trial. For years, the village talked about nothing else, there had never been anything like that there. But don't worry too much, Hanni will calm down again. A friendship of a quarter of a century should survive such a crisis. Wait and see, I will visit Hanni soon and put in a good word for you. But don't do something like that again, I urge you." I kept insisting that I was innocent, at least less guilty than Hanni. But she behaved as if she were the victim of a bomb attack. And what was my misfortune, to lose Hanni as a friend, against the tremendous misfortune of Hanni, who had lost her husband to suicide (or was it an accident after all?). And was ruined financially.

Out of desperation I called Hanni's ancient aunt Mimi in Ticino in Italy, whom we had once visited together, and howled and cried my eyes out like a castle dog while on the phone. (Why do castle dogs howl like that? Do they get lessons in howling from the lord of the castle?) The aunt lovingly comforted me, as only a really old person can provide comfort.

"Everything will be all right," she said, "a childhood friendship can't be broken by such a trifle. I'm sure of that. You are not a bad person, and you are so attached to Hanni, such a friendship is worth its weight in gold; how often is there one like that on Earth? For me, my schizophrenic sister was my best friend, but only when she took her medication, without her medication she could become like a fury. Well, that was bad, I tell you, you can't imagine such a thing, the scenes she made for me, fits of rage, comparable to those of my hot-tempered brother. I said to him when he arrived with that impossible bride, a saleswoman — Hanni's mother: "But you must not father any children." He didn't listen to me and fathered four girls. It's madness, given our family history."

When I no longer knew what to do, I sent my graphological report to all three, to Hanni, Heidemarie, and Anneli. In it, it said in black and white, that I was an altruistic person and would never get back what I gave.

Heidemarie called me and said: "Maybe you should call Hanni now, she's calmed down." And I called Hanni, who said: "Yes, you are altruistic, but you can also administer blows, for example when you told me 'how could you put me on the wrong train at the Bern train station'. After all, I'm only human, and a human can make mistakes, errare humanum est, and you scolded me when I forgot to change trains on the way to Zurich, yes, who do you think I am? A well-functioning machine?" And it was indeed so, I had complained, because I had just come from the States and had jet lag and was still dazed in the head. And already I seemed more guilty than Hanni, who was much more unfortunate than me, and so I apologized for my offenses and said I was sorry.

From then on, Heidemarie and I wrote each other letters regularly when there was a crisis with Hanni. And they became more frequent as time went on. Heidemarie had had an urge to be a fine lady since early childhood, Hanni had told me. As a child, she paid her younger sisters with her pocket money when she didn't feel like dusting. The silly-billies then did that for her. And Heidemarie sat down at the piano and pretended that she could play, although it was only the schizophrenic aunt who was musically gifted and who had received piano lessons. But Heidemarie had hit the jackpot with a marriage advertisement in the Zurich newspaper, and after her divorce she married a man ten years her junior who had built up a huge company for plastic containers. Now she could shop to her heart's content at Hermès and Prada and Gucci and Pucci, as I called it. And she looked like a fine lady, down to her hair, which she wore straight and long and light blond like the Lorelei on her rock, and with it the precious jewelry, the large pearl earrings with diamonds and the fine diamond rings on her fingers that flashed in the sun. Only she didn't sing like a siren. Once Hanni sobbed pitifully, because Heidemarie had visited her with Detlef and then sped off in a big dark blue Opel car to the south to a castle hotel, of which she had shown Hanni photos.

"She has her new husband, and all the money in the world, and even her ex-husband lives in her house, and I'm sitting here lonely and desperate and have nothing and no one." And I thought, you poor child, not only has heaven taken much from you, but it has also given more than abundantly to your sister. This is like being shot in the heart twice. But unfortunately, one is not dead after such shots of fate. You have to go on living and suffering with two poisonous bullets in your heart. No wonder Hanni sometimes went crazy with pain. Besides, Heidemarie liked to spread her wealth before Hanni by taking her on her shopping trips and buying her a handbag at Longchamp or a cashmere sweater now and then, but she bought herself three handbags at Hermès and seven dresses at Max Mara or whatever the posh stores were called that Annina also used to visit, but not me. I was forever Cinderella, reading Grimm's fairy tales about the good sisters and the bad sisters and what they do to each other. And Hanni's life seemed to me like a fairy tale, but not a good one like that of *Heidemarie in Luck*, it was that of *Hanni in Bad Luck*. And the more unhappy Hanni became — because of her sister's wealth — the more I felt the need to stand by her side as faithfully as possible, despite her occasional tantrums and the correspondence with Heidemarie behind Hanni's back. Because I knew why Heidemarie was so good and then again so cruel to Hanni: she was taking revenge for the years in childhood when Hanni had not only been the oldest, but also the most intelligent and the most beautiful in the family, but also the most haughty and the most scornful, Heidemarie often told me, a Hanni who loved to laugh at her sisters when they fell in the mud and got a beating from their father.

"You wouldn't believe how my sister treated me back then. I was a child with bad luck; my mother and father didn't love me. Once I got lost in the forest during a family outing and wandered around for hours until I arrived back home in the evening. My mother didn't even turn toward me from the stove to greet me, imagine that." I knew from Hanni that Heidemarie was an unwanted child and rejected by everyone. The parents had wanted a son after their daughter and got a second girl, instead, and made no effort to hide their disappointment.

"My mother didn't want me either," with these words I tried to comfort Heidemarie, and felt connected to her as well. However, this was fraught with danger. But thank God, Heidemarie's huge wealth — she soon owned not only the villa on Lake Zurich, but also a huge estate in South Africa, where she played golf, a large house in Cortina d'Ampezzo and a luxury apartment in Cannes — didn't have to be bad luck for Hanni, it could turn into her luck if Heidemarie finally made good on her promises and would buy her a nice home and would give her a monthly financial allowance, as she had promised so often. Still, it was only words up to now, but I thought to myself: One doesn't promise the blue heaven for years and watch the misery of the sister without intervening in her fate. In addition, Heidemarie also agreed to finance Bernd's engineering studies, which he never had to pay back, even if he didn't finish them. Heidemarie seemed to be the fairy bringing luck to the nephew, but he didn't appreciate the generosity of the rich aunt from the Gold Coast — as he called her — and, like his mother, he felt it was a humiliation to have to accept the money from her. And he dropped out of college when he failed an exam, even though he could have easily repeated it. Now he insisted that his dream job was to be a croupier in Interlaken (he had probably seen too many movies with gambling casinos for the rich people he hated), and so he began an apprenticeship there, while Hanni tore out her thick hair and Heidemarie flew off to Africa with the words: It doesn't matter what happens when I'm gone. Hanni complained bitterly to me that Heidemarie often didn't call her for months, because she was doing so well in South Africa playing golf, while she had to drive to her dark office every day. For Hanni had finally found a job through the mediation of her brother-in-law, with whom she had broken up years ago, I no longer recall why. Later I asked Heidemarie, why don't you call Hanni when you are in Africa?

"I am very happy there and have my own life and don't always have to listen to my sister's complaints," she said. "She didn't care about me either when her husband was still alive and mine was cheating on me with Michelle, she knew that for a fact. And when I moved out, she never asked my husband for my address."

"No, that's not correct," I countered. "Your sister didn't know you had moved out. Your first husband always claimed you were in town shopping."

"Oh, I see," Heidemarie said. "But when I moved back into my house — this time together with Detlef — she said to me that it was impossible to live with two men at the same time. But I didn't live with both of them, I just lived with them under one roof. That way, we saved a lot of money, which benefitted my son, who was studying at the university in Boston at the time. Studying in the States like that costs a fortune." She didn't have to tell me! And I remembered how haughtily Hanni had spoken of her sister introducing this new man, Detlef, to her as a lodger when she greeted him.

"What an unworthy appellation — a lodger — for the owner of an international plastic container empire."

"Well, I guess she didn't want you in the family to gossip about the arrangement, so she fibbed rather than face the sisterly malice."

"What do you mean, sisterly malice?"

"Well, just imagine, the two men — both the first husband and the second husband — went golfing together with my sister, and often with Michelle to boot, the ex-husband's twenty-year-younger mistress, who is still married to a German dentist who probably only married her so he could open an office in Basel. Because he doesn't care at all that she sleeps with my ex-brother-in-law."

"Maybe he's already got someone else, too," I suggested as a solution to the mystery.

"Could be," Hanni said, and I quoted a cheeky verse from our youth in Germany: In the old days, it was settled that everyone screwed his own. Nowadays, it's all tricky because everyone screws someone else. And then Hanni and I laughed like we did during puberty. Different times, different customs, we like to say. But who knows what the customs were like in the past? Old Aunt Mimi, who later comforted me so sweetly, had cheated in her youth on her first husband with the next, and when the first took her only son away from her — because, at that time, the father in Switzerland had all rights over the child and the mother had none — she went to the consulate in Bern and reported him because he had sold Swiss luxury goods like chocolate and cigarettes to the Germans at a profit during wartime. And she cheated on her second husband with her third, but cleverly prevented the second from changing his will shortly before his death in favor of his children from the first marriage. She even took the jewelry that had belonged to his Jewish wife, who took her own life when Hitler came to power in 1933. And this jewelry really should have gone to the daughter of the unfortunate woman. And Aunt Mimi soon kicked out the third husband when he became impertinent and tried to order her around. After all, the money came from her or, let's say, from the rich old builder she had inherited it from as his widow. The third one moved back to Cologne, where he came from. But later, he often visited her in Ticino (Italy), because divorced they got along well again and immediately forgot why they had gotten divorced. I think he remained her lover until his death, although, in the meantime, he had married someone else.

So, old Aunt Mimi, who is so good at consoling, was a sly old lady, and at the funeral of her schizophrenic sister she said to Hanni: "Lie and cheat as much as you can, kiddo. The world deserves nothing else." However, Hanni never cheated on her husband and never looked at another man 'covetously', as it says in the Bible. Karl-Hansi was the great love of her life. And yet, heaven punished her so harshly. Where was the higher justice in that, I would like to know?

"That's not just," my niece Rieke often said to me. And I answered: "Who says that life is just? The people who are demanding their assets back that were unjustly taken from them in the Third Reich are absolutely right, but justice has rarely existed in human history. For example, who returned to my grandmother Marie her great fortune that she lost in

1917 because of the Russian Revolution? Who speaks of justice when a child gets a hump or a harelip? And one child has beautiful long legs and the other short, crooked, ones. Some children have wealthy parents who can pay for their tutoring, and others don't. If there is a God, then he is unjust. Or we don't understand divine justice. Only the idea of reincarnation seems to be just. But we all don't want to believe in that." And I sit here, in Lüneburg, with my once intelligent mother, who stutters away, and none of my brothers show up, their wives neither, and I despair during this Christmas season full of Christmas decorations in the shop windows, which, in the past, always comforted me. If it weren't for my mother's next-door friend Erika, I wouldn't be able to talk to anyone. And where is my Aunt Käthe now? Where is my beloved cousin Anni? In the meantime, my brother Max has been here, and I asked him: "Can I sleep at your place when mom is no longer alive?" Then he had the nerve to answer me: "No, not at our place, my wife has problems with you!" As if his wife had no problems with him, or with her children, or with my mother, everywhere there were home-made problems. Only I am excluded, because I know the most about his marital problems. He's afraid I'm going to make friends with his wife and open my mouth and tell her this and that, which could hurt him. Because he dumped everything on my mother and me for thirty years. We were his wailing wall, just as this diary is now my wailing wall. Surely one has to be able to complain somewhere.

A few years ago, I had the stupid idea to drive with Hanni in the car (how I loved to drive with her!) to Morcote to my school friend Etta. Etta was the most beautiful in our class, our Princess Lorelei, and she had gotten Prince Roger, a grandson of the Swiss billionaire, who built an empire in Europe like that of the American mail order company Sears. But the old man couldn't part with his fortune with an open hand, and Roger's parents had to wait for the money until his death at the age of ninety-seven. By then, they were seventy themselves and gripped by the fear of old-age poverty, and they didn't give anything away with an open hand, either. But finally, the day came, when Etta and her husband, the famous brain surgeon Roger Herzog from the University of Marburg, could dive into the mountains of money like Scrooge McDuck in the Disney comics we loved so much back then.

Etta had not only been the most beautiful in our class, but she also had a strongly developed sense for everything beautiful. Her homes and her gardens were among the most enchanting I had ever seen. No wonder that I wanted to see her new house in Morcote. Together with Hanni, but she didn't feel like it at all, as it was to turn out. I had forgotten that she once told me that she didn't like going to class reunions because then she had to look at the houses of her classmates, while she no longer had one of her own. Which is quite understandable. Nevertheless, I went with her to Morcote because Etta, good-natured as always, had said: "Yes, you can come, we have two vacation apartments next to our house for our sons." Hanni had just moved into her late parents-in-law's house because it had a garden (albeit a tiny one), and she had owned one all her life and felt she couldn't live without it. But no sooner had she moved into the house, built cheaply in 1947, than she realized that the walls were too thin, and not sufficiently insulated. She froze cruelly all winter long, until Anneli gave her an electric blanket. When the cherries ripened in the summer, she bought a cherry pit remover — but for reasons of economy, one for only two cherries instead of the more expensive one for ten cherries — which she told her friend Peter. He burst out laughing derisively on the phone and said: "And you call me stingy, look at yourself, a cherry pit remover for two cherries, such a joke!"

But Hanni wasn't stingy by nature at all; she had been forced into frugality by her poverty. A big difference! Evil vengefulness awoke in Hanni, and she screamed at the man who wouldn't even let her have an ice cream sundae with her coffee: "Go to hell where you come from, you impudent ass!" Peter immediately jumped into the car and rushed over to make up with her. She stood in the doorway like a fury, she told me, and slammed the door on his nose. And fainted from exhaustion and despair because she had moved into the wrong house. Because not only was it insulated poorly, she also heard every noise the woman living above her made, who had a habit of stomping around in clogs from morning till night, which infuriated Hanni. She asked her to take off the clogs, but the woman, named Rita, insisted she was wearing normal slippers and without them she would get foot pain. Hanni's nerves were on edge when I visited her to take her to Morcote. And because she couldn't kick Rita out — the house now belonged to her unloved brother-in-law — she kicked out the tightwad, Peter. And, later, almost me.

Morcote is located in the Swiss Ticino on Lake Lugano and is a village for the super-rich and super-famous of the world. The owners of the splendid villas don't live there all year round, because they have many other splendid villas to visit in turn. The poor posh place stands empty, waiting for the guests with locked doors and boarded-up shutters. Romy's mother, Magda Schneider, had owned a large house on the lake, where her daughter had entered into the unhappy engagement with Alain Delon. That was long, long ago. And Romy is now dead and buried, just like her little son. On the way there, Hanni and I saw two large street signs. One said 'Retirement Home' and the other 'Cemetery'. These were the next stops for the ghost inhabitants of Morcote. We called it somewhat enviously "mort coté lac," death by the lake. A beautiful death, a rich death.

"You wouldn't believe how boring it is here in the summer when it rains. There's nothing to do, no movies, no stores, only two restaurants," Etta had told me on the phone. And her husband would drive his Ferraris around the neighborhood. When we got to her place, I saw that she was right. She wasn't a rich, spoiled woman who found fault with everything; she was an intelligent, bored woman who couldn't even buy her books in Morcote, dozens of which she devoured in the beautiful solitude. Etta needed to be doing something, but for that she had to go by car to Lugano, a pretty town with many stores where, unfortunately, people spoke Italian. And we had learned Latin in school, but not Italian. For this reason, Etta and her husband had been taking Italian lessons for years. But foreign languages are so hard to learn when you get older!

No sooner were Hanni and I sitting on the lovely back patio of their wonderful house overlooking the justly praised Lake Lugano, that I realized we shouldn't have come. Or just me alone. Roger looked grimly at the woman he didn't know. Etta, on the other hand, was trying to make friendly conversation. And I thought again of how beautiful Hanni had once been and how delightedly Roger would have looked at her twenty years ago. I suddenly remembered Remo, who had taught German at school for a short time and had automatically thought the prettier children to be the smarter ones.

After a while, Roger wanted to show us his Ferraris, but Etta cut him off: "Roger, women are not interested in cars." This was true and then again, not true. Because I had never seen a Ferrari and had never known a Ferrari owner. And

Photo of Morcote, by Fernanda Fabio and Mariana Leão

this man owned three of them. Therefore, I showed interest in looking at the Ferraris. We drove to Roger's car showroom, where there was one Ferrari next to another (or there were other makes interspersed that I couldn't make out), and he spread his arms and said: "Look at this wealth, there are at least thirty million Swiss francs here!" Hanni pressed her lips together, and I thought, let's get out of here, pronto. It was blazing hot and stuffy in the hall anyway.

Etta said: "You see, Roger, women are not interested in cars."

Later, we went for a walk together, and I was talking about old school girlfriends. That's when Roger said that he and Etta were done with the past, and they were both no longer interested in people from back then. Oh, what horror, given that I was such a person from back then! And I no longer understood the world: Roger had been the dearest and kindest of hosts in Marburg, and now he enjoyed insulting me. I wonder if he was also bored in Morcote? He talked about ice hockey and asked me if I was interested in it. And I answered truthfully that I was not interested in most sports.

"Well, what are you interested in?" he pressed me, angrily. In books, I thought, wondering what I should say in reply. Because he himself read only medical books and the weekly magazine *Der Spiegel*, as far as I knew. Finally, I remembered my war criminal father, and he was visibly interested in him. Men love war and war stories as well as cars and technology and ice hockey. Finally, we got along again, but then I saw that my poor Hanni was constantly walking around with her lips pressed together, and I knew I had to take care of her. So, after dinner we quickly went back to the apartment that Etta had made available to us. It was an expensive apartment that was simply furnished, but it only had one bedroom with a king-size bed. Now, I had often slept with Hanni in king-size beds, in Paris several times, in Florence and in Venice, but this time, she didn't want to be with me at night. She ran out of the room, distraught, and into the living room. I followed behind her: there she was, lying on the couch with her face pressed into the pillow as if she were crying. I tactfully left her alone in her despair and went back to the bedroom to wait for her. But she didn't come. She spent the whole night on the sofa in the stuffy, hot living room while I slept in the air-conditioned bedroom. I couldn't sleep much because I always had to think about poor Hanni. And in the morning, I dreamed of the war: high flames were rising from the bombed houses of Morcote.

The next morning, Hanni was silent at the breakfast table. She obviously wanted to go on with her sad thoughts, while I would have liked to know how to bring her to others. What are we doing here? I thought in despair and was glad when we left the happy place of the rich and beautiful on their way to the old-age residence and the grave.

Our next stop was at the home of my college friend Dodi, with whom I had shared an apartment in Lausanne. She now lived near the Château de Coppet of Madame de Stael, where I had often visited with her. Unfortunately, Hanni slept badly in the ugly hotel — which I had paid for dearly— because it was located directly on the busy country road. And she refused to use earplugs and a blindfold. I, on the other hand, slept excellently with their help. The next morning, she started to rant in front of the owner in the hotel restaurant during breakfast, saying that such a room should not be rented out: no guest could sleep in it because of the outside noise. When I tried to calm her down, she ran angrily into the garden, and I ran after her, suggesting that we go right back to Bern and not visit the Château de Coppet, nor go to my friend Katja's — she was the owner of the apartment in Vence — and go sailing on Lake Geneva with her and her husband in their boat on that glorious Sunday morning. As a result, I never saw our old college friend Henri again; it would have been the last time. But it had become painfully clear to me by now that Hanni couldn't bear to visit yet another beautiful house prior to the sailing trip, as we had planned.

On the drive back to the loathed house of her in-laws, we both kept silent. The next morning, we were talking together again when, at breakfast, she knocked out a piece of the expensive (where did she get the money?) new glass table with her key. Silently, she let her index finger slide over the damaged area. She seemed to remain quite calm. I thought, well, she is not angry with herself, and I can tell her what else happened on 9/11 in world literature, because the date of the terrorist attack happened to be also the date of her birthday. Immediately, she began to shout: "I didn't study like you and your girlfriends; you just want to instill inferiority complexes in me! Leave me alone with your stupid books!" The screaming didn't stop until I locked myself in my guest room in the basement and read my book about *Christiane Goethe* by Sigrid Damm for the rest of the time. In there, it said that on a September 11, Christiane threw a terrible tantrum at Bettina von Arnim in an art exhibition and threatened her with an umbrella. And Bettina called her a blood sausage gone wild, if I remember correctly. On the day of departure, we talked to each other in a civilized manner, and I thought, now everything is good. But at the train station, for some inexplicable reason, Hanni hid behind a station house with my small suitcase, and I yelled — already on the train — over and over again in terror: "Hanni, Hanni!" Finally, she came out and handed me the suitcase. Unfortunately, I called her a jackass: "Where have you been, you jackass?" When I called her from Chicago to thank her for her time with me, she brayed many times:

"Hee-haw, hee-haw, hee-haw! I jackass!" And slammed the phone down, hanging up on me. I understood then that it was time to put the many years of friendship on ice for a while, the ice the jackass goes on when it gets too comfortable.

Our second beloved cat lived for only ten years and came to a strange end. He suffered from diarrhea for a year and threw up daily, which incited Larry to fits of rage in which he accused me of overfeeding him. He put him on a strict diet. And I could hear my little kitten meowing in desperation from hunger, but Larry wouldn't back down until he found out on the Internet that he was wrong and Pumi was allowed to eat double the amount of cat food. By now he was emaciated to fur and bone, and he carried himself like a piece of fluff when I picked him up, which I ended up doing often, because from one day to the next he refused to go to his drinking bowl by the window or eat from his food bowl in the kitchen. I kept refilling that until he finally nibbled from it. I called the vet, and she warned me that he had to drink a lot, or we should bring him to the vet's office. But Pumi absolutely refused to drink when I carried him to the window and put him in front of his water bowl. He resisted with horror, as if he feared that the water was poisoned. What's wrong with him? I asked myself in despair. Then I watched him prance around on Larry's lap with strong legs, and I said to my husband: "He's not weak at all. He's afraid of something, but what?" And I put my hand on the radiator and said: It doesn't work, there's no heat coming out, that's why it's so cold here in the living room!" Maybe Pumi was suffering from the cold? Larry, however, didn't care about what I said. "It's always been like this," was all he said. Well, then, I guess that's God's will, I thought acceptingly, and put my book in front of my nose, my favorite means of escaping the tiresome world.

A short time later, on a Saturday evening — Larry was praying for the safety of all of us at the Catholic Church near us, Mary on the Lake — when I saw Pumi looking intently at something under our dining room table. I thought, is he seeing ants? And went to see what under our table might be attracting his interest in such a way. I saw a wiggling creature that I first thought was a hamster tail. And then I continued to walk along the table and also past the corner of the sofa until I saw the head of a snake that was looking at me calmly, without moving. I looked at it, just as calmly — outwardly calm, but I was livid inside me. A long snake on the twenty-second floor of our high-rise building. Overlooking the park and Lake Michigan. Hadn't I laughed at the beginning of my life in Chicago at a City of Chicago program on TV (German for Americans) in which a woman always repeated the simple phrases: "There is a snake in here. There is a snake in here." Where were there snakes in Chicago? I thought, such a joke! Wrongly so. Because here was a snake that had landed in my living room, over a foot long, looking at me with that look: Well, aren't you amazed? I was not only amazed, I ran to the phone and called the police: "There is a snake in here" I kept on shouting. But the police must be used to such calls, because the woman on the phone calmly said: "Call an animal shelter" and gave me several phone numbers. No one there answered the phone, because it was Saturday night. Next, I dialed the number of the entrance hall of our high-rise building, where a doorman was sitting.

"There's a snake in here, there's a snake in here!" I shouted desperately, as if I were already stuck in the throat of a python.

"There is no snake!" the man yelled back, but when I didn't stop yelling, he calmly said: "OK, we are sending someone up!" First, my husband comes out of church with our big weekend pizza in his hands. I open the door while screaming: "There's a snake in here." He sets the pizza down in the kitchen and sits down on our red sofa, wanting to laugh his head off: "I saw that one hanging in the window above Pumi's water bowl at eleven o'clock last night and thought: My stupid wife bought our cat a toy snake!"

There's a knock at the door, and I open it to one of the building's engineers. He has a flashlight in his hand and calls out sternly: "Where's the snake, here?"

"Come with me, now I don't know where it's hiding." Fortunately, the thought occurs to me to lift a large pillow that has fallen on the carpet, and under it the snake lies peacefully curled up.

"My God!" exclaims the engineer in amazement, "A snake, indeed! And here I thought that the woman was drunk! I've never seen anything like that in my twenty years in this building!" So, to him, I was an alcoholic who sees snakes! Larry and the engineer laughed uproariously and seemed very pleased to have such an unusual visitor. The snake, however, was fed up and thought, I'd better get out of here, and it moved along the wall and under the radiator, which gave off no heat. The engineer went after it with his flashlight and yanked down the rack — and there was the animal, lying on the radiator, letting itself be warmed.

The man pointed the beam of the flashlight at it with the words: "I have orders from the property management to guard it, so it doesn't visit more neighbors and give us a reputation as a snake-infested house! The cockroaches have already been enough for us." On his cell phone, he talked tirelessly with the woman from the administration who, I'm sure, had already made herself comfortable and was sitting in front of the TV in her house dress.

Larry called his best friend, who always knows what to do and immediately asked, what does the snake look like? "Reddish, with a black pattern," Larry said.

"It's a red corn snake and not dangerous at all, it lives mostly on mice." Thank God, it didn't think our Pumi was a mouse, I thought, and grabbed my beloved, totally terrified animal, the bottle of Saturday night champagne and a big slice of the pizza and rushed into the bedroom, slamming the door shut behind me:

"I don't care what happens after me, and the snake as the devil in paradise!" I called to both the men, who, by now, were talking animatedly. Probably about cars. Or the ongoing war in Iraq and Afghanistan. American-instigated wars. Three hours later, snake hero Larry came into the bedroom and said:

"It is gone now!"

"How?"

"An exterminator came and grabbed it behind the head with our spaghetti tongs and put it in the box he brought."

"Did it let that happen?"

"No, it fought back furiously and hissed a lot!" And I felt ashamed that I had acted like a hysterical woman. But, at least, I hadn't been drunk off my ass. My niece thought she would have behaved more somberly than I had.

"I am not afraid of snakes! What happened to the poor animal?" Unfortunately, I didn't know. My nephew told me one more story: His friend had had a python snake and a red corn snake. He put a live rat into the terrarium as food for the python snake, but it hid fearfully. And the rat angrily bit the poor corn snake into two pieces. I didn't want to hear anything more about snakes. But wherever I go, I tell the story of how the devil himself visited me in my high-rise apartment in Chicago. And how he scared my cat to death, so that we had to put him to sleep a short time later. All my friends asked: Where did that snake come from? I answered: "I don't know that, either." I asked it: "Who is your daddy? But it couldn't speak yet." A wise man corrected me: "It didn't know the language of humans, only that of snakes!"

Dr. Sacks: "It's no wonder that you don't get pregnant, Gorda. You don't sleep together often enough."

"I know, Larry always gripes for a week or more after every fight."

Dr. Sacks: "And what are the two of you going to do about it?"

Me: "We found a way."

Dr. Sacks, very curious: "What is it?"

"Larry went to the porn shop and brought back movies."

Dr. Sacks: "And they helped?"

"Yes, they helped for a while."

"And then no longer?"

"Less than before, but I made an interesting observation!"

"What's that?"

"People judge women differently depending on whether they are dressed or naked. Dressed, the skinny ones are the most beautiful, but naked, it's the round ones, the ones with full breasts."

Dr. Sacks: "And the men?"

"The erection looks ridiculous."

Dr. Sacks, astonished: "Why ridiculous?"

"It stands off the man's body in such a funny way, as if for the Hitler salute!"

Dr. Sacks: "A strange comparison. Not very eroticizing!"

"Yes, but it's true. All of Germany greeted the 'Führer' with an erect member back then! They had the manhood craze, after all: Women to the hearth, men to the front! Women birth the sons; men get the swords!"

Every year, I had a first-class meal with Remo at the railroad station restaurant in Bern. He invited me to join him. One day, he told me that he no longer slept in the bedroom with his wife, but was back again in his bachelor's room, which I knew well. His wife, Helene, had reproached him for not taking care of her and their three children.

"That's why she refuses me sexual intercourse, which is my right, after all! That's quite an impertinence!"

"Well, then take care of her and your children!"

"The noise at home drives me nuts, so I'd rather go work in the library." I knew that I could call him at his office anytime, even on weekends. And I confessed to him that, last year, I had suggested to Larry that he rent the apartment next door in the high-rise and that we hadn't lived together since. But in the evenings, he would come over to watch TV. We noticed with astonishment that our marriage went much better when we were apart than together.

"Are you still sleeping with him?"

"I don't want to talk about that, you're not my Dr. Sacks, after all!"

"Say, what do you say you drive home with me now, my wife is with the children at her parents in Schaffhausen!" And I went along. That's how I saw the apartment again that should have become mine and that I often visited in my thoughts, and which I never left. It was empty; the brother, Jean, had half of the furniture and silverware sent to America, where he now taught Latin and Greek at a prestigious university. Despite that, the apartment in Bern was still full enough with the precious things that I had not known to appreciate when I was young. But now I knew their value, having had to acquire all the household goods myself, first the cheap china and glasses, later the better china and crystal glasses.

Everything was "scrimping and saving," like my parents used to say after the war: "We can't afford that, we have to save for the desk!" Or the Persian rug or the large upright closet. Saving, saving, saving, that was my life in the States — and studying, studying, studying to get the praise from professors, that was rarely or never given in Lausanne. It was only in the States that I began to believe in my intellect, which had been beaten out of me by my mother while I was doing my schoolwork, and which, in Lausanne, crumbled under the relentless criticism of the teachers. It was no accident that it was only at the end of a long course of studies in the States that I found the strength to believe in myself. And scribbled the first poems on paper, threw the scribbles away, picked them up again and asked myself: Are they worth anything? Am I worth anything? Poor Gorda, all her life she has been condemned to search for her worth. "You remind me of my mother-in-law, and I never did like her!" This sentence of my mother had been burned into my brain for life.

I cried in Remo's apartment, always cried, until he poured me grappa and fed me bread and Viande de Grisons and poured some more grappa again. Nothing could calm me down until I fell asleep as if unconscious. Forever, I hoped. But I woke up again with a severe headache.

"Please, take me to Hanni's right now," I said. And we drove to Emmenthal to my dear Hanni, who comforted me and said to me: "How could you do this to yourself? Are you a masochist?" And Karl-Hansi gave her the day off ("you don't need to cook"), and we drove to Merligen at Lake Thun, and I thanked the heavens for my beloved friend Hanni, with whom I could laugh again at the greatest misfortune of my life: to have lost Remo and Switzerland. But I still had Switzerland when I was with my Swiss friends, not everything was lost. Hanni was my favorite, because she lived near Lake Thun and thirty minutes from Bern.

"You shouldn't see Remo anymore," she advised me. But I knew it would turn out differently.

"He doesn't sleep with his wife anymore," I told her.

"That's what all men say who want to have an affair," Hanni warned.

"But it's true with him!"

"How do you know?"

"I saw his room again, the rumpled bachelor bed."

"Did you look at the bedroom they shared, too?"

"No, I would never do that! That's where his wicked mother used to sleep in. How lucky Helene was not to have known her, the jealous dragon who wanted to save her last son from marriage and for herself. Surely, she would have hated Helene, too."

"You don't know that," said Hanni.

"Yes, you do know that," I contradicted. (Am I nuts? Do my wounds never stop bleeding?). From then on, Remo and I went to a different place in Switzerland every year, to Murten and Coppet Castle, to Winterthur and Sierre, and to the gravesite of the poet Rainer Maria Rilke. We talked about literature like we used to, about Rilke and Gottfried Keller and Conrad Ferdinand Meyer and Max Frisch and Thomas Mann. We talked like two people destined for each other by fate, because they can speak so well together. That is how Nietzsche

Merligen on Lake Thun in Switzerland

had put it: one should marry the person with whom one can speak wonderfully. And he wanted to marry Lou Salomé, whom the young Rilke also loved later on and who must have spoken wonderfully like Rahel Varnhagen and Madame de Stael, who never kept her smart mouth shut, to the amazement of all of Weimar. And Remo saw in me again a woman that was his equal and didn't fear that I might be superior to him. He enjoyed my silliness and my pointed tongue when I described acquaintances and family members to him with as much wit as possible.

"I hope you don't talk about me like that when I'm not around?" he asked me thoughtfully at one point. Then he laughed again, as if he were safe from me and my sarcasm. I read him my latest lyrics, and he admired and celebrated me as a poet at a time when no one had any idea of my talent, except perhaps Friederike.

"You are a real poet," he said to me solemnly by Lake Murten, raising his glass of Valpolicella and toasting me as if I were a laurel-adorned goddess of victory. But I was not a winner at all, only a loser in the game of life's great happiness: here I was sitting with the man destined for me by fate, but he had married someone else and gave her three children, who would make it financially impossible for him to leave them. "How could you bring three children into the world? I didn't even have the strength to have one!" But I knew why he had had three children like his brother (whom he tried to imitate in everything): he desperately wanted a son, and only the third child was one.

"Now everything will change at home, now I have a little son!" he said back then. But nothing changed at all, and on weekends, he continued to go to his office so he wouldn't have to put up with the noisy kids at home. He became exactly the father I had not wanted for my children, the absent, the unknown father.

"If I leave my wife, will you leave Larry?" he asked me in Sierre. And I will never get over the fact that I said no with the words: "You're impossible to live with!" If I said yes, I would now know whether he was serious about his words or not. Now I live with the uncertainty. As if that made any difference! We would certainly have become a very unhappy couple. But a couple, albeit a silenced one.

The Dean of German Studies, a Manfred Henning with a thick crown of black hair, had accepted me for the doctoral program of his prestigious university after I obtained my master's degree at the State University of Illinois. A university in the States is prestigious if it is private and expensive. Not prestigious if it is public and less expensive, but expensive enough. That way, democratic America provides for the timely separation of the population into rich and non-rich, into better and so-called less good universities. And when we ask in the States, 'where did you study?' we ask at the same time: Are you rich or not? There is no need to ask about the place of residence, which is also a property indicator. In the States, after the master's degree, you have to study for two more years and then take a big final exam before you are allowed to write the doctoral thesis, which is also a kind of habilitation thesis. Hence all the effort. It was with regret that I turned down the famously expensive university in a park-like suburb of Chicago, because it couldn't guarantee me immediate employment as a Teaching Assistant, which would have freed me from the tremendous tuition costs. Back then, we still sat then on the old chairs that Larry's dad had brought us from various bars and that my mother had painted black. And we ate off the cheap white china from the big department stores for the masses of poor people in the States, and we had wicker chairs instead of armchairs. And cutlery made of metal, and not a piece of real silverware anywhere. And our glasses shone uncut.

Despite our obviously modest circumstances and my rejection from the university, Professor Dr. Manfred Henning, the dean of the German studies department for the rich and beautiful, one day became a friend of our family. The recommendation from my old state university must have been so excellent that he forgave us the second-rate wine in the uncut glasses. He came to our house for dinner every Wednesday. Larry wasn't on duty until later the next day, he himself wasn't on duty in the morning, and my beautiful friend Annina was a grass widow during the week anyway, because her husband worked at a hospital in Ann Arbor as a surgeon and rented a small apartment there. He only came home on weekends. Annina and I would fool around on Wednesdays as if we were seventeen and untroubled by the weights of marriage on our hands and feet and hearts. But almost more enjoyable than the evenings were the long conversations I had with Manfred on the phone every day. His voice sounded exactly like Remo's, although he originated from the Black Forest and not from German-speaking Switzerland. And we talked about literature (he was writing a book about Rilke!) and I felt as if I were talking to Remo, but this time to an unmarried one and without the three 'interfering' children. I could conquer this man here in Chicago, and I would grasp the happiness, that I had so foolishly lost in Switzerland, firmly by the collar! At last, at last, I too would be happy like my friend Charlotte, who had named her daughter Gorda, albeit Elizabeth Gorda, and she was called Eliza, but Gorda as a middle name after all, and she was my beloved godchild. And Charlotte, after an ugly divorce battle, had gotten the man meant for her, a wonderful one whom I too could have loved, a kind of Robert Gernhardt, who was my dream man among the poets of Germany. Although my good friend Peter Rühmkorf was indisputably the greatest of them all. But the heart has its own reasons. And how seldom it wants to love where it should love! For women like me, life without love seems pointless: A life built on sand!

With Manfred, suns came up for me: it couldn't be a coincidence that he had Remo's hair, that his voice sounded like Remo's, and that he was writing a book about Rilke while Remo was managing the Rilke archive in Bern. Inside me, there was jubilation. I had been fated to have a second chance, just as my mother had gotten our wonderful daddy in 1946 after the suicide of her war-criminal husband, and I would get Manfred! Why he had never married, I sometimes wondered, because he was already at the age when my friends had their first marriage behind them and their second or third ahead of them. Oh, what the heck: Manfred had not yet found the right woman, namely me; he had unconsciously waited for me; he couldn't do anything smarter; we were guided by invisible spirits and were striving towards each other with the full force of fate! One day he said the meaningful words: "Come, let us (he actually said "us!") write some beautiful love poems together!" And I wrote poems for him that I still consider my most beautiful.

A Winter Night's Dream

My king
Wears a crown of
Black hair
I would like
To break off some pieces from it

I would plant it
Deep in
My garden
From it, soon would grow
An original German forest

He could slowly meander
To take in the air
To melancholically look upon
The stolen peaks

Then I would rustle
Tenderly down
From above I would
Keep my king
Busy in the woods

That way he would
Beg me for signs
And my smile, that
He would not see for
All the trees.

Dr. Lindemann from NDR Hannover, however, found the poem weak: too romantic. Too playful. Not worthy of a modern woman.

A few times, Manfred and I made out when Larry brought Annina home, but as soon as he heard him in the hallway, he went to say goodbye to him and me. Yet, at the time, Larry lived next door.

That's how years went by. Or so it seemed to me.

I began to desire him like Potiphar's wife desired young Joseph, which Thomas Mann describes sensitively, probably because he knew what futile desire meant, for he himself dreamed of boys when he lay with his fertile wife Katia. When reading *Joseph and His Brothers*, I have always had to think of how jealous he must have been of his brother Heinrich, who could simply go to a brothel to satisfy his preference for large-breasted and corpulent women. The time we lived in, on the other hand, forbade him Greek boy-love. Also, the smooches with Manfred took place very rarely, considering that we were destined by heaven for each other. Or were we not meant for each other at all? A student at my state university, who had previously been at the fine, expensive one, told me Manfred Henning was queer and supposedly had a relationship with the famous Thomas-Mann expert, Professor Dr. Ernst Pfennig. I asked him about it, he denied vehemently and said the homosexual act disgusted him.

"And why are you so close friends with him?"

"Because he is my father substitute; I never met my own, he was killed in the war."

"Mine, too," I said, even though I knew he hadn't fallen but had hanged himself, but at the time I kept quiet about our family shame. Unfortunately, soon after, under the influence of his favorite drink, Southern Comfort, he told me he had fallen in love years ago with a red-haired assistant who was writing a doctoral thesis on Erich Mühsam. She was married to a rich banker whom she would never leave. And there was another, older lover, who had suffered immensely because of the red-haired one. And, at home, in the Black Forest with his mother, the third one taught at a country school, although she had inherited a toy factory and didn't have to work. He has a whole harem, I thought; and, as a culture vulture and opera fan, also of Mozart's wonderful music in *The Abduction from the Seraglio*. Mozart here and Mozart there, what woman voluntarily joins a seraglio?

Slowly, my poems became desperate. Desperately beautiful.

The Abandoned Maiden

He
Is a flock of birds
That soared over my
Silenced garden
And that now trills and whistles
And chatters for my
Ear and eye and heart
And the tips of my fingers

He
Is a flock of birds
That eats my fruit
Leaving nothing for me and thus I remain
Without cherries and apples
Lost the peaches
Wonderful music
Playing inside me

I
Am a garden that's been eaten up
In the autumn, whose birds
Traveled into the heart of summer
See, I eagerly grasp,
For the white sheet

That icily forms a cloak
Of silence around my shame

I told Remo of my unrequited love for Manfred and added: "He is like you; I love you in him."

"Why don't you finally leave the man alone?" Remo growled impatiently. "Do you really still love me?" Oddly enough, it was my infatuation with Manfred that made it possible for me to love Remo without wanting to possess him again. I wanted an unattached Manfred. — Unattached?

I had to admit to myself that Manfred was at least as attached as Remo with his stable full of children. (Cornelia had always said that about her brother: He has a stable full of children). Manfred maintained relationships with three women, and he had a disreputable father substitute. I mean, Anaïs Nin also slept with her father, there was such a thing today. Maybe, just out of opportunism, he might let the old creep get to him. I say 'old creep' because I once spent an evening with him and some other professors and afterwards he said to Manfred: "I didn't know that Gorda was a hetera." Just because I spread a little charm around. Spread? Wasted!

For him, there would be no friendships with women, that was a puzzling sentence Manfred had said to me under the influence of Southern Comfort. And what was his relationship with me? This in-between thing of eroticism and friendship? Without alcohol, he was secretive like Remo ("a book with seven seals"), who always denied to still be sleeping with his wife or with anyone else. He only wanted to possess me. Such a liar!

I suffered like a dog abandoned by its master. In this confused situation, my brother Max told me that his boss had had the handwriting of all his employees examined by a graphologist in Hamburg. His own had turned out excellent. I asked for the address of this modern witch and sent her a handwritten card from Manfred. She wrote me in elegant, right-angled handwriting that she didn't do expert opinions for private persons, only for companies, but since she held Max in high esteem, she wanted to make an exception for me.

Here is the expert opinion on Manfred:

> It is indicative of an educated, but very complicated personality, difficult to get at. The writer has something to hide and hardly lets you see inside him. He is very controlled; he is therefore not very — not to say not at all — spontaneous. The intellect is dominant. Everything seems to run through the intellect. But for all his quickness of thought, the writer seems peculiarly lifeless. There is hardly any question of youthful freshness or even dynamism.
>
> He is not a person who cherishes contact with other persons, no matter how much routine in dealing with other people may be at play. He also lacks elasticity and, accordingly, adaptability — not the will to adapt, where it is opportune for him, but only there. Then he can certainly be quite diplomatic and doesn't have too many scruples in doing so. His self-esteem is highly unbalanced. Accordingly, he is easily hurt. This easy vulnerability must not — or rather: should only conditionally — be equated with sensitivity. The writer can even be very harsh. He is not broad-minded

and tolerant. If his sense of self were more stable and unified, he would not need to fear so much that he might show himself to be vulnerable. A tendency to present himself as something special and original will be present, as will a tendency toward understatement. The latter, however, is more likely to be considered as 'fishing for compliments'. A sense of achievement is particularly important to him — all the more so because he has little opportunity to live from his own substance and fullness of personality. Even though he can be witty and original, given favorable circumstances, he is ultimately not a cheerful person.

In his work, he is persistent and tenacious in the pursuit of his goals, also very thorough, this aspect possibly already exaggeratedly so. He is extremely ambitious. The ambition is a decisive driving force, not a vital drive. It is difficult to imagine him as a family man. Rather, he is a more of a lone wolf. For him, a perfectly natural and casual, uncomplicated, and tension-free life together will hardly be possible.

What a shock! This expert opinion hit my romantically sick soul with a clenched fist. Hadn't Goethe already known that everything romantic is pathological? This was the proof! And I sent the report to Manfred. Out of revenge? Out of sadism? He said very curtly: "Well, well," on the phone. And I was ashamed and out of a sense of justice sent my handwritten letter to the highly gifted Hamburg witch for appraisal.

Character assessment based on handwriting.

The range of interests of this agile and gifted scribe is very wide. With ease, almost effortlessly, Mrs. S. grasps the most diverse of phenomena and contexts. She grasps things both intellectually and intuitively. She is always responsive and open-minded and very easily motivated. And she is so dexterous and skillful that she seems to manage everything 'off the cuff'. She goes out into the world spontaneously, curiously, and restlessly. But she always withdraws into herself.

She doesn't dwell on trifles. Her vision is directed to the essentials. She thinks in long threads of thought, probably sometimes running the risk of getting too deeply involved in one idea or another. But there is also always an effort to be objective when making judgments. Her commitment can be very intense. Occasionally, her vital resilience probably lags behind the intensity of the commitment.

Her contacts with other people are, when viewed superficially, quite uncomplicated, casual, and easy-going. Thanks to her sensitive touch, she understands other people very quickly, even in more complicated relationships. She finds it more difficult to form deep and, above all, lasting bonds. They could easily be perceived as an impairment of her individuality. So it may be that the writer tries to avoid final ties more or less. When she feels more irritated (in the broadest sense), then she lashes out (which should not be understood in the physical sense). The diversity of impressions is great. One will have to regard it as a lucky coincidence that the writer has the ability to convert experiences into artistic forms. Thus she limits herself — in her inclination to the unlimited and infinite — time and again. And the inner restlessness is directed to goals and into paths.

Mrs. S. is youthful in her liveliness, naturalness, and immediacy. She will, however, also have to be a bit careful that she doesn't become a candle that is lit at both ends. But being able to express what she has experienced is certainly a great relief.

And I sent the report to Manfred. He only said: "How beautiful!" And I knew I had to kick my love addiction with the help of writing and wrote the story *Gerhild's Revenge*, in which the mysterious man himself gets to speak and explain himself.

Gerhild's Revenge

I am a neat person. I don't mean that in the superficial sense, that is, someone walks into my apartment and snap, everything is in its place. On the contrary, the uninvited guest might fall over boxes on the carpet, find food leftovers in the kitchen, the bed would probably have been left ransacked, books spilled all over the secretary, most of it surrounded by a dust-silk layer at rest — and yet I am a tidy person. That's what

I keep telling Gerhild when she talks about untidiness in private, referring to my workplace, which is none of her business, like everything else, but there are people who wipe dust-seeking fingers on other people's furniture for no reason, without a hint of justification. I said to Gerhild when she entered my apartment uninvited — I couldn't kick her out, after all, but next time I certainly will, if it happens again — the picture is deceiving, and again Gerhild said, you're untidy, and that's when I wanted to know from her whether I might have dirty dishes in the living room, books in the bedroom, cigarette butts in the dining room — and Gerhild looked as puzzled as all carelessly judgmental people for whom an insight candle has been lit. She had not yet heard the term 'order' interpreted this way. She laughed a little slyly, with which she wants to provoke me to further explanations, because she knows I don't like to explain, at least not when it's about my person; one thing leads to another in these explanations and the more clearly one explains, the more of an attack surface one offers the other, the more unprotected is the space that surrounds us. This was already the case in childhood: if you admitted you had lied, mother would say, you're lying again, so you'd rather not admit anything at all — and so my dorky brother became the family liar, while I, on the other hand, could say what I wanted; I was always believed. These are such life lessons. Only Gerhild doesn't want to keep to my rule of silence, she asks and asks, morning-noon-evening, she drills holes into my fabric of life, and so she also drilled that day, when she appeared uninvited at my place, inquiring what I understood by order. And so I explained to her twice, and for all that I use each room only for its specific purpose and for no other, I eat in the dining room, I smoke in the living room, I write and read in the study. You won't find any books in my living room, no food leftovers in the study, no full ashtrays in the bedroom, I stressed again, and Gerhild seemed to chew on the answer, at least she made chewing movements and otherwise kept her mouth shut, which gave me time to erect the wall of silence again; I had work to do, I grumbled, she would have to go — and she really did go, to my relief, although she was wearing violet, and violet is my favorite color, and I would like to be allowed to touch anything violet for a moment, like the irises that I prefer to have on my work table; yet Gerhild knows nothing of my color preference, she would even scoff at it, like at my so-called order, which is not so-called at all, but simply and par excellence means THE ORDER for me, the order that I need to have in order to be able to function, and I function splendidly, if one considers the immense number of articles that I publish annually in our magazine — such an article grows out of ten or twenty other articles, and how much time the writing of such a single ridiculously short-seeming essay devours, is known only to those who are themselves occupied with it, and since Gerhild doesn't write any essays — she is employed, after all, only part-time with us, sometimes in the morning, sometimes in the afternoon, just as she likes, she has no idea of real discipline and order, like all artistically inclined people have — at least that's what Gerhild says, although there certainly must have been very tidy artists who painted in their studio and not exactly in the kitchen — but Gerhild always emphasizes that she does everything in the same room, and with her, that is a kind of bedroom and living room and library room rolled into one. I saw it once, after a Christmas party at the office, which ended in Gerhild's apartment — with several colleagues, of course — with a drink of wine; I got a glass of Southern Comfort, of which Gerhild happened to have a bottle in the closet, although she couldn't know that this is my favorite drink and she also had Winston cigarettes in her linen drawer, when I ran out of mine, although Gerhild doesn't smoke at all; then I got to see her studio, which is also her bedroom and on the wall there were long rows of books, it's amazing what Gerhild reads, even my beloved Nietzsche was there, the *Birth of Tragedy* and a lot more — and actually, I saw on a small table plates with leftover potatoes and vegetables or whatever — so Gerhild eats and reads and paints in one room, which, for me, is a monstrous thought; I can only function if I do the right thing in the right room, i.e., read where reading is to be done and eat where I have a table intended for it and smoke where the ashtray is.

All my achievements have only been possible through this kind of division of life; I had to earn my own money for my studies, I studied in the evenings when others went out; you can only do that if you do what you do completely, if foreign fields of study don't carry over into what you are attacking at the moment, when one doesn't long for Southern Comfort in the study, think of one's books in the dining room, and dream of one's bed in the kitchen — where I am, that's where I am completely, I said to Gerhild, who pointed with her finger to her bed, which is, at the same time, a couch and several armchairs when you push them apart; well, I hate such multipurpose furniture and rooms and life. But I love Gerhild's paintings, there is no doubt about it, as much as her way of being upsets me, that's how unresistingly I adore her paintings. Yet, Gerhild's own kind of chaos also reigns in these pictures: you could say that each picture is simultaneously a still life and a landscape painting and a portrait — it's as if she superimposed several genres, there's always a face, often a familiar one to me, floating somewhere in the landscape or among the birds and flowers, because Gerhild 'utilizes' all the people around her, or whatever you want to call it; suddenly the face of my colleague Hansen appears in a vegetable still life — behind it North German moorland. Gerhild, you're going to be famous, I said, standing in front of just this picture; I was surprised at myself, at the verve while otherwise I am restrained, and Gerhild looked at me in amazement, as if a gate had opened in a barricaded castle, and immediately she wanted to push her foot in there, asking me if I actually had a girlfriend, but then I quickly spoke of the next picture, in which she depicts a mountain landscape, with several female heads superimposed on each other, which gives the strangest impression, as if at least four pictures had moved into each other, and Gerhild said, yes, these are my dearest girlfriends, unfortunately they all live in a different place. When I am old, I would like to have all three of them around me, just like they already live together in me now. And that is just the unrestrained element in Gerhild, which so frightens and attracts me; it disgusts me in life, and I find it enchanting in her pictures, and perhaps I am inconsistent in the artistic field, but everybody has their weakness, and better that way than the other way around, I tell myself — but Gerhild exploited this weakness in a flash and demanded time from me for a portrait — I can already say, she demanded, so sure was she of her cause and, of course, it was hard for me to resist, who wouldn't like to find themselves in a picture that will, one day, hang in a museum, of that I am convinced, but as soon as Gerhild had her foot in my door, she marched into my life, she opened windows and bolts where I like to see locked rooms. She sketched me after hours at the office, she sketched me at work, she did sketches during the birthday parties that are a regular occurrence in every major office. When I lifted my head, I saw Gerhild's bent over some piece of paper — she didn't show me anything at the time, I don't know how I looked on those pieces of paper — it gives one a strange feeling to be watched like that, a feeling of warm-and-cold; does she like what she sees or doesn't she? And in the evenings and mornings I would stand in front of the mirror longer, studying this chance face, which up to now couldn't or would not arouse my interest, and I tried to look with Gerhild's eyes, but then my own image blurred into those I had seen in her — clearly I am not an artist — but now we often stayed together in the evening, because of the drawings of course, and Gerhild took out the bottle of Southern Comfort she had ready for me, and we chatted more and more often, and he who chats, chats away, especially after three glasses of Southern Comfort, many a happily knotted knot comes loose in me; I don't pay that much attention to the effect of my words, Gerhild kept on asking holes into the fabric of my life, or did she instead mend holes in her image of me? as she said, it all depends on who asks and who answers, at least that's what I told Gerhild, that for five or ten or fifteen years, I didn't want to be too specific, I've had a mistress, but I don't take her with me anywhere — and why not, that's just completely and naturally my business, but Gerhild didn't stick to 'my business' or 'my private business', she kept asking, and since we were together so much because of the portrait — she said, she had started it by now — she kept poking around in my most intimate business, and that includes the women in my life, what do you mean five or ten or fifteen years, my dear, she said, she dared to call me my dear, I hate aloofness, and I call maybe four people in my life, you and my dear, apart from my closest relatives, you always evade, Jochen, she had the audacity to use my first name, call me Gerhild, and what can you do, aloofness or not, or should I say, you always lie, Gerhild said, laughing, I mean, it does matter whether you've been with her for five or ten or fifteen years, or maybe nine, I said thoughtfully, but then Gerhild interjected that it couldn't be nine, because I had met her at the time of the moon landing, and that would have been fifteen years ago. I said yes, I talk too much when I'm drinking. During the day, I don't feel obliged, in any way, to confirm what has been said, I often feel an urge to blur what seems to be clear; she is uncomfortably on my trail, I thought, and I prophylactically contradicted her, she would have had me confirm the moon landing date. Why should I have you confirm the moon landing date? Gerhild inquired, what do I care about the moon landing? I just remember very clearly how you spoke of your girlfriend at that certain time — that's not true at all, I said dryly and soberly and swore to myself to drink less, in general, but especially in Gerhild's presence, because in the meantime she wondered why I never brought my girlfriend to festivities. I would have a reason to hide her, and the only reason Gerhild thought of was that she was married, and from then on, Gerhild called her Isolde; she had the impudence to call the woman I love Isolde, because she knows that I love Richard Wagner, again such an artistic preference for the fuzzy, I, who value a clear line in my life above all, but just not clarity towards strangers; I myself never ask Anke about her husband, I don't owe Gerhild any explanation at all regarding why I keep Anke 'hidden', as Gerhild calls it — but in the meantime, Gerhild's curious questions touched another area in my life, my parents' house in the south of France, where I spend my summer vacations every year. Would I take Isolde with me? Gerhild asked. I didn't react at all for a few weeks, until I finally was fed up listening to it and let out a no, which seemed to satisfy Gerhild for a while, but then she circled back to the south of France again and whether I wanted to meet her in Marseille next year or the year after — I stuck to yes-and-no, which obviously annoyed her, and I told her, to distract her, about the trips I regularly take from my parents' house, to Vienna or to Italy. Were you alone in Venice? Gerhild suddenly asked, and I said no, and in Vienna? And I said no again, and in Florence? Then, my boundless stupidity finally dawned on me, and I spoke of something else, but now Gerhild was scanning my travels in southern Europe, whether with the parents, and if not the parents, the brother perhaps, no, no, I cried angrily, but now it's over, I have to go home. That way, I escaped my drilling and tormenting spirit — I have never met such an inquisitive person as Gerhild — I mean, so gratuitously curious, she probably refers to the fact of our, how shall I put it, nightly embraces, result of too much alcohol, which are extremely unpleasant to me during the day; it is incomprehensible to me how I can always forget myself like that; that's it: I forget myself when I drink, I become aloof and blurry like all average people. I told Gerhild, that's my Dionysian element, but during the day I don't know anything about it, often I have no real memory at all of these so-called hugs, which Gerhild holds under my eyes at highly inappropriate moments, she trumps with it as if she had some rights to derive from it, for example her questioning rage, her rummaging in my most private areas, which now include the women in my life — I was justifiably annoyed, when Gerhild told me one day that she now knew I had a second mistress in the south of France, whom she, from then on mockingly, as it seemed to me, called the beautiful Marianne — no, I wasn't immediately angry; at first, I was puzzled by Gerhild's subtlety, her talent for snooping, for keeping all the details I had carelessly thrown in, her ability to connect something I said two years ago with the latest material, while forgetting where I can, what's with this ridiculous accumulation of shabby plot fragments, my God, the garbage a life like that accumulates, you have to clean it out day by day to be able to breathe; happy is he who forgets, that's my favorite song, so I forget where I can, and here comes this woman, this Gerhild, collecting and preserving and cherishing that which I have thrown away and regularly confronts

398

me with it, when I would like to use my hands, white-as-heaven, for better purposes than to get rid of done stuff again — before I knew what was happening to me. I had told Gerhild, surely again under the influence of this unholy swill, that the French woman doesn't need to do anything because she is very wealthy. "Why don't you marry her?" Gerhild asked; to my irritation, she had taken to addressing me as 'Du', the German informal 'you', while I addressed her as 'Sie', the German formal 'you', and we conduct our conversations on this 'Sie-Du' level still to this day, even though Gerhild sometimes switches to the 'Sie' when we are with other people or in sober daylight, in which she, too, must become aware of our relationship in all its limitations, but in the evening, after a glass of wine, she was no longer capable of using the formal 'you' for me, Gerhild says. She would not bring herself to use the 'Sie', the formal mode of address; to do so, would be ridiculous, as ridiculous as my so-called order; Gerhild finds and finds no end when she gets her hooks into something, and I would always lie, five or ten or fifteen years, that made a tremendous difference, and whether one woman knew about the other, and it would be a joke that I didn't want to marry a rich woman because of the unfavorable power structure, and that I wouldn't take Isolde — I mean Anke — because I didn't think much of divorce — that I simply was domineering and selfish and cranky. But by then, I had had more than enough, a huge rage rose up in me: what does this woman actually want from me? What business of hers is my private life? She has barged into my circles uninvited; she knocks around in my garden with her cheeky hoe, she messes up my flower beds and tears down my fences, she talks about lying where I see discretion, which is a tremendously precious trait — while she shamelessly chats about her love affairs as if they were future paintings. She is an exhibitionist, and her questions have a castrating streak, which is why I have to reduce the nightly hugs to a minimum, if they can't be abandoned altogether because of my unfortunate Puntila personality, that self-forgetfulness that rises up under the influence of alcohol. I continue to explain to her this strange break in my being in the most matter-of-fact way possible, so that she will stick to the fact that she has no rights to claim my time and feelings during the day. I am completely connected to Anke, both mentally and physically, and in the summer, there are just Giovanna and Francoise — after all, I didn't marry Anke and don't owe anyone fidelity — I'm just human and I can't take any more complications, i.e., I didn't know anything about complications until now, only Gerhild points her cheeky finger at my inconsistencies, as she says, and I suffer all this in the name of art, because I was waiting for the birth of this painting, and every day, Gerhild promised me she would show it to me; so twelve weeks have already passed, but yesterday the time finally came, I saw it: And, unfortunately, it must be said, I have fought and endured, explained and denied and rejected in vain, Gerhild's painting is a disaster, it is outside the scope of her other work, it is a misfit, an outcast, a monster of a painting. This time, instead of the delicate, floating, interlocking, Gerhild has divided the rather large area into many small boxes, and in each of these squares is an embryo with features that are supposed to be similar to mine — but in my opinion, there is no similarity at all — and the disgusting thing about the picture is, that each embryo, or how should I call these disgusting creatures, is doing something, so one is reading, the other is writing and again one is eating, the next one is smoking, and a particularly disgusting one is puckering its lips for a kiss or what is that supposed to mean? And then there is a small male in the middle, such a small weather-vane male, that is colored completely in purple, in my favorite color, but which is hideous here, while all the others are blue or red and sometimes a little yellowed, this male drinks from a kind of bottle, in short: a horrible picture that I would not want to own in any case. From now on, I'm refusing any further sessions. Just now, the woman called, she's coming to bring me the miserable piece of work. That is a tremendous impudence of this person. I hope I still have a bottle of Southern Comfort in the house. I can't possibly stand her sober, or I'll throw her out.

She calls the painting *The Birth of Tragedy from the Spirit of the Bottle*, another outrageous impertinence. But the craziest thing is that she claims she loves me. She claims to be quite unhappy and to love me. Looks like we're in for some fun and games. A hysterical person!

And my poems sounded like this:

You are like a tulip

When, in my garden,
a stinging nettle stood
next to a tulip
I inevitably fell in love
With the stinging nettle

Oh, tulip, tulip,
I rejoiced,
why do you burn
My adoring fingers that adore you above all

Don't you know
That you are a tulip
I sobbed and pressed

The burning weed
To my fevering breast

Which, in its brainlessness,
Never knew anything about a tulip

While the young poet Goethe, before he found his sweetheart Christiane for his bed, was constantly on the run from the women who loved him back (Friederike, Lilli Schönemann, Mrs. von Stein), Heinrich Heine 'needed' the unrequited love (to his rich Hamburg cousins Amalie and Therese) in his youth in order to be able to write poetry. And one of his most beautiful poems on the subject of 'unrequited love' is *Lorelei*, which can almost be called a folk song of the Germans (based on the setting by Silcher — but who even happens to know the composer's name?). I was doomed to love and sing about stinging nettles, even if they grew in a huge Dutch tulip field. Finally, I was exhausted beyond belief by myself and my senseless loving.

Final requests

So take my wings then
Pluck them from me
I'm not going to fly anymore
Neither today nor tomorrow
Towards home

So break my feet
And carry me
I'm not going to walk
Neither today nor tomorrow

Away from my home

So extinguish my soul
Crush it
I'm not glowing anymore
Like I didn't yesterday and still don't today
I'm standing there empty

"What are you complaining about?" Remo had asked me. "You are writing, that's all that counts! And are you still loving me, too?"

"Yes, yes!" I cried desperately, thinking: I'm in love with a man I can't have back. I'm in love with a man who is a liar. And I'm married to a man who lives next door and would rather get drunk with his friends at his favorite bar at night than be with me. I'm a poetry-writing, unlucky worm! And I suggested to Remo that we stop seeing each other for a while.

Desperately, I wrote to Friederike: "I seemed as gifted for love as men seemed ungifted to be loved by me, therefore I feel like a genius swimmer doomed, for life, to practice in a drying bed."

The Desert Bush

Took all the water for itself
Was the ruler of the desert
Poisoned the ground wisely
For friend and for foe
So it stands alone
An arid ball in autumn
And sun to sun in spring -
So you stand alone

You have hogged all the water
You are the ruler of the desert
And even though you came in crippled form
It was always you
Blossom's sun scrawny ball
Sometimes desert's wages, sometimes desert's sorrow
Love: it was always you
You poisoned my life
With your delight

That reminds me: I invited Hanni to Chicago a few years after her husband died, paid for her — the ruined woman — the airfare, and lunches and dinners at restaurants. Larry was angry all the time because the visit interfered with his habits (crossword puzzles, Sudoku, going to the bar to get drunk). "I don't want to have to chauffeur you guys around all the time!" And he added: "She's butt-ugly, mind you! How can you talk about a great beauty! She looks like an old country wench! She could be my Polish grandmother!" Then I told him about her former Lorelei beauty, for which every man who saw her would fall. Larry just laughed derisively, and he started arguing with me in front of our guest.

"No, that restaurant is too expensive, we won't go there!" Hanni got annoyed with our quarrels and one day threw them at me, saying: "Do think about me! I don't have a husband anymore, and you're fighting with yours!" Yet, all these days I had thought only of her! After she left, Larry berated me for my choice of impossible girlfriends. On the way to the German restaurant 'Brauhaus', one of our favorite places, where we had also been a few times with Hanni, he said cynically: "She looks ten years older than you." In return for the compliment, I insulted him as being a macho man who only looks at women's faces, if not at their breasts and buttocks.

When the older waitress came to our table, she enquired kindly: "Where is your daughter today? Has she flown back to Europe yet?" Larry wanted to laugh his head off!

After the 'breakup' with Manfred, the house friend, I had gotten into the habit of calling Remo at the office sometimes, even though I didn't want to meet with him anymore. To my amazement, one day he said sharply to me: "Stop calling me! Don't you actually notice when people don't want to have anything to do with you anymore?"

"And you say that to the woman you once loved so much?" I asked him in disbelief and deeply hurt. I hadn't had any children and probably hadn't realized how much time had passed in the meantime since he had last asked me: Do you still love me? It's been years. And I pondered: What has happened in the meantime?

"Do you love another woman? Do you have a mistress?"

"No, of course not, otherwise I wouldn't have such inferiority complexes!" I believed him because I wanted to believe it. But he continued to answer the e-mails we sent each other in the meantime like the whole world networked on the Internet. And I suppressed the eerie feeling of belonging to the old rusty iron in his life. One day, he told me he had now put his life in order and packed up my love letters once torn apart in passionate anger.

"Where do you want me to send them? Or do you want to look at them again first?" Why would I want to see them when he could no longer bear to possess them? I said no and missed the last chance to meet him again. I was overcome one morning with a mad urge to ask him if he still loved me. I called him, and he cheered — as if he had been waiting months for this question —

"Yes, I love ... I still admire and love you! I've been regretting what I did to you lately, too!" Again, I wondered: What has happened? And I sent him the announcement of the finally published novel of our failed love. Then I sent him a yellow envelope with the pink book inside. The envelope came back unopened. I froze! Hadn't he said a few weeks ago that he still loved me? What was going on? My emails also came back unanswered. Return to sender. The unanswered emails hit me deep in the pubescent heart. On revient toujours à ses premiers amours (you always go back to your first love), the French call my type of Tristan-and-Isolde-fidelity. The computer remained silent and gave no explanations. He didn't answer the mobile phone. I left a message on his answering machine: "I'll be coming to Bern and to your house soon!" This threat didn't frighten him.

I had the publishing house send him the perfidious message: "I am widowed!" And I thought, he must react to that! But he didn't react. At least the message was not returned to sender. So, he existed somewhere in Bern. I was slowly going crazy. At the same time, repairs were taking place in our high-rise building, lasting eight hours a day. We, the residents, had to endure horrible months, during which we felt as if a giant drill was screeching in our mouths every day. Nothing helped, no earplugs and no noise-cancelling device over the ears like those worn by workers at the airport, which Larry had thoughtfully bought for me. I lay down in bed, not wanting to get up. Larry lay down beside me and said: "I'll take care of you." I wanted to die.

And would have died without Larry and Pumi. How long can you stand this? I thought: the screeching in the building and the silence in the computer? Is Remo still alive? And I dreamed how a huge black bird, or was it a fighter plane, was racing toward me through the open window. This is my end, I thought, frozen in the dream. And in life. One morning, at five o'clock, the phone rang. Hanni was on the telephone.

"Why are you calling me so early?" I asked her angrily. "We are still sleeping!"

"Gorda, I have something important to tell you!"

"What?"

"Remo is dead! I just found his obituary in the paper!" Larry looked at me questioningly from the bed.

"Remo is dead," I said, as if it were insignificant news: "Hanni just read his obituary!"

"I see," said Larry, as if the news meant nothing to him, either. And I went back to bed. And got up again and went to the living room to call Hanni back. But she was already gone. Remo had died on August 28. That was Goethe's birthday. And he had been born on the day when the shots were fired in Sarajevo and WWI began, although not in the same year. It was my mother who was born in the unlucky year of 1914.

Every day of the year is a day of joy and a day of misfortune! Now, on August 28, I would have to think not only of Goethe's birthday, but also of Remo's death. And June 28 was the birthday of my great love Remo, and that of the horrible WWI, which gave birth to the second even more horrible one. And, during the second one, a baby was born in the Third Reich, who was given the strange name Gorda, while the unfortunate father Adolf Suhr shot dead or had to shoot dead partisans at the Russian front, who knows for sure.

On August 21 — a week before Remo's death — I had tried once more to call him on his cell phone. This time, someone answered the phone and said, in a choked, feeble voice, the long-drawn-out word: Glüüüüüüüück … I pressed the off button, startled. This was not Remo, who always said, succinctly and clearly: Glück!! Was it his son? But then my phone rang, and I shouted into space: hello, hello, hello! And nobody answered. I guessed that Remo, on the other end of the tremendously long line, had heard my voice. But he said nothing. That was the last time, for both of us.

I had said to him years ago, instruct your family, they must notify me of your death. He didn't do it. Why not? Out of sensitivity? Out of sadism?

Hanni went to his funeral service at the St. Mary's Church in Bern and told me on the phone, for two hours, how it was. His three grown children sat on the left with their families, and on the right sat his wife with a baby on her lap. The pastor first read out a text from Remo himself, which he is said to have rewritten many times over — close to fifteen times. In it, he first addressed his loved ones with the words: "Dear family, if I may call you that?" (Why may? It was his family, after all!) Then he speaks of his love for his wife and thanks her for her faithfulness and her intelligent humor. He said he had not been a good husband, nor a good father, nor even a good friend. He had not contributed much to the upkeep of the houses inherited from the grandfather. Financially, he considered himself a failure. And at the end, he sent his regards to his five cats (why didn't he ever tell me that he and his wife loved cats like I do?).

After this damning self-portrait, the lady pastor said Remo had chosen as his funeral text Paul's First Corinthians letter: "But now, faith, hope, love, these three, remain; but love is the greatest of these." Yet, Remo had assured me again and again that he couldn't love. Not anymore, after his love for me. And that's why he couldn't write like me, couldn't become a writer,

Interior of St. Mary's Church in Bern, Switzerland

as had been his brother's wish and his own. "Had I spoken with the tongues of human beings and of angels, and had not had love, I would be like sounding ore or a ringing bell."

He kept being like sounding ore and a ringing bell.

But how beautifully this bell sounded in my ear when he encouraged me to continue writing.

After the pastor, an old friend of Remo's (was it Hans?) spoke, and he described him as a young Germanist: he described him as having been as very broad-shouldered and masculine as the other mind-eaten figures in the German-studies department were slouching and bent forward. (Oh God, I thought, he has read my book about our failed love! But Remo had sent it back unopened!) Then his brother, Jean, told of the close relationship between the two of them. He claimed that he was a surrogate father for Remo, because the real father had died early. They wrote letters to each other every week, which they carefully kept and filed away (Oh, if only I could read those — and maybe publish them! A piece of literature?).

"Remo's wife looks just like you, Gorda, I always thought that was my girlfriend sitting there!" said Hanni (is she trying to comfort me with that? Nobody can comfort me!). The brother, Jean, was so weak, that his wife had to lead him by the arm. And of all those present, she was the only one who cried, nobody else. His family supposedly was really happy, like at a wedding party, the adult children, their partners, and the grandchildren: everybody was talking and laughing. Only Remo's wife sat silently on her chair to the right of the altar, playing with the little fingers of the smallest grandchild.

And Hanni added: "The woman looks like nothing special, Gorda, I'm telling you: nothing special!" So, she looks like nothing special and looks quite like me? Had Hanni still not gotten over her dead husband's tactless remark: "Gorda, you are a beautiful woman!" How deep the poison dart must have pierced her heart, into her heart that is hating all sisters since childhood.

And didn't almost all my friends hate their sisters? Even my beloved Friederike, who has only good things to say about other people (the other day, we had such a charming letter carrier come to the house!), hates her sister, who is many years older.

"She is jealous of me and begrudges me everything. And my mother only talks about her problems, I'm sick of it! That's a matter for the lawyer!" she often says when it comes to her mother's joint inheritance, a phrase that doesn't fit at all with her amiable appearance and childlike voice. As if an angel were to start cursing!

And my friend Katja has not spoken to her sister for twenty years. And when her mother died, she found out that she had left everything to her sister, even her jewelry, Katja could only get a very small part of the inheritance with the help of a lawyer. "Quelle femme méchante!" (What a nasty woman), that's what Henri said of his mother-in-law. Or did he mean his wife's sister? And my friend Nadine argued with her sister for years by letter and telephone because of their love for their mother; both of them wanted to have their mother's love (because there was nothing to inherit from her) all to themselves and begrudged the other sister even the smallest piece of it. To this day, Nadine still doesn't know where her mother is buried; her sister punishes her in this point with silence. So Nadine has built a small altar for the mother in her bedroom: a photo in a silver frame, two candles around it and a fresh red rose in front of it. Her husband thinks this is excessive: after all, he lost his mother already when he was eighteen. And she should get rid of the altar. Which Nadine thinks is petty. And surely the urn with her mother's ashes would be on the mantle of her sister in Regensburg, where she currently lives, even though that is not allowed in Germany. Nadine has to take heavy antidepressants to be able to bear the vicious behavior of her sister; otherwise, she would suffocate from her anger at the evil sister.

My beloved cousin Anni doesn't talk to her half-sister anymore, because that one will inherit a huge fortune from her father, while his stepdaughter will go empty-handed. Even though Anni has two children while her half-sister has none. And the unjust grandpa has not considered his step-grandchildren (the only ones he has!) in his will either. This is our family pig Uncle Horst, with whom my brother Max quarreled so violently that our family broke up into two pieces. Two pieces that can never grow back together.

I am cursed to love my girlfriends too much because they are my 'sisters', the sisters I never had. All my life, I have longed for Anni, my first 'sister', from whom I was separated when I was five. Where all real sisters envy and loathe and argue and fight, I love (even Aviva?).

This morning, I had a terrible dream: Remo's mother had just died, and I was engaged to Remo; I was standing all alone among all the Swiss mourners and I knew Remo didn't want to marry me at all. He had lived with his mother for too long and had been spoiled by her for marriage.

Switzerland

Switzerland: Everyone had rejected me, the mother, the brother, the relatives, Remo's friends, above all Hans, who had a beautiful German fiancée, Ingrid, a blond beauty whom Remo's mother liked so much ("You see, Remo, you should marry her!" she must have said to him daily: "She's really beautiful!").

While I had been admired and loved as an exchange student in California, people in German-speaking Switzerland rejected me as if I were a leprous unperson — and in my own eyes I was turning more and more into a disgusting, leprous unperson every day.

On the old photos, you can see a heart-shaped face with downcast eyes and lowered corners of the mouth. That's me, next to the massive one of Remo. He is smiling, but is it a good smile like Pierce Brosnan's, whom he so resembles? No, it's the one of the man with the three Cs and the three Os (children, cooking, church — Obey, obey, obey). Where was the Gorda who danced the dying swan in front of the enthusiastic school in California to the song *I am a stranger in Paradise*? Where was the Gorda who became Miss Fehmarn at seventeen because she could swing her legs so beautifully to orchestral music (no matter what piece of music!). Died in Switzerland, buried in Bern's bed, and risen again in Chicago, in a strange city in a strange country and with new in-laws. But risen again! Miraculously! So, stop whining around here. Count your blessings, Gorda!

This morning, I had another strange dream (even though I hate it when people and writers tell me their dreams!): a man tries to force open my door and bites my hand as I try to close it. Suddenly, he turns from a burglar into a seducer and runs his hand over my breasts, and it feels so good and hurts so good, as if I were a young woman. And there's nothing to do but lie down ... Waking up, I remember telling Dr. Sacks that Larry and I now preferred to watch porn, in which young girls are raped.

"And that excites you?" he asked matter-of-factly.

Me: "Yes."

"Do you want to be raped?"

Remo and Gorda

"Only in fantasy, not in reality." But why do I desire men who don't want me, and those who do want me, I don't want them?"

"Do you mean Larry?"

"Maybe that one, too."

"You've built a wall around yourself that wants to be torn down. Where did that wall come from?"

"I don't know that either!" (Oh, how I knew!)

I made one of my most terrible trips shortly before my mother's collapse. I visited Almut Gernhardt in Tuscany, the widow of the poet Gernhardt, who was not only a poet, but also a beautiful man with much wit in his oratory. A man like I wished to have for myself. As only the 'others' got it, not me, with the family curse on my broad but weak shoulders. Even though Larry said at the time in Lausanne that he thought at the sight of me: Look at that woman's shoulders, she has the strength of an ox. And can work like an ox! (And then his disappointment in Chicago!). On the third afternoon, I didn't go to Almut in the main house because I was alone in the guest house and was afraid of the snakes she had warned me about. She wanted me to hit the floor with a stick to scare them away. So I stayed in my room and hoped she would come for me. But she didn't come until evening and reproached me. "I wanted to show you my husband's studio where he painted his pictures before you left." I had no idea of a studio that was to be in the main house.

"I was afraid of the snakes!" I defended myself. "And my knees hurt on the uneven, scrub-covered floor." But Almut remained upset, and I went to bed depressed, because I really liked the pretty, funny woman and wanted to keep her as a friend in my life. That didn't bode well. Besides, I was afraid that Remo's old friend, Hans, would pick me up by car the next morning, to go with me to the Adriatic Sea, where he owned a condominium. After Remo's death, I had found his address and phone number in the computer and called him. He was very surprised to hear from me again, after too many years to count. And he immediately told me the tragic story of the beautiful blond Ingrid, his wife, who had become an alcoholic, so that he had to pay three times for an incredibly expensive hospital stay for her (was he still sorry about the money today?). The neighbor lady was saying that Ingrid was already drunk at noon. But Hans doubted that, thinking the woman was jealous of his Ingrid. She was also to have said once: How could such a beautiful woman marry a man like you! That would have been an impudence! As if he were ugly!

And I thought: Yes, you were ugly with your thick wart on your right cheek and your stern, black-rimmed glasses around your little water-blue eyes! I pulled out the album of Remo and me in Chicago ("Why do you get the photo album?" Remo had asked angrily at the time. "And what do I get?"). There, I saw the many photos of Hans' and Ingrid's wedding with my fat 'mother-in-law' in them, Ingrid and her taking a pleasurable drag on a cigarette and laughing at each other, the way Mother Fortune (Glück) never smiled at me, her North German misfortune with the tragic facial features.

"What did Remo die of?" I asked Hans anxiously, over the phone.

"I don't know that, either. I moved near him two weeks before he died — at his request, by the way — and he tried to help me move. But he looked so emaciated and frail that I asked him: What's wrong, Remo, are you sick? No, I don't have anything, it's just old age, he said. And, a few weeks later, he was dead. His wife said it was stomach cancer, but Remo didn't want her to reveal any details.

"Just like with his mother. In that case he didn't tell anyone, either, that she had a stroke, not even me, his fiancée. He didn't even take her to the doctor until it was too late. He denied her dying, like he denies his own now." It must have been prostate cancer, I thought. He was ashamed. As soon as Remo's old friend stood in front of me in Tuscany, he held his palms wide apart to indicate how much I had grown in width in the meantime. In turn, he had lost all his hair. But I didn't point a finger at my head, which, unlike his, was still full of it. And I also didn't put my index finger to my right cheek, where I had no wart, not even wrinkles, while his face was covered with them. During the long drive to his apartment, to which he had persuaded me on the phone in Chicago, he began to tell me that Remo had been after Ingrid, that there was a photo of her lying devotedly in his arms.

Once, he said, she had called her fiancé in extreme fear, whispering over the phone: "Remo is standing in front of my door and keeps banging it with his fist. He wants to come in here! He's drunk as a skunk. Come right away and save me!" And Hans went to his Ingrid as fast as he could, but Remo had already disappeared. And I thought: I knew there was something between them! Remo could never talk about Ingrid without snickering ironically about her, as if she were a ridiculous person, which she was not at all, and once he even said: "She actually wanted me!" Only when Remo told me twenty years later that Ingrid had become an alcoholic, did he stop snickering. Back then, Hans wanted to leave her for another woman, and Remo said to him: "You don't leave a sick woman!" Hans remembered this sentence well, having immediately forgiven his friend for attacking his bride ("After all, he was totally sloshed!").

417

Afterwards, Hans told me about the wonderful sex he had had for seven years with a female journalist from Vienna; she, too, was married and had children and was not at all beautiful, not at all as beautiful as his Ingrid, but so inventive in bed, that is, sex from all sides, from above and below and behind and in front ("she liked to experiment, I tell you!"), he had never experienced anything like it, it was something completely new for him after the boring sex in marriage. And Remo had given him a book on how to prolong sex, that is, for hours, what previously lasted only minutes, not even minutes sometimes ...

And that's when I said: "Yep, in my day it took seconds with Remo. Often, I wondered why there was such a fuss being made about so little desire!" But suddenly, Remo could hold out for a long time, much too long for me; my only thought was, when will he finally be finished? I still have to finish to read the book for the French seminar on George Sand, but suddenly he found no end, unfortunately, at a time when he had already told me the three Cs and the three Os, so that I knew I couldn't stay with him as a house cleaner and now also as a sex slave; that was too much for me, because despite the seeming strong shoulders, I felt tired most of the time. I didn't yet know about 'food intolerances' (what a singular tapeworm word, in German!) and that I should avoid bread and dairy products. My mother had sent me to the doctor because of the ever-occurring weakness, but he looked at me with the look: She is only hysterical and there's is nothing wrong with her at all. A quitter!

"You are as strong as a horse," said another doctor who had been recommended to me by Friederike — who was also always tired — as being particularly sensitive and having a fine feeling for young women. I thought: She's as rough as a farm horse — and we parted, I disgruntled.

So, Remo had been after the beautiful Ingrid, the one with the blond curls, and his mother had certainly turned him against me: Gorda is not beautiful at all, just look at Hans' bride! And, indeed, Ingrid was more beautiful than me, but Remo and I had literature in our blood, and Ingrid did the tax return for a cheese factory, she had numbers in her blood, and maybe alcohol, but no poems. Remo and I belonged together, according to Nietzsche's law, while Ingrid and Hans got drunk together, but the drinking didn't harm Hans; only Ingrid got liver damage from it and died in terrible pain. She had also gone blind the last few years, and her daughter wanted nothing to do with her because of the drinking. And Hans had lain in various hotel beds with the Viennese journalist for seven years and had had wonderful sex, and at home he snapped out orders like a short Napoleon or like Remo after he had given me the engagement ring. Nowadays, I think that he feared it as a nose ring for himself. If I had married Remo, I would have gone blind, too, so as not to have to see what he was doing with other women, and in the evening, I would have staggered drunk into bed, like poor beautiful Ingrid into her grave.

On the way back, Hans said: "You say you dress modestly when you travel so as not to be stolen from as a rich woman, I understand that. But you don't have to appear in Turkish baggy pants and even in black, with a cheap bag as a travel bag, that's going too far. In Italy, women wear white and very fine materials like linen and silk; black is reserved for old mothers sitting on their benches in front of the house. So, do dress decent, when you travel in Italy and Switzerland. In the States, you might be able to walk around in clothes like that, but not here with us. They laugh at you. I always go to Italian stores that sell expensive merchandise cheaper, because of small weaving flaws that you don't even see. Look at my beautiful shirt, it's the very best cotton and here are the tucks, you don't have that in your horrible country. Americans have no taste, everyone in Europe knows that. My friend, Anna, who is a rich Milanese businesswoman and makes leather goods, especially bags, was upset about a tiny hole she found in my yellow cashmere sweater, most expensive quality, you couldn't even see the hole after I had it artfully darned for very little money. Such high standards apply in Italy!"

"I have rich girlfriends in Chicago, too," I returned flippantly. "Very rich ones, even, but they don't talk about clothes, they talk about the books we read together. You see, I direct a book club there!"

"What kind of stuff do you read?"

"We just read *Lotte in Weimar*, by Thomas Mann."

"I'm not interested in that kind of stuff, you know. I'm a specialist in politics and economics — and I can tell you that we Swiss won't be taking your European course. You can disappear into oblivion with the euro, we will not. We'll keep our beautiful silver Franc!" Then he asked me to give him one hundred euros as payment for the gasoline. At noon, while I was buying a sandwich in a store, the scrawny man kept eating chocolate, of which he kept many bars in the glove compartment. He had to save money, he said, the car had to be repaired, which had not been planned for in the budget and had cost him 200 francs. He's going to ask me for even more money, I thought, even though he had persuaded me to take this trip to the Adriatic with him. What a strange man, he also seems to be stingy. And I wondered how Remo could be friends with him. Remo, who was always so generous!

But actually, I knew the reason for the friendship: Hans talked incessantly, everything that went through his head came out of his wide mouth. He had verbal diarrhea, as Larry called

420

it. Remo, on the other hand, had put every word on a gold scale, before he opened his mouth. Hans had amused him with his crazy stories, as I had amused him with mine. And maybe mine were just crazy, and not funny, as I imagined in my arrogance. Hans was a chatterbox, and didn't my mother once even say to me: "You talk too much!" And I had also been reproached for it in the book club, and from then on, I preferred to let the others speak and felt guilty when I talked about my encounters with famous people. That annoys people anyway. And I had noticed that nobody called me in Chicago, probably because I talk too much on the phone. Larry prefers to look at his computer when I say something. So I live a lonely life in my poet's den, sitting in my favorite chair by the window overlooking the lake, which is like an ocean without a shore, like being in Italy at the Adriatic. And the beaches are full of young people in bathing suits like in Europe, only the beach chairs are missing and the umbrellas. That's why older people don't go there. Like me, they sit at the window and look out. And long to be in the park with the young people.

In the early evening, Hans dropped me off at Hanni's, and how glad I was not to have to be with him anymore. However, we had arranged to go to Remo's and Ingrid's graves the next day. Hanni now lives in a wonderful house with a view of the entire Emmenthal valley, green meadows and hills everywhere, and not a disturbing house anywhere. A view to behold. The rich sister has finally kept her word to help her, even if after Hanni's death, the house goes to the sister's son and not to her own. But still, Hanni lives like a princess again; the tiny cold and noisy house of the in-laws with the guest room in the damp cellar had hardly been reasonable for the daughter from a once rich home. Out of anger about it, she had put the boyfriend out and made me one scene after another during the last visit. But now everything is good again, I thought, now my friend is turning into the woman from before, into the funny, humorous one with whom I was able to laugh so well. With whom I was able to laugh well for decades!

After Hanni had shown me the multi-story house, and I didn't miss any opportunity to make exclamations of delight and excitement, we sat down on the spacious terrace for dinner and had before us the magnificent view all the way to the white peaks of the mountains of the Bernese Oberland.

"How lucky you are!" I said to Hanni, "this view is even more beautiful than the one from your old house, which you have always missed! Your sister is a treasure! It took a long time, more than ten years, but finally she helped!"

Now Hanni began to tell me that she had started a quarrel with the neighbors in the new neighborhood where she lived, because there was a trampoline in front of her house, on which the children played from morning till night with loud shrieks and whooping. And she couldn't listen to that noise. She said she had sent to all her fellow residents a plan of the neighborhood, on which it was clearly marked that the place in front of her house served as a turning place for cars and not as a playground the children — those were marked in other places. And so a Homeowner's Association meeting was called, and Hanni made it clear to them that she would not be willing to put up with children's noise all the time. She was asked if she didn't like kids. And she countered and talked about her own two children. But I knew that Hanni had always had only one child at a time (the age difference between the two was too great) and one child is like no child, and there is silence in the house (thinking, on the other hand, of Nadine's two, only thirteen months apart, every day is filled with screaming fights!). There were more HOA meetings, Hanni said, and finally it was agreed that the trampoline should be placed somewhere else every other year. A young woman had rung Hanni's doorbell and told her to move away, that she didn't fit into the neighborhood. All the young couples would have gotten along wonderfully, and they also partied together. Hanni was considered to be something of a thorn in the flesh. The next day, however, the young woman apologized to her by letter.

Hanni looked so haggard when she told her story that I felt obliged to calm her by saying, "I'm so sorry, you are absolutely right ... I understand you very well ... I would also have ... How can one bear such noise ... I really feel sorry for you ... What bad luck you have."

But secretly I thought of the woman who had lived above her in her in-laws' house and whose stomping, as she called it, drove her crazy. Is she pathologically sensitive to noise? I asked myself. And I recommended ear plugs to her again.

"I can't stand them, you know that!" Oh yes, at the hotel in Commugny she didn't want to stuff any in her ears and preferred to lie awake with a growing rage in her belly all night long because of the noise of the cars outside. The next morning, I heard the children's voices from the trampoline: how the little ones laughed and cheered, and I thought of my childhood in Lüneburg with Anni, when we sat together on the swing and whizzed through the air with much joyful noise and whooping. My heart warmed. How I longed back for my childhood with Anni. But then I remembered that these noises drove Hanni crazy and didn't remind her of summer and vacation happiness. What a pity for her. During breakfast in the kitchen, we heard nothing of the little children, neither in Hanni's bedroom nor in the living room, not even on the terrace was anything to be heard, only in the guest room and in the hallway.

"But Hanni, then you don't really have any problems," I said soothingly. "How easily you can sit down in the living room! You can't hear anything there!" But Hanni objected vehemently: "Already, when I stop my car in front of my door, which I have every right to do, then I have to be afraid that the children will run in front of it, and I might kill one dead!"

"Oh, I see," I said, "I hadn't thought of that." And then the bell rang, and Hans was at the door to take me to the cemetery. It's a beautiful cemetery with lots of old trees, just like I love them, only I didn't remember where the Glück family grave was. It had been by the cemetery wall, I remembered. By the entrance gate there was a cemetery nursery store with flowers and little white angels to comfort both the dead and the living. I bought a bunch of yellow roses and three little angels for Remo and Ingrid and Karl-Hansi. First, we went to Ingrid's grave. Then we searched along the wall for a long time for the grave of the Glück's. It was nowhere to be found, and the wall was so terribly long. I wondered if I remembered correctly. It had been so long ago when we — Remo, Jean, and Betty, and I — stood at Mother's fresh grave one November day. Hans and I had given up hope when suddenly I saw the name I used to love so much on a plaque on the wall.

"Here it is!" I cried out delightedly — and horrified at the same time. Remo's name was written in huge letters on the grave slab above the ground, with no indication of his date of birth or death. As if no member of the Glück family should ever be buried here again. Remo was the final line, just as Hanno Buddenbrook had once drawn it in the family book. I put one of the angels on the plate. He was reading in a large book, the book of fate. And while it had been closed to us at his mother's funeral, it had opened in the meantime, and horrified, I read in it the story of our separate lives. How could I have left him?

424

The man I loved more than anything! Had I not said to him: I already hate the man whom I may love after you! Now I was forced to live with him. In the States.

When Hans dropped me off at my friend's house, he demanded twenty Francs for gas, as if he were a cab driver and not an old friend of Remo's, who had paid all bills for him, as I well knew. Even though Hanni had just invited him to dinner.

He came at seven o'clock and looked out at the Emmenthal valley from the terrace, and we hoped he would say something nice now. Instead, he proclaimed that such a view meant nothing to him, that he had grown up with it, that his father, the internist, had had a house in the immediate vicinity. And that, as far as he was concerned, the houses of the new neighborhood were ugly from the outside, like toy blocks for giant children. But he deemed the inside the house to be quite acceptable, even if he didn't like the stairs — his knees would hurt on them — one would have to think of the future. Which future? I thought. The one in the wheelchair? Hanni looked disappointed. A tactless acquaintance of hers had said during the house tour that one could see the industrial area of the village — but one could only see it if one turned one's head far to the right and looked over the barrier, i.e. with the greatest effort, but who would make such an effort on a terrace with a magical view to the white peaks of the mountains of the Bernese Oberland?

At dinner, Hans and Hanni spoke Swiss German to each other, which I didn't understand. That way, I had time to take a good look at Hanni sitting there with her still pretty body in a skin-tight leotard blouse and how she laughed flirtatiously, turning her head back and forth: a young girl flirting, the beautiful young girl of back in the day. Which she wasn't anymore, unfortunately.

And Hans grinned with his wide mouth, and the wart on his cheek wiggled along with it, that is how violently he was laughing about the story presented in the most beautiful Swiss German, which Hanni produced for him. Of which I understood not a single word. Finally, I became impatient and wanted to know what they were laughing about (maybe about me?), and I asked them several times to talk in High German.

"I can't understand you!" But Hanni was having her Swiss German day and didn't care about my objection. She said: "That's not true, Gorda, you can understand us just fine! You understood Remo, after all!" That was true — but in the meantime, years had passed, and I no longer understood a word of the conversation between the two. She wants to charm him with her Swiss German dialect, I thought, because I told her that he loves their dialect so much and can't stand the High German enunciation. Maybe that's why he had become so rude to me on the trip to the Adriatic Sea and back? He was bothered by my North German way of speaking. Remo, unlike him, had spoken perfect High German — and why couldn't an intelligent journalist like Hans learn to pronounce Goethe's language without an accent? Surely that should be possible if his wife was from Germany and his mistress from Vienna? Or had both women learned Swiss German because of him? That's a possibility, I thought. This ugly man has a Napoleon complex!

He had told me that he had forbidden his Ingrid to have contact with her own sister, after the two of them had been on a trip together and had stayed at the hotel under her maiden name — Edecke. When he called there, no one knew anything about a Mrs. Stauffer.

"It was my own wife, my Ingrid Stauffer, a brazen impertinence! Well, I told the sister off! Never again did she travel with my wife!" When he stood at the door to leave, I thought for a moment that we should now ask him for the money for dinner, as if we were a restaurant. But of course, as a daughter from a good family, I kept my well-bred mouth shut.

Unfortunately, I warned Hanni about Hans, which didn't please her: "Watch out, he already has a girlfriend on the Adriatic, he just wants to sleep around, and he's stingy like your old boyfriend, who didn't allow you to order an ice cream with your afternoon coffee or a piece of cake. He asked me for gas money on two separate occasions. And at the Adriatic, the first night he let me take him out to a good restaurant, and the next night, he put a tiny piece of meat in front of me, a morsel like that, you know, and the strawberries he had bought weren't there. Where did they go, I asked him. He wanted to save them for later. When later? I went straight to bed, of course. To my own bed in the guest room!"

I had to think of how, the following morning, he had angrily ordered me to pack immediately, we were going back; it was raining, and the radio had predicted bad weather for the next few days. I knew, of course, why he was angry and wanted to leave immediately: I had not come to see him that night. On the phone from Bern to Chicago, he had pleaded with me for weeks: "Don't be like that, I can still really do it right; take advantage of your last chance!" But I didn't feel like taking advantage of my last chance, especially with Remo's old boyfriend, the husband of the beautiful Ingrid, to whom Remo should have been engaged to if matters had gone according to his mother's wishes. Or would she have made trouble with her too? At the Adriatic, I had lost my appetite during breakfast, because I thought of the two dead people (hopefully they lie in their graves separately and not together somewhere ...). I was glad when I was back in the car and on the way to my beloved Hanni. Then my girlfriend said into my thoughts: "No wonder that Hans didn't want you. Just look at how you look!" I quickly went to bed, so as not to have to explain.

The next day we went into town, to an exhibition on the life and work of Robert Walser. I struck up a conversation with the friendly director and told her loquaciously (I am a chatterbox!) that I was from Chicago but that I had once been engaged in Bern to a man who had written his doctoral thesis about Conrad Ferdinand Meyer, on the wonderful Conrad Ferdinand Meyer.

"Oh, you must mean Doctor Glück!" She laughed out loud! "Everyone knows him here; he was known for his affairs — he had a young mistress for twenty years who didn't marry because of him. The poor thing hoped he would get a divorce for her sake. But he didn't, he didn't have to, his wife tolerated everything. Be glad you didn't marry him!" I thought I was going mad! And I went mad for a moment.

"Let's go!" I said far too curtly to Hanni: "It's too hot for me in here!" The woman had shot me in the heart, in the poor adolescent heart that didn't want to learn and didn't want to know about statutes of limitation and the decades that had passed when he had last told me that he loved only me. You're crazy, Gorda; you get over a love, even the so called 'great' one, or else you have a screw loose somewhere. You belong in an insane asylum; all that silly romantic nonsense isn't worth a damn. This is too ridiculous, even the chickens are laughing! Or even worse: the gods! I didn't need this gossip from Bern, after the visit to the cemetery with Hans. The Lord save me from further strokes of fate! But heaven still had more in store for me.

The next day, Hanni and I were sitting peacefully by Lake Thun, eating a big sundae, and drinking a pot of coffee, as usual. And I felt safe with my friend in my beloved Switzerland, which had become my second home. Unfortunately, Chicago, never quite felt like my third home. Back again in her beautiful house — so much nicer than my apartment in Chicago — Hanni showed me some clothes that the rich sister had bought her, and four pairs of expensive shoes, until the angry sentence escaped me: "My God, is she trying to buy you?" And, of course, I shouldn't have said that. Hanni winced in fright. But it was true that earlier she had mocked Heidemarie's clothes mania, and now she was talking about Hermès and Gucci and Prada as if they were her personal go-to-staples. She was visibly transforming before my eyes into her patroness, the sister.

And I said: "I can't afford this expensive stuff, but I don't care, either. All my rich girlfriends in Chicago talk about is books!" Then Hanni showed me a photo of a big, beautiful house that was on her living room table: "Look, here's my childhood home. My friend, Elsie, the former waitress I told you about, said to me: 'You often look so haughty, as if you were something better.' I want to show Elsie what kind of home I come from. Then she'll know who I am. She'll be surprised!" Better leave that alone, I thought, if you want to keep her as a friend. Thank God I kept my mouth shut. It was more than enough for me to brag about reading with my rich girlfriends.

At dinner, Hanni got that haggard look on her face that I knew so well. She always got it when she talked about her sisters who had stolen her inheritance. And already she started with the old familiar topic, because she was supposed to pick up her younger sister from Zurich in two days. And she complained again about her father's unjust will and that two of her sisters, who had inherited the two houses, had left and had never helped her in her misfortune after Karl-Hansi's death. I had heard that many times now, and I drank quite a bit to distract myself. I was quite happy when her son unexpectedly came home and greeted me warmly, or so it seemed to me. Unfortunately for me, I showed him my latest book. He asked ironically: "Well, then you've been showing off horribly with your books again! What is it about? I'm sure that I'm not interested! Here's a book that captivates me!" And he showed me a book, by Konsalik, I think. I looked at Hanni, who kept her eyes lowered. She always lowered them like that when she wanted to hide something. And here, she wanted to hide the fact that she was teaching her son that I was a show-off and was always talking about my books. In the same way, she had described the rich aunt from Zurich to him as a pretentious, conceited goose. And he claimed that he wouldn't let such a person pay for his studies — although that wasn't true, he had accepted her money, but dropped out of college because he had failed an exam that he could easily have repeated. Typical family lies. And now he was studying at his mother's expense, but she could only finance his studies with the help of her rich sister.

"No, I'm not bragging!" I said fiercely, and, as if caught, he bolted and ran down the stairs to the basement, where he had a nicely converted, renovated apartment.

"You have an uncivilized son!" escaped me under the influence of alcohol: "And your sister says so, too!" I should have spared myself these sentences. Hanni flared up like a snake that has been kicked by a horse, and hissed: "How dare you call my son uncivilized!"

Immediately I tried to calm her down: "Please, forgive me, I didn't mean it!" I kissed her goodnight in reconciliation and said: "I love you."

"I love you, too," she replied. And I thought all was well again. How wrong I was! On the last morning, we sat comfortably at the breakfast table on the terrace, because the night train to northern Germany didn't leave until evening. Then I packed, while listening to the sweet voices of the little children on the trampoline. How I would have loved to stay! But I knew that my mother was not well, and I had to go home. "Something will happen to her soon," I said to Hanni prophetically. We drove once more to Gunten and Merligen and looked at Lake Thun which, on this day, was colored deep blue like the high mountains surrounding it. I felt comforted in the Swiss paradise. In the distance, we saw the beloved Niesen, which I surely — as I know now — will never see again.

In the early evening, — unfortunately too late, as always — we drove to the train station of Bern, to the station where I had stood hundreds of times with Remo. And now he would never stand there again, not even with another woman. To get to the parking lot, Hanni and I had to go through an underpass where the paths were painted on with white stripes.

"Oh God!" she said suddenly: "I'm going the wrong way." She should have backed the car up, but since there were no vehicles to be seen far and wide, she continued to drive the wrong way until she reached the parking lot. At that moment, a car that had been parked against the wall approached us very slowly. A young man came out, showed us his police ID, and said:

"May I see your driver's license?" Hanni immediately got into a wild excitement, because we were in a hurry, the train must already be on the track and would be leaving shortly.

"We're going to be late!" I said anxiously.

That's when Hanni yelled at me: "Yes, Gorda, I know, and it's all your fault!" She showed the policeman her ID, tore the suitcases out of the trunk, grabbed the smaller one, and sped off in a huff. To my amazement, the young man bent over

View of Niesen from Gunten

laughing! It was perhaps his first day on the job as a traffic cop, and he thought Hanni's reaction was funny.

"See," I said to him: "now it's my fault!" And I wanted to add: "Be nice to my friend, her husband took his own life ..." Then he asked me:

"Where are you going in such a hurry?"

"To Lüneburg," I answered.

"Do you live there?"

"No, in Chicago."

"How did you get to Chicago?"

"I'm married there."

"And what are you doing in Switzerland?"

"I visited my girlfriend." He would have liked to chat with me some more, that was obvious. But I hurriedly took the big suitcase, and said to him:

"Goodbye!" and ran after Hanni. She was already waiting irritably by the escalator. The train was at the platform, ready to leave. Hanni helped me to lift the suitcases, gave me a kiss, and hurriedly disappeared back to the policeman. Oh, then all is well, I thought, she gave me a goodbye kiss. But nothing was well. When I called her a week later to tell her my mother had had a stroke and was in the hospital, she screamed like a banshee: "Gorda, I've been driving for thirty years and more without ever making a mistake. It's your fault that I have to go to the district attorney and have my driver's license taken away for three months! On top of that, I'll get a huge fine! And it's all your fault! I never want to see you in my house again!!!"

Horrified I called the daughter, who said to me: "That's how she always does it. She is never to blame for anything. Why don't you drop her! She'll always get fits like that; I've had to put up with her all through childhood and adolescence. If you think she'll apologize to you, you can wait until the day you die." Let her go, let her go! These words hit me right in my childhood heart. Into the childhood heart, that once loved Anni so ardently.

One day, Dr. Sacks said to me:

"Gorda, don't you realize that you are whining a bit much? You should write down all the good things that have happened to you in your life! Count your blessings, as they say here in America!" I'll do that now. Count my blessings! I thank heaven that I didn't become Hitler's daughter like poor Svetlana became Stalin's daughter. I thank heaven for giving me a handsome and intelligent mother who, as a war criminal widow with three half-orphans, was able to find a man to marry her after the war, because there were few men then. So many of them had died in the war and remained in captivity or were missing, as it was called. And the young girls wanted to get a man, too. My mother was over thirty years old at the time. Her chances of remarrying were slim. But she had to, she always said, because she had not learned enough to support herself and the three children. She pleased our stepfather's mother, who was also a very intelligent and well-read woman, so much that she persuaded her son to marry this widow and her children.

I thank heaven that our stepfather Wolf Selig had syphilis in his youth, which was treated with Mercury at that time, which made him incapable of fathering children. That way, he appreciated us three children and didn't consider us as annoying souvenirs. I thank heaven for this stepfather, a handsome man and civil servant with pension rights, as my mother pointed out, who largely left the upbringing of her brats to his wife and never beat us, just bossed us around a bit with phrases like: "Close the door! Do I have to keep saying that?" Or: "Lights

434

out. Remember the electric bill!" Or: "Can't you do the dishes with less water?!" But other than that, he gave us a nice home where we didn't give a thought to being war-criminal orphans. Yes, I — the youngest child — didn't even know it.

I thank heaven that the unknown paternal grandfather bought three houses in Lüneburg in the best business area in 1905, which his wife — our grandmother — inherited after his death (the son had been paid off with his studies), and which she passed on to us three grandchildren, at a time when most Germans owned little.

I thank heaven that we were young when we inherited; Max seventeen years old, Heiner fifteen, and I, twelve. Today, children have to wait until they are very old to get their inheritance. That way, they can just afford a better retirement home.

I thank heaven that our stepfather seemed born to manage our houses: righteous, orderly, industrious, and thrifty. He had a lot of fun turning the war-ravaged property into a stately home that allowed my brothers and me to study, furnish our apartments, and travel to foreign countries. I was even able to study in Switzerland because of it.

I thank heaven for all my nephews and my niece Rieke, who is something like my substitute daughter, since I couldn't have children.

I thank heaven that I couldn't have children because Larry came home drunk during many years of our marriage. And I had to prove to myself with endless study that I didn't remain a fool in spite of my mother's beatings over schoolwork.

I thank heaven that I married a Catholic who always believed in the sacrament of marriage and therefore didn't leave his sick wife. In fact, once a woman on the plane asked me some advice on how to cope with food intolerances (what a word!): How come your husband didn't leave you? Obviously her own had, and she looked so chagrined about it.

I thank heaven that my husband is a doctor who, one day, found a cure for my frequent migraines, which made my life more bearable, because before that I lay in bed for days at a time with blackouts and earplugs in my ears.

I thank heaven that Larry and I never divorced, although I recommended to him that he rent the apartment next door. That way, all he had to do was come over and everything was fine again.

I thank heaven that Larry doesn't drink so much anymore, because by now he throws up or suffers from diarrhea after getting drunk.

I thank heaven for my German women's club in Chicago, which makes it possible for me to live in the American city almost as if it were a German one, where I speak German, think German, and write German (even though I do swear in English!).

Everything wrong and yet everything right! I write German poetry in a time that doesn't appreciate poetry. In a country that doesn't understand it and for an audience that finds modern poetry confusing, if not chaotic or obscure.

I thank all my girlfriends for showing me what snakes are writhing in my chest. For an Eastern sage has said: "If you meet a person whom you admire, emulate them. But if you meet a person with many faults, look inside your own chest!" This diary that is full of snakes is the chest I look into every day.

I thank heaven that Remo acted like a macho man even before we were married, so that I didn't have to experience a nasty surprise marrying him.

I thank heaven that I have a lawyer brother who has managed the houses in Lüneburg just as exquisitely as our stepfather, which is why I have an allowance that enables me to write and publish and give away books that hardly anyone wants to read, let alone buy.

I thank heaven that the war criminal father hanged himself from the bed sheet in the prison in Wuppertal before it came to the trial. Thus he couldn't be hanged in Nuremberg.

I thank heaven that I learned of his crimes so late that I had the strength to go on living and didn't take the sixty sleeping pills.

I thank heaven for the poems that suddenly gushed out of me when I didn't know whether to seek a position somewhere in the States or stay with Larry and become a poet.

I thank my beloved friend Friederike for finding my poems and prose beautiful, because otherwise I would not have continued to write.

I thank heaven that my mother found my stepfather's lover's love letter in his jacket before he could divorce her, as he apparently intended to do.

I thank heaven that my mother became his widow and not the deeply humiliated wife he abandoned. And that we were able to add to her modest pension.

I thank Dr. Sacks for his years of loving attention that allowed me to tell him things I didn't want to talk about and write down stories I would have preferred to keep to myself. Even though the wall around me never quite came down, it started to crumble with his help. And I thank him for forgiving me when I didn't want to meet with him in Frankfurt: I don't need a father in bed, too, I thought (in contrast to my spiritual doppelganger Ulla Hahn).

I thank heaven that I have not become as ugly as Hanni might have wished. And that I have a strong chin and not a receding one like the wonderful writer Eudora Welty, because a receding one is worse, Larry says. He thinks mine is beautiful.

I thank heaven for him waiting patiently for me in Chicago, for no one else is waiting for me, only my young tomcat.

I thank heaven for my mother's last companion, the art painter Rudolf Führmann, who left her his entire treasure trove of paintings, many of which now decorate my apartment in Chicago, where they console me daily for not having stayed in Europe.

I thank heaven for all the good things I can't think of at the moment ....

My life has become a Grimm's fairy tale, all grim. In the afternoon, I go to the hospital where my mother is sleeping away. In the morning, I do the shopping for her and me. And since she can never return to her apartment, I asked at the nursing home at the spa park if there was a room for her there, and fortunately one has become available with a view of the huge park, which at the moment looks like a Christmas winter wonderland: all the bare trees and bushes are covered with thick white sheets glistening in the sun. The stores are bustling with pre-Christmas activity in the stifling heat. I have to wait in long lines and sweat runs down my temples and back. Then I get diarrhea from fear and have to run to the bathroom. Back into the queue, which has become even longer. A hard-to-bear life during a time which, for me, belonged otherwise to the most beautiful times of the year. I feel lonely and abandoned.

No longer do I have a mother whom I can tell everything, even if she didn't want to hear what I had to tell: "You have to deal with your worries alone. You only upset me! Leave me alone with your stories!" Or she would give me sage advice that, unfortunately, I didn't always follow: "My advice to you is

438

this: don't fight back. If you say something critical to someone, you'll only get it back. They'll always find something!"

My beloved sister-in-law, the diet chef, wrote me not to turn my mother against my brother Max; he was her last support. I ask myself where she gets that idea? He is her last support? And I am sitting here at her bedside, and he hardly ever shows his face. His wife, the doctor, not at all, anyway. She told me she has a lot to do in her practice. My beloved niece has gone to India for half a year with a friend. Heiner can't come because he is so ill. Larry recently said on the phone that he is dying. And I say to his wife: Why don't you come here once more? And don't add: It might be the last time. But I think it. Heiner found a doctor who assured him that he could still live for years with his chronic pneumonia. They now believe him. Even though Heiner's doctor said to his wife: "You need to prepare your husband for his death." How do you prepare your husband for death? Nobody can do that. You can't even prepare for your own death. And if you tried, every day, every minute of the year, after all, you still wouldn't be prepared. You are never prepared. I read books about reincarnation every day to comfort myself. But I cannot be consoled. And not prepared. Losing my brother, in addition to my mother. And everyone's love, because no one seems to love me. Forever the unloved child.

Yesterday, I bought a lamp and curtains for mom's room in the nursing home. I have a long list of things to buy. For which I have to stand in the unbearable lines. And then the thick winter clothes that make standing in line even harder for me. What I would love to do most is put my body to bed with my mother and send my spirit shopping. My spirit should buy the underwear and the wardrobe and the small television because the big one doesn't fit in the little room in the nursing home. Max asked me what I wanted to do with the big one, if I wanted to take it with me to America? No, I want to have it for company in my loneliness in my mom's apartment. It's talking from the answering machine. And the people in the answering machine are my visitors, who stand by me in my despair, when the family doesn't.

Now I'm sitting here, writing, at my mother's bedside, instead of sitting in one of the cafes watching the young people doing their Christmas shopping. How they laugh and show each other the packages. And I have to be happy if my mother stays alive.

Mom's closets are wonderfully tidy. She's obviously been preparing for death for a long time. Only in the corner where I have my stuff, writing notebooks and manuscripts, there is chaos. It's not only Larry who is a hoarder, so am I, though not quite as bad as he is. A fastidiously neat partner couldn't have put up with him. I, too, have fallen off the German way. We have a 'Polish economy'.

Today, I found the unpublished autobiographical novel by Rudolf Führmann that Mom told me about. I am now starting to read it, and I'm feeling like I am together with him and my mother again, as I did when it poured every day in July and Rudolf prepared a French 'Christmas dinner' for us in the evening, because he had learned to cook during his years in Paris. With lots of garlic in the sauce and on the salad. I could speak to him in French, and he had read endlessly and was politically informed. A man to marry. "Don't take him away from me!" my mother said to me. But I didn't want a father in bed. She didn't have to worry.

Yesterday, I went to visit Rosie and Richard. Rosie served the fresh homemade bread with the crispy crust, as usual, and the delicious herb butter with garlic to go with the filet. But even before dinner, I could tell they both wanted a fight. Rosie asked me in a sharp tone why I hadn't cleaned up the stain on my pants. I had not noticed it at all. Then, at dinner, Richard started asking again: "What are you saying about Rosie? What are you saying about Rosie?" I couldn't tell them, after all, that the cab driver had said Rosie was so brusque and arrogant in the store that no one in Lüneburg would buy from them. So, instead, I said what I actually said many times: Rosie was so intelligent and gifted that she would have easily passed the High School Exam (Abitur). So what if she would have needed some tutoring in math? Most of us did need it. Even her intelligent handwriting showed that.

But Richard didn't take no for an answer to my praise this time, and over dessert he opened up to me: "This is the last time we're getting together!"

"What?" I asked: "You're telling me this after thirty-three years of friendship?!"

"Your superficial relationship with Rosie was never a real friendship!"

"I'm sure it was!"

"No, you just imagined it!"

"Thank you for dinner, and now I want to go home. You don't have to come to my mother's funeral!"

"You won't take away my right to go to my cousin's funeral, will you?"

"Yes, stay away! Stay away forever!" Then Richard took me by car to my mother's apartment, his old bachelor apartment, where we once laid in bed, in love and making out. Long, long ago.

Just before getting out of the car, he snapped at me: "Do you actually know the truth about your father, the war criminal?!"

"Yes," I shouted angrily: "I know it, and do you know what you deserve now? A kick in the ass!"

On the street I shouted louder and louder: "A kick in the ass! A kick in the ass!" There I was standing in front of his house, and the neighbors were looking down from their windows at a woman screaming in despair. A woman, to whom Richard once said: "You are the only person I know who is never saying a wrong word." Now I've finally said it!

Mom is dead.

End of the diary.

Addendum by Geertje Suhr

Only after my mother's death did I find the strength to write about the unknown war criminal father without hiding behind the mask of a Gorda Selig. I called the report "Baby in the Third Reich."

Baby in the Third Reich

When an American woman said to me: "As a German, you are guilty of the crimes of the Third Reich," I replied: "I was a baby in the Third Reich, how can I be guilty?"

"But your parents are guilty," she objected adamantly.

"Do you know how old my mother was when Hitler came to power?" I asked her.

"Well?"

"Eighteen years old. And my friend Petra's mother, for example?"

"Well?"

"She was thirteen years old, and ten years later, her husband was killed in the war. War widow at twenty-three years of age, with two children." All guilty?

Chancellor Kohl has spoken of the 'mercy' of late birth. My mother often made fun of this grace, as did most Germans at the time. Because everyone was supposed to be guilty, the early-born and the late-born. Or all innocent? Or did the Germans, who hardly believed in God, detest the Christian word 'grace'?

And it did seem to me a grace to be born late, preferably forty, sixty, hundreds of years after the twelve years of the Thousand-Year Reich, the devil's kingdom, one should rather say. Guilty to the third and fourth generation, it says in the Old Testament. And in the New Testament?

I belong to the first generation after the 'Great German Fall of Man'. And I have felt guilty, although I was only a baby in the Third Reich. When did my feelings of guilt begin? I must have been fourteen years old when I saw Alain Resnais' film on TV at my aunt's house. I think it was called *Through Night and Fog*. Or simply *Night and Fog*. There sits the young girl, almost

Still from Alain Resnais' film *Night and Fog*, 1955

still a child, watching railroad trains stuffed full of hideously emaciated people staring out of the cars with their huge, suffering eyes. Living skulls on their way to death. Then, again and again, piles of corpses. Pits full of corpses. Gas chambers and piles of corpses. American or English soldiers next to piles of corpses. Horrified faces of young women next to piles of corpses. They hold their noses. They run away. The girl goes into the next room and says to her mother and aunt: "Come over here, I see something terrible here. How they gassed all these people." The mother lowers her eyes. The aunt stares into her coffee cup. Neither one of them get up.

"Yes, yes," says the mother.

"Leave it be," says the aunt. "We've heard that before."

The girl knows: she will never forget these piles of corpses. Not until death. And she will say a hundred times and more to her mother: "How could the Nazis gas millions of people? Didn't they have a conscience? That will never be forgotten, not until the death of mankind. This is the most horrible thing that people have ever done to people."

And the mother lowered her eyes. And never said anything. But at some point, she said: "It was the English who invented the concentration camps. It was during the Boer War. A lot of people died there..."

"Boer War, Boer War!" I shouted. "That excuses nothing!"

And my mother kept her eyes lowered. The history of my feelings of guilt started at age fourteen, in front of my aunt's television. The feelings of guilt that I sometimes denied, like that time in front of this American acquaintance with my defiant words: "I was just a baby in the Third Reich."

I was quite elderly when I learned that I was not just any baby in the Third Reich, but the child of a Gestapo and Waffen

SS man. My mother kept that from me for a long time. She was able to keep it quiet for so long because he was probably a Nazi, but thank God, not high enough to carry one of those names that reek of excrement. My last name is not Himmler or Heydrich or Eichmann, just Suhr. I must have been about eight years old, when we had to write our first curriculum vitae in elementary school: Name — first name — year of birth — place of birth ... father's name — father's profession — year of birth of father — year of death of father, if any, as with so many fathers at that time.

"Write, he died in 1946," my mother said.

"What did he die of?"

"He died," my mother replied, looking stern. I didn't ask any more questions. I was proud of my birthplace, Prague. It was called the Golden City, my mother had told me. So I had not simply been born in little Lüneburg, like my mother, or in bombed-out Hanover, where we had moved after she remarried, but in a city that was called golden because of its great beauty. A golden dream of a city with a great castle, the Hradschin, and the Charles Bridge with the many statues of saints on it. My mother had engravings of the castle and the bridge on her wall and books about Prague in the bookcase. I sometimes looked at them and listened to her when she told me about the beautiful city: there was always peace there, the bombs fell elsewhere, in Hamburg and Düsseldorf and Frankfurt. Prague, however, was golden and holy and was spared the bombs. It was an island of peace. That's why many movies were shot there during the Third Reich, *The Golden City*, for example. Movies that starred Hans Albers and Willy Fritsch and Christina Söderbaum. When Berlin was bombed, the Ufa movie company could no longer shoot there. And my mother once saw the great Ufa star Hans Albers in Prague.

"He had wonderful ice-blue eyes," she said. My mother spent the best years of her life in Prague. She was only twenty-four-years old when she moved there from Berlin, really at her partying age. Only, most of the men were away fighting in the war and couldn't join the party. So, you took what you could get. Cigarettes and schnaps. And some men, the lucky ones, were always exempt from the prescribed killing. Even the man who was to become my father, was no longer in Prague, but had been called back to Berlin.

"What did he do in Prague?" I asked my mother.

She answered: "I don't know." He was not allowed to talk about it. He had to swear an oath that he would say nothing.

"But if I could tell you, you wouldn't want to know," he said. And my mother lowered her eyes. My God, what could they have done there? I asked myself, afraid. 'They', that was the German occupation force of countries that Hitler had brought home into the Reich, that is, Austria and Czechoslovakia and Poland and France. Germany was in the process of unifying Europe. What Napoleon had not succeeded in doing, Adolf Hitler now wanted to do: he wanted to create a giant German empire, with himself as the leader from the highest graces, a thousand-year kingdom of happiness. And the Germans were the master race, because they had the best blood, and at the bottom were the Jews with the worst. Blood could be good and bad; it was not simply 'a special juice'. It was not the character that counted, but the blood, and the blood of the new rulers was Aryan, and no longer blue like that of the nobility, and above all, not Jewish, although Christ had Jewish blood. However, no one spoke of this anymore. Especially not the Bohemian lance corporal, as old Hindenburg disparagingly called him. But he still made him chancellor, even though he had not won the election in the least, he got only thirty-three percent of the votes. Thirty-three percent too many, as we know today. And so fate took its course.

But there was always peace in Prague, and my mother was young and not interested in politics, like most young women. But, later, she was even more interested in them, probably to make up for the stupidity of her early years and to prevent the reign of a second Hitler. Only the compulsory task of having to bear children in the Third Reich was a burden for the young women. My nominal aunt Lisa, my mother's best friend in Prague, said to me: "We were of one mind, your mother and me. We didn't want to have children, one after another, forever. The party people came by regularly and asked us if we were pregnant again. That annoyed us terribly."

Just as many years later, in China, they asked: "You're not pregnant again, I hope? One child per family is enough." My mother also wanted only one child, and after the second she was totally fed up. It was the middle of the war, after all, and bombs were dropping everywhere, though not in Prague, but in the news they said they were dropping everywhere else, and at the third pregnancy my mother became radical and had an abortion, even though Hitler had made abortion punishable by death. He needed warriors for the next war. With the fourth pregnancy, she found no doctor willing to risk his neck, and so she resigned herself, like it or not, to her fate — and I had no choice but to see the darkness of the world in a Prague hospital on February 8, 1943. Stalingrad, which had been occupied by the Germans, had just fallen back to its Russian owners, on February 2, 1943, in fact, and my mother once said to me: "We knew the war was lost when you were born. And Hitler had taught us we would all be killed by the victors."

Her life from then on was like doing the feeding and diaper changing on a volcano. Walking with the baby carriage through the beautiful city, and on the left, a child holding your hand, and on the right a child on wobbly little legs and no future for any of us.

"Where was our father?" I asked my mother.

"He was back in Berlin and didn't want to do what he had to do. When I still lived there, he always had asthma attacks in the morning when he went to work." And at night he would scream, and once he choked her so much that she was terrified.

In 1939, when the war started, he would have preferred to go to the front so he wouldn't have to do what he was doing. But they wouldn't let him go. He knew too much, they said.

"What did he know?" I asked my mother.

"I don't know that either," she said. "He had sworn an oath that he would keep his mouth shut. But in the end, they sent him to the front, because he wanted it so badly."

"That was in November 1942," my Aunt Anne said to me, many years later. "That's what he wanted, you know, he preferred to go to the front. I never saw him again after that."

"Where did he work in Berlin?" I asked my mother.

"He worked at the Secret State Police," she answered, lowering her eyes. "He was a lawyer, after all, and he applied to the regular police and to the other one there, too. Unfortunately, the other one answered with a 'yes' first, so he accepted right away. You don't know what times were like, there was no work ... A week later, he gets the 'yes' from the regular police. If it had been the other way around, his life would have been better." Truly? Years later, my aunt said: "He wanted to work in the law firm in Lüneburg where he had been trained. By a Mr. Meier. But then Hitler issued a new law that you could only work as a lawyer in a law firm if you were related to the owner. Your father was no relation. And so he had to apply to the state.

I never heard about that law again." Did that really exist? And my mother's best friend, Lisa, whose husband had been in the mounted SS police in Prague, said to me: "My husband was also a lawyer. Hitler wanted to have as many lawyers around him as possible." Probably because he was in the process of rewriting the law. All these young lawyers first had to be converted to the laws of the Third Reich. The Ten Commandments appeared in brand new brown garb and were hardly recognizable.

> The first commandment was now called: Thou shalt have only one God, and his name is Adolf Hitler.
> The second: Thou shalt not make unto thee any graven image, save Hitler's picture on the wall, and the bible is now called *Mein Kampf.*
> The third was called: God is now called 'Providence'.
> The fourth: On Sundays, thou shalt be ready for parades at any time to honor Adolf Hitler.
> The fifth: Don't honor your parents and grandparents if they have Jewish blood. If you are Jewish, leave the Holy Third Reich as soon as you can.
> The sixth: Thou shalt not kill, other than your numerous enemies, and I, Adolf Hitler, will tell you who your enemies are. First and foremost, the Jews, but then also the Communists, the Gypsies, the mentally handicapped, the homosexuals, the Slavic subhumans, all the archenemies of the German national movement and the Great German Reich ...
> The seventh: Thou shalt not commit adultery, unless your husband or wife is Jewish, in which case you must separate from them as soon as possible, lest the curse of Providence strikes you. Or that of Hitler.

The eighth: Thou shalt not steal has become: Yes, steal as much as you can from the rich Jews, for they have acquired their property unlawfully.

The ninth: Thou shalt not bear false witness now means, slander as much as you can when it comes to Jews and other enemies of our beloved fatherland.

The tenth: Thou shalt not covet thy neighbor's wife and other property, unless it is the Jews, then take from them their Aryan oxen and donkeys and their Aryan wives and servants. What do you mean by stealing when dealing with Jews? We simply take back what belongs to us.

That had to be drilled into the young and older lawyers first. You can't rewrite ancient laws overnight. Nietzsche called it the revaluation of values. But thanks to Providence, everyone hated the Jews, the Germans and the Austrians agreed on that, unless they were Jewish. Then they were unlucky.

Hitler may well have been Austrian, but the Austrians also wanted a Greater German Reich free of Jews, and thus the new Messiah met with hardly any resistance in either country.

"Jews out!" that was shouted from everyone's heart.

My mother could hardly speak, so paralyzed had she been by a couple of strokes, so one evening in her nursing home we watched the news on television. They were about the Israeli heirs of the department store owners in Leipzig who had been expropriated in the Third Reich. Suddenly, my half-dead mother came alive and screamed:

"You see, all this belonged to the Jews! All that! All of Leipzig!" I was very astonished at this outburst, because all my life my mother had never uttered a word against the Jews or Israel. To the contrary.

And now she screamed: "Everybody hated the Jews! Everybody! Everybody! But no one wanted them to be killed. No one! Maybe send them away or something, but not kill them!" Soon after, she herself was dead.

I grew up after the war without any trace of anti-Semitism. Probably living among nothing but old Nazis. There were no Jewish people around me; they had been gassed or had fled in time. I knew nothing about Jews, not even that they had to choose names like Rubin or Bernstein, and, of course, I didn't have any knowledge of the ugly caricatures of Jews in the newspapers of the Third Reich. Just as little as my girlfriends knew them. If in the Third Reich, and long before that, it was said that the Jews had murdered Christ, now in confirmation classes we were told about the amazing fact that our Savior had been a Jew.

For me, Anne Frank was the archetype of the Jewish girl with her large sad dark eyes and tender sensitive mouth. And I would have loved to write the wonderful sentences in her diary myself. My heart belonged to Anne Frank. And when, at the age of fifteen, I wanted to go to America as an exchange student with the American Field Service, I angrily told a committee of teachers that we must never forget the crimes of the Third Reich. Nothing like that should ever happen again. Never! And I almost cried for all the murdered Jews of the world, especially for my beloved Anne. But the other students contradicted me and said that we Germans should no longer look back, only forward. Thank God, the Third Reich was over. And what good would it do to stir the old porridge?

And the teachers looked around delightedly. And I thought I would never get to the States. But the teachers obviously wanted to stir up the old broth after all, and sent the stirring Nazi child, the daughter of Gestapo and Waffen SS man Suhr to California. "I am small, my heart is pure," I could have prayed this children's prayer even at sixteen in California, that's how little I knew of our family disgrace. And that was a great luck. For, how could I have carried such tremendous guilt on my meager teenage shoulders? And never could I have innocently and naively loved Miss Bernstein, our Jewish drama teacher, nor she me, if we had both known what I know today. And never would I have suggested *The Diary of Anne Frank* as the play of the year in her class in 1960. The German exchange student child with the pure heart wanted to be Anne Frank in front of the entire American school only fourteen years after the great war between Germany and the United States. And lay out the German guilt in front of the Californian teachers and students and play the guiltless Anne and not be a child of her murderers.

It was not until much later that I understood why Miss Bernstein didn't want to perform the play — and when she was finally persuaded, she gave me not the part of Anne, but that of her mother. Yet, I looked remarkably like Anne, I thought, with my dark eyes, black-brown hair, and thin lips. But the student who was supposed to play Anne had blue eyes and golden hair. That didn't fit at all. She looked wonderfully Aryan, as they would have said in the Third Reich.

Although I was very disappointed at first not to be Anne, I liked playing Anne's mother, because I always liked acting. I still think today that I should have been an actress, and not a lonely, unknown poet of the German language working away in exile in the US. Then I wouldn't have to report on the family disgrace that robs me now of sleep, night after night. At that time, I proudly wrote to my mother from California about my role as Anne Frank's mother. What do you think this woman thought; the woman who was the mother of three children fathered by a murderer? I don't know. Thank God. It must have been terrible what she went through, every day of her postwar life. And every night. She often screamed when she was dreaming. I was very afraid of those screams!

She had some protection: the wall of silence she herself had built. Like that of all Germans. And her remarriage in 1947 to my stepfather, who was the only father I knew. And he was not involved in the crimes of the Third Reich. Although he had also been a member of the SA. He had to prove that in 1934, when he wanted to become a civil servant for life. Are you in the party or in the SS or in the SA? he was asked by the state culture department in Hanover. And if not, he would have to apply for membership immediately, it says in a letter in his files, which I took after my mother's death. And his certificate from 1938 being awarded a civil servant bears the gruesome signatures of Hermann Göring and Adolf Hitler. He also had to swear an oath of loyalty to Hitler. Like all officials and soldiers of the Third Reich. The devil knows exactly how to catch souls ...

The signature of the power-greedy Hitler is relentlessly jagged and falls to the right. That would suggest depression, it says in my graphology book. Perhaps he suffered from the sacred task of ridding Europe of Jewish vermin. And Goering's handwriting seems quite normal, considering that he had to take more and more heroin over the years to fulfill his murderous duties. What does Stalin's writing actually look like? And that of Mussolini?

Hitler, who swallowed masses of pills, Goering, who was addicted to heroin, Goebbels, the devilish womanizer who limped like the devil himself, the perfidious Jew-hater with the heavenly name Himmler, the opportunistic villain Heydrich, who later became the Reichsführer of Bohemia and Moravia and thus of Prague; what a select staff of criminals formed the top leadership of the Thousand-Year Reich when my mother was young and pretty and man-addicted and politically unsophisticated like most young girls at any time, as I was at her age, too. Only, she lived in a time that didn't allow her to be politically unsophisticated, even as a very young woman. As such, she had to become guilty for not protesting, for not leaving the country that was about to commit the greatest murder in human history.

And the ambitious man she had married, seven years her senior, had joined the SS and the party soon after Hitler came to power. Then, as a young lawyer, he joined the Secret State Police in Berlin. His path into the Great German Guilt was preordained.

"You know, he was pathologically jealous," my mother told me.

"One of his friends would often come by our house after work and then eat some cookies from a bowl in the living room. And your father would yell: 'Who ate our cookies here again?' I mean, such a few cookies and then this fuss! But we were poor then, even though your father was in government service. Everybody was poor then. I used to walk fifteen minutes home from the streetcar stop because I wanted to save the dime for changing trains. So those cookies were a thorn in your father's eye. And finally he kicked his friend out of the apartment with the words that he shouldn't come back, or he might get something. Because of those few cookies. And that's how it always was, whether a friend was eating cookies with us or drinking a glass of wine. And when a man is that jealous, he drives you into the arms of another, I can tell you that. That's a law of nature."

It was in Prague that my mother experienced her first orgasm. "Suddenly I heard myself screaming," she told me, when I was already not too young for being told that, "thinking, who's screaming? And there it was myself."

"And who was the man?" I asked her.

"Oh, some soldier on leave," she said throwing it away: "I don't even remember his name." So I didn't ask any further. Questions were not welcomed, anyway. Many years later, my brother, who was five years older, told me that our mother had had an affair with dentist Müller.

"She locked us kids in the nursery, with a bucket to pee in and some sandwiches, when he came." My mother told me one day that this dentist Müller had wanted to marry her after the war, after she had become a war criminal's widow. "But I didn't want him," and she added: "he always got it on with his receptionist." What I didn't know was that she herself had been that married man's receptionist. I only knew that she had always wanted to be a dentist, but her parents would not have had money for her education. Probably it had not been an unknown soldier who had elicited this cry of pleasure from her, but the handsome dentist Müller, whom I knew from a photograph taken in Prague, in which she was walking beside him, laughing merrily. And on the other side of him, her very young sister. She, too, is laughing merrily in these dark times. Youth always finds something to laugh about.

I, too, wanted to have fun in my twenties. How we laughed in the last year of high school! About God and the world. But our world was harmless, and politics took place in peaceful little Bonn, and we didn't talk about it; Sartre and Simone de Beauvoir did that for us, they had both gone through the bad times. And maybe they too had not been in the resistance enough and had not helped any Jews get out, as I read in a book

Mother walking next to dentist Müller and her younger sister

by one of their Jewish friends. Maybe they were so obsessed with politics because they suffered from feelings of guilt like so many German writers who had grown up in the Third Reich, for example, the famous ones born in 1929, Peter Rühmkorf and Hans Magnus Enzensberger and Christa Wolf. Too young to be guilty and too old to be completely innocent. A lifetime of standing around between the chairs of guilt and innocence and never being able to take a seat. That must be difficult.

And then Günter Grass, a little older than the others, the great accuser of the guilty Nazi generation, and, in the end, he had still been in the Waffen-SS, although, without his doing, he became innocently guilty, and never fired a shot. His friend Peter Rühmkorf collected enemy leaflets when he was fifteen, and that was punishable by death, he told me, and, at night, he secretly listened to the BBC station under the bed covers. That, too, was punishable by death. That's why he said he had been in the resistance as a youth. In general, all of Germany had suddenly been in the resistance. How many of my acquaintances told me that when I had to confess to being a murderer's child! "My parents were in the resistance," they said, but no proof was offered. No parent had emigrated or been imprisoned in a concentration camp or murdered. And that would have been the only convincing proof of having been in the resistance. The criminal heads of state in the Third Reich didn't waste a lot of time with resistors. There are supposed to have been well over a hundred assassination attempts on Hitler. Did any of these heroes survive the Third Reich? I don't think so.

I wish I could say that Suhr had died on a meat hook after the twentieth of July 1944, like the father of Wibke Bruhns. That would have been an honorable death. And I could be proud of such a father. And yet, there was a way out for desk murderers and concentration camp guards. They could say they preferred to go to the front to fight and die for the holy fatherland. That was the only way out of the murder misery, as far as I know.

Some years ago. I watched an interview on American television with an old man who had worked in a concentration camp as a young man. He had to take the clothes, money, and jewelry of the Jews. Much of it was stolen by the guards, although there were heavy penalties for it. Because, by law, the looted goods belonged to the looting country Germany and not to some ridiculous boys who had to do the dirty work in the concentration camp. And this old man on TV had also eagerly helped to steal and had hidden the loot in a locker. A German bad guy must have ratted them all out, but the man interviewed had been notified in time and was able to make his loot disappear. The others, however, received severe punishments. Even in a country of criminals, order must prevail.

"Why didn't you have to go before a court after the war? You worked in a concentration camp, didn't you?" the interviewer asked the old man.

"I didn't want to work there and had enlisted to the front. But my request was rejected. After the war, I was able to show the rejection notice as proof."

"Did you ever suffer from guilt during the war or afterwards?" the American asked him.

"No, never!"

"And why not? There were women and children murdered in the concentration camps, after all."

"It was war," the old man answered, "women and children were being murdered everywhere. That was nothing out of the ordinary."

I once heard in an old interview on the radio how Elie Wiesel said to an interviewer, I think it was Studs Terkel: "The desk killers and concentration camp people could report to the front, nothing happened to them if they did, not even to their families. So, for them there was a way out, and that's why they're all guilty and have no right to say they had to obey an order."

My unknown father chose this path and enlisted to the front long before I was born, my mother told me. But he was with the Gestapo and so guilty that they wouldn't let him go, he knew too much, they said. Until they let him go in November 1942 — and at that point he came from a relatively peaceful Berlin, where total war had not yet broken out, to the worst of all fronts, the Russian one in Kiev. On November 19, 1942, the Russians had begun their counteroffensive, and it led to the so-called fall of Stalingrad on February 2, 1943, six days before my unfortunate birth. That was the turn of the war, and Kiev, where Suhr was fighting or murdering in the Ukraine, whatever you want to call it, was also under vicious fire. And in November 1943, exactly one year later, the Germans had to vacate Ukraine. That's how Suhr came to Toulouse in the south of France, which the Germans had occupied only late. There he was allowed to shoot partisans again.

I learned what he had done in Ukraine from a book by Uwe Timm *Am Beispiel meines Bruders* (*In My Brother's Shadow*). Behind the German front in Russia and Poland, i.e. in the East, where the Slavic 'subhumans' lived, there were special commandos, which didn't exist on the Western Front, and they shot so-called partisans. These were all who looked Jewish, all who held a rifle in their hand or looked somehow suspicious and Slavic. Meaning, everyone and anyone.

In the Ukraine, the desk murderer Suhr became a direct murderer with hands dripping with blood. While he had worked before in a manure bucket in the Reich Security Main Office in Berlin, he now ended up in a cesspool of the Waffen SS elite troops in beautiful Ukraine, that Ukraine with the waving cornfields that Hitler claimed for his beloved Aryan people. What was Suhr thinking when he went from the manure bucket to the cesspool? "Should I better have stayed in Berlin?"

I don't know.

When, after my mother's death in 2000, I called my nominal aunt Lisa, the last survivor of the Third Reich I knew, and told her about my gruesome discovery that Suhr had worked for Eichmann for a while, she said:

"It wasn't quite that gruesome. We also had very good times in Prague. And I knew Eichmann personally. I was invited to tea with him once." She still seemed pleased about this tea invitation from above.

"At least my father enlisted to the front," I said through tears: "He wanted to leave."

Then she screamed at the top of her lungs: "Stop bragging, here! My husband wanted to leave, too! But then they said to him: be careful or your life and that of your family is in danger!" She continued to snarl: "Your father was too soft, you hear, too soft! He was like you! And the Jews are always to blame for everything, after all. Even still today. Look at the world! Look at Israel! Always the same!" That was enough for me, and I hung up!

Aunt Lisa had been my mother's best friend in Prague — and also later in life. The two of them had lived together in Prague in a large villa that had a beautiful garden with a fountain and a sandbox in it. There we little Nazi children splashed and played, the daughter Mona and the son Jens of Aunt Lisa and my two older brothers and later me and the child of my Aunt Anne, who had been something like my twin sister, since she was only five months my junior. We wandered hand in hand through our innocent childhood in the same little dresses. The stately villa probably once belonged to a rich Jewish family, my aunt Anne said to me after my mother's death.

"There was a glass elevator in the house for the paralyzed daughter, because she couldn't climb the stairs." And I always see in my mind's eye the poor Jewish girl, a paralyzed Anne Frank, floating up in the glass elevator. What happened to her and her family? Hopefully, they escaped from Prague in time, and didn't wait long to emigrate until it was too late. When the German invasion of Poland began on September 1, 1939, it was too late. That's when the borders closed. Until then, Eichmann and his men, and thus also Suhr, collected information about the Jews in order to persuade them to emigrate. At first, they were not to be murdered. They just wanted to be rid of them: They were stripped of their belongings, their German passports, and made into stateless people. Then they were left with fifty Reichsmark, a few suitcases with clothes and linen, and nothing but out with them to the foreign countries that were stupid enough to take in this 'human vermin'. But the other countries also suffered from the virus of anti-Semitism and didn't want to accept Jews without difficulties. They already had enough, they claimed. When my mother visited me for the first time in Lausanne, where I studied from 1966 to 1971, she suddenly pointed to a place on the opposite shore and said: "There lies Evian. That's where the foreign countries decided they didn't want to take any more Jews ... at least not all of them ... and so ..." She suddenly fell silent.

Geertje Suhr's birth house in the lower right corner of the photo
(now the Slovak Embassy). The Villa Petschek, now the American
Embassy, can be see in the upper left corner (curved building)

What I didn't know at the time was: and that way, Hitler and his clan of murderers decided to deport the Jews to their deaths. That began in the fall of 1941, and on January 20, 1942, the infamous Wannsee Conference took place, the murderers' conference, at which Eichmann alone, without his suupport staff, was allowed to be present. Later he proudly reported that he drank cognac with his superiors, the vain Jew executioner; how nice, he was allowed to drink real French cognac with the high murdering rabble. Proud as my nominal aunt Lisa, who was allowed to drink tea with the Eichmanns in Prague. Was my mother there, too? She didn't tell me. For her, Prague was paradise, where there was no war and no Heydrich raged, until he died there in an assassination attempt and a whole town, Lidice, had to atone for it.

"Do you know," I said to her, many years later, "that the Germans in Prague were murdered by the Czechs in May 1945?" My mother lowered her eyes.

"When did you get out?"

"Your father sent a truck for us in time, and Aunt Lisa and I drove through all of Germany with you children. The country was completely destroyed. Beautiful Dresden — you know, your father and I took our honeymoon there — a huge heap of rubble!" The city, a jewel of Baroque architecture, was no more. In Viktor Klemperer's diaries, I read how horribly Dresden was bombed by the Allies in February 1945. The war ended in May of the same year. The destruction of the city had not even been necessary for war reasons. It was an act of revenge against the German women, children, and old men — the young ones were all at the front — for Hitler's millionfold crimes against humanity. How many suffocated miserably and burned to death? But miraculously, the Jew Viktor Klemperer and his 'Aryan' wife were saved, both of whom otherwise would

Dresden as viewed from the tower of the Rathaus (City Hall)
looking toward the south with the scultpture Allegory of Grace
or Goodnees (foreground) by August Schreitmüller, 1945,
showing destruction of the city. Photo by Richard Peter (1895-
1977), from the collection of the Deutsche Fotothek

have been deported to the concentration camp the next day. Something good came out of the terrible. Viktor Klemperer survived, and with him his diary, in which he bears witness to the terrible period from 1933 to 1945, when the Germans became a nation of murderers.

I cried when I read that, in the summer of 1941 he had to wear the yellow star that was to demote this fine, cultured man to a third-, no, fourth-, no, fifth-class human being. The beautiful Star of David burned on him like a mark of Cain.

And I cried even more when I read — it was already after my mother's death — in a book about Hitler and his bureaucrats that my biological father was one of the collaborators who wrote the text of the decree stating that from now on Jews would have to wear a yellow star. It was signed by Heydrich, not by Suhr. A small consolation for me. My niece had told me to read the book *Hitler's Bureaucrats: The Nazi Security Police and The Banality of Evil* by Yaacov Lozowick, saying that her grandfather Suhr was in it. I was fifty-seven years old at the time and had long been married in the United States to a man of Polish descent when I learned that I was the child of a man who had worked for Eichmann for a time.

When I was twenty years old, my Aunt Anne in Lüneburg had shown me my biological father's last letter, in which he bids farewell to us three children.

"He took his own life," my aunt said, sobbing loudly.

"Your mother wanted to tear up the letter, but I took it for myself. Your father was a wonderful man, and if your mother had not married him, I would have."

"Why did he take his own life?" I asked my mother, distraught.

"He didn't want to do what he had to do. He would rather go to the front, he said. And so he went to the Russian front.

And when that collapsed, to Toulouse, France. From there, he had to bring the German troops back to Berlin when the war was lost. Hitler's last order was: No prisoners will be taken. All those who carried out this order received the death sentence at Nuremberg. Your father hanged himself in prison. And I had a second chance in life ..." She paused, lit a cigarette, and continued:

"You know, right after the war, chaos reigned everywhere, many families lived apart. You could still find a husband there. That was only for a very short time. There were so many young widows and then the girls who had never married. And very few men. And that's when I met your father — Daddy, I mean, your stepfather — and married him. That saved me. As the widow of a so-called war criminal, I was not entitled to a pension for myself and you children, even though your father had been a senior government official and civil servant appointed for life. I desperately needed a husband and a father for you three children. I had not learned enough to get us all through. So my marriage to Daddy was a great good fortune for me and for you kids."

But this happiness had not been such great good fortune, either. She was happy when she dropped her children off with her parents and went to work every day in a translation office. After her remarriage, she and her new husband had to move away from her family and Lüneburg to Hanover, where he worked as a trainee teacher at the State Ministry of Education. From then on, she sat alone with the unloved child of the unloved dead husband in the tiny apartment, while my brothers and my beloved cousin Anni stayed with the grandparents in their native Lüneburg. She was feeling unhappy and lonely, and, as a result, she dealt with the poor child in a strict and vicious way. Strict and vicious had been the preferred educational method of the Third Reich anyway, as the Swiss psychoanalyst Alice Miller writes in her books. 'Black pedagogy' she calls this well-known sledgehammer method: "Blows to the back of the head increase the ability to think!"

The new stepfather preferred to disappear to a bar in the evening, as he was accustomed to do as a bachelor, instead of staying home with his ever-smoking and reading and ill-tempered and still-young wife. For my mother, happiness was nowhere to be found in Hanover. As a married woman she was doomed to unemployment. That was the thinking of that time back then. She found relaxation only in books and cigarettes. And on Sundays, she hiked across the fields to a farm in the distance, where her old friend Lisa from Prague was staying with her children.

"We always had to tell each other a lot," Aunt Lisa said to me on the phone as a very old woman: "After all, we could talk to each other quite honestly about everything." Even about Prague, of course, about all the parties and flirtations and affairs, about all the things they didn't tell us kids about. Maybe they also railed about the Jews when they were alone, so they could open their mouths honestly and talk as they had gotten accustomed to in their anti-Semitic youth: "The Jews are to blame for everything, even today! Just look at Israel and how the Palestinians are being treated. A scandal!" But in front of us children, they never uttered a word against the Jews and Israel. There was not a trace of anti-Semitism left, only the eyes were always lowered when Eichmann was mentioned. And when his trial took place in 1960, my mother lived with constantly lowered eyelids — and said nothing, as if she had never known him and even though, perhaps, she had tea with him once. And when my stepfather came home one day and said that today he had found the file of the father of one of my brother's schoolmates — he was to be promoted — on the desk at the Oldenburg Ministry, where we now lived, he refused to sign it, because B. had been a real Nazi pig in the Third Reich.

"I mean, a real pig," he said, laughing in the elation of his knowledge that he himself had not been such a pig, even if he had been in the SA as well. But the producer of his stepchildren had been, and perhaps Daddy had never known that, or only a little bit, and he had repressed that too, just as most other things about the Third Reich had been and were being repressed. For example, that April 20 was Hitler's birthday. That was a real holiday, with joyous parades and numerous fireworks. But my mother never said: "Today is April 20; that was Hitler's birthday, there were always celebrations and parades all over Germany," so there was never a nostalgic look back. It was only when I became friends with the German Petra T. in Chicago that I was enlightened about this. She said to me one day: "My brother is a real bully, no wonder, he was born on April 20, and that's Hitler's birthday."

And when we later met Karl-Heinz Jakobs at the Goethe Institute in Chicago, the writer from the GDR who eventually had to leave the country because of his protest against Biermann's expatriation, he mentioned that he was born on April 20, 1929. Petra and I screamed, as if from the same mouth:

"But that's Hitler's birthday!" He laughed in amazement and asked us: "Why do you know that?" Because simply nobody who had the grace to belong to the late-born generation, knew about Hitler's birthday and the glorious national celebrations on that day in the Third Reich. "As a child, I always thought I was something special," Karl-Heinz Jakobs told us with a smile: "I mean, all of Germany celebrated my birth, after all!" And while he grew up with the diabolical doctrines of the Third

Reich and later shook them off, Petra and I, who were both born in 1943, remained untouched by the celebrations and hatreds of the Third Reich, untouched by hatred of Jews and contempt for the Slavic peoples who were to serve the Aryans as slaves in a giant Holy German Empire that wanted to unite all of Europe and even Russia under its heel.

In a fit of black humor, I once said to my husband, whose ancestors had all immigrated to the States from Poland: "What Hitler didn't manage to do, I did: make a Pole my slave!" In fact, after he retired, he took almost all the housework off my hands, saying that I was doing everything wrong and was obviously too stupid to do it. And we laughed as if at a joke, but it was a sad joke. When I fell in love with my future husband, Jack, in Lausanne, and told my mother on the phone from Switzerland, she asked me as if shot out of a pistol: "He must be Jewish. Or is he?"

"No, no," I reassured her, "he's Catholic, Polish Catholic." And I thought she asked me such a question because we are Germans and suffered from German collective guilt. But now I know that she was afraid that she would have to inform me that I was the child of a murderer of Jews. Such a marriage could have led to a catastrophe. The catastrophe, that one day we would find out the truth about my unknown father. She must have wondered what would happen if it came out that Suhr had worked for Eichmann for a while (from July 1, 1941 to November 1942).

But thank God, Jack was only Polish-Catholic. And not Jewish, though he did have a Jewish last name — which I didn't know at the time — and we in Chicago regularly got letters from Jewish associations asking us for donations to Israel. Once, one asked me on the phone for money for a tree in Israel. And, to this day, I regret that I didn't donate the sum, but gave as

470

an explanation for my refusal that we were not Jewish, we only had a Jewish last name.

"I wish you good luck with your campaign," I added.

"Thank you very much," he said politely: "I will remove your name from our computer list." Now there is no tree of mine growing in Israel. I really should have donated a forest! And I always think: how could you refuse such a request? Were you crazy? Something as beautiful as a tree of mine in Israel! It would have been even nicer if I could have donated a hospital or a children's home ...

To dampen my guilt a little, I gave my Israeli friend's daughter, whom I had loved dearly since childhood, a gold bracelet with a diamond bow on it — Jack had given it to me at the beginning of our marriage. And later I gave her the matching necklace with the same diamond bow as a wedding gift. I explained the 'lavish' gift to Rebecca by saying that I had always worn the jewelry when I roamed the stores of Chicago with her mother — both of us still young women. Now, I said, I was too old for the delicate jewelry: it belonged on the arm and neck of a beautiful young woman.

Rebecca's mother, my friend Assia, is the most beautiful woman I have ever met in my life. To this day, she still possesses the perfect face of Nefertiti, with huge dark sultry eyes and a perfectly formed body that dwarfs that of a Venus de Milo. I have been close friends with that beautiful woman for thirty-seven years now. She is Jewish and was born in Israel, her parents having immigrated from Poland. Her father was a dentist there. And neither of us knew until the year 2000, that I was the child of a murderer of Jews. The Jewess and the German murderer's child, close friends for thirty-seven years. And I cannot tell her what I learned that night in September 2000 about the criminal deeds of Sturmbannführer Suhr. How can I burden her with that? Our friendship would be over. How could she continue to bear my closeness — I can hardly bear it myself.

For a few months, I withdrew from her and no longer answered her calls. But then I felt shabby: she didn't know why I was hiding, after all. I had to conceal the truth out of tact, but I had no right to torment her. And I went back to answering the phone and met her in town and paid her luncheons, a tiny gesture of reparation for the evil actions of the SS man who defiled me with his genes. And Kurt, Assia's husband, during the time of his retirement, wrote his memoirs and gave them to me to read. There, I learned about his childhood in Berlin and his poor Jewish parents: not all Jews were rich, as Hitler and his comrades claimed, frothing at the mouth. Kurt's father had gone from door to door with a vendor's tray to sell his haberdashery. As a very young man, Kurt had joined a Zionist association and managed to get to safety on one of the last ships to Palestine. And his poor parents and sister, born later, died in German concentration camps — probably, because he doesn't know for sure where they stayed.

"And just imagine," Assia said to me indignantly, "after the war he flew from Israel to Germany, to this atrocious country that had his family and half our people on its conscience. He wanted to work there as a surgeon in a hospital. Can you imagine that? I said to him, I will not live among such criminals. I threatened to separate, otherwise we would be living in Germany today and not in the States. Doesn't the man have a sense of honor?" And, in fact, Kurt never reproached me for being a German.

He just asked me once: "Do you have the impression that we Jews are different from other people?"

"No, I don't have that impression. Maybe a little more intelligent, but not different."

"How could Hitler do what he did?" he asked me, me of all people.

"I can't explain that either," I said: "He was evil. And evil is mysterious." He was evil, and evil is mysterious.

Again and again, I watch programs on television about mass murderers who kill for no reason, just for the fun of it. And sometimes they even eat the corpses of their victims for the fun of it, like the mass murderer Jeffrey Dahmer from Milwaukee with the Aryan-blond angel face; he looks so guilt-free, as if he couldn't harm a fly. And he has had his way with the corpses and then put them in a freezer, in pieces, for later consumption. And Adolf Hitler was also such a man, even if he was a vegetarian and didn't touch animal flesh. But he touched human flesh all the more. Millions and millions of pounds of human flesh. He never showed his face in any concentration camp, not even at the front, I think. Let other poor pigs murder for him. He was devilish and mysterious at the same time with his lust for murder and destruction. For a while, people in Germany were asked to look for a Hitler within themselves. Does he really exist in all of us? That is unimaginable to me. But my unknown sperm donor worked for the devil. And whoever works for the devil does devilish things, whether he wants to or not. I hope with all my heart that he didn't want to. That, in normal times, he would have remained a normal, decent person, even if contaminated by the virus of anti-Semitism, because the whole era was contaminated by it.

At first, I didn't like my husband's Polish surname — I didn't know for a long time, that it also sounded Jewish — because in German, it is not simply called Potash, but may also be bastardized as pot-arse or pot-ass. And my cousin by marriage, Karin, once jokingly said to me: You pot-arse with ears! Who wants to be called pot-arse with ears? The Polish Potashs had added the h to the end of their name so they wouldn't be called Pot-arse in the States, otherwise their name would have been Pot-ass in English. Potash, on the other hand, sounded harmless in the States. I think with shame that, at the beginning of our marriage, I suggested to my husband that we change his name to Ashley; I liked the name. It was the first name of Scarlet O'Hara's great love in *Gone with the Wind*. So we could keep half of his original name after all, the Ash. And only the Pot would disappear. But pride comes before the fall. One day, I found in the newspaper a list of fifty of the most hideous names in the States. At the top of the list was Adolf Suhr. Suhr sounds like sewer in English, my husband explained to me. And Adolf was not only Hitler's first name, but also one of the many first names of my murderer father, Suhr. When I later learned what this Adolf Suhr had done, I wrote the following poem in despair:

Nomen est Omen

Suhr in English
Means cloaca
And is the nastiest
Name in the States
Adolf Suhr
Is in the top spot in the list
Of fifty winners
In being horrible
And was the name
Of my unknown sperm donor

Geertje Suhr
Daughter of Adolf Cloaca Sewer
Hitler Dachau Auschwitz Himmler
Lord in Heaven
Heydrich Eichbaum
Oh man
Buchenwald, oh Buchenwald

Germany, your forests
No beautiful land in those days

Stay away from me
I wouldn't take you even if you paid me for it
Adolf hanged himself

I felt doused with liquid manure, and from then on was glad to bear the innocent, Jewish-sounding name Potash. And I would never have chosen the name Suhr as a writer if I had known what a criminal Suhr had become in the Third Reich. I would have named myself Schmidt after my stepfather, because he had been my father anyway. And I also grew up as Miss Schmidt and not only as Miss Suhr. And in my old age I felt it to be a shame to have been born in Prague, in the wonderful golden city, and no longer a distinction. Prague, how attractive that had been, as attractive as my Dutch first name Geertje, which no one in the States could write and which they thought was a man's name.

"You are really a nice person," the husband of a French friend in Chicago said to me: "If only you didn't have such a horrible first name." I had been born in Prague, a child of the German occupation forces, and my father had worked there as commander of the Security Police and SD from June 22, 1939, until he was ordered back to Gestapo headquarters in Berlin on May 28, 1940. And every year I went to Berlin with my mother — that must have been about twenty times — and she never said to me: That's where we lived, and we did this and that here, and your oldest brother was born in Berlin. She kept silent about the years there, as she did about everything in the Third Reich. The white snow of silence lay over the entire filth of the Thousand-Year Reich, which had lasted a whole twelve years. And I have to thank her for that silence: how could I, as a young person, have borne such an ugly 'truth'?

These days, I can hardly bear it as an older woman, even with five years of therapy behind me with a Jewish psychologist from Riga, who had a number burned into his skin in the German concentration camp. His wife's as well. He met her there. Year after year, I cried in front of him, in Chicago, because of the Great German Guilt. And finally, he said to me: "My God, I didn't realize how much the youth in Germany suffers from guilt. And now I also understand why so many young Germans go to Israel to work in the kibbutz. That was inexplicable to me before." And he told me not to be so generous with my money, that would only lead to people taking advantage of me, but not respecting me.

And I said: "I know, I'm still saving the Jews with everything I do." He looked so dumbfounded, as if I had slapped him, out of the blue, and he said to me almost a little harshly: "Well, that's enough of that, now. I don't want to hear another word about it. You are not guilty; you were a baby in the Third Reich. But your parents, that's another story."

Yet he had always defended my mother: "No wonder, if the married women had lovers. If the men insisted on going to war, then the abandoned women had a right to have lovers." And I didn't even know at that time that I had been the child of a murderer of Jews. Would he have given me absolution, even if he had known about my murderer genes? I think, yes, he really didn't believe in the punishment of other members of a family for the crimes of one member of the family or family liability. He believed in my character, and he knew it was not evil or mysterious, just naive. I wanted to save the Jewish victims posthumously with my small, good deeds. And in a dream, I once stood in front of Hitler and shot him.

And Dr. Zaks asked me: "Do you have the disposition to be a murderer?"

And I answered: "No, I don't think so. It's only Hitler that I would have liked to shoot." And maybe Göring and Goebbels and Himmler and Eichmann, I add today. And all those who worked for Eichmann, that is, including Suhr, so that he would be stopped from further murdering. And what I commit here on paper is patricide. I execute Gustav Adolf Ernst Friedrich Suhr. You are not supposed to write anything bad about your father, a dear friend told me; one's father is holy, whatever he did. But I don't think so; rather, you have to earn the designation 'father' before it becomes holy. And the Gestapo and Waffen SS man Suhr didn't deserve the word father. He is not my father, and consequently, he is not holy to me, and I execute him here on paper, because he shot me in the heart with his crimes. And such a wound never heals; it festers and proliferates and bleeds away until the day I die. And if there is an afterlife — and what do we know about what there is after death — then my spirit will roam around in the afterlife with this festering wound in my chest.

I only hope that I will never meet the murderer Suhr or the murderer Eichmann or the murderer Hitler there, because that would imply that I would have to have been banished to hell with them. Therefore I want to go everywhere, only not to hell with these devilish monstrosities, rather into a hell-tub filled with scalding water or into the steaming bathtub, like the mother of Alexandra Senfft, the poor Eri Ludin, who put an end to her mental agonies around her murderer father Hanns Ludin by falling into boiling water. Or maybe it was indeed an accident, as the daughter seems to hope.

And I thank heaven that I would not have known and perhaps would not have gotten to know and maybe even learned to love Suhr; like poor, desperate beautiful Eri, who had been a father's child and loved him ardently until he was hanged by the Slovaks shortly after the war. There, as a German envoy, he had signed a deportation order that sent seventy thousand Jews to their deaths. And the Ludin family had always doubted his guilt in order to be able to bear his fate and their own.

Oh, I would also like to be able to doubt the guilt of my father, and I cling to the fact that he tried to get out of the Eichmann murder group and reported to the front, even if at the front, there was no honorable defense of the fatherland, but a mass murdering. Among all the desk murderers around Eichmann, he was the only one to report to the front. And they didn't want to let him go, as my mother said. During his interrogations after the war, Dieter Wisliceny — also an Eichmann collaborator — stated that Eichmann had never let any of his people go. In 1944, he had personally stated to him: "We are all in the same boat, and no one is getting out." But he concealed the fact that Suhr got out of his murderer's boat in November 1942, and went to Kiev, into another boat of murderers. I don't think he was allowed to decide where he wanted to go. In any case, he made an effort to get out of the Eichmann boat — and for that I kiss his guilty forehead before I put a bullet in it. And I will try not to destroy myself psychologically for his guilt, as poor Eri Ludin destroyed herself all her life with her affairs, her alcoholic excesses, and her screaming and raving all night long. And, finally, the fall into the boiling water and the horrible death in the hospital wrapped from top to bottom in gauze bandages like a living mummy. Alexandra Senfft has called the book about her mother *Silence Hurts*.

But speaking and writing also hurts, it hurts me immensely to have to write all this down. At night, I sleep badly, have constant nightmares, and take Valium and pills against my depression. In the evening, I can't wait to open the bottle of wine to wrap my poor soul in a gauze made of alcohol and chemicals:

"Sleep, you poor child, sleep, it's not your fault. You were just a baby in the Third Reich." And the punishment of other members of a family for the crimes of one member of the family (family liability) was abolished with Hitler; at least I hope so, although an acquaintance said to me after the ghastly night in September 2000 — I had shown him the book with the revelations about Gustav Adolf Ernst Friedrich Suhr: "You three children should rightly have been drowned, a friend of Wiesenthal's said, because your father also killed the Jewish children." And whether the houses that my brothers and I had inherited had been 'looted property of the Third Reich'? And whether the probably precious painting I had given him, under which my mother had died, a genuine Flemish drawing from the eighteenth century, was 'looted property of the Third Reich'?

"No," I said, "my mother got it from a rich friend; her husband's family had owned the newspaper in Aurich. And surely, neither woman knew how valuable the drawing was." After all, I didn't know it, either, and had given it to him as a gift, even though my mother had died under it in the nursing home. I gave it away, like so many other things in my life, in order to be a good person, in order to pay off the huge debt of guilt of the Germans at least a little bit with my modest good works. But now I was suspected of possessing and giving away looted property of the Third Reich. And the recipient of the gift(s) became my accuser — and perhaps I should have been drowned like a mangy kitten or stuffed into a sack and shot, as happened to one of my mother's cousins, in front of his tender son, in order to harden him for life — probably in the sense of the Third Reich. But the son had never been grateful to him for this lesson, on the contrary. And I detested my mother's cousin for a while, although I had once had something like the hots for him for a few weeks, when I was twenty. You're an awful person, I thought — and never again did I feel his charm to be charm, more like a cheerful mask over the ugly face of the Third Reich.

"The houses come from my grandfather and have been in our family since the beginning of the twentieth century," I told the acquaintance, who was perhaps believing in punishment of other members of a family for the crimes of one member of the family and is currently giving a course at the university on the children of the great criminals of the Third Reich. After that, maybe one about the grandchildren? He mentioned my case, he said to me, though without mentioning my name. And he spoke about me with empathy. And I would have to be grateful to him for wanting to have anything to do with me at all, unless his father was also involved in the crimes of the Third Reich. But he didn't know that for certain, like most of the children and grandchildren of the Third Reich. After all, the old Nazis had let the white snow of concealment fall softly down from the sky everywhere. "Snow falls softly at night," is the name of a beautiful Christmas carol, and it is not the snow at Christmas, but that of yesterday, the snow of concealment of the Great German Guilt.

When Suhr was sent to Kiev, in November 1942, to one of the most terrible military fronts, the Russian one in the Ukraine, because there special commandos behind the front additionally murdered what there was to murder among Jewish people and Slavic people — all this fell under the name of 'fighting partisans' — he got miserably and completely drunk immediately after his arrival with the help of a bottle of cognac, or so it says in his files which my niece gave me some time ago and which came from the Federal Archives in Berlin. Totally, miserably drunk he insulted his future colleagues: They probably didn't know what work was on the Russian front. And he also insulted a married woman, who was present, with the following derisive words: "You there in the red dress with your indecent body!" He must have expressed himself — even though he was totally drunk, — very clearly and understandably.

His letter of apology states verbatim: "I have already noticed two or three times, as a student that, according to statements by my comrades, I made speeches and had conversations in drunkenness like a sober person, but on the next day didn't know what I had actually said in detail, nor how I had behaved." Suhr, who had sobered up again, was told by his comrade, Dr. Schlierbach, about his improper behavior. He was 'horrified' and 'completely dejected'. Suhr continues to whine in his files, because he had insulted people who were 'dear and worthy' to him and of whom he had a high opinion. He must have apologized at length to all concerned for 'the appalling expressions' of his behavior. And, of course, he was aware of how much hard 'work' was being done on the Eastern Front. Besides, he had only just arrived in Kiev and had not been able to form an objective picture in this respect. His two-day journey had exhausted him completely, and in general, he had been in poor physical condition. He had lost twenty pounds recently (apparently without reason). I wish that Suhr, filled with French cognac, had been right, and that there had been more partying and drinking going on at the Eastern Front, and, for my sake, sleeping around with the attractive women there, whom he must have mentioned according to the woman in the red dress, instead of German efficiency brilliantly proving itself in the murder and manslaughter of thousands of so-called partisans.

In any case, after the expiration of his probationary period, which was shortened from half a year to a few months, Suhr threw himself with zeal into his murder duties. From then on, always and everywhere, he was exemplary in his leadership qualities, his organizational skills, his ability to crack down wherever it seemed necessary. All his documents prove this, and nowhere can I detect any sign of weakness in him that could be a consolation to me during this time of bleak reading of his files. But there was something else that made me breathe a sigh of relief for a moment: in 1940, he had applied to be allowed to emigrate with his wife and two sons (I didn't yet exist) to the African colonies that Hitler wanted to bring home to his giant German empire. Would Suhr have liked to disappear from this Third Filthy Reich? Did he hope he could escape from the brown dust to a better African dream world? Or did he just want to rule over the black 'sub-humans' on a warmer continent? I don't know. In any case, my mother had already started learning Swahili in Prague — she knew a few words up until the end of her life that I have forgotten. *Out of Africa* is the corny title of the beautiful book by Isak Dinesen (or Tanja Blixen), that has also been published in English.

If Hitler had won his Aryan *Lebensraum* war, I would be sitting today in German East Africa and not here at the window of my Chicago apartment, looking not at the waters of Lake Michigan but at lions and elephants and zebras, if they had not already fallen victim to German thoroughness. And my housework would be done for me by black 'sub-humans'. And I would believe in my Aryan superhumanity, and I would read no Thomas Mann and no Marcel Proust and no Else Lasker-Schüler. Instead, I would read *Mein Kampf* every day. And on my wall above the fireplace, there would be Hitler's portrait in large format. Or would I have learned to think for myself and rebelled against the evil stupidity of the Third Reich? I don't know. And it makes me quite sick sometimes: would I have been able to resist the Zeitgeist of that time? The anti-Semitism, the chatter about Aryan blood, German racial superiority, the fanatical nationalism, and the disgusting Darwinian struggle for the so-called *Lebensraum*?

I hope that Suhr's bender in Kiev was an act of rebellion against the imposition of having to shoot innocent men, women, and children. I would have liked him to get drunk and lash out every day and then put a bullet in his own head. Because there was nothing else he could have done to escape his duty as an angel of death at the Russian front. Whoever proved to be disobedient to the Waffen-SS was quickly put aside: off to the concentration camp or shot on the spot or hanged from the nearest lamppost. The Waffen-SS didn't wait around long where punishments were concerned, and even relatives may eventually be punished, like the mothers, at home with their numerous children, who had been conceived for the Führer and the fatherland and the next genocide. One must think of the future, the infertile Hitler thought. He who wants to murder many, also needs many murderers' hands.

In November 1942, Suhr escaped to the front in Russia, in order to not to have to continue murdering for Eichmann. After the war, he was wanted and captured as a war criminal because, according to my mother, he carried out Hitler's last order: "No prisoners shall be taken." That is, he shot the prisoners, which was a violation of the Geneva Convention. But what happened to his successor, Otto Hunsche who, after Suhr's departure in November 1942, took over his position in Berlin as a desk officer in Jewish Affairs (which should probably mean Department of Robbery and Murder)? He continued to live undisturbed, as a lawyer in the Adenauer Reich until, following the Eichmann trial in 1962, he was put on trial and sentenced to five years in prison for assisting in the murder of six million Jews! And as far as he was concerned, that was still too much. He appealed against the verdict and promptly received twelve years in prison, still a modest punishment for his unimaginable crimes against humanity.

After the war, Hunsche's secretary recalled that her boss had said that in case of defeat, all members of Eichmann's department would have to kill themselves. But they didn't do that, not in the least. Eichmann lived for years under a false name in the Lüneburg Heath region, where he ran a chicken farm — and then he disappeared for many years to his family in Argentina. It was not until 1960 that the Israelis abducted him from there and put him on trial in Jerusalem. Like Hunsche, the other desk perpetrators, Krumey, Nowak and Wisliceny, were not brought to trial until many years after the war. And a large number of the mass murderers never were. They lived undisturbed in West Germany until their deaths and died a natural death in their beds, which had not been granted to the victims murdered and gassed by them. *The Murderers Are Among Us* was the title of a film in post-war Germany. How much it corresponded to the truth, the growing young people couldn't know: that perhaps their fathers and uncles and their fathers' friends had become murderers in the Third Reich.

When I can't sleep at two in the morning in Chicago, I often call my Swiss friend Johanna in Belp near Bern, who is having breakfast at nine o'clock in the morning. And I tell her about my murderer father, and she listens to me patiently and tells me, to comfort me, that her Swiss father had also become a member of the SS. And it came about like this: her grandparents owned a cable factory in the Eifel region in Germany, and the children of the family grew up as exiled Swiss in Germany. One night, Johanna's father got drunk with his German friends, and, in his drunken stupor, he let them talk him into joining the SS. He put his signature on an SS membership list. The next morning, he realized that he had committed an immense stupidity and fled with two suitcases to his native Switzerland. There, the lucky man was able to stay throughout the war, married a Swiss woman, and in 1944, my beloved friend Johanna was born in Lucerne. After the war, he returned to the Eifel with his wife and their two daughters — in the meantime, a second daughter had been born — to rebuild his father's completely destroyed factory.

But what is even more interesting is the story of her aunt, her father's sister. The aunt, who was called Mohr all her life, experienced the Allied carpet bombing in the Eifel, and, as a young woman — she was perhaps in her early twenties — fled on her bicycle to Cologne to the Swiss embassy which, by then, was already housed in a makeshift building, since the actual embassy had been destroyed by a bomb. She managed to get on the last ferry across the Rhine just in time, and on it happened to be the Swiss ambassador himself. The fine, elderly gentleman took the pretty young girl under his Swiss wings — and she was allowed to take a bath in the embassy, completely filthy as she was, and sleep in a nice bed with clean linens, while her Eifel home was being turned into a pile of rubble. In gratitude for his fatherly help, she married the man who was probably much too old for her, and she was safe for the time being, because the Swiss embassy in Cologne was under diplomatic protection and had an excellent bomb shelter. Her husband was close friends with Adenauer, who had been imprisoned in Cologne by the Nazis. Once a week, he drove to the prison in his ambassador's car to bring Adenauer food and letters.

But the most amazing thing is that one day — long after the death of this uncle de Wys d'Alba — Johanna saw a film about Adenauer's life on Swiss television, in which it was mentioned, among other things, that the Swiss ambassador de Wys d'Alba had saved the lives of many Jews in Cologne. He had been something like a Swiss Schindler. And when Johanna visited me in Chicago, she came to me with a long newspaper article about her uncle, who was now also known in Switzerland. That's when I introduced her to my Israeli friends Assia and Kurt with the words: "This is the niece of the Swiss Schindler." Kurt laughed sheepishly. There, we stood together, peacefully and friendly, the German-Jewish man whose parents and relatives had been gassed in the Third Reich, the niece of the Swiss Schindler de Wys d'Alba, and the child of the desk murderer and war criminal Suhr. I still get goose bumps when I think about it. I, with my filthy genes, have been friends with these people for many years. What an irony of fate. And yet: How nice that there is such a thing.

The last companion of my mother, who was widowed for the second time in 1970, the painter Rudolf Führmann, was a communist in his youth and had to flee to France immediately after Hitler came to power in order to escape from Hitler's murderous thugs. After the German troops entered Paris in 1940, he joined the French Foreign Legion and was sent to Africa, where he fought against Rommel. He was eventually captured by the Germans and given a death sentence. Instead of being shot to death, he was allowed to dig up mines with the other POWs. Most of his comrades got blown up in the process. He, however, miraculously survived and was able to view his death sentence with his own eyes after the war. For this brave life, he would have earned a knighthood from the Queen of England if he had been a Briton. And in Germany, the Federal Cross of Merit, first class. Or an even better medal.

What hasn't Suhr murdered, to collect all those ragged medals? For example, the "Knight's Cross of the Iron Cross as SS-Obersturmbannführer and Commander of a Combat Group with the Commander of the Security Police and the SD in France, etc.," December 11, 1944. That is the seventeenth entry in his magnificent list of awards and honors bestowed upon him by the devil himself and his sub-devils. Well, he was 'capable', just not on the good side. When I was three months old, he was awarded the Wounded Soldier Badge in Black on May 31, 1943 (number thirteen on the list). Exactly three years later, on May 31, 1946, he hanged himself in a prison in Wuppertal to avoid receiving the death sentence in Nuremberg. I am grateful to him for that. Better to execute the death sentence on himself than to leave the work to the executioners. Perhaps he was even convinced of his guilt. I hope very much that he didn't die fully feeling convinced of his perceived innocence. What he thought about his life in prison, I don't know, and I will never know. I don't possess any of the letters he must have written to my mother during the long war, and of which Wibke Bruhns possessed so many when she wrote her impressive book *My Father's Country*. Or like Alexandra Senfft, who chronicled the life of her poor mother Eri Ludin.

My unsentimental mother must have destroyed them all. All I have is a tiny German-French paperback, on which he wrote F. Suhr on the first page. And I can't find that anymore either, only a single loose leaf is left of it. Suhr came out of the muck of the Third Reich and, after committing suicide, was burned to a heap of ashes that is buried in a Lüneburg cemetery, where I don't want to lie near him, that much is for sure. I'd rather be with my stepfather Wulff Schmidt and my spiritual father, Rudolf Führmann, and with my mother, the survivor of three men: one a murderer and war criminal in the Third Reich, the second relatively innocent, even if he had been in the SA, and the third completely innocent and a victim of the Third Reich.

After the war, the writer Ernst von Salomon wrote a very famous book at the time, titled *The Questionnaire*, in which he says that he met the former German envoy to Slovakia, Hanns Ludin, in the prison camp before he was extradited to the Slovaks. They executed him for sending seventy thousand Jews to their deaths with his signature. According to Ernst von Salomon, this man belongs among the best that the Third Reich produced. He was full of idealism and love for the fatherland. He cultivated comradeship, loyalty, and decency, even in the prisoner-of-war camp among a bunch of brutalized old fighters. He voluntarily reported to the Allies, to take his guilt upon himself, so that his wife and numerous children would not have to be ashamed of him. But they were ashamed of him all their lives and were not at all grateful that he didn't continue to hide until the amnesty in the Adenauer era and thus would have remained in the family as father and breadwinner — like so many other criminals of the Third Reich did.

Since I cannot have Suhr speak for himself, I quote Hanns Ludin in his place, according to the words of Ernst von Salomon: "I have thought often about what you said about Hitler ... about the Führer. I didn't want to listen to it, I didn't want to tolerate anyone talking about him the way you did. I didn't want to, because I didn't want to appear as if I were looking for the easy way out, to shift all the blame onto him and hide behind him." And further: "I haven't found the measure for him yet. Maybe I'll never find it, maybe history will never find it, either. Sometimes I thought he was a genius, sometimes I didn't know if we weren't being led by a madman. Sometimes, I thought he was demonic, sometimes morbid.

But none of all this is right, not right is also your expression: 'lemur-like'. If I try to find a valid word for him, it is that he was 'deviant', a man who couldn't stand the light, a man in the shadows, coming from the shadows and speaking out of the shadow, and pushing everything that wanted to come to the light back into the shadows. And yet, I couldn't get away from this man. If I felt something, felt something with certainty, it was that he was a man with a destiny, a man of destiny, which I have never been able to understand as anything other than a huge shadow. But other than him, I have never met a person who was as fateful as he was; and since it was the fate of the Germans for whose sake I wanted to live, he had to coincide with the Germans for me. Maybe it would have been hubris, what he, what we perished from, but certainly it would have been hubris of me, had I presumed to approach him for what was to be done with my schemes. I couldn't choose him, he was there. I couldn't choose the people to whom I belonged, they were there; everything was there with all its faults and weaknesses, I had to love it with all its faults and weaknesses. If I became guilty, if we all became guilty, we became guilty out of love."

Today we would say that he was talking a load of nonsense; the children and grandchildren of the Third Reich, who cannot even imagine how so many decent people could fall for such a fanatical murderer and clown figure as Hitler. Horrified, we look at old newsreels: and you believed in this cheap smear actor? An Austrian, born in Braunau and raised in Linz and coming from a backwoods family, without much schooling, he acquired his little knowledge by reading, in Vienna, as the Austrian historian Brigitte Hamann writes in her book *Hitler's Vienna.* He absorbed the fascist ideas of his time with his mother's milk and his beer. Early in the morning, he often stood in line at the Vienna Opera box office to snag one of the cheap standing room places for Wagner's *Ring.* That was his musical education: murder and manslaughter among the Germanic gods. And that's how he saw himself: as the Wotan of his time, or as the emissary of a Providence that had assigned him the task of saving the glorious blond Teutons in their struggle against the tuberculosis-infested rich Jews.

And this third-rate actor, Hitler, had to take lessons in High German from a professional actor, so that he would not have lapsed unaware into his beloved Austrian dialect — and thus would hardly have seemed Nordic-Aryan to the Germans. His High German was a late-learned theatrical High German, and his fanatical roars and fist-swinging acts were carefully practiced by him in front of the mirror. Nothing about him was genuine, he was not a full-blooded Aryan, he didn't even know who one of his grandfathers had been. We still don't know today. He was not tall and blond, rather of puny stature and dark-haired and brown-eyed. And he may even have been homosexual, this murderer of homosexuals, as one historian claims.

He had picked up nerve damage in World War I, and he survived during World War II with cocktails of pills, without ever having gone to the front. Nor did he visit the concentration camps. He was too squeamish for that. He would certainly have become sick to his stomach. And this sensitive person didn't touch animal flesh, because he was disgusted by animal flesh. He loved his German Shepherd dogs so much, unfortunately not the people, especially not the Jewish ones. And instead of saving the Aryans from the Jews, this Austrian Wotan staged a *Twilight of the Gods* with Wagnerian brilliance: there the whole madness of the Third Reich, the bad tastes of blood and soil, the *Lebensraum* drivel has been driven to hell in a symphony howling with dissonances, never to return. At least let us children and grandchildren of the Third Reich hope so. Hitler's crimes have helped to eradicate the virus of anti-Semitism in the Christian West of the world to a high degree. And the state of Israel has also risen again, as the Bible predicted. And maybe the Bible is right in everything, and we should be afraid of the predicted apocalypse. We would have deserved it.